Sexy, seductive and powerful.

These words—along with *compelling, attractive* and *larger-than-life*—are perfect for the strong, passionate men Ann Major writes about. These men will do everything—and anything—to achieve their goals. And when that goal is a particular woman... Well, she'd better be ready to be swept off her feet!

What better example of Ms. Major's expertise with heroes than Prince Alexander Vorzenski, Boone Dexter and Morgan Hastings? These men discover there are some things that even they can't control...like their growing desire for three extraordinary women.

Join us as the adventure begins!

ANN MAJOR,

author of nearly forty novels, is a premier Silhouette Desire author, and has written for the Silhouette Special Edition, Silhouette Intimate Moments and Silhouette Romance lines, as well.

Her larger-than-life characters, compelling plotlines and sensual prose have touched the hearts and emotions of millions of readers all over the world. Whether she writes a simple love story or a more intricately plotted tale of romantic suspense, she always delivers. Her books have repeatedly placed at the top of national and international bestseller lists.

Ann lives in Texas with her husband of many years and her three college-age children. She has a master's degree from Texas A&M at Kingsville, Texas, and has taught English in both high school and college. She is a founding board member of the Romance Writers of America and a frequent speaker at writers' groups.

Ann loves to write; she considers her ability to do so a gift. Her hobbies include hiking in the mountains, playing tennis, sailing, reading, playing the piano, but most of all, enjoying her family.

ANN MAJOR

DAZZLED!

Published by Silhouette Books
America's Publisher of Contemporary Romance

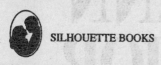

SILHOUETTE BOOKS

RECYCLED PAPER

ISBN 0-373-20165-6

by Request

DAZZLED!

Copyright © 1999 by Harlequin Books S.A.

The publisher acknowledges the copyright holder
of the individual works as follows:

DAZZLE
Copyright © 1985 by Ann Major

MEANT TO BE
Copyright © 1982 by Ann Major

BEYOND LOVE
Copyright © 1985 by Ann Major

Visit us at www.romance.net

Printed in U.S.A.

CONTENTS

Dear Reader,

I am DAZZLED to get to write love stories for you.

The other night at a party, a woman told my husband, "I never read romance novels."

How sad. My answer to her might have been, "I feel so sorry for you. You have missed some of the greatest novels ever written."

I would have said that these books celebrate women, that they are as luscious as chocolates and as delightful as bubble baths. Of course, some of us can't make a steady diet of chocolate and don't have time to take constant bubble baths.

I try to write stories that are spiritually and emotionally restorative. The shelves of Texas's largest cancer hospital in Houston are full of romance novels... because they offer heart and hope to those who need courage.

When people say love stories don't deal with important issues, I wonder what is more important in our violent world than hope and love? I am not talking about naiveté or romantic love or sex. I am talking about love between children, individuals, cultures, races and nations.

Love heals, transforms and inspires the soul.

With love, I offer these stories to you.

Ann Major

DAZZLE

To the special families I married when I married my husband—the Cleaves, the Brakebills and the Acords. The lives of these people have been indelibly interwoven with mine, both their joys and their pain.

To Helen and Wilbur for being wonderful grandparents.
To Kitsie and Kent for running their "Acord Hotel."
To Connie and Dave for their love.
To Gini and in loving memory of her Mark.
And to Rusty, Dinah, Lisa, Missy and Cathy for giving so much to me.

Chapter One

The slim, golden girl walked lightly across the exquisite perfection of gleaming teak joinerwork on the yacht's deck. In one hand she carried a large brown envelope that had just arrived by special courier, and in the other hand a drink she was being careful not to slosh. When she saw Alexander she stopped abruptly, her mind in turmoil as to what to do.

Gazing down at the dozing man, she thought he looked dangerous even in sleep. He could be so unpredictable, so wild, so terribly reckless. Since his wife ran away seven years ago, he did exactly as he wanted as if he had no care of the consequences.

Tina's courage fled. The address on the package was familiar. Whenever Alexander received something from this Mr. Henson he would glance at it and then tear it to shreds with a pretense of indifference, but he would be brooding and difficult for days.

She remembered his abominable mood of the night before and made the cowardly decision not to wake him. She knelt and slid the envelope stealthily beneath the *Financial Times*. Then she set an iced soft drink garnished with a sliver of lime beside the stack of mail and newspapers.

A moment later Alexander awoke. When he opened his eyes, Tina was gone, though her fragrance lingered upon the things she had touched. He saw the drink and stretched a dark arm toward it. He was surprised she'd ventured on deck. He wondered idly if it was a peace offering because of their quarrel the night before.

He did not see the fat brown package beneath the *Times,* hidden as cozily as a time bomb.

Sipping the tart, fizzling drink, he reached for a section of the *Times* and began to read with the fascination of a man who'd long been married to the business world. He frowned as he noted Dazzle's stock had fallen a point while Radiance's had risen.

On first glance, he did not appear the entrepreneur at all. Prince Mikhail Alexander Vorzenski had the look of a pirate about him. He was tough and lean, a tall man who was so powerfully built and so awesomely male, he made even the tallest woman feel small and enchantingly feminine. His eyes were piercing gold; his broad, white smile deliciously and disturbingly cynical. He had the stormy good looks most women find so attractive, and his teasingly bold manner told them he knew it. He could be arrogant and insolent when pushed, and cynical when confronted with maudlin sentimentality in others or himself. Despite his charisma and his easy smiles, he was a difficult man to know well. Women had the feeling that he deliberately closed off that most vital and exciting part of himself, but this aura of mystery only made him all the more fascinating, especially when they caught stirring glimpses of his passionate, hidden soul.

He was so charming, when he chose to be, that women forgave him all these faults and many others. Into his arrogance they read self-confidence, and into his insolence, a sensitive temperament. In his cynicism they saw intelligence. When he was dominating, they defended him by saying that this only made them feel cherished and protected, but none of these women understood him.

Only one woman had glimpsed beneath his surface hardness. Only she had discovered the lovelessness of his childhood, which had made him the proud and lonely man he was. Born of parents who had no time for him—his father a titled playboy, his mother a workaholic—Alexander had thrown himself into sports in his youth, playing to win because he wanted to gain the brief approval of his parents. Only Liz knew that business was a game to Alexander and that winning had become supremely important to him because his mother applauded only the winners.

For the briefest time Liz had shown Alexander a world where love could be had without the need of conquests. He'd glimpsed the fulfillment a happy family life might have brought him. After her, he was harder and lonelier, his victories in the business world more ruthless than before.

Alexander was, as usual, thinking of the business problems that faced the international perfume company he ran. Though he lived his personal life with reckless indifference, he was dedicated to his company. He was ostensibly vacationing, but in truth he'd left Paris so that he could isolate himself and concentrate on several very disturbing realities he'd just become aware of.

The sun gleamed in a cobalt sky and warmed the sheer

rock cliffs. It was summer, and Alexander's skin was bronzed from skiing in the Swiss Alps, where snow lingered even in July, and from having just sailed from his elaborate villa in Sardinia's secluded Porto Rotondo.

Alexander stretched his long, lean frame on the narrow strip of navy towel he'd thrown down upon the foredeck of his immense Swan, the latest and loveliest of all his yachts. In the marine world, the name Swan has a connotation similar to that of Rolls-Royce in automobiles, Rolex in watches, or Godiva in chocolates. It is a reputation based not upon fabulous price alone, but on quality.

Prince Alexander, who'd sailed all his life, was very pleased with his new yacht, with the way it had sliced through the Mediterranean the previous afternoon like a freight train in twenty-seven-plus knots of wind, its lee rail dipping under a single reef.

He was a man who sought the very best of everything. It was a fact of his character that he demanded nothing less from himself or the men who worked for him.

His strength served him well. If it were not for the sheer ruthlessness and drive of his powerful personality, he would have long ago lost the presidency of Dazzle Ltd., the vast family-owned international company he controlled, for there were those who wanted to take it from him. Indeed, his hold on power had never seemed so perilous. There were officers in the company who said he was too hard, that he took too many risks. They wanted to go back to the slow pace of the old days. They said that these were good times, that on the downside, Alexander would bring the company to ruin. Worse, they said, he was a pirate, a man who disregarded all rules but his own. Others still blamed him for what his wife, Liz, had done seven years ago.

Alexander's power was intact only because Dazzle had

prospered under his leadership. The majority of the board was afraid to get rid of him; his successes had been too brilliant and too timely. His enemies were watchful, resentful. Dazzle, a leading manufacturer of perfume in England and Europe, had been sailing through rough seas for the past few years, and it had taken an iron hand at the helm.

A sudden reversal of fortune had made many who had cheered his successes forget them in the wake of a series of disasters that had struck the company. The worst and most recent had occurred only ten days before. The explosion in one of Dazzle's top-security chemical labs in the Alps had rocked the very foundations of Dazzle. Alexander was blamed by several board members for the incident because he had personally overseen the installation of all the security measures at the plant.

Alexander rolled onto his stomach. He felt strangely restless. He wished he hadn't agreed to this party Tina had demanded. He wanted to be sailing, not tied up at a mooring. He lay back, watching the pink pages of the *Financial Times* ruffle when he tossed it aside. The article in the *Times* about Dazzle and the explosion had not improved his mood. The journalist implied that arson was at the bottom of the tragedy, and publicity of that nature was the last thing Dazzle needed.

A week ago Alexander had flown to the site himself and examined the black debris; he'd talked to the injured men and to the Swiss police. What he'd learned had shaken him.

Alexander tried to relax. The quiet, familiar sounds of the Mediterranean came to him: the gentle lapping of wavelets against the snowy fiberglass hull, the distant purr of the incessant summer traffic of Monte Carlo, the roar of a nearby ski boat slicing through the dimpling, gleaming waves, and the gentle laughter of one of his more enchanting female guests, who graced the grand salon below. Suddenly these peaceful sounds were shattered as a passionate tirade of Greek music blasted from the salon.

Mon Dieu! Did they have to play that? He combed bronzed fingers through his thick, black rumpled hair, brushing aside the lock of hair that had fallen across his brow. Alexander frowned wearily at himself for his reaction to the music. What was wrong with him? He felt so unamused by all the things that had once so amused him. He should be glad his guests were having a good time. It was rude of him to ignore them, but he'd invited them for Tina. He hadn't come to the Mediterranean to entertain the same sort of people the perfume business forced him to associate with in London and Paris.

His mistake was that he'd invited Tina. She was like a child who demanded constant entertainment—incessant flirting, gambling or partying. He shouldn't have brought her! It was just that he hadn't wanted to be alone with himself, with all the memories he normally kept himself too busy to face, and with the great unresolved mystery that still haunted him.

He hadn't realized until yesterday how completely unsuited to his personality Tina was. Tina abhorred the peace and silence he sought, and last night she had dragged him to the main casino of Monaco to play the roulette wheels. He'd strolled restlessly among the gamblers, pausing in the Salon Rose where he'd looked up, observing with cynical amusement the unclad nymphs floating about the ceiling smoking cigarillos. Unfortunately he'd grown bored with the ceiling long before Tina had grown bored with roulette. When he'd retrieved the sulky and losing Tina, she'd dragged him to the equally opulent and crowded Hôtel de Paris. She'd stopped be-

neath the bronze statue of Louis XIV's horse and whim-
sically stroked its extended golden fetlock for luck as was
the custom among gamblers in Monaco. Afterward she'd
insisted upon at least stopping at the frenetic Café de
Paris. There Tina had gambled away the last of her, or
rather the last of his, loose change in the slot machines
between her too-frequent Bloody Marys. Later, things had
been even more difficult than usual between them.

Ice tinkled against crystal glasses as a never-ceasing
abundance of expensive liquor was consumed by the
prince's guests on his yacht. Tina and her friends drank
heavily for ones so young. He had no common bond with
any of these people.

Why then did he hang around with shallow pleasure-
seekers who bored and dissatisfied him? Why did he
choose for his companion a woman of Tina's inclinations
when his own passions were neither shallow nor visceral?
Alexander shrugged these questions aside; the last thing
he wanted to dwell on was their answer.

The papers beside him began to flap. A brisk westerly
gust would have sent newsprint flying had Alexander not
seized them. Curious, he secured the *Times* beneath two
magazines and examined the bulky envelope. In bold
black letters Henson's unmistakable scrawl flowed across
stiff, brown paper: "Raymond Henson and Sons, Private
Investigation Ltd."

Alexander's pulse thudded with startling violence. A
terrible premonition gripped him as he ripped open the
package.

"Liz! Damn! What a hell of a time for her to surface!"
he muttered savagely, knowing even before he spilled the
contents of the envelope onto the deck what they would
contain.

Seven years ago Alexander had hired Raymond Henson

to find his wife when she'd run away. Alexander had
wanted to find her to prove that he was innocent of the
destruction she'd deliberately wrought upon Dazzle and
upon him, but when he'd failed, he'd managed to salvage
his position in the company. He'd reshaped a world for
himself that no longer included her, and he'd continued
his search for her for one reason only. When she'd left
him, she'd been pregnant, and he was determined to find
his child.

Alexander was accustomed to Henson's monthly reports. The slim white envelopes that invariably contained
a single carefully typed page that informed him there was
still no trace of Liz's whereabouts had arrived with un-
faltering regularity—until now.

Three glossy photographs, a sheaf of typewritten pages
neatly clipped together, and an exquisite, handsomely
packaged twelve-inch doll lay before him. He studied the
photographs first; two were of Liz.

He lifted one of them and stared at it, his handsome
face hardened by his grim determination not to be affected
by her. Even on paper she dazzled like a brilliant jewel,
tempting him from his harsh stance. Her slender, pale face
was vibrant with emotion, her black eyes ablaze as she
tilted her chin at the defiant angle he remembered so well.
She was talking to someone that Henson had not photographed. Alexander could almost hear her voice, that incredibly silken and yet so very American sound that could
fall sexily hushed against his ear.

He remembered the brief time he had had with her, the
only time in his life he had not felt alone. A flare of
intense excitement shot through him. There was another
feeling too—an overpowering relief to discover she was
alive.

How was it possible that a mere photograph could make

him feel electric with tension? Hatred, he'd been told, was as powerful as love.

She still wore her red hair the way he liked it, rippling like a mane of fire over her shoulders. He remembered suddenly the silken touch of it, the scent of those perfumed tresses falling across his pillow when he'd slept with her in his arms.

On closer inspection he noted she was thinner, as though her life had not been easy. Her bright hair accentuated the extreme pallor of her cheeks. Yet there was an air of gallant bravado about her that would have triggered his admiration had he not instantly stifled it.

She was dressed in one of her wild and extravagant costumes that no one but Liz could have carried off. Apricot silk swirled around her body. The dress looked like an Indian maiden's, its hem edged with the most exquisite and lavish of embroideries.

The male in him noted that the fabric clung to the uptilted shape of her breasts and to the slim curves of her hips. In her bright hair she wore a headband twined with strands of gold and trailing with white feathers. It was outlandish. Ridiculous. It was Liz.

The second picture was a close-up of her face. For the first time Alexander noted a new sadness, a vulnerability in her expression that he had never seen before.

He set the pictures quickly aside, not wanting any further contact with a woman who'd brought him so much pain.

The third photograph was of a boy uncannily like the boy he'd been himself at the age of six. A surge of fatherly pride swept Alexander. It was an emotion more intense than any in his life. He gazed at his son with rapt eagerness.

For seven years he had waited for this. At last, a picture

of his child! He remembered how he'd hungered for his own father's regard when he'd been a child, and never received anything but indifference. His father had been too busy womanizing and racing cars and spending the allowance his rich French wife indulged him with in gratitude for the title their marriage had brought her.

His older half brother, Paul, had resented both his mother's second marriage as well as his young half brothers, and, therefore, had ignored them when they were growing up. Servants had raised Alexander and his younger brother, Sasha; kindly teachers and coaches had played father in wearying succession to the little boys starved for love. When Alexander had become a tennis star in college, his mother had taken a mild interest in him. "I think you've got the instincts of a winner," she'd said proudly after he'd become an amateur champion. "Welcome to my world. You have a job at Dazzle when you graduate." He had accepted her offer, glad for the chance to prove himself and win her approval.

Alexander wondered about his son. Who did his own child turn to? Did he long for the father he had never known? Or had Liz taught the child to hate him? Was he being brought up by servants and neglected?

In the photograph the black-haired child, his golden eyes alight with daredevil exhilaration, stood on the edge of a precipice formed by a rock above a pool. It was obvious he had every intention of jumping. A look of terror contorted the Indian features of the girl behind him, who was trying to dissuade him. Then Alexander saw Liz in the water, her bright hair flowing loosely, her arms encouragingly outstretched toward the child.

Alexander drew a quick, sharp breath. Idiotically he wondered if the boy could swim, if the pool was deep, if it was sanitary. He felt new fury toward his estranged wife that she could be so reckless with his son. But then Liz had always been reckless. If she hadn't been, she never would have dared to marry him and attempt to destroy him.

Alexander stared at the picture of his son. He did not hear the Greek music, nor did he feel the sea breezes, cooler now because of the sinking sun.

He wondered if Liz had deliberately allowed herself to be found by Henson. Did she realize how dangerous it would be for him to associate with her right now, even if his interest were solely because of his son? Was she trying to complete the task she had almost succeeded in accomplishing seven years ago—his destruction and that of Dazzle? If so, she'd unerringly placed the most tempting of all baits on her hook when she'd let Henson get close enough to photograph the child. Despite the danger to himself, Alexander was inexorably drawn to the child. He scarcely understood his feelings; he didn't realize that all his life he'd yearned for someone to love, that what he'd once sought from his father and his older brother, he would now seek from his son. Alexander knew only that he had no choice but to go after him.

At last Alexander read the report. Henson had located Liz because he'd received an anonymous tip that Jock Rocheaux was traveling from Paris to Mexico City nearly once a month, and the reason for his trips was to visit Liz Vorzenski.

An anonymous tip. So Liz had wanted to be found. Alexander bristled at the thought of Jock having anything to do with his son. Damn Liz! How could she be blind to the kind of man Jock was? Superficial charm concealed his reptilian cold-bloodedness.

Jock was Alexander's own first cousin, and they'd been boyhood friends. Together Jock and Alexander had been the most promising junior executives at Dazzle. The first break in their relationship had occurred because of an unfortunate incident involving a young woman they had both been dating.

The severe rupture happened on a hairpin curve at a speed of over two hundred kilometers an hour. Jock decided winning a certain Grand Prix tour on the French Riviera was worth any price. Unfortunately the price had been Sasha. Jock had floored the accelerator of his race car and sent Alexander's younger brother, who was driving the car beside him, hurtling through a barricade and over a cliff in a ball of crystal flame.

Alexander publicly blamed Jock for Sasha's death and used all his stature in the company to have Jock thrust out of it. In the end Jock resigned in a rage and went to Radiance, Dazzle's rival....

Alexander continued to read. Henson reported he had nearly returned from Mexico City without discovering anything until he'd happened upon a collection of exquisite dolls in a department store. The doll he enclosed to Alexander was a model of the shepherdess in Zurbaráns painting in London's National Gallery. The scarlet dress was a replica of the gown Liz had designed from the same painting for herself to wear on her wedding day. Henson had discovered the sloping L, Liz's signature as a designer, hidden upon the heel of the doll's foot. Henson had learned that a hacienda in the mountains outside of Mexico City was the factory where the dolls were made. Jock had visited the village near the high-walled, Spanish colonial hacienda several times. When Henson staked the place, he'd photographed Liz and the child.

Alexander set the report aside. The sky was lit with fiery brilliance. Greek music swirled in the soft evening air. Soft waves caressed the white fiberglass. He came back to his world with the jolt of a man who'd traveled a long way.

Everything was the same, but everything was different. Liz had come back into his life. Once, in a moment of dark anger, he had promised her the most terrible revenge.

Now all that mattered was his son. He would go after the child even though to do so held monumental dangers for him. He would take his son away from a mother who would no doubt be no more than the most destructive and shallow influence upon him. What kind of woman fled to an uncivilized Mexican village and tried to bring up a child far from the heritage that was rightfully his? To raise a child without the cultural and educational advantages he was entitled to was neglect. What kind of woman deliberately denied a child his own father?

The stereo stopped abruptly, and the passionate Greek music was replaced by the clear sound of Barbra Streisand's voice. Tina's mellow laughter soared above the haunting notes. The deeper tones of a man's joined hers, and Alexander heard their enjoyment of one another without a trace of jealousy.

Alexander lifted a black brow. It was not Tina and her latest admirer that caught his interest, but the lyrics of the familiar song. From his Russian father, he had inherited his passionate response to music, a response he frequently sought to conceal, for it embarrassed him.

Tina must have changed the record. She was the only American on board, and she was as avid about Streisand as Liz had been. Sometimes Tina forgot that he did not want Streisand played.

The voice sang of lost love and all its deep anguish, and suddenly Alexander remembered the song; it had been a favorite of Liz's. The melody and its sensuous lament affected him, bringing back a tantalizing fragment of the glorious time he'd shared with her.

A wave of passionate longing washed over Alexander. It was a feeling that only one woman had roused in him. He knew with an acute, aching pain all that he'd lost, just as he knew how empty his life was without her. Tina was no more to him than his latest friend, and like all the others before her, she was a mistake.

No woman could replace the one woman he'd lost—not that he wanted to replace her. That was the last thing he wanted! He wanted to be free of her! Burning deep in his soul was the torture of a memory that was still too vivid—his unforgettable, his blazingly bold, his terribly defiant Liz. How he had loved her in those twelve brief weeks he had had with her.

He'd thrown her out in one blind moment of rage. He'd accused her without once giving her a chance to defend herself. But the evidence of her treachery had seemed so blatantly irrefutable.

If only she hadn't burst into his office to give him her news at the exact moment he'd just been confronted with the incriminating evidence of her betrayal. If he had had even an hour to cool down before he'd seen her, he might have handled everything differently. He'd been hurt, furious, sick with feelings of betrayal. He'd lashed out with all the violence of his nature, and he'd never behaved more brutally toward anyone.

He would never forget the way she'd flung herself from him. She'd run out into the rain. From his window he'd watched her slender form disappear in the gray, slanting storm, and he'd wished passionately that he'd never met her. He never wanted to see her again. She'd deliberately sought to destroy him, and she'd very nearly succeeded. She'd jeopardized his career, divided the board of Dazzle and brought the company itself to the brink of ruin. Because of her, his own family allied themselves with his enemies against him, even his brother, Paul.

Strangely, when Alexander's anger had abated, the only thing he could remember with crystal clarity from that terrible scene was the shattered hurt of her beautiful face when she feebly protested her innocence before he'd overridden her protests with accusations so vile that the lovely look of vulnerability had died in her luminous black eyes, and she'd merely stared back at him with a smoldering defiance he hadn't then realized was significant. Then she'd run away. What he hadn't known at the time was that she was pregnant; Henson had found that out.

At first he'd wanted to find Liz. He had to! He spent a fortune trying to find her. He wanted to try to understand why she had betrayed him. Now all the urgency was gone, and all he wanted was to have her out of his life, and out of his son's life as well, he amended.

Once she had laughed up at him, "Money won't buy everything, my darling. But it can buy freedoms most people can't begin to imagine." She had smiled enigmatically. "You can escape so completely when you're as rich as we are."

He'd thought she was speaking of *his* fortune. He hadn't known then who she really was and that she was incredibly rich herself, and that she knew all about money, that she who was such a bold, free soul was an expert at escaping, that she'd lost herself in countries, in cultures, in out-of-the-way niches in the world for months on end during the rebellious years of her youth when she'd defied her family. There had been so many secrets she had kept from him.

Once he had wanted to know everything about her. That

time was past, despite any tricks his sentimental nature might play on him. All he wanted now was his child.

He could never want Liz again! He hated her for what she'd done, because above all things he despised disloyalty. He'd loved her, and she'd deliberately tried to destroy him.

His hatred had warred with his love for seven years, and in the end the harsher emotion had stifled the gentler. He'd never met another woman who mattered to him. How many women had there been? Beauties, heiresses, international celebrities, and so many of them Americans, had shared his company all because *she* was American.

The press said he had a taste for free-spirited American beauties. Tina, like so many of the rest, was American. But not one of them had made him forget. He didn't want to see Liz again, but he knew he had to confront her. She was no more than an intense memory he couldn't quite put behind him, a breathtaking illusion that had never really existed.

The music enveloped him, and his fierce mood was suddenly too overpoweringly painful to be endured. Alexander hated thinking of Liz. In seven years his hate and love had become as hopelessly twisted as a snarled vine. He felt violent and impotent at the same time, each emotion feeding and magnifying the other.

The haunting words seemed to go on. Was that song never going to end? Tina! Damn her! If it weren't for her, he'd be sailing instead of bitterly awash in memories!

Suddenly he had an immediate target for his explosive anger. He sprang to his feet. He ran lightly across the gleaming deck, his hard body lithe and fluidly graceful. He took the varnished teak stairs two at a time.

He burst into the throng of revelers near the bar and ripped the record from the turntable. There was instant silence. For a breathless moment not even an ice cube dared to clink in the glasses gripped with paralyzed, bejeweled fingers.

The faint odors of the Greek foods the caterers had brought on board at Tina's whim assailed him, mingling in unappetizing chaos—sizzling suvlaki, trays of pastitso, heaps of dolmathes, and the inevitable tiropitaki.

Alexander's head was pounding. Instead of comforting him, the silence was thick and suffocating like wads of warm cotton stuffed smotheringly against his face. Tina swirled her gilt head to glare at him in annoyance.

Alexander stared at her, sharply seeing her as though for the first time. She looked very young with her straight, cornsilk hair and with her wide blue eyes. Her flawless, honey-toned body was covered (if one could call it covered) by a crocheted string bikini. She was far too young for the sophistication of her lifestyle, he thought. She belonged on some American college campus in Colorado or Wyoming and not on a perfume magnate's yacht cruising off the south of France.

The moment between them was long and still.

His other guests watched with mild interest. Intense emotion was a novelty to them, and it was exceptional in their cynical and worldly Mikki, as Alexander was called by his intimates.

"Mikki, what the hell?" Tina began sulkily before she broke off, suddenly not daring to go on as she met the full force of Alexander's angry gaze.

His tanned, handsome face was as fierce as that of a warlord. He wanted to smash everything in the room. The pupils in his golden eyes had dilated. They blazed like black fire.

"I told you never to play that record in my presence, Tina," Alexander said in an ominously soft tone. He cracked the brittle plastic and let the black shards fall to the carpet. "You know I don't like American music." The fact was he liked it too well; Liz had taught him all her preferences.

There was a terrible, suppressed violence about Alexander, in his low voice, in the dangerous stillness of him, and Tina did not dare to defy him.

Then he was gone, leaving them to stare after him in mild, bored confusion, until one of the younger women, who'd been drinking too much, tittered a bit nervously as she exhaled a deep breath. "I never saw Mikki like that before! He's so…so magnificently pagan," she stated with a touch of breathlessness. "When you tire of him, Tina, darling, why don't you give him my number in Zurich. Passionate men can be so amusing in bed."

Tina's acid response was lost as the wild Greek music resumed.

In his cabin, Alexander made two telephone calls. One to Paris and the other to London. He refused to listen when his brother Paul told him it was impossible for him to postpone his return to Paris, that important decisions that he alone could handle had to be made. Alexander overrode every protest and gave orders for his Lear 55 to be flown at once to his private airport on his estate in Grasse.

He would go to Mexico City and catch Liz by surprise. She would not best him again. This time he was determined he would be the winner—no matter what it cost him. Dazzle had long been Alexander's life, but even if the price were the presidency itself, he would pay it to remove his son from the care of that irresponsible and destructive woman.

He would hire a nanny, tutors. He would have to find out what the best schools in England were. Hell! It suddenly occurred to him that he didn't know a thing about little boys. Well, he could learn.

Alexander had no intention of allowing Liz to pursue the disastrous course of raising his son as a half-savage in a remote Indian village in Mexico. Nor would he allow Jock to hold any influence over the child.

What in the name of God was Liz thinking of?

Chapter Two

The edges of Mexico City's smog reached the pine forests on the green mountain slopes, bringing with it the diesel smell from the distant city. Beneath the forest on the gentler terrain farmers were cultivating their terraced cornfields, some with primitive wooden plows. The peasants of the village called this annual breaking of new land the *barbecho*. The poorer farmers who still used the ancient Aztec cutting and burning system of hoe culture, locally known as *tlacolol*, were weeding their fields, which hugged the steeper slopes where a plow could not be used.

It was the rainy season, and the air was crisply cool and damp. Liz wrapped her *rebozo* more tightly about her shoulders and sipped her first cup of coffee that morning. It was strong, the way she liked it, and it tasted rich and delicious.

An unopened letter from Jock lay on the table beside

her treasured photographs of her beloved Cornwall. Quickly she slit the envelope and then set it down without reading it. The letter would contain the inevitable demands. "Marry me. Leave Mexico and come to France. Forgive your father. Forget Alexander." Sometimes Jock enclosed a gossip magazine photo of Alexander with some young beauty to emphasize that the husband she had so passionately loved had long since forgotten her.

Because of Jock, Liz knew how wildly Alexander lived. She'd kept every photograph Jock had sent, studying those handsomely chiseled yet so coldly remote features, her heart filled with the pain of a woman whose hopeless love refused to die. It was little comfort that Alexander looked no happier than she despite his glamorous companions.

For the thousandth time she thought about marrying Jock. She did not doubt Jock's love, though her own fondness for him scarcely reciprocated the passion he professed for her. But if she married Jock, she would have to resolve the complex mess she had made of her life. She would have to face the issue of divorce.

The coffee cup clattered as she set it in its saucer. Divorce Alexander? Divorce the man she'd loved since the first moment she'd seen him? Even now she lay awake in the night, her dreams filled with sensual memories of him.

She was a fighter, and yet she hadn't fought for Alexander. She'd run away, because to fight for him had meant she had to fight him. Loving him as she had, she hadn't possessed the strength for that battle. Now, she knew that if ever she had the chance again, she would do anything to regain his love. However, she'd never have a second chance. Alexander did not love easily, and having let his guard down with her once and been hurt, he was not likely to do so again. He was vulnerable, but he shielded himself with an armor of ruthless hardness.

The haunting vision of Alexander's burnished maleness, his jet dark hair, his golden eyes, rose in her mind's eye. She saw him again as she'd seen him that first night. They'd met at a beach party in Deauville after a sailing regatta he'd won. Of course he'd won; that's what mattered most to him—winning.

Their meeting had almost seemed preordained. It was ironic that it was Mimi, her father's mistress, who had suggested a holiday on the coast of France.

Mimi had said, "A few days together…away from your father…will give us the opportunity to get to know one another."

Liz had wondered if Mimi sensed that she felt uneasy in her presence. Mimi had always been friendly, and yet from the first Liz had felt a reticence toward her. Even her father had noted it. He had said, "It is not easy for a man like me to live alone, Liz. I know Mimi is…different, but that is often the case with famous actresses. There is this ego problem."

Perhaps he was right, or perhaps it was only the normal jealousy a daughter might feel toward her father's mistress who was years younger than he. Nevertheless, Liz had not wanted to go to Deauville, but she had not known how to refuse.

They'd come late to the grand old château, which was aglitter and alive with laughter and music and dancing. Mimi, who was famous in France, was immediately in the midst of a throng of autograph seekers, and Liz was left to herself.

Liz noticed Alexander at once, even before he'd noticed her.

Women were swarming around him. His black head

was thrown back and he was laughing. Yet even from across the ballroom she sensed a loneliness about him that only someone who had suffered as she had could understand. She knew too well what it was like to be with friends and yet to be alone, to be lost in a world of money and opulence and success. She fancied that none of the people he was with really understood him, that in some curious way he deliberately kept himself apart from them. Suddenly she'd felt the heat of his gaze upon herself. He smiled boldly because he'd caught her looking at him.

She flushed with an odd, embarrassed sensation. His male eyes ran over her dramatic gown, and his smile broadened. She was overdressed for a sailing party, but then she usually overdressed. He liked to win. That was his way of seeking attention, and she liked to dress outrageously for the same reason. Only the way he looked at her made her feel self-conscious, as though she'd blundered.

Her bodice of burgundy velvet studded with bugle beads and sequins tightly encased her full breasts and tiny waist. Puffed and slashed Renaissance sleeves gave the impression of a Tudor princess. Naturally all the other women were wearing slacks.

Liz tossed her head defiantly and moved quickly away. She was deeply conscious of his eyes following her, and an oddly breathless sensation made her slow her pace. But she was curious about him, and she had whispered excitedly in Mimi's ear a few minutes later, "Who is that man dancing beneath the potted palms? The conceited one with the black hair who looks so like a pirate?"

"A pirate!" Mimi's features froze. Her throaty voice didn't sound like her own. "You have been buried in Cornwall. That's Mikki Vorzenski. He's no pirate, *chérie*, but a real prince. He's the new president of his family's fragrance company, Dazzle. Quite a yachtsman too. A winner at every game he plays, or so it seems. In the game of love, they say he is a despoiler of women. Roger told me that his own family has exiled him to London. You must stay away from him.''

"Mikki Vorzenski!" Liz murmured. "Oh, no." A terrifying hollowness in her stomach made Liz feel sick. Of all men, he was the one she was bound to avoid.

Her attraction horrified her because her father had warned her and had made her promise to avoid him. ''Mikki Vorzenski and I are old, old enemies, my child. He is a ruthless thief in the perfume world. He would like nothing better than to hurt me through you.'' Her father had made it clear that he wanted her to marry Jock.

It was inevitable that Liz would have met Mikki Vorzenski in France. What Liz could not have anticipated was her own instantaneous attraction to him.

She remembered Mimi's words. ''A despoiler of women.''

Mimi had disappeared.

One of the young women beside the prince was leaning forward so that her breasts spilled invitingly against her thin T-shirt. ''Mikki,'' she cried laughingly, ''dance with me.''

"Another time, Monique."

It appeared likely that a number of the young beauties would have jumped at the chance for a little despoiling.

And how was she different from them? She understood them only because the same urge lay within her. Liz stumbled toward the door. She could not stay and chance any encounter with him.

Liz hurried blindly across the ancient cobblestones of the darkened garden. Heavy footsteps thudded behind her. Suddenly she was jostled hard against the lean body of a man who'd been running as swiftly as she. For a stunned instant she forgot her fear.

She was at once profoundly aware only of the man. She felt his warmth, his masculine strength when he touched her. She caught her breath at the dangerously provocative sensations his hard, groping hands evoked.

"Oh, excuse me," he said quickly, the warm, rich sound tickling her earlobe. "I'm terribly sorry." But of course, he was not sorry at all.

His touch lightened; his arms slid around her tiny waist to steady her. The strange desire for him to mold her against himself nearly overcame her.

She looked up into the passionate fire of his golden eyes, and she froze. Her black eyes went darker with recognition. She knew he'd followed her deliberately.

"Are you all right?" he asked in that deepest, that most melodious of voices.

She was afraid, but she nodded hastily. Her fingers still gripped his arm for balance. She liked to touch him, to hold on to him. She caught the faint scent of his musky aftershave mingling with the fresh male scent that was uniquely his own, and she liked that as well.

When she flung herself away from him with sudden, fierce determination, she noted that he was breathing hard, as though her nearness was as oddly disturbing to him as his was to her.

Liz was struck with the awesome electric quality of his male charisma. The way he looked at her set her on fire. The way he touched her made her feel thrillingly alive. And he was a stranger. She remembered who he was. Oh, if only he *were* a stranger.

His molten eyes held hers, as though he could not look away, as though he too were unexpectedly affected by her,

as if he couldn't stop himself from having feelings he
didn't want to have.

That night of their first awareness—one for the other—
would be forever frozen in Liz's memory. She had never
been so immediately aware of another human being as
she was of this striking man, her father's enemy, whom
she'd chanced upon in a summer ballroom amid the crumbling grandeur of an ancient château.

Liz knew then, as a woman always knows, that he was
just as deeply affected by her.

"You're Mikhail Vorzenski, aren't you?" she gasped
in a trembling tone. She dreaded his answer.

"Yes, I am." He smiled warmly. "Who are you?"

She couldn't possibly tell him. Some friends of his
called to him, and she seized the opportunity and escaped.

She escaped France and her father and Mimi as well.
She hid for a week on a Grecian island.

Alexander pursued her to London. It took him a month
to find her. It was late on a golden afternoon when Alexander strode into Liz's shop, Isobel's, with that air of
bold confidence he always wore. Liz heard the little bell
jingle faintly as the door closed against the jamb.

Leaving a customer in the fitting room, she ascended
the stairs and observed him without his knowledge as he
browsed restlessly, perusing a grouping of hazy jacquards
inspired by the Gobelin tapestries, and a table of velvet
blouses with circular yokes recalling the filigree bib col-
larettes from ancient Egypt.

Alexander lifted a negligee from a low table. It was
little more than strips of jade chiffon hanging from a
plumed neckline. His low, male chuckle filled the shop as
he let the nightgown float back to its place on the table.

It did odd fluttery things in her stomach to watch so masculine a man finger such delicate lingerie.

Liz spoke at last in a strangled voice. "Have you found something that interests you, sir?"

He spun around as though electrified by her presence. She was just as profoundly affected by his, though she was determined to deny it.

"Definitely," was his dangerously smooth reply, which he punctuated with a smile that was even more dangerous. His golden eyes were direct and bold as they met hers before they lowered and swept her body with possessive insolence.

Liz stumbled backward with a gasp. He ignored her sputters of indignation and continued his raking scrutiny.

He stared at the mad pulsebeat at her throat and the faint tremor in her hands before she clasped them together. His mere presence was an assault upon every sense in her being. How dared he come here? She retreated into the deep shadows at the back of the shop in an effort to feel safe from him. Then she realized that there was no safety anywhere.

"Do you always undress a woman when you look at her?"

"Only a woman I want," he said, shrugging his wide shoulders lazily. There was laughter in his pleasantly deep voice. "Why did you run away from me in France?"

"You should not have come here," she said, and her words were low and desperate. She was afraid her eyes betrayed the treacherous excitement he aroused within her.

"Why shouldn't I?" he asked, moving nearer. "I always go after what I want."

She shrank against the wall. Her breasts tautened as if

in response to his nearness. "Because I told you I wanted nothing to do with you."

He smiled into her glare. "I don't believe you." She moistened her lips, and he watched the curl of her pink tongue as though he found it tantalizing.

She rallied. "I have a customer downstairs. How can you stand there and tell me what's in my own mind?"

"Why not, when you won't?"

"You really are too much," she managed, trying to back away, an impossibility because of the wall behind her. His lean, dark body loomed threateningly nearer. She forced her gaze from the expanse of his broad shoulders, from his large but surprisingly lithe body.

"Look, I'm sorry that you find it so objectionable that I don't want to have anything to do with you."

"That didn't sound much like an apology," he chided silkily.

"It wasn't." She turned toward the back of the shop.

"Not so fast." Deliberately he stepped toward the door, blocking her escape. His grave eyes held hers. "I find it objectionable because you don't really know me." He spoke quietly, all the mockery stilled for the moment in his handsome face.

"I know of you, Mr. Vorzenski, and that's more than enough," she retorted. Her tone held dismissal, but there was a betraying quaver in her voice.

"You don't strike me as the kind of woman who usually lets other people do her thinking for her," his deep baritone taunted.

Her back stiffened, and she thought he knew he'd found a weak place in her armor. She dared a glance at him, her expression softening subtly.

"You're making a mistake," he continued, "to rely on hearsay when it would be so much more interesting to learn about me from firsthand experience.'' Again there was that dangerously seductive silkiness in his low voice that left her shaking.

"The last thing I want, Mikhail Vorzenski, is to learn about you through firsthand experience,'' she muttered, her thick dark lashes downcast.

"Is it?'' Golden eyes flashed with amusement. "I wonder?''

Her cheeks were aflame. "I told you, I know all about you.''

"Not all, surely? But that is why you intrigue me. You know about me, so I must learn about you.''

"I don't want to intrigue you.''

"But you do. The moment I saw you, I wanted to know you. When you ran away, I was determined to find you. It was not easy.''

"Such selfish determination is deplorable,'' she flung out hastily.

"Really?'' Again he looked amused. "You prefer indifference or weakness in a man then? A boy, perhaps? Or a sissy?'' His eyes that knew too much slid over her, those golden male eyes that viewed her with such disturbing intensity.

Everywhere his gaze touched her, her skin flushed as if singed by a tongue of flame. Despite herself, the faint beginnings of a smile played at the corners of her mouth. "I did not say that.''

"You implied it.''

"How am I going to get rid of you?''

"Perhaps you are not.''

"What do you want?''

"Only the reward that I deserve for my trouble.'' Again he smiled.

"I should have known.''

"Oh, I don't want money."

She hadn't imagined that he did.

"What do you want?" Her voice was a tantalizing whisper.

"You."

The single word was direct and bold—like the man.

Before she could give into her sudden wild impulse to escape him, it was too late. He seized her hand and drew her to him.

The shock of his touch compelled them both.

His heady masculine scent enveloped her. A powerful, unconquerable force bound them one to the other in a spell of electric enchantment. She was breathless, and so was he. The tension drained out of her as her fingers curled around his in mute acceptance.

Nor did she draw her hand away as he turned her slender fingers over in his palm and brought them to his lips caressingly. His mouth was pleasingly warm and vibrant against her flesh, and she shivered from the heat of his slow kiss.

She looked into his eyes, and all her timidity was gone. Her black gaze was bold and hot and wanton.

"Hold me," she said suddenly, "tightly. Oh, tightly!"

With a half-smothered groan, he crushed her slim body against the awesomely lean power of his. Her delicate body accommodated his even more perfectly than she could have ever imagined. In that first rapturous moment, the world stood still.

They'd both come so far, traveling through two lifetimes of loneliness to find each other.

She held herself motionless in his arms, her pulse hammering wildly and her breath faint and shallow. She did not speak. Her face was pale and still. Her only movement was the quick downward flutter of her long dark lashes over her eyes.

His hands slid over the soft flesh of her arms. His warm breath stirred in her perfumed hair. A thousand needs pounded in her body.

He lowered his mouth to possess hers, but she reached up and brushed his lips with her fingers.

"Not now," she said breathlessly, "not now." But her eyes caressed the sensual curve of his male mouth with a desire as heated as his own.

"Have dinner with me tonight," he said hoarsely.

"This is all so preposterous." Her husky whisper of protest was the most passionate assent any woman had ever given him.

The whole length of her body was heated by the contact with his.

"Seven, then?" he asked. "Wear that red dress you wore in Deauville."

She nodded. Her black eyes were still fastened upon his dark face, most of all upon his lips.

"The shop closes at six-thirty. I'll be ready then." There was a blistering eagerness in her that warred with the lingering traces of her fear of him.

"Why are you so afraid of me?" he asked suddenly. "Why did you run away?"

"Because we cannot be."

"But we are," he said forcefully.

"Yes," she murmured. "And that is more frightening than anything." In agonized passion she nuzzled her face against the warmth of his throat, and his hands moved caressingly through her hair, pressing her head even more tightly against him to reassure her.

They dined in the Grill Room of the Connaught, considered by many to be the most desirable and exclusive public dining room in London. How Alexander had obtained his favorite table in the bay window on such short notice, Liz did not ask. But she knew that the Grill Room was sold out, lunch and dinner, every day and that the most sought-after tables were the two in the bay windows. There were, in all, only eleven tables in the room. The black-haired, black-tied Giancarlo Bovo escorted them discreetly to their places.

The superbly prepared game and woodcock might as well have been cardboard, because they scarcely made an impression on the striking couple at the window table. They had eyes only for each other.

Liz was aglitter in the elaborate wine red gown with the slashed Renaissance sleeves. Her red hair was plaited in coils, which were wound high upon her head in an elaborate coronet of gleaming braids. There was a wildness in his eyes every time he glanced at her that made her blood flow as hotly as lava.

"If I'd known we were eating in the Grill Room, I would have worn something less extravagant," Liz said softly, tilting her face so that the golden light illuminated her flawless beauty.

"I'm glad you didn't," Alexander replied with one of his easy, warm smiles.

"This hotel prides itself on the understatement," she murmured.

"You couldn't look more perfect."

She studied the strong line of his jaw, the brilliance of his golden eyes. He was studying her as well, and she colored with pleasure beneath his intense, hot gaze.

Long silences such as this one fell between them from time to time, moments of hushed, expectant excitement that were powerful, unspoken eroticisms.

"What am I going to call you?" she asked a little breathlessly after one of these prolonged silences.

"Everyone calls me Mikki," he said.

That name jarred; that was the name her father had taught her to hate and fear.

"I don't want to call you what everyone calls you."

"My mother calls me Mikhail."

She frowned, and he saw that she didn't like that either. "What about Alexander?"

"No one calls me Alexander."

"Alexander." She said his name softly, sexily possessively, and then she smiled. "It's a shame to have a name that no one uses. I will call you Alexander."

"What will I call you?"

"Why, Liz, of course."

"No choice?" he asked. "No last name even?"

"For a long time I have preferred not to use my father's name." Her expression was momentarily shadowed, her fleeting smile enigmatic. *Tell him,* a tiny voice sounded in the back of her mind. "No choice," she said in a strange, tight voice.

"I'm beginning to wonder if there isn't a basic unfairness in our relationship." His golden eyes flashed with amusement.

She laughed. "I certainly hope so, if it's in my favor."

"I'm not used to being dominated by a woman," he teased. His fingers wrapped the velvet warmth of hers across the table.

Her eyes met his. "No, I don't suppose you are," she whispered. "It will be a new experience."

"One must always seek...new experiences," he murmured, bringing her fingertips to his lips, having forgotten for the moment the restrained, formal atmosphere of the

Connaught. "They say it is the secret of retaining one's youth."

"Is that what I am to you, a new experience?"

"That, and much more." There was an acquisitive gleam in his eyes when he spoke, and a certain teasing look as well.

She knew what he meant, and her fingers tightened upon his with an eagerness that more than matched his.

Afterward they'd gone dancing at the Savoy with the Thames sparkling behind them. Alexander was an excellent dancer, and Liz drifted happily in his arms as a piano tinkled softly.

Later they talked, holding hands, their voices soft and hushed, their faces rapt and golden in the dim candlelight. The ice melted in their untouched drinks, and their kindly waiter left them to themselves. Time passed quickly, as if on wings.

Alexander made himself deliberately charming, and Liz forgot the danger of him. The loneliness of the past year, her grief, her mother's foolish self-destruction, her own mad flight across a far-flung world—all these things were swept aside in the breathless thrill of her excitement.

Liz talked to Alexander easily, making light of the succession of tragedies that had befallen her. She told him everything, everything except her damning secret. She spoke of her childhood in Cornwall, the simple pleasures she'd found on those golden beaches with the man she'd loved as a father. She did not say that only recently she'd learned that man had been her stepfather. She brought to life Killigen Hall and all its wonders. She told him, as well, of her despair that her mother had planned to sell her childhood home.

In his turn Alexander talked of his own life—a cosmopolitan world so different from hers she could scarcely imagine it. It was a world of high finance, of the struggle for power, of world-class yacht races, of resorts and beautiful women. Unlike her, he did not mention his childhood or his parents. He spoke of Sardinia, his occasional happinesses there before his brother Sasha's death. His was a fast-paced, exciting world, but it was a world of loneliness and emptiness as well.

They talked as if they'd always known each other. Why had her father warned her of this wonderful man? Alexander made her feel as she'd never felt before—beautiful, desirable and infinitely precious. He looked at her with glowing eyes that were as warm and radiant as firelight. She did not know that her face mirrored the rapture and thrill in his.

The hour was late when he took her hand in his and turned it over. He brought her palm to his lips and caressed it with a warm kiss that sent shivers throughout her body. His eyes met hers with a look that made her emotions rocket sky high.

"Liz, you know what I want, don't you? More than anything?"

The excitement that rushed inside her was hot. She dropped her eyelids. She was at a loss.

"Look at me," he said. When she did, he murmured, "I'm in the mood to follow the most dangerous inclination."

"Dangerous." Odd that *he* should choose that word. She trembled.

"I-I don't understand."

"I think you do."

There was no mistaking the sound of passion in his deep voice.

"You could have any woman."

"But I don't want just any woman."

"This is all so new to me," she heard herself say.

"The way I feel tonight is new to me," he admitted.

"You've had many women, while I—"

"They were not you. Until I saw you in Deauville, I never understood the instinct of other men to pursue one woman and forsake all others. I do now." His voice changed subtly, an edge of regret and cynicism having crept into it. "Of course, I can't promise I'm the changed man a woman like you deserves. I've lived a different sort of life for too long. I can only say I don't want to hurt you, that you are special to me, Liz. I don't know if that's enough."

He made her feel like a queen. The flickering candle had burned low in its pool of wax. Her fingers squeezed his. He'd been humble and honest, while she... She dismissed her guilt, and gave in to the tumultuous wonder of her feelings for him.

"It's enough," she said. "More than enough, for now."

"Will you come back with me to the Connaught?"

She did not speak, but she did not have to. They both knew the answer. It had been inevitable from the moment they'd first met.

Chapter Three

When Alexander and Liz arrived back at his hotel, and she knew they were going up to his room, her mood altered subtly. He was so sophisticated, and doubtless he preferred women who were experienced. She had never been with a man before. She knew only that she wanted to be with him. To delay, she insisted on walking up the handsome, six-story oak staircase to his suite rather than using the elevator.

"I love the Connaught," she said, tilting her head at a defiant angle when he protested the climb. "It's like a great English country house. It doesn't have all those empty, endless, Kafkaesque tunnels punctuated by anonymous doors other hotels have. I love the oil paintings and cupboards with china figurines. Have you seen the mounted stag's head?"

"I can't say that I have," came his dry reply.

"Then we must walk up."

He looked past her and eyed the stairs suspiciously as though he wished he were living in a hotel with dull halls rather than fascinating ones, but he did not deny her her wish.

She dawdled, delighting in the discoveries of a chinoiserie cabinet, a tall case clock and an old map encased in a thick, plain frame. She laughed when he confessed he'd passed these treasures every day on his way to and from Dazzle without noting them.

When they came to his door, she grew silent. He was silent as well, and she wished he would think of something careless to say that would put her at ease. He led her inside, and when he locked the door, she blushed beneath his warm gaze. Her boldness was gone. She seemed overcome with shyness at being alone with him in the quiet intimacy of his hotel room. Her gaze made a frightened sweep of the vast bedroom, lingering with misgivings upon the bed.

She wished that his bed had not been carefully turned down by the maid, that the embroidered linen mat had not been placed beside the bed so that the guests' bare feet would not have to touch the carpet when they retired at night and rose the next morning. The room was obviously ready for the retirement of its occupants.

He came to her and circled her with his arms to reassure her, but she lightly skipped out of his reach.

He left her alone while he shrugged out of his jacket. He went to the bar and splashed brandy into a crystal glass.

"Would you care to join me?" he offered.

She did not answer him because she didn't hear him. She was standing beside his desk, where his research papers on Dazzle's latest fragrance were spread out. She could not stop herself from staring at them. So, her father had been right. Dazzle was preparing for a new launch.

It reinforced exactly who Alexander was, and why they could have nothing to do with each other. Perhaps it was not too late to stop this madness between them.

Alexander was loosening the knot of his tie when she glanced up. The lamplight gleamed in his shining black hair. He turned to her; his dark face was flushed with some emotion she did not understand. She felt as guilty as a traitor to have looked at his papers. In the mirror her skin was as white as flour against her jewel red gown.

He strode to her, and she jumped away, too guilty and upset to speak to him. A tremulous silence hung between them. He caught her frightened glance and held it.

She forced herself to calm down. Of course, he could have no idea that she could understand his papers, that she was as inexorably linked to the world of gums, flowers, essences, concretes and absolutes as he. He would think her too ignorant of the business to understand perfume formulas. He did not know who she was, so he could not possibly realize his danger.

Shakily she dragged her eyes from his. "I must go," she choked.

"What?" Her behavior was incomprehensible to him.

"I don't know why I came out with you tonight, why I came up here," she whispered, trying to race past him. "I've made a terrible mistake."

He ignored her words. Reaching out, he caught her slim shoulders and pulled her against him. "What's wrong, Liz?" he demanded. "You must tell me."

"I can't explain."

Inscrutable golden eyes met her wavering glance. "We're no longer strangers on the street. I thought we

were becoming friends." There was warmth in his gaze.
"More than friends."

"You and I can never be friends."

"But why?"

She stared at him in mute anguish, giving him no answer. She was quivering like a frightened animal, and after her warmth all evening she understood why he was at
a loss.

Despite her fear, the heat of his body against hers
aroused her like a drug. Neither was he unaffected. She
felt the rapid unevenness of her breathing. She was trembling everywhere her body touched his.

"Alexander, you must forget we ever met. Let me walk
out that door, and don't come after me. You will never
be sorry."

"You're wrong, Liz." He laughed softly. "I would be
sorry every day that I lived. You can't leave me."

"I must!" She struggled to free herself.

Then he did the only thing he could to stop her. He
pressed her even closer against his body so that she felt
the heat of him and his need of her. Easily he captured
her hands, which pushed against his chest, and twisted
them gently behind her waist.

"Alexander..." She pleaded weakly that he stop even
while her pliant softness shaped itself to his hard contours
with womanly readiness, even while he seemed to sense
something deep within her was yielding and that her excitement was causing her to lose control.

"Oh, Liz, can't you understand that there's no reason
for you to be afraid? Not of me. If you'll only tell me
what the trouble is, I'll help you."

His mouth brushed the softness of her hair, then across
her forehead and eyebrows, trailing at last to her trembling
lips. He kissed the velvet skin of her throat. Ever so softly

he won her from her purpose, stroking her body, finding all the secret places where his touch aroused her. Desire quickened under his expert titillation.

She felt wanton and yet shy toward him. His hands slid into her hair, and she felt his fingers freeing the pins, uncoiling the braids, until the silken mass flowed freely.

"I did not want to go to the party in Deauville, but when I saw you, I knew you were my destiny," he murmured, his lips trailing along the smoothness of her brow. "When you ran away, I was desperate to find you. Don't leave me tonight, not when I want you with me forever. I need you, Liz. I've never said that to a woman before."

His gaze was filled with stark longing, and she reached up and touched his face lovingly.

"I won't leave you, Alexander."

Gently he wrapped his arms around her and led her toward the bed. He removed her rich gown, and when next he held her she felt the smooth hardness of his bare skin against her breasts. Her nakedness seemed strange and scary, and yet thrilling.

"I-I've never been with a man before. I hope you don't mind," she whispered shyly.

"Mind?" Alexander's laugh was soft and tinged with desire. "Liz, that just makes you lovelier, my sweet virgin."

He lowered his black head and possessed her lips with slow, passionate mastery. His tongue played across the edges of her warm wet mouth. His hands moved against the satin warmth of her flesh, hands that knew too well where and how to touch a woman. His mouth smothered the passionate moan that erupted from her lips.

She clung to him. He seemed pleased when she let her tongue mate with his, when she pressed her trembling body even more tightly against him. He gazed into slanting eyes that had gone dark with a passion. Her hand came up to his roughened cheek and she caressed him with infinite tenderness.

"I love you, Alexander. I don't know how that's possible, but I do." Her black eyes seemed filled with love, and sadness too. "I don't want to hurt you! Not ever. That's why I'm afraid."

He took the hand that brushed his cheek and kissed it gently.

"Hurt me? How could you ever hurt me, my darling?" Her obvious concern for him accentuated his tenderness.

Alexander bent and kissed her. He lifted her into the bed and quickly stripped off his own clothes to lie beside her. She had watched him in fascination, blushing at the bronzed power of his body, at the magnificence of his muscled shoulders, the flatness of his hard belly, at the swollen shaft of his manhood.

He gathered her shivering body into his arms. He was gentle and loving, restraining his own passion, arousing hers. He learned the feminine secrets of her, kissing her everywhere with hot exploring lips until she was scarlet with embarrassment even while little whimpers rose from her throat.

The time that followed was filled with the rapture and wonder of discovering one another.

Alexander crushed her to him and abandoned himself to the full glory of his desire. She returned his kisses feverishly, running her hands over his powerful body, reveling in the hard pleasure of his muscular frame, savoring the ripple of muscle and sinew beneath the light tracings of her fingers.

She gave herself to him, opening her body for his, emitting a soft sob of ecstasy when he came to her and showed her the wild thrilling joys love could bring to a woman.

Afterward she lay weeping silently in his arms, too deeply moved to say anything. Now she knew what she had wanted that first moment in Deauville when she'd watched him across that glittering ballroom and caught that hungry look in his golden eyes, and when she'd felt the strength of his arms on her body in the courtyard. She'd wanted him like this—wild and powerful and yet possessive and gentle.

Her languorous black eyes opened slowly to meet his. "I love you," she whispered.

Alexander's eyes shone with tenderness, and his fingers lazily caressed her cheek. "Marry me," he said.

"I—"

"I love you, Liz. I can't bear to live without you. Until this moment I've been alone."

This from a despoiler of women. She smiled shyly and reached up and kissed him because suddenly she knew that she couldn't live without him either. She had no one except him. She could not go back to that barren loneliness now that she'd known the glory of being close to him. Liz gave him a tremulous yes, and the temptation to confess her secret trembled on the tip of her tongue. Her courage failed her, and she lay in tortured silence, her omission a fatal step in the destruction of their love.

"Do you realize you've promised to marry me, and I don't even know your last name?" he probed gently.

"My last name," she choked, "is Killigen." It was the truth, and yet it was a lie. She found that she could no longer meet his gaze.

After he'd conquered her reluctance, there had been no stopping their soaring passion. She had known from the moment his name was whispered to her in Deauville that their love could never be, and yet she married him without telling him who she really was.

Now, seven years later, she was in Mexico alone with her two children, and he had his wild bachelor life in Europe. How blindly stupid she had been. Liz clasped her fingers together beneath her thick shawl to conceal their trembling.

Just thinking of Alexander could still bring a faint tremor to her body. She wasn't ready to confront him in person. Crumpling Jock's letter, she threw it, unread, in the trash. She would have to keep putting Jock off, at least for now.

From the balcony, Liz could see the peasants walking up the winding road from their village to open the doll factory. They dressed as they had for centuries, the women with their dark-colored skirts and high-necked blouses, half-aprons, and rebozos, the men in their white cotton jackets and trousers, straw sombreros, leather huaraches, and sarapes.

Once these primitive surroundings had seemed alien to the thoroughly modern Liz, but now they were home. Here, with the help of a village midwife, Liz had borne her fraternal twins. The children were miniature replicas of their parents. Alex was bronzed and dark and muscular, as Alexander must have been as a child. Samantha, with her carrot red hair and beanpole slimness, was bold and mischievous. This was the only home they had ever known, and despite her own sense of isolation and bouts of homesickness for Killigen Hall in Cornwall, Liz had sought to make it a happy one.

Jock said the children would have more advantages in France, but she was not sure that was true. Mexico was not without a rich cultural heritage.

This morning the twins were sleeping even later than usual because Liz had driven into Mexico City to pick Samantha up from a visit with friends the previous night.

The children frequently slept until nine because Liz liked them to stay up in the evenings when she could spend time with them. She lunched with them during the siesta hour as well. During the mornings a tutor came and worked with the children. In the afternoons they had the run of the hacienda under Esmeralda's doting supervision.

Liz sank back against the creaky leather of her handmade Mexican chair and savored this rare moment of relaxation. She was thinking of the excitement of her recent trip to New York, her first trip abroad since she'd come to Mexico. With a thrill of pleasure she remembered the buyers' enthusiasm for her dolls. "Exquisite," they had said. "Museum quality." "Delightful." Their praise was the fulfillment of a secret personal dream she'd conceived in this mountain village. She was going to have to work harder than ever to be able to fill their orders for her dolls.

The morning stillness was pierced by a sudden, ear-splitting shriek of despair that startled Liz out of her reverie. The sound came from the doll factory, and a wave of alarm rippled through Liz. Besides her twins, her factory was the most important thing in her life.

Liz jumped up. Her shawl slid to the floor, but she did not notice it. The thick, roughly woven Mexican cotton dress with its lavish, jewel-bright embroidery work was long sleeved and warm.

A second scream erupted from the factory, and this was followed by a tumultuous chorus of cries.

What in the world could have happened?

Chapter Four

Her bright hair flying, Liz raced down the sun-splashed corridor. She crossed the courtyard, which was shaded by ancient poplars and draped with scarlet bougainvillea. Even before she reached that part of the hacienda she had converted into her doll factory, she saw the telltale signs of trouble.

Water trickled in a steady stream from beneath the doorway and pooled on the pink tile floor of the courtyard. She heard the muted cries of hopelessness. Not bothering to remove her huaraches, Liz sloshed through the water. When she opened the door, her heart caught in her throat.

Eyes from a hundred brown faces turned toward the tall, slender woman who looked far too young to be shouldering her massive responsibilities. To them she had always been like a goddess since she first stepped onto their mountain and moved into the dilapidated, high-walled hacienda that had been partially destroyed during the Revolution because it had once belonged to the most hated of all the *caciques*.

Liz surveyed the destruction. The entire factory was floating in three feet of water. Doll dresses, tiny wigs, spools of golden braid, beads, miniature shoes and hats, the machines—everything was soaked.

Juan, Liz's foreman, shushed the others to silence so that he could speak. "Señora, the water tower on the roof broke and flooded the factory." His low, Spanish voice held both anxiety and defeat. He was a man whom life had defeated too many times. "We have lost everything."

Liz felt as lost and defeated as they did. She had hundreds of new orders that had to be filled within the month, and they were already running behind. During the rainy season the villagers needed time to seed and cultivate their fields. She was too lenient with her workers, excusing them from duties to tend their land when she should have insisted that they come. She even excused Juan when he didn't work because of his drinking, but the peasants' lives seemed so relentlessly hard to her.

She thought of New York, where she'd found the vast new outlet for her dolls. She'd come back with hopes of expansion, and now this. If she disappointed her distributor, a hard man who would not tolerate failure, he would lose faith in her.

She waded through the water and picked up a sodden doll garment and a tiny soaked silk flower. She fingered the limp petals of the ruined flower reverently. She was overwhelmed by despair. Years of her own work and frustration stood behind her dolls. She remembered the loneliness and isolation she'd endured in this strange country that was so far away from England and everyone she'd loved.

Nor would she be the only one affected if this calamity

were allowed to destroy everything she'd worked for. The desperate Mexican villagers depended upon her factory for their livelihood. She was responsible for them. The silk flower was a symbol of their ruin as well as hers.

She felt the stinging fire of tears behind her eyelids, but she fought them back. She set the little flower on a table and smoothed the petals tenderly. She did not know what she could do to salvage her factory, but when she looked up, Liz's dark eyes flashed with the fierce determination that was her heritage, the heritage of the father she sought to deny.

"I will not give up. *We* will not give up," she said so softly they scarcely heard her.

Her Spanish was awkward. She had learned to speak the tongue the way she always did everything—by simply plunging in and doing it. But the people who worked for her loved the soft sound of her voice despite her confusing conjugations and hopelessly jumbled pronouns. They heard strength and hope.

Long ago, when Liz had first come to the deserted hacienda, the people had regarded her with suspicion. When she saved a child dying of malaria by driving the infant and his mother into Mexico City for medical help and remaining with them through the crisis, the hearts of the villagers softened. They gave her their sympathy when they learned she was pregnant and alone, their respect when she'd begun her factory, and finally their love because of her treatment of them. She had brought them work, hope and a new beginning. They could not know that by helping them, she had given herself the same things.

"We will have to work together," she continued haltingly because she had to pause to keep her voice from breaking, "as we always have. This will mean long hours.

Six days a week. You must bring your cousins from other villages to help you in the fields. No vacations for a while if we are to clean this place up, dry everything before it mildews, and repair the machines. But if we can satisfy our New York distributors, it will mean a bigger factory very soon, better machines, more jobs, more money for you."

Now there were smiles instead of dark looks of despair. For an instant she was filled with doubt. There was a much easier way to save the factory. One telephone call to an opulent flat in Paris. One telephone call to her father and Mimi.

The mere thought strengthened her resolve. It would be easier to lose her factory, easier to starve, easier even to watch the villagers and their children starve than to call him. With an effort she forced Roger Chartres and Mimi from her mind.

Liz beckoned Juan and gave him specific orders. Then she telephoned Manuel Rodriguez, her partner, who was in Mexico City, and told him they had to have more machines at once. She carefully concealed her desperation. He would learn how bad things were when he returned.

"At once?" Manuel asked. "Liz, in Mexico you must learn the word *mañana*."

"There are many things about the Spanish language that are beyond me, Manuel. The meaning of that word is one of them."

She hung up to the sound of his laughter.

She would succeed by herself. Already the demoralizing feelings of defeat were subsiding, and her fierce will to win despite all odds was taking over.

Liz worked long into the afternoon, racing between her office and the factory, making uncountable decisions as to what could be salvaged and what should be thrown out. It was a painful process.

An entire shipment of fifteen-inch dolls resembling miniature princesses from imperial Russia, all lavishly costumed to attend a dance in the tsar's Winter Palace, were soaked. The research that had gone into the creation of these dolls had been monumental, the labor in their gem-studded diadems, gossamer veils and rich ball gowns awesome. Now they were ruined.

Ruined as well were four dozen Japanese samurai dolls. These dolls were the finest and most authentic Liz had attempted to design and manufacture. They were dressed in rich brocade, and their equipment included the traditional two swords, a suit of armor fashioned of leather, metal plates, and silken tassels. Embossed miniature helmets hid heads of real hair. Clean-shaven chins reflected the samurais' fastidious customs. Liz had spent three months pouring over library books before she'd completed her design for the model of this doll.

She forgot about lunch and the siesta hour until Esmeralda tiptoed into her office. Then Liz's stomach growled ferociously as she realized it was long past the hour she usually had lunch on the balcony with the children.

They must be starving! She couldn't imagine why they had not bombarded her office an hour earlier, as they usually did when she became engrossed with her work. The spicy aroma of chile and tortillas drifted from the kitchen.

When Esmeralda said nothing, Liz glanced up and saw the misery contorting Esmeralda's face. With the instincts of a mother who realized her twins' numerous imperfections, some charming and some of them not so charming, Liz knew that a new catastrophe had struck.

"What have the little rascals done this time, Emmie?" she asked lightly, for she was an indulgent mother.

"Nothing, señora," Esmeralda wailed. "The little angels are gone!"

Panic rose like a hot wave in Liz's throat.

"Gone?" Liz's tired mind refused to accept a new crisis. "Surely it's one of their games."

"No, señora, they are gone. Even the burro Pablo. I left them in the meadow to ride Pablo, but he was being so stubborn he wouldn't move. When I came back they were gone."

"When was this? Have you looked everywhere for them? Someone must have seen them. Did you go down to the village?"

"I'm crazy with looking for them, señora. Mario told me he saw them with a gringo. *Un gigante.* A giant. He took them into the forest, Mario said. They were laughing as though they were friends. I am afraid of the forest. I cannot go after them."

Liz's fingers gripped her ledger. Esmeralda, like many of the other villagers, believed in all the gruesome local superstitions regarding the cliffs, mountains and forests. The villagers believed in a world filled with hostile forces whose goodwill and protection must be secured. The rain god would withhold rain if he were neglected. *Los aires,* the spirits who lived in the water, might send illness to those who offend them. The superstitions regarding the mountain were so ridiculously frightening that Liz had never paid any attention to them before.

Liz looked past Esmeralda to the thick pine trees that climbed the steep slopes. Liz was not frightened by legends, but the forest and the mountain were dangerous with their unexpected precipices and cliffs.

A giant who laughed? Was there some reality to this?

Liz remembered a foreigner she had seen in the village the week before. But none of the village men were giants. Only one man that she knew fit that description. Alexander was six feet four, his body so thickly muscled he would seem a giant to someone of Mario's smaller stature. She remembered her husband's broad grin, the pleasurable rumble of his laughter, and she was shaken.

"Oh, no! Don't let it be Alexander." Liz sank back, gasping. Was the man who'd come upon her last week, when she and Alex had gone swimming, someone Alexander had sent to find her?

She could fight the loneliness of exile. She could fight floods and the constant lack of money, but she could not bear to lose her precious darlings.

Had Alexander found her hiding place? Had he come and kidnapped the children? She had read stories of fathers doing that. What if he took them and went away as she had? She felt a twinge of guilt as she thought how he might twist her actions of seven years ago. But what she'd done had been different. Alexander hadn't wanted her, and he hadn't known she was pregnant. He hadn't wanted children from her. He'd sent her away, vowing the most terrible revenge if he ever found her. But what if he'd changed his mind? What if he wanted them now? What if he took them? With his vast resources, how could she fight him? Would she ever be able to find Alex and Samantha again?

Liz's stubborn, resilient will rallied. She mustn't allow herself to panic yet. The man last week did not have to be in Alexander's employ. The children were probably perfectly all right. She was overreacting because she was already in an anxious state from the flood.

Liz rose. She stood a head taller than Esmeralda. "Tell

everyone we must search for the twins. I will go into the forest myself."

"But the giant, señora!"

"If he is so terrible, Esmeralda," Liz erupted, "do you think I will leave my defenseless children in his care in the forest?"

The brook gurgled as it flowed over amber pine needles and splashed over black lava ash. The shadows in the forest were darkening; the sun had sunk behind the lavender peaks. A sliver of moon hung in the sky. Liz had been walking for hours, and she was exhausted.

"Alex. Samantha. *Queridos.* Oh, my darlings. Where are you?"

Liz called the names repeatedly, and when there was no answer, her terror increased. Never had her bold, mischievous children seemed so vulnerable and in need of protection.

When she stepped on a twig that crackled, she screamed, so brittle were her nerves. She felt so tired and emotionally drained, she did not know how much longer she could go on. At last she sagged wearily against a tree and listened to the silence. For the first time she grew aware of the darkness. From somewhere deep in the forest came a sound that didn't belong. She strained to hear it again, but there was only the swift flapping of a winged creatured in a branch overhead, the rustling of leaves and the hootings of an owl.

Her teeth began to chatter. Just when she thought she must return to get flashlights and warmer clothing, Liz heard the sounds of childish laughter mingling with the pleasant, deep resonance of a man's voice.

"Come on, Pablo. This way." Samantha was coaxing her pet, who was renowned for his stubbornness.

The chilled night air swirled around Liz, but her relief was so profound she scarcely felt it. She was about to call to Samantha when the velvet warmth of an all-too-familiar, amused male voice came to her.

"You're sure this is the way back, Samantha? Burros usually have a better sense of direction than people do—though I hate to credit this ragtag animal with any superiority."

"No, Daddy, I'm not sure," Samantha admitted. "Maybe Pablo is right."

"Daddy." The word that was so casually uttered by the daughter sliced through the mother's heart. Liz began to quiver, and was rational enough to know she was on the verge of hysteria.

It couldn't be. He couldn't be! Not here! Not Alexander! Not with the children! Had he come to take them away?

"Alexander?" Liz cried his name with hushed fear as she propelled herself into the darkness toward the voices.

"Liz. Is that you?" Her own name and his question with the husky French intonation reached out and enveloped her like a warm caress. Only *he* could make her name such a sensuous sound.

She saw him then, walking in the moonlight, and she stopped as though a witch had frozen her with a spell. Everything seemed to happen in slow motion, as though the purple darkness of the night had somehow enchanted the forest and everyone within it.

The children's laughter at Pablo's hoarse snort was fuzzy and sounded far away. Liz was aware only of Alexander beside them, holding Pablo's reins and the children's hands.

Liz felt his intense, devouring gaze. There was a look of astonishment scrawled on his handsome face. Their eyes touched before she looked quickly, too quickly, away. In that split-second glance she memorized every detail of his appearance.

He was as stunningly charismatic as ever. His hair was as black as the deepest shadows; his golden eyes were molten with hot, unfathomable emotion. It seemed he could not tear his gaze from her.

His face was leaner and more uncompromising than it had been in youth. The hard experiences of life had carved his features, imbuing them with roughhewn strength. He was as compellingly handsome as she remembered, but the aura of rugged power he had always exuded had intensified. He was as awesomely virile as ever. Worldly cynicism curved his sensual mouth into a bold, insolent smile as he regarded her lazily. Yet there was about him a new and terrifying remoteness, a fierce determination to win no matter what the price.

Her heart began to pound like a frightened rabbit's. She went hot and cold.

All the emotions that she'd told herself were dead came alive like the searing, raw pain of an open wound, and she knew how terribly she had missed him, how terribly she still loved him. She wanted to rip away that chiseled mask he wore. Her independence these past years had been a valiant charade. She fought back the desire to beg for his understanding, to beg that this time he believe her.

Instead she stood stiffly before him. Pride silenced her and made her tilt her head upward defiantly, so that her gaze was almost level with his. She would not beg him again.

She struggled to fend off the overpowering emotions he so effortlessly engendered, feelings that left her weak and vulnerable and unable to fight him. But fight him she would. He represented danger. He could be hard and cold to his enemies. He might take the children from her.

"Mommy! Mommy!"

The spell of enchantment that bound Liz and Alexander was broken. The children sang in unison as they raced toward her. When they tumbled headlong into her arms, she knelt and cradled them against her breast, grateful for the security of their nearness. They were wriggling and breathless in their excitement.

"Pablo ran away, and Daddy came! We got lost in the woods chasing Pablo, but we weren't scared because Daddy was with us. Why didn't you tell us Daddy was coming, Mommy? Why didn't you?"

Liz hugged them closely, silently, frantically. When she gave them no answer, they shrugged free and peered at her with solemn, uncertain faces before they darted back to Alexander.

She felt bereft by their rejection, and she was in a state of bewilderment as she stared at her children clinging to their father. Never before had she had to share her children's loyalty. How had Alexander won their affection so quickly? It was an ominous sign.

"Daddy said you might not let him stay with us," Alex said. "We want him to." There was a mutinous note in his voice.

"Darling, how could he possibly stay?" Liz reasoned lamely. "Daddy lives far away. Besides, he's too busy." She glanced helplessly toward Alexander.

"He'll stay if you let him," Samantha cried passionately. "Mommy, please!"

Liz did not know what to do. Alexander's silence was no help. Why didn't he tell them it was impossible for him to stay?

It was terrifying that he could obtain an emotional hold

over the children so quickly. Might he use longer periods of time to turn them against her?

As always, Alexander read her easily. His features hardened. She felt the thorough rake of his narrowed eyes sweeping chillingly downward over her body.

"It's getting dark, and the children are cold," Alexander said curtly as she stood up. "I think it might be best if we went back to the hacienda before we tried to talk."

It was a rational remark, but his tone of command sparked anger in Liz. "After seven years, you and I have nothing to talk about," she lashed out, speaking in French so the children wouldn't understand.

He responded in French that was as rapid and deadly as gunfire. "The hell we don't! I've come because of my children."

"Don't use them for an excuse. You couldn't possibly care about the children. You scarcely know them. You don't even know how to love in the first place."

A muscle spasmed in his jawline. "I do care about my children," he stated coldly.

Fear made her reckless. "Well, you have no rights at all where they're concerned. You threw me out when I was pregnant."

All of his careful control disintegrated, and she moved nearer, she realized how stupid she was to provoke him.

"No rights, you say? I don't know how to love, you say, as if you do? You damned little..."

He was a tower of coiled fury looming over her, and for a minute she thought he might strike her. She cringed as he fought for control, and she noticed that the children were afraid and upset. Their faces were crumpled in misery.

Alexander glanced uneasily toward the children and

saw their white faces. He swallowed his furious expletive even as he seized Liz by the shoulders and pulled her against his lean body.

His hard arms circled her tiny waist, and her hips were ground tightly against him. The heady scent of his maleness mingled with his cologne and enveloped her. Everything about him came back to her in a poignant rush.

She felt the heat of him, sensed his masculine toughness. Only her fury prevented the bold intimacy of his embrace from being a dangerously stimulating sensation.

Brown fingers tilted her chin so that he could inspect her face. She was afraid, and her mouth felt so parched she couldn't speak. When she trembled, it was his rockhard body that supported hers. She felt branded by the muscular power of his body. She licked her lips and he watched the motion of her tongue with hot, dark eyes.

His brows were drawn together in a deep frown as he studied her, his mouth twisted in sardonic anger. His expression was as intense and primitive as that of a predator who had stalked his prey and captured it.

There was danger in his hard look, and suddenly she was afraid. It was as if she were facing a stranger instead of the husband she'd slept with, the husband whose children she'd borne. His deep, golden eyes continued to rake her with frightening intensity, his penetrating gaze stripping away her defenses until her very soul lay dangerously exposed.

"No," she murmured breathlessly. "You should never have come. Let me go. You must. Be reasonable, Alexander."

He held her so close that the hushed warmth of her soft voice brushed the dark skin of his throat. Her hair sprayed like tousled silk upon his bare brown arms. She struggled wildly, but only became more hopelessly and intimately entangled with his steel-tough body. He did not release her. Instead he threw back his black head and laughed down at her harshly.

At last he stopped laughing. "I must? You really are too much, Liz. Why must I do anything you say?"

"Because..."

"I owe you nothing, my dear." She was very aware of his hands searing her bare flesh. "Let's get something straight," he said hoarsely. "I wouldn't have thrown you out if I had had the slightest idea you were pregnant. No matter how I felt about you, do you think I could deny my own flesh and blood? You deliberately left without telling me you were expecting a baby. When I found out, I spent seven damned years looking for you."

"I came to your office that morning to tell you," she replied quietly, "but you were already out of your mind with rage. There seemed no point then."

"Of course I was angry. You'd wrecked Dazzle and me in one staggering blow by stealing Paul's formula and giving it to Jock! Why, Liz? Why did you do that? What was worth all those lies and treachery, not to mention outright criminality?"

His brown face appeared contorted through her blinding tears. "I had nothing to do with that," she whispered. "I tried to explain. I couldn't have done that to you."

"No?" There was a jeering note in his hard voice. His fingers tightened cruelly on her shoulder blades, and he pressed her so tightly to himself that his body seemed to consume hers. "Then how did Radiance steal and launch the perfume Paul had been perfecting for more than three years? Explain why Jock named that particular essence Liz. And while you're at it, tell me those photographs used in that launch aren't of you, my darling wife. Tell me you weren't the model for Radiance in that stinking, crooked deal! Tell me you aren't Roger Chartres's daughter! Liz, why the hell did you try to destroy me?''

The anger in his voice was fierce and frightening. She realized with a sinking heart that seven years had changed nothing.

"Let me alone," she moaned. "You won't believe anything I say, so why should I defend myself?''

He held her as tightly as ever. "Answer me, Liz.''

"I didn't…''

He gave her a hard shake. "I don't want your lies. This time I want the truth. Why?''

She was stung by his stubborn belief that she was so heartless, and she couldn't bear his bullying demands when he wouldn't even listen. Her fighting spirit returned, and she struggled, trying to break his grip. Kicking him again and again, she wrenched her hands free and pummeled his chest. She cried out in rage and misery, begging him to release her. Her fragile body writhed against the steely might of his arms until her heart pounded as though it might burst. At last she gave up. Against his strength, hers was as nothing.

"Tell me, Liz, was Jock your lover?''

"No!'' The single word was explosive. She yanked a hand free, and would have slapped him had he not caught her wrist just in time. She was panting in fury. "How could you even think that?'' she cried. "There's never been anyone except…except…you.'' Suddenly that angered her more than anything. "You rotten—'' She bit back the rest of her sentence. What right did he have to answers from her now? How she wished she could return Jock's love. How she wished there had been many, many other men. It was all so hopeless. Her thoughts clouded as a terrible dizziness swept her.

"Let me go," she pleaded. "I feel so strange. I can't breathe. Please. Alexander, I think I'm going to faint."

The brutal disappointment of the flood, the hard work, her terrifying search for the children, and Alexander's fierce anger had all taken their toll.

His hold seemed to loosen, and yet she did not fall. She felt curiously weightless. His grave face blurred in a nauseating whirl.

She relaxed, but even his strong arms could not keep her from sliding into a void that brought swift, black oblivion.

Alexander lifted her into his arms. He stared into her still face. Her flaming hair fell across his shoulders.

"Why, Liz?" he drawled in a voice that was strangled by torture, repeating the question that had haunted him for seven years. "Why did you do it, when I loved you so?"

Chapter Five

Alexander strode with Liz in his arms. The children and Pablo trailed behind in a disorganized scramble. Liz felt excessively light and delicate against his body, and Alexander felt remorse at his treatment of her. She looked so innocent and sweet. His rage was gone and in its place was a baffling tenderness.

Samantha's curiosity bubbled to the surface with questions that intensified Alexander's guilt. "What's the matter with Mommy, Daddy? Why is she sleeping now? Why did she get so mad at you?"

"Your mother's tired, Samantha," Alexander replied gruffly, answering the first question and evading the second. Samantha's eyes, so like her mother's, remained doubtful.

The hacienda was brilliantly lit against the deeper blackness of the mountains, and as Alexander climbed the path leading to the front gates, Esmeralda, Juan and several other Indian peasants walked out of the house. Curious, worried black eyes accosted him with a thousand half-formed suspicions.

"My wife fainted in the forest," Alexander drawled in his heavily accented Spanish, emphasizing his relationship to her. "The shock of losing the children and seeing me again after our long separation was too much," he began. Deciding that their señora had come to no harm, they nodded in swift understanding and immediate acceptance of him while he marveled at how naturally the word "wife" slid from his tongue even in a foreign language and how right it felt to call Liz that.

Alexander could almost read the villagers' minds as they stared first at him and then at his son, Alex, who bore the irrefutable stamp of his paternity.

They were thinking, The señora's husband has come. Despite the seven-year separation he is the rightful man of the house and must be treated with respect.

In the village it was not the custom to question a man's behavior. The peasants' acceptance of him made Alexander accept his position in the household as well.

Liz's head stirred groggily against his shoulder. "I'm all right, Alexander. Put me down," she mumbled faintly.

Ignoring her request, Alexander commanded her servants with the ease of a man used to giving orders. "Take me to my wife's bedroom and bring hot tea and broth in case she's hungry."

Maria scurried to the kitchen while Esmeralda took the children. Juan led Alexander up winding tiled stairs to the señora's spacious bedroom, which had views of the valley and mountains.

Alexander kicked the door open, stalked inside and gently laid Liz upon her great, hand-carved Mexican bed. Juan lit an oil lamp before shutting the door, leaving the couple alone in semidarkness. The enormous chairs and ornately wrought candelabra cast flickering shadows upon the stuccoed walls, but Alexander could see the evidence of Liz's talent for making any room charming. Brightly colored Indian rugs covered the tile floor. Childish artwork decorated one wall, and he realized that their children must have inherited her artistic talent.

He saw the photographs of her beloved Cornwall on her worktable. Shelves were filled with the original models of the dolls Liz had designed. Snuggly baby dolls in yellow organza sat beside Mimi from *La Boheme* and two stern Amish dolls. Southern belles in ruffled hoop skirts stood next to the dolls from her International series. Goya portrait dolls smirked from their corner. Alexander scarcely noted them.

He brought the lamp to the bed, and Liz blinked from its brilliance. She flung her hand weakly over her eyes to shade them but the movement exhausted her. Her fingers fell away. In the golden light her cheeks were pale, her lush, half-parted lips temptingly rose colored. Her tousled red curls pooled in a riot of waves upon blankets.

He knew he should leave, but he felt intensely concerned. He hoped this was nothing more than exhaustion. It was not in him to hate someone who was so weak and defenseless.

"Alexander." Her voice was a soft whisper that stirred long-forgotten intimate memories.

He could feel the low thudding of his pulse. He had not contemplated what the effect might be upon himself were he to find himself alone with her in her bedroom, accepted by all in her household as her rightful husband.

"Come here," she begged. Her low tone was sexy. It was the way she had always spoken to him in bed.

He turned. His eyes moved over her, from the enchanting beauty of her face to the creamy flesh of her throat. She was irresistibly lovely. Her breasts rose and fell beneath the stiff Mexican cotton gown. For countless seconds he just stared at her. Then he leaned over her, his great body powerful above her slender form.

"Is there something you need, Liz?" he questioned gently.

"Alexander, is it really you?" she murmured, her anger gone because his was. Her voice held an aching tenderness that Alexander was incapable of ignoring. She lifted her hands to his cheek and caressed him wonderingly, inflaming him with her gentle touch. Her softly glowing eyes held his.

He had to get out of here at once. Still, he remained while her fingertips traced the curve of his hard jawline before outlining the edges of his earlobe with featherlight strokes. His skin was alive with sensation.

Alexander groaned inwardly and brought his own hand up to remove hers. Curiously, instead of removing it, his warm fingers wrapped hers. He brought her fingertips to his lips and kissed them one by one while he stared deeply into her eyes.

What was happening to him? This was the woman who had deliberately tried to destroy him. She had kept him from knowing his children for seven years. He had no business staying with her like this.

His blood throbbed as with a fever. He could fight her harsh words, but her gentleness was too potent a force for him to resist. He knew if he didn't go soon he would heartily despise himself in the morning.

Not that he had the slightest intention of remaining until morning. He would leave her quickly. He had only to make sure she was comfortable for the night. She was the mother of his children, and his unexpected appearance had given her a shock. If he hadn't taken the children into the forest, she would scarcely be in this state.

When he thought of the children she had given him, his bitter attitude toward Liz lessened. He had expected Alex, but Samantha had been a glorious surprise. Alexander wondered again how Henson had missed the lively little girl who reminded him of Liz. He already adored his daughter. He wanted desperately to play a vital role in the lives of his children.

"I'm so sleepy," Liz said dreamily. "So sleepy." Her black lashes lowered and lay still against her pale cheeks.

He viewed the stiff cotton gown twisted about her body and realized the bulky fabric was probably uncomfortable.

"Sit up, Liz," he whispered. "I know you're tired, but you can't sleep in that dress. Let me help you take it off."

She nodded weakly and sat up so that Alexander could lift the gown over her shoulders. He noted how soft and warm she was when he touched her.

Alexander tossed the dress over a chair and turned back to her. Her eyes were closed, and her dreamy expression gave her the look of an angel. Her form entranced him. Her waist was as tiny as a wasp's, her hips slimly curved. Beneath her lace teddy he saw the dark crests of her nipples. He remembered her wildness in his bed, her total lack of inhibitions, which had shocked even him at first. He remembered the way she had made love to him with her lips. He remembered the golden afternoon she'd seduced him in that secret Italian grotto on a tiny island off the coast of Sardinia.

He inhaled deeply, thrusting the memories to the recesses of his mind. He had to get out of there. He was rising to make a swift exit when her hands circled his neck. She fingered the inky tendrils that fell over his collar. A single fingertip twirled a ribbon of soft blackness around its pink nail. Every muscle in his body froze.

"Alexander, do you remember how it was between us?"

A bolt of desire shuddered through him as she lowered her hands and moved them across his shoulders, drawing him back down to her. He hated himself for his weakness.

"You don't know what you're doing, Liz," he said hoarsely. "This is madness."

His lips hovered inches from hers. Her uneven breaths whispered against his mouth, low and seductive, irresistible in their wanton invitation.

"There was always madness between us, wasn't there?" Her hands moved lower, touching him with the expertise of a woman who knows every vulnerable area of her man. "Alexander, you're the most magnificent man. Is it so wrong of me to want you? I've been alone so long and I'm still your wife."

"I didn't come here because I wanted you." He expelled the cruel words roughly, but his skin burned from her caresses.

"Really?" Her silken tone mocked him.

He couldn't think when she touched him like that, with her fingers circling lightly over his body. She slipped the strap of her silken teddy downward until the honeyed orb of her breast was revealed, her pouting nipple thrusting tantalizingly upward.

"Liz, don't do this!" he groaned, but he didn't prevent her trembling fingers from unbuttoning his shirt.

A strip of bronzed male flesh was exposed, and she leaned forward and slid her tongue across his warm skin, trailing a blazing, liquid path from his throat to his navel. She continued to kiss him there, her head buried against the dark hair of his stomach. He felt the flicking movements of her tongue, the warmth of her breath tickling his body, driving him insane with need.

"Alexander, stay with me."

"God, I want you, Liz. Damn you," he muttered forcefully, gathering her body in his hard, bruising arms. "I can fight everything but this."

"How do you think it's been for me?" she cried. "I still loved you when you drove me away. I tried to forget you, but when you're here, holding me, I can only remember how it always was between us. I want to know if it's still the same, if it's really over between us, if you really hate me as much as you say."

His dark face flushed with fury as well as desire. She was deliberately tempting him despite her knowledge of his dislike. Well, she'd pushed him too far. He despised her, and nothing she could do or say would ever change that.

"It's over, Liz."

"Is it? Then walk out that door, Alexander," she taunted softly. "That's all you have to do to prove it."

The violence of his emotions was unforgivable. Hesitating, he stared into her smoldering black eyes and was lost.

He felt the intimate pressure of her soft body beneath his. Desire surged in his blood in a powerful pulsing sensation. He had to have her, despite everything that had passed between them.

He seized her and pulled her roughly against his chest, hating her, loving her, wanting her, despising her. His arms were ruthless iron bands binding her against his tough male body. "You wanted this, Liz, remember that."

He crushed his mouth against hers, pressing his tongue deeply into her mouth. He was on fire with passion and anger, and his burning need consumed her as well. His hands forced hers to circle his neck. She trembled as though suddenly afraid of the overpowering emotions she'd aroused.

His fingers were tangled in her hair, and he jerked her head back. The lamplight shone on her pale face and in the gleaming blackness of her eyes.

She'd taunted him with the memories of their past love. She wanted to know if he hated her. She'd dared to defy him by saying all he had to do to prove his hatred was to walk out the door. "Prove it," she'd said.

Well, he'd prove it, and there was a better way of showing her how he felt than walking out the door.

He ripped his clothes apart, not bothering to fully undress before he flung himself over her. His hands forced the ridiculous lace garment she wore downward, uncaringly shredding the flimsy material in his haste so that her body was fully exposed. He touched her everywhere but without even a trace of the infinite tenderness he'd once so lovingly shown her.

She lay very still, the expression on her lovely face uncertain, her body stiff beneath his hard hands, as if, too late, she sensed his callous intent. Then she began to struggle.

"Stop it! Stop, Alexander. I won't be treated so."

His harsh laughter mocked her desperation. "You were the one who wanted this, my love."

"But I did not want—"

Her words of protest were stifled by his hard mouth claiming hers. His caressing hands roamed over her with intimate familiarity until at last her body reluctantly responded. He lowered his mouth and kissed her white throat. His palm cupped her rounded breasts, kneading its tip into a hardened bud. Her flesh felt hot beneath his lips and hands as though her passion washed her with waves of fire.

She fought him, but her strength was that of a child, his that of a giant. Mercilessly he overpowered her. He caught her flailing hands in one of his and held them high above her head. His mouth covered hers, and when she tried to twist her face on the pillow, he held her lips with his relentlessly.

His legs were long and muscled, his thighs like iron. Tears streamed down her cheeks, but her sobs were muffled from his kisses. When at last he released her lips, she muttered with a terrible sadness, "You've grown hard, Alexander. There's no softness left in you. You're a stranger."

"If I'm hard, Liz, you have only yourself to blame. If we're strangers, whose fault is that?"

She was silent then. His mouth found the rapid pulse-beat in the hollow of her throat. His hands moved over her bare arms, her waist, down her thighs, savoring every lush curve before his knees forced her legs apart.

Alexander's blood throbbed with the beat of a pagan drum. The sweet female scent of her stimulated every sense in his being until his desire consumed him.

He paused and kissed her with all the thorough, ruthless passion that was his nature, the heat of his punishing mouth insolent and demanding. She was shuddering, but her hands had raised to circle his neck again as if she were driven by a hunger as fierce as his. He felt her fingertips caress him.

He kissed her again and again until she was limp and unresisting, until her body melted against his. He soared on hot, flaming wings in a wild black night, and she came with him.

Her breathing was as labored as his. Their desire built

into a wild crescendo of spiraling needs. For a timeless moment their hatred fell away, and they were lovers again, each glorying in the taste and the sensation of the other.

He took her then with the swift blind need of a man who'd been too long without the one woman he wanted. For a fleeting moment he glimpsed heights he'd thought he would never see again. His mouth moved over her in moist, intimate exploration, seeking all the intimate feminine places that would bring her the most pleasure. Then desire overcame him in a shattering burst of glory. In that final moment he crushed her beneath him as she whispered his name in complete surrender.

Afterward they lay in the hushed darkness without touching. His passion spent, Alexander's anger toward Liz returned. It was even more intense than before, augmented by the gnawing memory of a passion he had not wanted, augmented by the deep feeling of self-loathing for what he'd done. He should never have let this happen. There could be no closeness with her.

He had used her, not as the wife he loved, he reassured himself swiftly. She'd given him physical release, nothing more. Despite what had happened, nothing between them was changed. He felt no closeness with her, only a deep, unremitting coldness. Still, a new, unnamed unease lingered.

He slanted a hard glance in her direction. She lay as still as death upon the woolen sarapes. For an instant he wondered if she was unconscious. Then he saw the flicker of her lashes and the faint glimmer of her eyes behind them. No. She was awake, despite her exhaustion and his rough treatment. Liz was too bold to shrink from unpleasant realities. She was staring at the ceiling through her narrowly slitted eyelids. He wondered what she was thinking.

He remembered suddenly the long, languid lovemaking sessions of their past, so different from the violence of the present. He remembered the loving hours afterward, those balmy moments of satiated glory. He recalled the rapturous afterglow when they'd clung to each other after their wild excesses.

Now they lay without touching.

Despite the crisp mountain air sifting through the partially opened windows, the room was stifling. Alexander rose abruptly, turning his back on the silent woman on the bed. He did not want to think of the past or of the present. He wanted no part of Liz. He had not meant for this to happen, and he swore that it never would again.

Chapter Six

Liz snuggled beneath the coarse cotton sheets and thick pile of woolen blankets and sarapes. Sunlight streamed into the room, its brightness indicating the lateness of the hour. Why hadn't she heard the children? Why hadn't Juan sent Esmeralda to summon her so she could handle any emergencies involving the factory?

Liz sat up, shading her eyes with curled fingers. The leaden weight of anguish lay upon her heart. With her fingertips she felt the crusted residue upon her cheeks from the countless tears she'd wept during the long night. She'd scarcely slept. Every time she'd wakened, thinking futilely of Alexander's passionate dislike for her, fresh waves of sadness had swept her.

How could she have been so foolish as to believe he felt anything other than hatred? He'd been like a stranger in her bed, using her brutally to satisfy needs he did not even want to have.

When he'd left her lying in the chill darkness, she'd felt the most profound emptiness because she realized how deeply she still loved him, just as she realized how hopeless her feelings were.

Last night there had been no union of their souls, only the fierce mating of their bodies. His callous passion had shown her all that she had lost, but it had strengthened her longing to regain it, however futile that possibility seemed. If only she could have hated him for the way he'd used her in that time of wild darkness. Instead a part of her had reveled in it. She should feel ashamed for the way she'd seduced him against his will, but stronger than hatred or shame was the memory of his passion.

The furious rush of water splashing in the shower came to her, and she realized with a start that Alexander must be taking a shower. In her shower. Her heart fluttered in wild panic; he might walk in at any moment.

The shredded teddy lay on the floor where he'd thrown it. It would never do for him to find her like this. Her hair was disheveled and she knew she must look horribly wan. She leaped out of bed, picked up the torn garment and went to the dresser, where she hid it in a drawer. She worked swiftly, smoothing the worst tangles from her hair, wiping away the salt of her tears, dabbing blusher on her cheeks and putting on lipstick.

From her closet stuffed with outrageous clothes she grabbed the most dramatic garment of them all. The robe was a daring swirl of scarlet crepe de Chine with the sleeves cut out from the waistline. A wide sash made her waist as tiny as an hourglass. The robe, like many of her designs, was flamboyant rather than practical, but it was just what she needed to wear to make her appear bold and confident when she felt so uncertain.

Liz had designed the robe for her spring collection for

Isobel's, her boutique in London. She'd never worn it before. She'd kept the original for herself when she'd sent Ya Lee, her London manager, the designs. Always when she was designing, Liz used her own secret fantasies as an aid to create clothes made to appeal to the woman who wanted to feel excitingly different.

Liz opened the drapes and looked out on the purple mountains and the broad valley. But this morning, the peaceful landscape did not bring harmony to her troubled mind. At the sound of the door, she spun around, her heart jumping chaotically.

In the sunlight her hair was spun flame. She was unaware of how extravagantly beautiful she was, because her attention was focused on the lean, dark man framed in the doorway.

He was unsmiling, his harsh stare as menacing as his lovemaking had been the night before. Well, at least he was not indifferent to her. Even his hatred was preferable to that.

It took all her willpower to maintain a surface calm when she felt so shaky inside. She did not know that the light from behind her outlined her body through the soft fabric of her gown. She was aware only of the swift intake of his breath, of a baffling intensity about him.

"Hello, Alexander," she said in a deliberately casual voice.

He said nothing, but there was a vital, sensual element in his hard, assessing gaze. His eyes lingered on her, following her as she moved from the long windows.

The force of his male virility seemed to capture her, and she felt a sudden breathlessness in the pit of her stomach. The way he looked at her made her feel positively undressed.

"Come in," she invited, not knowing what else to say.

He stepped inside, and she was never more aware of how sexually appealing Alexander was to her as she watched his lazy, swaggering grace. Determined not to be intimidated, she tilted her chin defiantly.

Still, her senses registered his physically disturbing state. His blue shirt was half-buttoned, and a strip of his deeply tanned chest was tantalizingly visible. A sheen of dampness from his recent shower clung to his jet dark hair, and he smelled fresh and masculine. If only she could go to him. She wanted to touch him, but his remoteness quelled such impulses.

"It's a beautiful morning, isn't it?" she said composedly, as if there were no secret desires in her heart and no hatred in his. She walked to the rattan table and chairs by the corner window and sat down. "Did you sleep well?"

"Well enough." He hadn't slept a wink. It was irritating the way she looked so glorious and rested. He sank negligently into an overstuffed chair across the room.

"I'm glad. Sometimes that's difficult in a strange bed." She rushed on to cover the awkwardness between them, but, of course, she didn't cover it at all. If only he would quit looking at her like that. "I suppose you've already seen the children?"

"Yes. They're with their tutor now. You must see them soon. They're worried about you and filled with questions."

She laughed lightly. "I can imagine. They're not used to their mother showing any weakness. In the forest, I was scarcely my usual serene self."

"Your usual serene self? That's certainly a new one." His soft voice mocked her.

She merely laughed at his jibe and continued with her chatter. Alexander stared at her, scarcely listening. She wasn't going to show any signs of her true feelings about last night, he realized. Had she been badly hurt, shocked? Was she resolved now, as he was, that it had long been over between them, that such tactics as she'd employed were useless on him? Or was last night no more to her than a bit of untidy emotional refuse to be hastily swept aside and forgotten now that it was obvious it had served no purpose? He wished he could forget it as easily as she, but the sight of her in that wildly dramatic gown, her feminine curves enhanced by the bright soft silk, affected him. Nor could he stamp out the memory of the light from the windows outlining too clearly the shape of her body. His blood was still beating violently from that first vision.

A knock sounded, and Liz called out a cheery welcome. Maria stepped inside carrying a tray with coffee, marmalade and two servings of warm *bolillos,* a hard Mexican bread. The better Liz's humor, the worse his grew.

"You'll join me, I hope, darling?" Liz invited her now-scowling husband with the sweetest of smiles.

"I've eaten," came his terse reply.

"Then I hope you don't mind if I do?" she said, buttering a bolillo while she sipped her rich black coffee. "I'm starving. You may remember I always am in the morning when I've been enormously excited the day before."

"Enormously excited!" He lifted a dark eyebrow in irritation. How dared she skirt that sore subject so cavalierly. It goaded him that she appeared so unruffled, indeed so bold, as if that disgusting episode last night had given her immeasurable confidence.

She completely ignored his dark frown. Indeed, she seemed to thrive on his bad humor. He watched her smear a dab of marmalade on a slab of bread.

"I'm afraid this is going to be a busy day once I get started," she continued in the same bright voice.

"They've all been clamoring to wake you for hours, but I wouldn't allow it," Alexander replied testily.

Startled by this unexpected thoughtfulness toward her, she glanced at him. His cutting gaze slashed her. Whatever softness had motivated him was scarcely apparent.

"There seems to be a bit of confusion downstairs," Alexander said, "that only you can resolve."

"That's putting it mildly, I'm sure. You see, Alexander, the water tank on the roof flooded my doll factory yesterday, before you came. But enough of my problems. I know you didn't come to Mexico without some purpose. It's time we got down to what brings you here. What do you want from me? Why have you come?"

She crunched off a bit of bolillo.

"I've come because of the children."

She swallowed the tasteless, half-chewed bit of bread crust in her mouth. "Of course, but what does that mean—specifically?"

He shot her a dark look. "Specifically—divorce and custody rights."

She dropped her fingers from her bolillo and clasped them together. She did not like the businesslike way he spoke of the children, as if they were just another profit-and-loss statement to be analyzed, another game that he could play and win.

He continued with savage intensity. "Our marriage was a mistake from the beginning. We were only together two months."

"Twelve weeks," she corrected faintly.

"And separated seven years. Not much of a marriage. We have no choice but to legally end it. Naturally I would prefer sole custody of the twins, and I'm willing to make a generous settlement if you agree. You can go on living in whatever bizarre lifestyle you're currently caught up in, but the children will have stability. I will give them the best schools. They can spend their summers in my villa in Sardinia or one of Maman's châteaux in France. Liz, you've scarcely managed to teach them a smattering of French. They're growing up with illiterate Indians.''

"They're only six, and they speak both Spanish and English fluently,'' she retorted coldly.

She was seething. "Bizarre lifestyle,'' he'd said. How could he refer to Esmeralda and Maria as illiterate Indians? Didn't he see that they had loved her and cared for her when he had thrown her out?

Her voice was dangerously low, poorly concealing her anger. "I'm sure you've discussed this with the children.''

"Why should I?''

"You mean their wishes would have no impact upon you?''

"I did not say that.''

"Did it ever occur to you that it might do them irreparable damage to be separated from me? You cannot manage children the way you manage employees in your factories, Alexander. You say you will give them the best schools. Children need much more than that. Your mother, for all her dull ability to be everlastingly proper—a trait, I thank God, I lack—''

"Leave my mother out of this!''

She sprang to her feet, her hot temper flaring. "I won't! All she gave you were the best schools, those glorious villas you're throwing up at me, châteaux, and money. That's why you're hard, Alexander. That's why you could throw out a woman who loved you without a qualm. You turned your back on me when I needed you the way she turned her back on you when you were a child. You didn't care that I was hurting! I won't let you ruin my children the way your mother ruined you!''

Alexander leaped to his feet and crossed the room. He towered over her.

"Stop it, Liz. You're hysterical."

"I'm not hysterical! I'm angry! A while ago you called Esmeralda an illiterate Indian. I'll tell you something that you in your insufferable narrow-mindedness will never believe. Esmeralda's a far more compassionate human being than you are."

"Are you through?"

"No. I would not have opposed a reasonable custody arrangement until you said these things to me this morning. Yesterday I saw that it was a grave error on my part to take the children so far away from you despite the hostile circumstances of our separation. I was sorry for that."

"And now?"

"I wish you'd never come here." She whirled away from him, her fists clenched against her stomach as she stalked toward the windows. She heard his heavy footsteps right behind hers. Was there nowhere to hide?

When she turned to face him, he was directly in front of her. The ruthless set of his jaw was grim with purpose.

"If you try to take the children from me on a permanent basis, I'll fight you. You can't buy me or my children the way you buy everything else in your life, Alexander Vorzenski."

'I suppose that's because you've already sold yourself to Jock.''

Liz slapped him. She was so furious, so deeply insulted by his bitter, hateful remark, she did so without forethought of the consequences, and she instantly regretted her action.

He stood silent and unflinching, but she sensed the violent emotions surging beneath his taut features. Her own hand stung with pain; she could see the imprint of four slim fingers upon his cheek.

She'd gone too far. Too late, she knew it. Liz tried to escape him, but before she could manage one step, his large hands lashed out and seized her forearm in a viselike grip, hauling her against the muscular wall of his chest.

"You shouldn't have hit me," he growled as she gulped for air. "You invite like violence on yourself."

Her fragile bones threatened to break under his crushing hold. His fingers wound painfully into her thick hair, pulling her head back so that the curve of her neck was exposed clear down to the rising swell of her breasts. It was a seductive pose that awakened fully his marauding male instincts. His head moved closer and she could feel the heat of his suddenly irregular breaths against her skin.

"I'll scream, Alexander," she cried, "if you don't let me go." Her heart was fluttering against her rib cage like a trapped bird beating itself to death in a cage. "After last night, I don't want you to touch me ever again."

"Don't you? And last night it was you who wanted this."

When Alexander had first seized her, he had no thought other than bending her to his will, but her nearness was provocative. The scent of her, the feel of her body pressing close intoxicated him. Even the passionate fire of her anger aroused him. He lowered his head toward hers instinctively.

In a frenzy Liz tried to twist away from him, but her hair, caught in his hands, was yanked painfully. His mouth came down brutally on hers. His kiss was ravaging and frightening in its hard demand. His arms pressed her body against his thighs and made her intimately aware of his driving male hunger.

"I'll hate you forever for this." She gasped out the words beneath the smothering pressure of his mouth.

He released her lips. "Do you think I care? Stop fighting me, Liz."

He jerked her even more tightly against himself, knocking the breath from her lungs. His arms wrapped around her; his hands molded her curves to fit the hard contours of his torso and thighs. He kissed her more deeply than before. His anger and passion raged with the force of a wildfire swept by a savage wind, consuming everything in its path.

She screamed, the sound stifled against him, as the insolent plunder of his lips made her completely his. His hands moved beneath sheer silk and caressed the warmth of her. He was shaking as if overpowered by the storm of his own emotions. Fierce, unintelligible endearments were whispered against her ear. His mouth evoked wild pagan feelings she'd never felt before. Her arms went around his neck, and her lips trembled in a wanton response.

Something melted within Alexander, gentling the angry tide of emotion. Rage and the desire to hurt no longer ruled him. The bruising force of his embrace changed subtly, and the hands that wrapped her so closely exerted tender mastery instead of punishment.

Perfectly attuned to Alexander, Liz instantly sensed the difference. His embrace was more dangerous than ever. Sensual longing flamed under the wanton expertise of his mouth, beneath the intimate exploration of his hand gently kneading her breast. She felt her resistance ebb. In another moment she would be lost. He would carry her to bed. A repetition of her surrender last night would be the final, unendurable humiliation. She had to stop him before it was too late. Her tattered pride gave her the strength to wrench free and stumble backward.

She felt empty and terribly alone. Her back was to him. She couldn't bear looking at him. His roughly carved face was too dear. She longed to be in his arms, and to assuage that need she wrapped her body tightly with her own. Her heart beat in wild longing. She couldn't let him know how shatteringly vulnerable she was.

From behind her his voice came, husky, gentler. "Liz—"

This new softness from him was more than the disturbed state of her nerves could handle. Liz turned around. His amber gaze startled her, compelled her. His hand reached toward her, not in anger this time but in—

She was never to know what would have happened had they not been interrupted just as his arms slid around her waist and shoulders in hungry possession.

She felt herself drawn intimately against him; his lips seared her brow in the tenderest of kisses. There was an embarrassed cough from behind the half-opened door. Her cheeks were flushed as she called out shakily, "Yes?"

Alexander drew a sharp rein on his own emotions as Juan stepped inside. To Liz's amazement, Alexander did not release her, and Juan accepted their embrace as perfectly natural between man and wife.

"Señora, you must come at once to the doll factory. We need your help, and that of the señor too, if he is willing."

"I don't think the señor is particularly anxious to help me," Liz snapped hastily. "He came here to—" She felt Alexander's fingers tighten on her skin and thought better of completing her sentence.

Stung because he was feeling extraordinarily loving toward her, Alexander responded without thought. "Of course I'll help!"

Liz stared at them both in helpless confusion, suddenly realizing the trap in which she'd been caught. Without meaning to ask for Alexander's help, she had, and now that he'd said he would, she had no choice but to accept. The very last thing she wanted was him running things in his high-handed fashion in her factory. It was bad enough that he was determined to make trouble about the children. Bad enough that she was in constant danger of letting her own needs for him humiliate her.

When Juan left, Liz said hotly, "You don't have to, you know."

Alexander dropped his arm from her shoulder with a pregnant emphasis. It was evident that he was now in control of the physical desire that had mastered him only minutes before.

"I said I would."

"But—"

"Leave it alone, Liz. Maybe it's for the best. It's obvious when we try to have any sort of reasonable discussion about our personal situation, things get out of hand."

"They wouldn't if you—"

"Liz, stop it. Get dressed in something that isn't—" His eyes ran over her body. The gown clung to every curve. He still wanted her. He wanted to make love to her as wildly as he had the night before.

Damn her! Why was she so beautiful? Even in anger she was magnificent. She had the most extraordinary eyes when she got mad. He had never seen eyes so brilliant in any well-bred woman's face before. They reminded him of the way she was in bed, all softness and fire, hellcat wildness and demure loveliness.

He wanted to touch her again, but he didn't dare. He'd just learned once again the foolhardiness of that. When he held her, his need for her became unbearable. He was determined never to give in to his weakness for her again.

She was so bold and completely determined not to be dominated. No other woman besides, of course, his mother ever opposed him. He was so used to getting his way with women, he wondered if he knew how to fight her. He had forgotten how to handle Liz—if he had ever known.

She was as damnably difficult as ever. He didn't know how he was going to get around her. But there had to be a way. He was determined the children were his and his alone.

Now all he had to do was convince Liz.

Chapter Seven

"I won't have you turning my factory over to Manuel Rodriguez!" Liz said heatedly.

Alexander endured her temper with the infuriating calm he'd shown all week. There had been many tantrums since he'd started trying to avert the disaster her factory was headed for.

"Why not? He's the best man for the job."

"It's my factory! I suppose you think nothing of telling me I'm not running it properly."

"Nothing at all," he replied cheerfully. "You have absolutely no managerial talent, Liz."

"No managerial talent!" she shrieked. "I built this factory from nothing."

"Lower your voice, my dear," he said, suppressing a smile. "I'm sure you don't want to be heard in the furthest market stall in the village."

"I don't care who hears me," she shouted louder than before. "Nor in what market stall."

"That's becoming all too obvious. Whether you like it or not, you need my help, darling. You've gotten yourself into a hopeless muddle."

She crossed her arms across her chest and glared at him, detesting his smug attitude. "Well, I don't like it. You're destroying everything. First you ruin morale by firing Juan."

"You should never have hired him in the first place, my love. He's all wrong for his job. He drinks. He has a negative attitude. Besides, I'm nearly positive he's been stealing."

She was trembling violently now. "And then you threatened to fire anyone else who didn't show up for work. Alexander, these people have land to plow."

He shrugged. "You have a factory to run, and you can't run it with the chronic absenteeism you've been tolerating."

"Then you started paying overtime, which I can't afford."

"Yes, you can once we get things organized and running efficiently. Look, Liz, actually it's amazing how well you've done considering your deplorable disorganization. The only thing that's pulled you through this far is your bullheaded determination and the unique charm of your dolls."

Bullheaded determination! "I'm glad you think I've done something right!" she snapped.

"Well, damn little. Your dolls are underpriced. Your machinery is dilapidated. New equipment would save labor costs. You have no distribution system. Shopkeepers just come here with a basket over their arms and collect what they want. Yes, I know Manuel has made a few calls on some stores in Texas and California, but that hardly counts. Then you went to New York and got your first real break, but that was the sheerest accident.

"You have a good product, but without the right publicity and a sales force, you're doomed. I can start Manuel on the road to straightening all this out. The guy's really talented at getting the maximum out of your employees. He understands them. He knows when to be hard, and you don't."

She was infuriated at him for criticizing everything she'd been proud of. The most unforgivable of all was that in her heart she knew he was right.

"Liz, don't you see, without the factory to manage you'll be free to do more research and create more dolls. That's where you should focus your time. You're a designer, and I'm beginning to believe you're a good one." He admitted this last reluctantly.

His compliment, delivered in such a manner, did little to mollify her.

"All week you've been criticizing me and countermanding my decisions," she cried angrily.

"Have you grown so stubborn and strong willed here in Mexico without a man's guidance that you can't listen to reason?"

"Of all the chauvinistic things to say. The last thing I need is a man's guidance, especially yours. A woman is equal to a man in every way."

"Not in every way, surely, darling?" A grin stole across his features, and his gaze drifted pointedly down the curve of her long neck to where her breasts spilled out from beneath woven silk. "That would indeed be a most lamentable state of affairs."

She blushed furiously. Her skin beneath her blouse felt

as if it were on fire. "You're deliberately twisting my words."

"I was merely trying to understand your meaning," he replied innocently. His eyes lingered like a hot caress on her body. "You were saying?"

His manner was excessively polite. Irritatingly so. He kept looking at her in that warm way of his, disrupting her train of thought.

"I-I was saying," she stormed, "that you've ruined everything. My employees, even Manuel, now look to you as the boss. The señor can do no wrong. They think I should be pleased. They constantly praise you to me. If I say what I think of you, I'll appear shrewish. I have to go along with your decisions because everyone else approves of them."

He lifted his eyes to the sky as if seeking a divine assistance. "Ah, the ingratitude of woman. In one week I've cleaned everything up and held a disaster sale, raising more capital than even she believed possible. Everyone here but her is thrilled with the reams of fabric, yards of lace and satin ribbons, dainty braids, and the thousand tiny buttons I ordered. As if I like playing with dolls."

"And as if the exorbitant prices were nothing," Liz added grumpily.

It was true that everyone was grateful for what he'd done. They said it was a miracle the way he'd obtained the sewing machines she had been unable to get. That rankled. No one objected to his hiring twenty skilled seamstresses from Mexico City temporarily. They explained when she questioned the wisdom of this extravagance that she had said the New York orders had to be filled. In short, he'd taken over her world, and everyone except her was pleased. Even the children turned to him now before they turned to her.

In public Alexander treated her as though she were his beloved wife. He was affectionate and courteous. His hand would linger at her waist as he helped her to sit down at dinner. His gaze brushed her lovingly, and always when it did, her pulse leaped before she remembered he was pretending. She hated herself for craving his attentions, for seeking to be near him when others were present so she could enjoy his lavish little gestures of kindness. She would not have minded his taking over her world had he genuinely wanted to make a place for her in it.

When they were alone, however, he was even colder and more remote than ever. The hot anger he'd shown her in the beginning was concealed, and she almost thought she would have preferred it to the icy wall of reserve he had erected between them. When she grew angry about the way he had usurped her power in her own household and factory, he laughed. When she said he was too strict with the children, he merely continued doing as he pleased. Once when she tried to explain she believed too many restrictions would curb the children's natural initiative, he laughed. "So that's your excuse for letting them run wild."

As always, any criticism from him stung. "But that's the way children learn!" she'd cried defensively.

At just that moment Samantha burst into the room holding a snake behind the head. "Is he poisonous, Mommy?"

"Good Lord, Samantha!" Alexander gasped.

"No, darling," Liz calmly replied, examining the snake. "You're carrying him beautifully, dear. Where did you find him?" Liz had proceeded with a zoology lesson while Alexander gaped. "Why don't you show him to your father, dear. He's positively bug-eyed with curiosity."

"Not with curiosity, love," came the deep voice.

Liz realized that he did not approve of her child-rearing methods.

Alexander refused to be drawn into quarrels or any real intimacy with her. Why was he staying, then? Since their argument about the children, he'd said nothing more about divorce and custody.

Not only was Alexander running her factory, but he conducted Dazzle's business over the phone. He drove into Mexico City and dealt with the local Dazzle distributors. Liz knew there was a crisis in Paris, but he did not confide in her. He just stayed on at the hacienda as if he weren't the head of an international company, as if he had nothing better to do than to concern himself with the shape and cut of a doll's wig and the yardage required for a miniature ball gown.

Liz knew that Alexander was running her factory to occupy himself while he was here, until he did what he'd come to do. She felt like she was living in a state of limbo. Every day that he remained she felt more drawn to him, and yet more terrified.

The sound of his wife's laughter floating up from the courtyard came to Alexander as he poured over Liz's account books. He was expecting a phone call from Paris or he would have already joined Liz and the children for lunch. It was the siesta hour, and the workers who lived nearby had returned to their homes for the two-hour interval. While Liz and the children waited for him below, they were playing games in the courtyard.

Alexander shut the ledge and strode out onto the balcony to watch them. He leaned heavily against the black grill railing. It was a brilliant day. Beneath, the exotic trees were bedecked with splashes of reds, oranges, blues and yellows.

Laughing wildly, Liz threw a ball to Samantha, who squealed with disappointment when she missed catching it. Alex scampered to it and picked it up as it rolled past, but Alexander was not watching his son. He was gazing instead at Liz.

Her exuberance matched that of the children. Never had his mother played with him when he was a child, Alexander thought. Liz's black eyes sparkled with excitement. Her cheeks were flushed. Her hair was parted in the middle like a Mexican señorita's. Narrow golden loops glimmered at her earlobes. She was wearing tight jeans and a thin blouse. When she moved, he watched her breasts swaying full and unrestrained beneath the fabric. His skin flamed at the sight of her, and he forced his gaze toward his children. But his thoughts remained on his wife.

Despite the problems at Dazzle, Alexander had decided to give himself a few days to decide what to do about Liz and the children. After his quarrel with her about custody, he had chosen to avoid a snap decision. He could not afford to make a mistake where his children were concerned. The last thing he wanted was to drag them through a lengthy court battle and the inevitable publicity such a trial would bring. So for one hellish week he had lived with his wife in order to spend time with his children. He had thought he could ignore Liz by concentrating on the problems of her doll factory, the impending crisis at Dazzle and the children; but she had haunted his thoughts night and day.

He had tried everything he could think of to put her from his mind. Even when he worked so hard that he collapsed in his bed in a state of exhaustion, he lay alone, thinking of her.

Every time he looked at her, he stripped her in his mind. The memory of her breasts, her long slim legs entwined with his, and her wanton responsiveness drove him wild. A thousand times a day he wanted to take her in his arms. When she smiled up at him so innocently, he wanted to kiss her violently even if it was in the middle of the afternoon. At night he dreamed of her. In his sleep she came to him and placed her slim hot body over his. Her tongue and mouth ran crazily over his skin until his passion for her would jolt him into consciousness. He would awaken in a hard sweat, his breathing ragged, his anger against both himself and her, savage due to the torment she caused him.

How many nights had he sprung from his bed aroused by the vision of her soft, scented loveliness, consumed with the mad intention of going to her room and taking her by force. Instead he would pace the balcony bare-chested in the cold night air, pausing to stare at the moonlight slanting across the jagged black mountain peaks, waiting until his sanity returned.

Was he crazy—wanting this woman after what she had done to him, this woman who should be abhorrent to him?

Yet in the daytime, when he was not goading her about the mistakes she had made in the management of her doll factory, she was the last thing from abhorrent. He goaded her often, though he considered it a poor revenge for the torment she had unknowingly caused him. She, however, always treated him kindly. She had given him the most attractive rooms in the hacienda. She personally kept his rooms and clothes clean and orderly. His favorite dishes were prepared. Despite his desire to keep her at a distance, he found he relished being with her in front of others. Only then did he allow himself to "pretend" that he felt toward her as he would toward a cherished wife. Then he could touch her lightly without fear of the possibility of his caress deepening. When he was alone with her, he forced a coldness in his manner because he was too conscious of the forbidden intimacies he desired.

He watched her constantly, searching her personality for the faults that should have warned him long ago of her deceitful nature. But to his amazement, he saw nothing but sweetness and courage in her.

One afternoon when they were talking about the factory, she had explained the terrible dilemma the villagers had been in when she first came to Mexico. With an ever-increasing population, there was not enough land. Many families had to move. She went to nearby Mexico City, where their plight was desperate in a city already choked by the multitudes of unskilled laborers pouring monthly into the capital from every part of Mexico. Other villagers migrated to the United States. Still others worked as *braceros,* temporary farm workers, in other parts of Mexico and the United States. This meant that the men were separated for long periods from their families.

There was poverty and overcrowding in the schools. Liz had seen how talented the villagers were. She had marveled at their handcrafts in their markets. There were velvet paintings, pottery, silver jewelry, onyx ashtrays, handwoven blankets, embroidered clothes, leather sandals, bullwhips and carved wooden animals.

One morning in a market stall, as she fingered an exquisite obsidian statuette of a rain god, she had envisioned her doll factory. At first the factory was a barely formed dream, but it was something she could not dismiss. She'd felt alone; she'd desperately needed something to do. She wanted to help these people who had been so kind to her.

When she recounted the initial thrill of her idea, Alexander had felt awestruck. From nothing she had started a business that could expand into a giant. Her factory had grown every year, employing more villagers at higher wages.

Alexander learned from that afternoon's conversation how to make her accept his proposed changes, which she had been fighting. If he used the argument that to follow his advice would insure a more rapid growth and thus a greater benefit to the villagers, he could always win.

He thought of Liz more often after that discovery. How could she be so compassionate to these people when she had been so treacherous to him?

To the children, Liz was warm and loving and patient. No matter what she was doing, she allowed the children to interrupt her. She rarely scolded them, and they loved her. To his amazement, he had discovered a framed picture of himself in each of their rooms, and he'd learned that she had taught them to love him. That was why they had instantly accepted him.

When he took the twins on outings without her, they talked constantly of her, asking him why he had not brought her along, begging him for money to buy her some little gift, and all too often he found that he was missing her himself.

He loved watching her with the children. When she knelt over their beds to kiss them good night, he would stand in the doorway. When she took them horseback riding in the forest, he would trail behind them, but that was partially because her stallion, Villano, was so unmanageable.

When Liz first mentioned Villano, Alexander had commented suspiciously, "Villain. I don't like that name."

Liz had tilted her head in that defiant way of hers and laughed recklessly. "You won't like the horse any better."

And he hadn't.

Leave it to Liz to own the most dangerous animal that galloped on rusting horseshoes. One thousand pounds plus of irascible, unpredictable, neurotic horseflesh. Villano had a fiendish dislike of saddles, bridles and riders. He had innumerable phobias, especially of fire. At the whiff of a cigarette he went insane. The only human who could gentle him was Liz.

Thus, whenever his family went near this prancing black demon, Alexander accompanied them, and all too often he found himself enjoying himself—because he was with Liz.

Never having known the joys of family life before, Alexander found that this need in himself to be part of a family gave his wife an ever deeper power over him. He was beginning to see that it would not be possible for him to separate Liz from the children. He loved them too much to deprive them of the mother they loved.

Much to his surprise, he had discovered that Liz hadn't seen or spoken to her father since she'd run away. If she had stolen the formula for Roger, why were they now estranged? Roger had come to him once in London after Liz had run away, and begged him to tell him where Liz was. At the time Alexander had not trusted Roger enough to believe he did not know where his daughter was.

Alexander saw no easy solution to the problem of custody. A sacrifice or a compromise would have to be made.

At just that moment Samantha threw the ball wildly and it headed straight toward Alexander. He reached out to catch it, and as he did the weight of his body jammed hard against the railing. There was a ripping sound of metal grating against tile and stucco as a rusty bolt loosened.

Liz screamed. She was a blur as she raced up the stairs.

He felt himself falling, and he grabbed wildly for the stucco pillar.

He pulled himself back onto the balcony just as Liz reached him. "Oh, Alexander," she said in relief. "I'm so glad you're all right." Alexander pulled her to him. The forbidden comfort of her embrace was treacherously pleasurable.

Looking past her shoulder, he saw the hard square Saltillo tiles beneath. He had narrowly escaped a serious accident.

The scent of her came to him, lavender soap mixed with jasmine. Her firm body against his own stirred all his old, unwanted yearnings. Breathing heavily, he set her roughly from him so that she fell against the white stuccoed wall.

"I should have repaired that railing a long time ago," she said shakily. "You could have been killed."

For an instant he almost believed she cared.

He regarded her for a long moment, carefully masking his emotions. "Look on the bright side," he said cheerily at last. "You would have been a very rich widow."

She paled, and he saw the glimmer of tears in her eyes before she dropped her gaze and turned, then descended the steps slowly to join his children in the courtyard. She did not see the involuntary reaching of his hand toward her before he stilled it.

He pivoted abruptly, went inside her office and kicked the door shut. The memory of her face would not leave him, her black eyes filled with pain and yearning.

He slammed his hand hard against the wall. A shaft of pain stabbed clear to his elbow.

Damn her! Damn him for wanting her! And damn the world for being what it was!

The phone began to ring. It was Paul. The news from Paris was devastating. Alexander was suspected of having caused the fire in Dazzle's lab himself, but when Paul demanded that Alexander return, he refused. Before, it had been uncharacteristic of him to put anything before Dazzle. Now it was suicidal.

The hacienda was jammed with revelers, the courtyard filled with the sound of guitars and marimbas as amateur village musicians played Mexican folk music. Juan and Alexander sat at a small table.

"Despite what you and Liz say, Manuel, I do not trust Juan," Alexander said. "He has been making threats against us in the village plaza when he has been drunk on pulque."

"He is a braggart. He will do nothing."

"I'm not so sure. You know I didn't just fire him. I offered him another job, but he felt he was being demoted and quit. He threatened me, and I had to throw him off the place."

"Forget Juan. He took advantage of your wife's gentle nature. He will do nothing but drink more pulque and shout in the plaza." Manuel smiled. "Why should he be the only one to have that pleasure? Join me in another *copa de tequila.*" He leaned across the table and tilted his bottle toward Alexander's glass.

Alexander nodded. Perhaps Manuel was right and he should forget Juan. He drained the glass with one swallow.

"It is good, no, *mi amigo,* the tequila?" Manuel asked, mixing the Spanish linguistic structure with his English. "A man can forget his problems."

"Then pour me another, my friend." Alexander's swarthy face split in a slow white grin as his gaze fell upon his wife dancing beneath bright paper-shaded lights in the

courtyard. He lifted his glass in a mock salute toward Liz.
"To the end of my problems." Alexander drank deeply.

The fiesta was in celebration of the village's patron
saint. There had been a parade in the village streets.

Liz was dancing with Alex. Her hips swayed in sensual
rhythm to the Latin beat.

The tequila was not working, and then Alexander's
thoughts twisted cynically, and he knew it was working
too well. His head was swimming, and yet after the long
days of constant tension, it felt good to relax. His only
problem was Liz. He knew he should not watch her. He
should concentrate on what Manuel was saying, but her
every movement was so gracefully provocative that he
could not drag his gaze from her. Surely there was no
other woman on earth who moved like that. He thought
of the way she moved beneath him in bed, and he wanted
her with a tearing ache that made him reach for the bottle
of tequila.

She was dressed in a gown of lavender lace that was
cut like a peasant dress, exposing her slim shoulders, en-
hancing the curvature of her breasts. The silvery sound of
her laughter came to him. How could she laugh, when she
put him in hell?

"The Mexican people, we love fiestas," Manuel was
saying, the tequila making him loquacious. "In our village
we have fifty-two fiestas a year, *mi amigo,* each lasting
three to four days. There are the barrio fiestas, where each
barrio celebrates its patron saint. Then we have the holy
days of the Catholic church. Naturally we can go to the
fiestas of other villages and towns outside our *munici-
pio....*"

Alexander was not listening. He was watching his
daughter. Beneath the broken piñata, Samantha was
scrambling with a horde of children for the best prize. She

looked wild and untamed, a miniature version of her mother as she seized several pieces of candy and grabbed for more.

His daughter was going to be a handful when she grew up. She would need a father's protection.

"You know, *mi amigo,* you're a smart man except with women," Manuel said, interrupting Alexander's thoughts. Manuel would never have dared so personal a remark had he not been very drunk.

"You think so?" Alexander muttered.

"I know so. You watch your wife as a man who wants no other man near her. But if you don't mind my saying, your wife is not the kind of woman a man should leave for seven years."

The tequila dulled the glimmer of Alexander's rage. "It was her fault we parted," he retorted coolly.

"But how will you accept it when your coldness forces her to marry the other Frenchman who sometimes comes?"

"Damn you in hell!" Alexander exploded, leaning across the table. "Don't talk about my wife and other men!"

Too late, Manuel saw the danger of the subject. "Easy, *mi amigo,* I meant only that a man must guard that which he wants from those who would take it. She loves you, and she has taught the children to love you. Your wife, she make everyone happy here. She bring us the factory. She love the children. If anyone in the village have a problem, he comes to the hacienda because he know she will help. But no one can help her. She has been sad. I see it often in her eyes. But when you came, she started smiling."

Alexander shrugged and sank back in his chair, pouring himself another tequila. Out of the corner of his eye, he noticed that Alex had joined the romp beneath the piñata. Liz was leaning against a tree, watching the children, her slippered foot tapping out the beat of the music.

"Excuse me, my friend," Alexander muttered. He was tired of listening to Manuel, and the tequila had loosened his iron control regarding Liz. "I haven't danced with my wife in a very long time."

Manuel merely smiled.

Alexander knew it was crazy of him to go to Liz when he'd been drinking. He was sure he would regret it, but he could not stop himself.

She did not hear his approach because of the music.

"Liz—"

She started. He saw the flashing light of her black eyes in the shadowy darkness beneath the tree.

"Dance with me, Liz." It was crazy, asking her to dance when his need for her was pounding in his blood. His hand touched hers.

"No. Please."

She was tense, ready to run from him, but he pulled her into his arms.

She forced herself to meet his gaze. "Alexander, please let me go."

"Darling, don't you see that I can't." His arms tightened around her body, and he began to dance. She moved in time to the music with the fluid ease he remembered so well. He did not hold her close, not at first, but he was aware of her body, tantalizingly near. It took the most terrible control not to crush her against himself. Her fingers brushed the skin beneath his collar; her other hand was folded tightly in his. He breathed deeply, liking her touch, needing it with a fierce hunger he was not sure he could continue to deny.

She sighed, and he realized she was even more nervous

than he was. They danced without talking, and slowly their bodies eased together. Her head lay against his shoulder, her hair an amber cloud, sweetly scented against his cheek. For song after song they swirled together in the darkness, far from the others, wrapped in each other, neither daring to speak.

At last he stopped dancing, but his hand lingered on hers and he pulled her further into the darkness. They walked up the stairs and along the balcony until the drumbeats of the music were as faint as heartbeats.

He paused, forcing her back against the wall. He placed his hands on the stucco beside her face and leaned toward her, his weight on his arms so that she was imprisoned by his body. Her face was tilted up toward his, her lips lush and innocently inviting, though her lashes were lowered. He wanted to kiss her, to make wild, violent love to her, but some last shred of sense restrained him.

"You've been drinking, and I think a great deal," she said warily. "Too much."

"Tequila. They say it turns a man's blood to fire—like a woman can." His husky voice was suggestive.

"Do you think it wise—to drink so much?"

"No wiser than to allow the wrong woman to fire one's blood." With his thumb he traced the softness of her cheek, then the curve of her lips, urging them open. He groaned when her mouth parted and she accepted the gentle invasion of his fingertip.

Her heart began to pound under the exploration of his fingers.

In a low voice he said. "You see, my love, I can't keep my hands off you."

"You shouldn't drink if it makes you do things you regret."

"You sound too much like a wife. I'll drink as much as I please, damn you."

She flinched, but her voice was soft. "Alexander, I don't know what you want, why you danced with me, why you're talking to me like this, touching me like this."

A muscular denim-clad thigh inserted itself between her legs, and she was arched against him. She lifted her head, subconsciously inviting his kiss. His mouth hovered near hers.

She felt the tantalizing whisper of his breath against her lips. "I don't want to feel this way. I don't know how in the hell I'm ever going to get you out of my system." One of his hands slid down her throat and brushed the tip of her breast.

She squeezed her eyelids shut with pain from what he said, even as her nipple hardened from his light, casual touch.

His mouth closed over hers in plundering demand. He lifted her body against his. She gasped as his mouth trailed from her lips downward to scorch her breasts through thin gauze with hot damp kisses. Her legs felt weak and unable to support her, but he was holding her and it didn't matter. Nothing mattered except the dizzying sensations his lovemaking evoked.

At last he drew away. He stared at her, his eyes fierce, his body pulsing with unwanted desire.

She choked back a half-sob, so intense was her longing for his love and not just his passion.

Her hand reached tentatively toward him, and she curled her fingers into the smooth darkness of his hair. "Alexander, oh Alexander, what in the world are we going to do?"

The sadness in her voice reached him and stayed his passion.

"We need to get out of each other's lives," he muttered. "But that seems more and more impossible."

"What do you mean?"

"I mean that our children need both of us. They love you, and they need you. But they need a father as well. They need more discipline. I want to resume our marriage. Come back with me to London." His voice was cold. He did not speak of the hot insanity that thrummed in his blood.

"But you don't love me."

"Love is not the only basis on which a marriage can be made," he went on, still in that cold tone she hated. "Men and women choose to remain married for practical considerations every day."

Practical considerations! That was a euphemism if he'd ever heard one to describe the taut fire in his loins.

"But I don't want that sort of marriage," she said.

He made the mistake of looking at her again. Her throat was naked and slender. His gaze trailed lower to the thrusting bloom of her breasts above her lace gown. "Do you think I do?" he said hoarsely. "The children need both of us, and I must admit that I want to watch them grow up. I've already lost six years. It confuses children to separate them months on end from one parent so they can be with the other."

She bit into her lip and said stubbornly, "It would not be a real marriage."

"It would not be without advantages to you. I would help you with the children. As long as you were discreet, you would be free to do whatever you wanted. I will help you with your factory so that the work you have started will continue. And, Liz, you will be home, in England." He didn't say "home with me," but he thought it. It took all his willpower not to drag her into his arms and convince her with his mouth and body.

But would it feel like home, she wondered desperately, when he was so set against her? He had said that as long as she was discreet she would be free. Nothing he could have said could have brought her more pain. She would be his wife in name only. She could not live with him, loving him, if she meant nothing to him.

"Alexander, what you ask is impossible." She flung herself away and ran, her slim form disappearing into the darkness.

From the courtyard beneath came the gay music and the sound of laughter and dancing.

She was right, of course. A marriage between them would be a living hell.

He stormed down the stairs, illogically angry at her for her answer. He remembered the softness of her, the scent of her. God, did he ever think of anything else? He'd forced himself to speak to her coolly, formally. The whole time his desire had been a hot, electric force barely under control. He'd said he wanted her because of the children. That was a laugh. Every time he looked at her, she aroused in him an avalanche of passion.

What he needed was another drink and a woman in his arms. He asked Esmeralda to dance, and then he asked every woman at the fiesta. He drank and he laughed and he swore, and still the vision of a flaming-headed goddess lingered on the fringes of his inebriated mind to taunt him with her forbidden beauty, to remind him that it was a tall, slim body he desired and not short, brown, rounded ones.

It promised to be a long, hellish night.

Chapter Eight

A dog barked outside the hacienda. Liz lay awake, listening to the sounds of the night. She'd scarcely slept since she ran from Alexander all those hours ago. She'd thrown herself upon her bed and sobbed for all that they had lost. Eventually she had gotten up and undressed for bed and fallen asleep, but a short while ago some noise had aroused her.

She thought of the children and, remembering the noise, a vague unease crept into the back of her mind. She decided that before she tried to go back to sleep, she would check on them. She slid from the bed and pulled on a thin robe, then tiptoed silently across the room out onto the balcony.

Her hand floated lightly along the balustrade as she made her way toward the children's bedrooms, which were past Alexander's. She was almost past his shadowed door when she heard a low male chuckle.

Her heart stopped.

Alexander was leaning nonchalantly in his doorway, his chest bare. In one hand he held a bottle of tequila. The hot scent of the alcohol came to her. Too late, she remembered the times she had heard him pacing outside on the balcony.

"So you can't sleep either?" His voice was lazily slurred, and she realized uneasily he must have gone on drinking after they'd parted. He stepped into the moonlight, baring his teeth in a smile. An aura of danger surrounded him.

"I was going to check on the children," she said tautly.

"Ever the virtuous mother? Perhaps it's time you played the role of wife as enthusiastically." His eyes were fixed on hers. They were hot, and darkly intense.

She shrank against the rail as he loomed nearer. He wasn't going to let her pass. "I wanted to make sure they were all right."

His hard eyes swept her insolently. "And I was flattering myself that it was me and not the children you were coming to see."

"You're very drunk. Go to bed before you do yourself some harm," she said, her voice harsh because she was afraid.

"Always thinking of others, my love?" he taunted, moving so near she could smell the tequila on his breath, and also his warm male scent. His black hair swung loosely across his forehead. "I can see you're disgusted because I've been drinking, but it was you who drove me to it."

"Don't blame me because—"

"Who else?" he rasped. "I thought only to drink until I could forget you, but I want you more than ever." He held the bottle up. "Betrayed—even by the bottle." He laughed softly and turned back to her.

The passion in his voice sent an odd shiver through her. She did not try to prevent him when he slid his arms around her shoulders and held her tightly against himself.

Seeing her unexpectedly in the darkness had tapped all the feelings he had been fighting to contain for the past weeks. He'd come out onto the balcony because he could not sleep for thinking of her. And now she was here, in his arms, arousing in him an uncontrollable white-hot blaze of passion.

"I want to take you to my bed and make love to you." His voice was a husky whisper in her hair. "Every night I lie awake thinking about you, about your breasts, your long legs, about your silken skin. I want to touch you, to kiss you. Damn you, Liz. No other woman—"

Her hair fell over her shoulders like a net of fire. It was an act of instinct, of terrible hunger that drove his fingers deep into the soft, shining thickness to bring her face closer to his. His mouth hovered inches above hers, burning her lips, caressing them with his breath before he brought them even closer. Against his chest he could feel the warm touch of her breasts, their quick rise and fall, the rapid beating of her heart.

"Alexander—"

His hard kiss cut off her words. His tongue plunged into her mouth, boldly, intimately, exploring, tasting the inner sweetness of her. When at last he released her, she stumbled back toward the safety of her room.

He swayed unsteadily, but his eyes were alert, dangerous. The moonlight shone upon his face, revealing his turbulent passion. She turned to flee, but he ran after her. He caught her just inside her door. He gripped her arms so hard, she knew they would be as bruised as her lips, which his mouth possessed again and again with savage hunger.

He forced her back against the doorframe, his muscled body pressing into hers, and he kissed her so hard and so long she thought she would faint. His hard mouth coaxed hers into parting, permitting the entrance of his tongue. Again he tasted the honey sweetness of her mouth. Her breathing quickened in arousal, her mouth moving under his, her heart pounding as his fingers explored her body, caressing the length of her spine.

His hands fumbled with the fastenings of her robe, removing it, so that it fell rippling from her shoulders in a pool at her feet. He was sliding her nightgown off her shoulders, his palm cupping her breast. Dreamily she twisted her body, her softness absorbing the hard structure of his hips, the long columns of his thighs.

"Alexander, someone might see—" There was an eagerness in her own voice that betrayed the scorching desires of her body.

"No one will see, my love."

He lifted her into his arms and kicked the door shut behind him. She clung to him, wanting him with the same driving need that possessed him.

"You are my woman. You have always been my woman. There has never been anyone except you."

"Someone once told me that you were a despoiler of women," she said with a giggle. "I'm beginning to believe—"

In the darkness he laughed. "A myth, my love. There's only one woman I want to…despoil."

His lips sought hers, and she was desperately willing, mindlessly in want of despoiling.

He laid her upon the bed, and stripping quickly out of

his trousers, he settled himself on top of her, his knees on either side of her hips.

His hands trembled against her skin as he removed her gown. He kissed her everywhere, his tongue and mouth moving along her throat, beneath her hair, to her breasts and then lower down to her more sensitive flesh, flicking along the inside of her thighs. His kisses were slow and hot now that she no longer resisted.

"Oh, Alexander, don't kiss me there."

"Despoilers don't take no for an answer. Love, I'm determined to live up to my infamous reputation."

His mouth nuzzled, and shivers of excitement coursed through her until her whole body tingled with erotic quivers. When she thought she could bear no more of the exquisite, pulsing rapture his tongue and mouth evoked, he pushed her down on the bed and covered her body with his. His desire raged out of control and his hands moved over her, arousing her to new heights, carrying her with him into a whirling world of dark desire.

With his hand, he made sure of her readiness before he entered her. Then he could contain himself no longer, and he took her with the shattering force of a man too long starved for the one woman he wanted.

Afterward he lay with his body still pressing into hers. His hands cupped her face, and he bent to kiss her perspiring brow.

He wanted to talk to her, but he could not find the words. He could only stare at her in speechless wonder and watch as she fell asleep in his arms, exhausted, clinging to him, too emotionally spent for anything other than sleep.

He lay in the darkness, thinking, and as his passion ebbed, the enormity of what he had done to her crashed down upon him. He remembered his violence toward her on the balcony. She had not wanted him. He remembered the way he had run after her. He had forced her because he'd been crazy with drink and desire. It didn't matter that in the end her passion had matched his.

He had taken Liz, his sweet and gentle Liz, with anger. He had used her against her will. He had overcome her with sheer physical strength. Then he'd carried her to the bed, and after that she had not fought him. He'd been an animal with no thought but for his own need, and he hated himself for what he had done. How could he possibly face her when he could not even face himself?

Slowly he slid his arm from beneath her head, carefully so that he did not wake her. He smoothed her hair upon the pillow, brought the sheets over her body, and then the sarapes. Quickly he dressed, and then he strode from her room back to the comfortless solitude of his own.

"Mommy, but I saw him!" Samantha cried. "It wasn't a dream!"

"Why would Juan come into your room in the middle of the night?"

"He was looking at me like he was mad, and he smelled awful, too. Then there was a noise on the balcony, and he ran away."

From outside Liz's office came Esmeralda's voice. "Samantha?"

"*Aquí,*" Samantha trilled, dashing outside to join her brother and Esmeralda for breakfast beneath the papaya trees.

Feeling slightly worried, Liz watched her daughter bound out the door. The child was subject to nightmares, but she had been more adamant than usual about this one. Of course, like all the others, this dream was no more than a product of her overly active imagination. At least it was not so terrifying as usual.

Liz returned to the stack of invoices and opened her checkbook, but it was impossible to concentrate. She thought of Alexander, hoping that things would be different between them.

She remembered him as he had been last night, his eyes hot, his expression dark and sensual as his strong arms had pulled her tightly against his masculine body. He had wanted her terribly. The memory of his excitement made her shiver. How would he act when he saw her? What would he say? What would she say to him? He'd been wild and angry, not the indifferent stranger he'd seemed for the past week. His embraces had been hard and demanding, but they had stirred the deep carnal desire in her. Afterward her sleep had been the dreamless sleep of complete fulfillment. But now...

She'd been up for hours feeling crazily mixed up. She felt shy with excitement and anticipation at the prospect of seeing him again. She felt thrillingly expectant, and yet at the same time terribly afraid.

At the swish of soft cotton skirts and a soft, *"Perdóneme, señora,"* Liz glanced up and blushed.

It was only Maria entering her office with her breakfast and coffee on a tray.

When the woman left, Liz poured herself a cup of coffee. Again she tried to work, but she was far too agitated, so she just sipped her coffee and waited. When at last she recognized the heavy tread of Alexander's footsteps, she froze, her heart fluttering. Hot color scorched her face. She did not dare to look up even though she was aware of him standing in the door, hesitating as though he felt as awkward in her presence as she did in his.

Her stomach knotted. Why didn't he say something?

Didn't he know that he was killing her with his silence? She remembered the violence of his lovemaking, and a thousand doubts formed in her mind. Was it to be even worse than before?

His rough voice broke the silence.

"I'm sorry, Liz, about last night. I was half-crazy with tequila. I swear I never meant for that to happen, and it won't again."

Her gaze shot up. Did he regret— His eyes were remote, unreadable. Guilt and self-loathing made him look grim and angry, and Liz's heart began to beat fearfully.

"I—" Her throat was too dry for speech.

"I'll be returning to London tomorrow. We'll have to work out a custody arrangement and the details of our divorce later. You'll never have to see me again."

"Of course," she managed.

She continued to look at him, scarcely able to think for the despair and hopelessness tearing at her.

Alexander wanted to tell her that she had never looked more beautiful to him than now when she was lost to him, that the thought of leaving her forever brought him the most unbearable pain. He had thought he hated her, but he had been wrong. He had never stopped loving her, and the last thing he wanted to do was hurt her, no matter what she had done to him. He hated himself for last night, and he was determined to leave her so that he could inflict no more anguish upon her, even if it killed him.

He longed to lean forward and curve her body against his. More than anything he wanted to explore again the sweetness of her mouth, to feel the glory of her response, to know the exquisite delight of her hands and lips running wild over his body.

He said only, "I'll be with Manuel in the factory if you need me this morning. And later I'll tell the children."

"All right." How did her voice sound so calm, when she felt that she was flying to pieces inside?

When he had gone, Liz blinked against the tears that betrayed the ravaging grief in her heart. What a fool she had been to hope. It was obvious he despised himself as well as her for what he had done. If he hadn't been drinking, he would never have come to her.

She buried her face in her hands and wept. She still wanted him, shamelessly, hopelessly. No matter how hard she tried to put him and her desire for him aside, she couldn't. She had led him on, tempting him with her dancing, with her laughter, with her kisses. All week she had dressed for him, worn her hair the way it pleased him.

Everything was her fault. If she had not been so forward, perhaps none of this would have happened, and he would have stayed longer. Perhaps somehow she would have found a way to reach him. Until he came, she had never realized how much the children needed him. Who was she trying to fool? She had never realized how much she still loved and wanted him. And now it was over. As this thought sank remorselessly in upon her, she began to sob more passionately than ever.

Things grew worse as the day progressed. She couldn't concentrate on her work. After Alexander talked to the children, they ran screaming and crying into her office, blaming her, begging her to make him stay. As if she could.

"Daddy is going away without us!" they cried.

"I know, my darlings," she said, her voice leaden.

"You must stop him. If you would only tell him you don't want him to go, he would stay," Samantha said.

"You don't understand." Liz could think of no words to explain that it was because of her that he was leaving, and not because of them. "I can't ask him to stay," Liz said woodenly.

"Are you going to divorce him?" Alex asked.

"Yes."

"But why?"

"Because he wants to, and it's for the best. We haven't lived together for seven years."

"You haven't tried. Neither of you have." Alex hissed in disgust, sounding older than his years. "The least you could do is try. That's what you always tell us."

"I know, darling, but this is not the same. Not the same at all. Someday when you are older, you will understand."

"I'll never understand!"

The hours dragged. The children blamed her, and they were solemn and tearful as they followed their father around like frightened puppies.

Alexander avoided her. When she visited the factory, he left, and no matter how long she stayed, he did not return until she departed.

She took no pride in the hum of fifty sewing machines working simultaneously, nor in the hum of the industrious hairdressers, cobblers and stitchers busily at work at their tables. In a daze she watched her sewers plunge their hands time after time into boxes of silky blue and gold fabric, run gathering threads on their machines so that the miniature garments bloomed like flower blossoms into Cinderella ball gowns.

Feeling useless and out of sorts, she wandered through the factory, past boxes of brown felt elf shoes for Peter Pan, gauzy white aprons for Alice in Wonderland. Other cardboard boxes were marked "Pearls for Elizabeth I" and "Wands for Fairy Godmother."

Carlos, her hatter, and his three apprentices were in a

room by themselves, twisting straw into perfect miniatures of Edwardian bonnets. In another room Imelda was busy making her tiny ruffled parasols. Her daughter Lucinda was rolling small stockings rightside out for a thousand small feet.

Liz realized Alexander had worked wonders in the short time he'd been there. Despite the flood, never had the factory run more efficiently.

For once she did not care about the factory. Her thoughts were concentrated solely upon Alexander. This was their last day together, and he wouldn't come near her. Her heart was breaking from his coldness, but pride kept her from going to him. She was terribly conscious of his every activity. She knew that he took his lunch with Manuel in the factory and his dinner with the children in the room she had set up as his office.

Alexander took innumerable overseas calls, handling them with a calm ease that maddened her. How could he conduct business as usual when she was an emotional wreck? That evening he took the children into Mexico City without her.

After watching the last curl of dust behind her red Fiat, Liz returned to her design room, but she listlessly eyed the fabric samples and the model she was constructing of a new Hawaiian doll. A dozen research books were piled beside the model, and she decided to try to make a few sketches for the doll's costume. For an hour she sat, sketchbook and pencil in hand, without drawing a single line.

At last she gave up and went to the living room, where she sank down on her favorite chair and stared out at the darkening sky. She switched on the television, and Mimi Camille's husky purr filled the room, bringing back more powerfully than anything memories of Roger and the time

Liz had spent with him in France. It was one of Mimi's early French films, with subtitles. Mimi played the part of a demonic woman with the face of an angel. Liz turned the set off abruptly, as always the mere sight of Mimi affecting her negatively. The last thing Liz needed was to think of Roger. Later it began to rain gently. She went to bed, but she was still awake when the Fiat chugged into the drive.

Alexander and the children came upstairs. The children's voices were sleepy, his gentle and reassuring. Esmeralda helped him put the children to bed, a ritual which Samantha made as long as possible. She cried that she was afraid, and begged for glasses of water. This was the way Samantha frequently acted when she'd had a nightmare the evening before, but because her father was leaving in the morning, she was even worse than usual.

At last the children were quiet and Liz heard the sound of Alexander as he walked to his room, the shutting of his door, his movements from within, the creak of his bed when he lay upon it. She wanted to go to him, but she did not. She lay miserable and lonely, never supposing that he might be as miserable and lonely as she.

How was she going to stand living without him for the rest of her life?

"Mommy!" Samantha's cry was a thin wail of terror that jolted Liz awake.

Liz jumped out of bed and ran outside. Moonlight flooded the balcony and courtyard. Beneath she heard a muffled sound on the cobblestones.

The cry came again from Samantha's room, and Liz ran more swiftly, her thin nightgown clinging to the shape of her body, the tile floor freezing cold under her bare feet.

Alexander's door opened, and he stepped outside wearing only a pair of jeans.

"It's Samantha," Liz said, unconsciously reaching for his hand, and he ran with her to their child's room.

Samantha was sitting up stiffly in her bed, bundled in her innumerable sarapes. Alexander swept her into his arms, cradling the shaking child against his chest. Liz leaned over and stroked Samantha's tangled hair.

"What is it, Samantha?" Liz asked gently.

"He came back!"

"You had your bad dream again?"

Samantha's black eyes were wide in her white face. "No! This morning I told you it wasn't a dream, and it wasn't!"

"What are you two talking about?" Alexander asked.

"I told Mommy that Juan came into my room last night, and she wouldn't believe me. She said it was a dream, but he did come! I knew he did, and tonight I bit him on his hand when he put it on top of my mouth."

"That was very brave, Samantha," Alexander said soothingly. "What happened then?"

"I told him I would bite him again if he didn't let me go. He dropped me back onto the bed and ran out."

In a voice of steel, Alexander said, "Liz, hold Samantha while I check on Alex."

He left them, returning almost instantly, his handsome face dark with alarm.

"Alex is gone. I think Juan took him."

"Oh, no! Juan wouldn't—" Liz bit back her cry of anguish. She remembered Juan's terrible anger when Alexander fired him.

"I'm going down to tell Manuel. First we must search the hacienda. If we don't find Alex, I'm going after him."

"Send for Esmeralda. I want to go with you."

"No."

"But I think I know where Juan might have taken Alex if he has him. He has a *jacal* on the edge of his plot of land on the other side of the forest. It's a little cornstalk hut where he sometimes stays when he's drinking or when he doesn't want to walk home from his field to the village. I don't think he'd take Alex to the village. We'll have to take Villano." She looked at Alexander pleadingly. "You've got to take me with you!"

The wild, desperate look in her eyes broke his iron resolve to refuse her. He knelt beside her. "Alex is all right, Liz. We'll find him." He took her hand in his. "Go get dressed." To Samantha he said, "I'll wait with you until Esmeralda comes up."

Liz dashed to her room and dressed in the darkness, pulling on jeans, a wool sweater and a Mexican poncho. When she reached the courtyard, Alexander called her.

"Liz! Over here!"

Alexander was leading Villano by the long reins of his bridle. Sensing something was wrong, the black horse snorted and pranched skittishly upon the uneven stones.

Liz wished she had a mango to give him, and she began talking soothingly in Spanish. *"Villano, por favor. Cálmate, mi querido."* She reached up and stroked his neck as Alexander jumped onto his bare back. The horse tried to nuzzle her hand in search of the fruit she usually brought him. Alexander reached down, grabbed Liz by the shoulders and swung her roughly up behind him.

"Hang on," he ordered, and she obeyed, circling his waist with her arms, lacing her fingers together against his belt buckle and burrowing her cheek tightly into his back.

Alexander dug his heels into Villano's sides, and Villano neighed, backing sideways, before he jumped forward, plunging into the darkness in a mad gallop.

"Take the first dirt road to the left," Liz cried. "Juan's *jacal* is at the end of the road."

The moon was hidden by the black mountains, but its silvery light peeped over the jagged peaks. Hooves pounded upon the hard road, and loose stones flew in all directions.

When they headed up the twisting mountain road, so overgrown it was scarcely more than a path etched between fields and forest, Villano ran more slowly, the weight of two riders and the steep incline draining him. Suddenly, when they rounded a curve to enter a patch of forest, the horse jerked his head wildly. Alexander urged him forward, but Villano reared.

"Damn fool—" Alexander jabbed his heels more deeply into the horse and slapped his neck with the reins.

"I smell smoke," Liz screamed. "It's no use whipping him, Alexander. Villano is terrified of fire."

"Naturally." Alexander leaped to the ground and helped Liz down. Her body slid along the length of his.

"We might as well let him find his own way back to the hacienda," Liz said. "He'd only hurt himself if we tied him here."

"How much further is it?"

Liz peered into the darkness. "Just ahead where that orange—Alexander!" She gripped his sleeve frantically. "Juan's *jacal* is on fire!"

Their gazes touched in mutual terror. Then they ran toward the billowing glow, Alexander quickly outdistancing Liz.

Liz reached the flaming jacal in time to see Alexander push a drunken Juan to the ground and dash inside the inferno. She waited in an agony of suspense.

It seemed an eternity before Alexander reemerged, carrying the limp child in his arms. Liz screamed in horror. The back of Alexander's shirt was on fire.

"Alexander!"

Ripping off her poncho, Liz ran to them and began beating Alexander on the back. When the flames were out she flung her ruined poncho onto the ground.

"Alexander, are you all right?"

He stared at her, the lines of his face grim, his mouth a grimace because of his pain. "It's Alex," he muttered, "that you should worry about."

"Is he—" The fear inside her choked off her words. Feeling more helpless than she ever had in her life, she stroked the brow of her unconscious son. "Alex, can you hear me? Darling, Mother's here."

Alex's face was terrible in its stillness and waxen pallor.

"His pulse is very weak, Liz," Alexander said gently. "We have to hurry and get him to a doctor."

From behind her came Juan's drunken voice, muttering brokenly, "Fire no on purpose, señora. The cigarillo, I dropped him. I never hurt the niño. I only want to scare the señor."

Alexander was too concerned about Alex to express his rage. He turned his back on Juan and strode down the road that led to the hacienda.

Liz ran to keep up with him. The long walk home on that rutted road was interminable. Alex never regained consciousness.

Liz watched Alexander lay her child gently upon the couch in the living room, and in the light of the lamp she saw for the first time how pale he was. There was an angry bruise across his jaw, and she wondered if Juan had struck him.

"Stay with him while I get the car," Alexander com-

manded. "You'll have to give me directions how to get
to the nearest hospital."

While he was gone, Liz held Alex's limp hand in hers.
He felt so cold, so lifeless.

For the first time she wondered if her child was going
to die.

Chapter Nine

The doctor worked slowly, slicing Alexander's shirt from his back. The immaculate blue-tiled treatment room seemed an oasis of peace in the overcrowded hospital. In the hall outside, the emergency waiting area was packed with a throng of families and patients. Babies cried, mothers tried to corral small children, nurses scurried with trays of medications, and doctors were summoned over the p.a. system.

As the scissors flashed, Dr. Gomez spoke of Alex's injuries. "The boy's had a severe shock, señores. He received a concussion. The burn on his arm is serious. He suffered smoke inhalation, but he will recover."

Liz exhaled in relief. Then she looked at Alexander. Her husband's dark face was pale. He winced as the doctor examined his injury, and Liz realized he must have been in pain for hours.

As the doctor pulled the last strip of cloth from Alexander's back, Liz bit into her bottom lip. "Oh, Alexander, I didn't realize you were hurt so badly," she said in a choked voice. Gently she took his hand in hers as she gazed at the blackened welts and blistered flesh.

Alexander gripped her slim fingers instead of rejecting them. The doctor gave him a shot for pain and began to cleanse the wound. Alexander went whiter, and the pressure of his grip increased.

"You are going to have to change your husband's dressing every day, señora, so this burn will not become infected. He will be on antibiotics, but the nursing care he receives is very important. He needs to take it easy for four or five days. By then I should be able to release your son from the hospital, and the worst will be past for both of them."

When the physician left the room, Alexander said, with a weak smile, "Well, I guess it won't be so easy for you to get rid of me after all."

"I don't want to be rid of you," she admitted softly.

His golden eyes met hers, and for once they did not gleam with cynicism at her kindness. "I could return to my hotel and hire a nurse."

"Alexander, please, stay with me."

"I never thought I'd hear you ask me to stay with you again," he said, his voice almost caressing. Again she felt the increased pressure of his strong fingers around hers.

He smiled at her, and an odd, thrilling sensation swept her. For no reason at all, just being with him like this meant everything to her.

"Funny how things work out," she murmured, and she turned away, too proud for him to see that her face was illuminated with joy.

She didn't know how deeply her concern touched him,

how fiercely he fought the wave of tenderness he felt toward her.

The hour was late that night when Liz and Alexander returned to the hacienda. They had both been reluctant to leave Alex alone at the hospital even though he was doing well. Finally they had compromised and returned home, but only after Esmeralda had been summoned to stay with the sleeping child.

Liz helped Alexander get ready for bed. He said his back was hurting despite the pain-killer shot, and he held himself stiffly, watching her as she pulled back the sarapes and sheets of his bed. She flushed as she felt his eyes upon her. The simple things she did to the bed, plumping the pillows, smoothing the sheets, seemed to take forever under his piercing gaze.

It wasn't what she did that interested him, but the swaying motion of her hips when she walked, and the invitation of their upturned roundness when she bent over the bed. She suspected his thoughts with a discomfiting accuracy that annoyed her.

"Well," she snapped when she was done with the bed. "Are you just going to stand there watching me, or are you going to undress and get into bed?"

"I would definitely prefer the latter," he said with sparkling eyes and a devilish white smile, "providing you join me."

"I—I didn't mean *that!*" she cried hotly. "I meant I'm dead tired, and I think you should be thoughtful and accommodating for once and go to bed like a good patient before we both collapse from sheer exhaustion."

"It's a good thing you avoided the nursing profession," he said dryly. "Your bedside manner leaves something to be desired."

She bit back the angry retort that sprang to her lips. "I suppose you're right there," she agreed grimly. "I haven't the patience to be a nurse."

"Ah, but you have other talents, my love, that more than make up for that lack." His voice was pitched low and was deliberately suggestive.

She knelt and poured him a glass of bottled water, in her fury splashing more onto the table than into the glass. Then she shook a pain pill out of its bottle with an explosive rattle and set it beside the glass on the bedside table. Without looking at him, she said, "I'll leave you to undress if there's nothing else you need."

She was at the door, anxious to make her escape, when his husky voice stopped her. "Who says there's nothing else I need?" She cocked her head defiantly, and he went on. "Liz, I hate to ask you, after all you've done, but would you help me undress?"

Her eyes lifted to the golden brilliance of his. She regarded his grave face with suspicion, and she thought she detected the trace of a smile at either corner of his lips. Like hell he hated to ask! Her nerves gathered in weary knots. She was about to refuse.

"I'll understand if you won't, of course, since you don't have the sensitivities of a real nurse," he said smoothly in his softest, most provoking tone, "but it hurts like the devil every time I move, Liz." At her doubtful look, he groaned. "It really does, but I don't want to bother you further. I'll sleep in my shoes."

He really sounded quite pitiful and humble—so pitiful, in fact, she suspected a trick. Still, he had saved Alex, and the thought of him sleeping in his shoes was more than she could stand. If she allowed that, she *was* heartless!

Liz walked warily toward him. "What do you want me to take off?"

"Everything."

The one, hoarsely uttered word was provocatively dangerous. Her heart began to hammer wildly.

Was he really in such pain? The doctor had given him a shot that should have left a giraffe reeling. But if he were, she couldn't bear the thought of leaving him.

Liz walked slowly toward him. The room was charged with the primal force of their sexual tension.

As if in a trance, she took his hand and led him to the bed. She knelt beside him and with shaking fingers began to work the laces. Fumbling, she clumsily knotted them.

Alexander watched her, misinterpreting her distress as distaste for him. No doubt, that was a result of his rough treatment the previous night. He felt guilty; nevertheless, his senses reeled at her sweet-scented nearness. He saw the movement of her breasts against her sweater. He longed to drag her into his arms and use her as her womanliness was made to be used.

Odd that he felt so drawn to her even after this hellishly long day. Maybe it was just that he'd been afraid for Alex, and now that the danger was past, he was still keyed up. He remembered her sweetness in the hospital, and he knew that, whatever the reason, he wanted her more than ever.

He ached for her, his injury and the long night having done nothing to quell his desire. Every muscle in his body tautened with suppressed desire.

She jerked the laces free at last and removed his shoes. He felt the softness of her fingers against his calf and ankle as she rolled the first sock downward. Then with the same tantalizing slowness, she peeled the other sock off. When she was done, she hesitated, a small sigh of relief escaping her lips.

She glanced into his eyes, then quickly averted her gaze, but not before he saw that her cheeks were flushed. Each knew that he could release her, if only he would.

Glancing down at her bright, demurely lowered head, he said mercilessly, "You know I always sleep in the nude."

Her voice was a whisper. "Yes. I remember."

"Undress me," he ordered, his voice ragged.

She jerked herself upward and too briskly attacked his belt buckle.

"Gently," he cautioned with a tight smile, whitening.

She instantly regretted that she'd hurt him.

"I'm sorry," she said in a low, muffled tone.

His brown hand cupped her chin, and he tilted her face. He saw his own passion mirrored in the luminous glitter of hers. Slowly and tenderly he lifted her lips to his, which were blazing hot with desire.

"Alexander, you're hardly in the condition for this sort of thing."

A hot, pulsing fire hardened in his loins. "I think I'm, er, a better judge of my condition than you, love," he said on a vibrant chuckle.

His mouth moved to each corner of her lips in turn. Then he explored her eyelids, the lush curl of her closed lashes, the winged arch of her brows. He nuzzled the curve of her silken earlobe.

Just as an uncontrollable shudder made her shiver, he removed his mouth. She moaned with suppressed longing as he pressed her into his body, burying his face in her hair.

They clung to each other, their bodies hot and shaking. She could feel his pulse thundering at the same mad tempo as her own. Silently they held one another. It was their first moment of mutual tenderness in seven years. At last Alexander put her from him.

"You were undressing me," he said as if nothing had changed between them, though everything had.

She unbuckled his belt and unfastened his pants. He stood up, and she, still kneeling, lowered his slacks over his hard muscular thighs. He groaned as her hands trailed over his legs.

His briefs came next. Trembling fingers moved beneath the elastic waistband. She lowered them slowly. At the sight of his exposed maleness, she never faltered as she removed this last, most intimate item. When she finished, her hands lingered caressingly once more upon his body until he was breathless with unbearable need.

Then her lips followed the path of her hands, gently exploring his thighs until, at last, her mouth claimed the satin hardness of him in a passionate, damp nuzzle of complete possession.

He clasped the back of her head, prolonging this moment of complete intimacy. She kissed him until his breathing was harsh and ragged.

"I love you, Alexander," she murmured. "I always have, and I always will. Can't you please believe me?" He felt the heat of her breath against his aroused flesh.

He wanted to believe in her love, but he could not.

His failure to answer her brought tears to her eyes, tears which she quietly suppressed. She was too proud to go on pleading.

When she rose, he said gently, "Sleep with me tonight, Liz. More than anything I want to fall asleep in your arms." His voice changed, and she heard the hint of humor as his hands moved over her. "Not quite more than *anything.*"

He'd rejected her love. He wanted only her passion.
But, though he didn't believe her, she'd caught an inflec-
tion in his voice that was almost tender. It wove a spell
around her that she could not resist.

"All right," she murmured uncertainly.

Hot golden eyes watched her every movement as she
stripped.

She moved into his arms, and the fusion of their warm
bodies was heaven.

"Alexander," she whispered as he drew her down onto
the bed beside him. "You're forgetting your pain pill."

"I won't be needing it with you in my arms," he said
as he positioned her beneath him. "Ever the diligent
nurse," he mocked as his body slid provocatively against
hers.

"And I thought you didn't like my bedside manner."

"There's nothing I like better than your bedside manner. Unless it's your in-bed manner."

"Alexander, you said that it hurt like the devil every
time you moved."

"Perhaps I exaggerated the pain just a trifle, my love."
At her frown, he grinned sheepishly. "But that was only
to win your sympathy." His grin broadened. "And to win
your kisses and the pleasure of your sweet, warm body."
Before she could protest, his mouth closed over hers, and
he moved his body erotically over hers, crushing her in a
tight embrace and thrusting deeply inside her until their
passion built to shattering ecstasy.

The next morning Liz awoke buried beneath the
warmth of Alexander's body. Maria was tapping lightly
on the door.

"*Ahorita, vengo, Maria,*" Liz whispered, careful not to
disturb Alexander, who was at last sleeping deeply.

Alexander's head lay against Liz's white shoulder. Her

legs were entwined with his, and she felt warm and safe and happier than she had in years.

Carefully she disentangled her body from Alexander's, and brushing the rumpled darkness of his head with a kiss, she rose. She dressed hurriedly and went to the door. Casting a lingering look at Alexander, she felt a curious protective feeling toward him. His rugged face was abnormally pale. There were gray circles beneath his eyes.

Alexander was infinitely precious to her. She would have to tell Maria that he was not to be awakened. Stealthily, Liz opened the door and slipped outside, closing it behind her.

Maria began speaking rapidly in Spanish.

"Señora, the other Frenchman, Señor Rocheaux, is downstairs."

Remembering the enmity of the two cousins, Liz felt a wave of alarm that Jock had come while Alexander was there. Her husband must not confront Jock while he was still injured.

Liz said coolly, "Please tell Señor Rocheaux I will be down in a moment."

Ten minutes later, Liz swept into the living room where Jock was having tea and bolillos. Jock chuckled when he saw her. She wore satin harem trousers edged with gold-threaded georgette flounces, and a ruffled blouse. The material was diaphanous, and the graceful outline of her body was revealed beneath the softly flowing, richly incandescent fabric.

At the sight of her at the door, Jock rose and crossed the room to join her. He lowered his golden head and kissed her hand. This old-fashioned gesture was typical of Jock, who radiated charm with the fire of the sun god. All his life women had chased him, and Liz knew he was fickle, never dating for long any of the beauties who clamored for his attention. She had been the only exception.

Jock was more classically handsome than Alexander, whose piratical look made him appear dangerous. Jock, on the other hand, fit the image of the urbane man-about-town. His was a complex personality. He was suave, brilliant and cultured; his tastes ran to the eclectic. He was a race car driver, an opera devotee, a womanizer, an artist and a gambler. Despite his charm and sophistication, it was an unwise man who underestimated Jock. In business he was ruthless.

Jock had perfect, chiseled features, indigo blue eyes, and golden skin. There seemed nothing hidden nor mysterious about him. He was tall, though not as tall as Alexander, and smooth in manner and temperament, unlike her more volatile, strong-willed husband.

Jock's blue eyes slid over Liz. "You're looking like—" He paused, searching for the right word in English to describe the whimsical quality she inspired in him. "Like some exotic, Arab, forest naiad."

"An Arab—with red hair? And a forest naiad as well?" Liz laughed lightly, deliciously. "I'm not sure that hodge-podge of images is altogether flattering."

He smiled in that open, easy way of his. "Like all women, you seek compliments."

"Naturellement," she replied in her French, which was every bit as atrocious as her Spanish.

Trying not to wince at her flat accent, he squeezed her hand. "Ah, *chérie,* you deserve them. You are unique. Beautiful, flamboyant, courageous. Most of all, you are fascinating."

"Stop!" she cried teasingly. "I feel positively stuffed on compliments now." The gilt clock on her desk chimed. "My goodness, I didn't realize it was so late." Liz chattered rather frantically, but while she did so, she wondered why Jock had come without warning. He usually wrote or called.

He let her rattle on for a while, and suddenly he broke in, his low voice serious. "You're different, Liz. There's a radiance about you that I thought you'd lost forever when Mikki threw you out seven years ago. He is here now, isn't he?"

Her still face told everything.

"I thought so."

"You can't see him, Jock. He's hurt, and—"

"And you're concerned about him?"

"Yes. He was injured carrying Alex out of a burning hut last night."

"Don't worry, Liz, I have no wish to see him. I merely wondered if he was here. Dazzle is in a state of absolute chaos, and for three weeks the president has been out of the country. There are even rumors now that he was personally involved in the explosion at Dazzle's lab in Switzerland. Rumors that have not been quieted by his lengthy absence. Damned peculiar. Preposterous behavior for a chief executive. I've known Mikki all my life, and I decided there was only one thing in the world that could make him shirk his mammoth responsibilities. That one thing is you, Liz. Does he want you back?"

"No. He came here because of the twins. He still believes that I'm guilty of stealing Paul's formula and giving it to you seven years ago."

"I can see you're determined to change his mind."

"Yes."

"That may be more difficult than you realize. Mikki is stubborn. This whole thing is as crazy as that time he accused me of having something to do with Sasha's death. Hell, the guy drove over the cliff himself. He was trying

to force me over it. It was either my life or his. It was a
choice I made in a split second, but Mikki wouldn't believe me. Sasha was after me, Liz.''

''Why?''

''I never knew. Sasha had always resented my closeness to Mikki. Mikki and I were once the best of friends,
you know.''

''What happened to change that?''

''A long time ago we made the mistake of falling in
love with the same girl. Mikki and I were participating in
a regatta at Deauville, and we met an enchanting woman-
child named Rochelle in a seaside café. She was an exquisite little thing, with blue eyes. Her skin was olive
gold, her hair as black as a raven's wing.''

''She must have been beautiful.''

''More than beautiful. Unforgettable. She was solemn
and passionate, quite different from the girls we had
known before her. We both courted her, but when it came
time for her to choose between us, neither of us could
bear the thought of losing to the other. We were two
young, callow, egotistical fools. So we dropped her, each
of us loving her, neither of us thinking how she might
react.''

''What happened?''

''She wrote us a desperate love letter, and we realized
we'd broken her heart. Mikki said it was foolish for all
three of us to be miserable when two of us could be
happy. We decided to let her choose. Rochelle was a very
sensitive girl. We went down to Deauville to tell her, but
we were too late. Two days before there had been the
most terrible accident. Rochelle had been found dead one
morning, having swallowed a handful of sleeping pills
that proved a lethal combination with the alcohol she'd
drunk at a wedding party the night before. We blamed

ourselves, and the guilt over Rochelle was the first wedge in our relationship. After that the easiness between us was gone. Then there was Sasha. Now we've been enemies so long I can scarcely remember when we were not. But I didn't steal that formula from Dazzle. Why should Radiance steal a perfume when we can develop our own fragrances? I believed that formula was ours, developed by our chemists, when I launched it. I didn't know you were married to Mikki, or I never would have gone on and used your face or your name with our launch. That made me look quite absurd when everyone found out you were married to the president of Dazzle. Roger nearly fired me. When accusations were made that Radiance had pirated Dazzle's formula, Radiance's reputation suffered immeasurably, not to mention my own. Roger withdrew the product from the market immediately, and he refused to discuss his decision or to let me investigate the matter further. But I've explained all this to you before. Your marriage was a secret then. You told no one."

Liz had turned her back to Jock, and she was staring at the awesome majesty of the purple mountain.

"I told one person."

"Who?"

"I'm still not ready to reveal that."

"Why not? Maybe it would shed some light on all this. Maybe I could help you."

Liz was very pale when she turned from the window and faced him. "No one can help me, Jock. Alexander believes that I deliberately tried to destroy him. I have always believed that I was the victim as well. I think it's time I return to London and Paris to find out what really happened and confront the person I believe is responsible."

"Sometimes innocence is impossible to prove."

They regarded one another in silence.

"You know, Liz, you never ask about your father or Mimi when I come."

Liz stiffened. She did not want to think of Roger and Mimi.

"They would give anything to hear from you, *chérie.*"

Liz hesitated. "How are they, then since you are so determined I should ask?" There was no warmth in her question.

"They miss your terribly. They don't understand your silence. They want to talk to you, to see you again. They are curious about the outcome of your pregnancy. Roger wants grandchildren so much. It's senselessly cruel of you to deny him the twins."

"What have you told my father?"

"Nothing."

"Good."

"But—"

"Jock, leave it alone."

"It's been hard on Roger, Liz," Jock persisted. "Mimi's been in the hospital several times the past few years."

"I didn't know."

"Roger kept her illness out of the papers, but he's been alone a great deal. He needs you."

"No! He doesn't!"

Jock had never been able to understand Liz's unreasoning coldness toward her father. When Liz had first discovered Roger was her father, there had even seemed to be a deep, instantaneous affection between them.

Jock knew the whole story, of course—that Liz's mother had been Catherine Carruthers, the famous American movie star in the fifties who had become the mistress to globe-trotting Roger Chartres, the French perfume magnate who owned Radiance. When they conceived a child, Roger had refused to marry Catherine. In desperation Catherine had married Ashley Killigen, a member of the English gentry. They had gone to live at Killigen Hall in Cornwall, where Catherine had given birth to Liz.

Catherine had always remembered Roger as the grand passion of her life, and she did not bring the scholarly Ashley much happiness. Catherine was a restless, lost soul, and the only real love Liz had known as a child came from the gentle Ashley, whom she adored. He was a famous archeologist, and he had taken Liz on digs all over the world. When he died, her mother had run off with a younger man. When Catherine put Killigen Hall on the market, Liz became permanently estranged from her mother.

Liz had felt bitter and adrift. She had had her shop, her career as a designer, her lifelong hobby of collecting dolls, but nothing else. There had been no one she could turn to. For a time she'd run away to Argentina and Brazil, living in the Andes with Indians. When she returned she went to work in her shop. It had been then that her real father, Roger Chartres, had come into her life, astounding her with the news that he was her father, that she was his only living child and his heir. He had invited her to France, brought her into Radiance, settled a fortune upon her, introduced her to Jock and tried to convince her of the wisdom of marrying Jock.

Ironically, Liz had repaid Roger's generosity and trust by marrying his greatest rival, but Jock knew that Roger had forgiven his daughter.

Roger had been enraged when he learned that Mikki had thrown Liz out. Six months later, when it was apparent she had totally disappeared, Roger grew so desperate that he humbled himself and went to talk with the son-in-law in London he detested, despite the bitter dispute over the formula.

What transpired between them behind the locked doors of Mikki's office, Jock never knew, but after that Roger never spoke ill of Mikki again. Even now, when the newspapers hinted that Mikki had had a part in the explosion of Dazzle's lab, Roger defended him. "The journalists are crazy. He didn't do it."

Jock knew he should let the subject of Roger and Mimi drop; Liz's mind was completely closed against her father. But for some reason he did not.

"Liz, do you resent Mimi so much that you have decided to have nothing to do with your own father?"

Liz trembled. It wasn't that she resented Mimi. Her feelings were more complex than mere resentment. "I don't resent Mimi. In my short acquaintance with my 'real' father, I realized he is the kind of man who will always have a beautiful, smiling face before him. My mother once fulfilled that role. Now he has Mimi."

"There is much more to Mimi than a beautiful face or a smile."

Liz shivered. Maybe that was what had always bothered her. Mimi was not the person she presented to the world.

"Mimi's real story has never been published," Jock said. "She grew up in Marseilles on the waterfront. She clawed her way from the pit of her hellish birth and degrading poverty to the dazzling pinnacle of world stardom. She is a very strong lady who knows how to get what she wants."

"You mean she sleeps with rich men now as indiscriminately as she once slept with poor."

Jock shrugged. There seemed nothing more he could say. As always, Liz refused to listen to any defense of her father. There had always been some difficulty between her and Mimi. It was not like Liz to be bitter and unfair. As always, he wondered why.

"So there's no chance for us?" Jock asked at last, changing the subject. His voice held resignation. "I can feel the difference in you. Mikki—"

She moved into the circle of his arms because he was a dear and cherished old friend, and he was French and expected her to.

"It's always been Alexander, Jock. I wish things could be different. I really do. If only it were you, and not Alexander." She kissed him gently then on the lips in parting.

"Yes, if only," he murmured, aroused by the warmth of her lips. He released her mouth reluctantly. "Will you tell Mikki I came?"

"I don't think so. It would only upset him to know that we've been together, however innocently."

Neither of them knew that someone was watching them.

Chapter Ten

It was a beautiful evening with lavender skies and an orange sunset. A week had passed since the night of terror, a week in which Juan had been arrested, a week of constant togetherness between husband and wife that had deepened the bond of love Liz felt toward Alexander.

Alex had come home from the hospital the day before, and though the child was pale and listless, he was improving.

Liz enjoyed tending to Alexander. She hoped that by showing him kindness, he would feel her love.

That particular evening Liz stepped into Alexander's bedroom to collect his supper tray and saw that he was sitting barechested at the writing table. Without his shirt, he exuded a primitive maleness that made him seem even more dangerous than ever.

His supper tray was untouched.

"Alexander!" He looked up and met the challenge of

her gaze. There was warmth in his eyes. "You haven't eaten your soup like I told you to."

He eyed her stiff form. "Obeying orders is not my strong suit," he said easily. "I'm tired of eating chicken soup."

"But it's so good for you. You delight in being deliberately difficult."

"If wanting to eat something for dinner besides chicken soup is being difficult, then I'm difficult. This is the third night in a row."

"Alex is eating his soup. He's six, and he's much easier to take care of than you are, Alexander. He does what I tell him."

"Perhaps, my dear, you should use different tactics on a man than with a child. Maybe he likes it when you're bullying and hard with him. I don't."

"I'm never bullying and hard with him," Liz cried. "I have to tease him and tempt him with things he likes."

She moved into the room, her skirts swaying over her hips as she began straightening things. Golden male eyes gleamed with new intensity as they trailed over her curves. "Perhaps I could be persuaded to eat too, if you were soft and teasing. If you tempted me—with things I like," he said in a beguiling, silken tone.

The back of her neck went hot. She flushed scarlet and felt shivery because his words and his voice stirred her senses alarmingly. She avoided looking at him while she brought herself under control.

"I might even eat cold chicken soup for the third night in a row," he murmured devilishly. "Why don't you come over here and tempt me?"

She snapped the stem of a flower she'd been adjusting in the vase by the window. She whirled around to glare at him. "Frankly, I don't care if you do starve." Those were just words. Her heart was pounding like a startled bird's as he rose and moved nearer.

His mouth twitched with suppressed amusement. "That's obvious. If you really wanted me to eat, you'd bring me a steak or some tantalizing French dish with a rich sauce."

There was something in his manner that alarmed her.

"All right! I'll bring you a steak or veal swimming in cream and mushroom sauce. Whatever you want. Right now."

"I don't want a steak or veal—right now."

"What do you want?"

"Why do you always ask questions when the answer's so obvious?"

When he moved toward her, she felt like running, but he caught her arms. His mesmerizing gaze told of loneliness and overwhelming need, of hopelessness and of desire. She saw as well a flicker of his old warmth and regard.

If only...if only he could love her again.

His hands moved slowly over her body, making her skin tingle. Very gently his fingers slid along her throat under her chin, and he tilted her face for his inspection.

"Liz, it would be so much easier if I could hate you."

She scarcely breathed. In the hushed silence she was aware of his rough fingertips moving against her flesh, in her hair, over her body. He knew too well how to touch a woman. He lowered his black head to hers with a suppressed groan, and she closed her eyes as his mouth covered hers.

The contact was intimate and sensual, bringing the thrill of sexual arousal. She trembled under the force of the earth-shattering emotions that shuddered through her.

At last his mouth released hers, but his hands on her

back continued to press her into the angular contours of his body. His voice against her lips was a husky tremor that told her he was as shaken as she.

"Liz, Dazzle is in the midst of a crisis I need to resolve. I've got to go back to London immediately, but I want you and the twins to come with me even though I can't—" He hesitated. He didn't want to hurt her.

She opened her eyes and looked into his and saw his doubt and desire and compassion.

"Make promises that you can't keep," she finished.

Her skin was flushed with the blooming, soft warmth of a velvet rose. He buried his face in her hair. "God help me, Liz, I can't go back without you," he muttered raggedly. "I ache for you. I burn for you. The board will lynch me, but when I think of those seven hellish years—"

The pain in his voice ripped her emotions and filled her with guilt to know that she caused him such torture.

"I don't know how I feel about you," he said. "I need time. But the children want to come, and I don't want to leave either of them, especially right now, not with Alex convalescing, not with the possibility of Juan's relatives seeking some sort of revenge for my having pressed charges against him."

"How can I leave the factory when so many people here have come to depend on me, Alexander?"

"Liz, I can help you improve the managerial structure of your factory so that we can oversee it from abroad."

"It won't be easy for you, Alexander, if I come back. Your family, everyone at Dazzle believes I betrayed you."

"No," he agreed, "it won't be easy—for either of us. But think about it, and give me your answer tomorrow. I want to leave the next day."

She thought of the long, empty years that had separated them, of the gulf of misunderstanding that still separated them. Quiet tears filled her eyes.

"I don't need to wait until tomorrow to tell you," she answered huskily, knowing she would do anything, promise anything in order to stay near him. "Alexander, I'll come back with you."

"Thank you," he said softly, brushing her lips with his fingertips.

His expression was grave, and when she read the doubt in his eyes, she began to sob.

"Don't cry about it, Liz. Just let me love you now,"

He whispered hoarsely as he possessed her lips.

Liz clasped Alexander, careful of his bandaged back. She clung to him in wild, dizzying abandon, withholding nothing, giving herself totally.

Her mouth moved from his lips to touch every intimate place of his body. No woman had ever made love to him as she did in that long wild night.

At one point he said, "You're a talented little despoiler yourself." She merely laughed.

Trembling fingers stripped his clothes from his hard body and caressed him until he was feverish and shaking with male need. The scorching, featherlight fingertips were followed by the molten, seductive tracings of her flicking tongue.

Where had she learned to love a man like this? He wondered as her silken tongue slid over his skin, arousing blazing, shivery sensations. He had not taught her. Yet she had said there had never been anyone else.

As she kissed him, her wanton tenderness was like a flame licking at the thick block of ice that had encased his frozen heart for seven years. Something inside him melted with each stirring kiss, with each velvet caress, until the pleasure of that moist tongue was too exquisite to be borne. He dragged her into his arms once more.

He pulled her down on top of himself, cupping her breasts with each of his hands, plunging deep within the warm bonds of her flesh as her hair spilled in a sweeping mass over his face. He plunged again and again, wanting to lose himself in her, wanting to love her forever. They soared like the blaze of a comet's path across a hot, star-filled sky over a wild, restless sea. Alexander brought her to peak after peak of sobbing surrender. Trembling waves of excitement washed her body, leaving her breathless and shattered, limp and softly, breathlessly loving as she tenderly kissed his damp cheek. It was that last gentle kiss that pushed him over the fine edge of control. When the curl of pink tongue licked his earlobe caressingly, he could hold back no longer, and he took his satisfaction in a shuddering burst of glory.

Afterward, as he lay in her arms, he experienced a feeling of total fulfillment and contentment, and he knew that even in the darkest hour of her betrayal, he had never stopped loving her. He cradled Liz gently in his arms.

Feeling ridiculously happier than he had in years, Alexander awoke the next morning and reached for Liz only to discover she was gone. Then he heard her voice drifting up from the patio. Her Spanish, which was always atrociously ungrammatical, was even more so when she was excited. No one could murder the beauty of a Romance tongue more enthusiastically than Liz. She was arguing passionately with Manuel over the solution to a problem in the doll factory. Alexander listened to the fervor in her voice with a lazy smile, recalling her wild sensuality of the night before. This morning she was equally impassioned. He longed to see her, to kiss her again, to press her against his body, to hear her ardent voice change into husky whimperings and moans.

This morning he was hungry to see her again. He thrust the sarapes aside and got out of bed. He stripped and strode into the bathroom. When he discovered the hot water was off, and he was going to have to shower and shave without it, he cursed Liz and Mexico and everything he could think of in a loud, roaring voice that could be heard clear to the doll factory. Fortunately this abusive storm was in French, and only Liz, who doubled over in laughter, understood him.

"Is it a national pastime to turn off the burners of the hot-water heaters everywhere in Mexico?" he railed. He was still grumbling to himself and dressing hurriedly because of the chilled air when Samantha skipped into his room. Behind her Maria carried his breakfast tray. He glanced at them both with annoyance because his hunger for his wife burned in him savagely. Maria spread out the sumptuous meal and laid a copy of the *Excelsior* beside Alexander's plate while Samantha chattered brightly. Alexander felt trapped and out of sorts, yet there was nothing for it but to eat breakfast. Samantha would be crushed if he left without eating.

Samantha sat opposite her father at the table and watched in silence as he ate *huevos rancheros* and sipped his coffee while he skimmed the financial section of the newspaper. She did not understand his mood. Usually he was so attentive. Today none of her usual gambits entranced him.

"How's Alex?" Alexander asked absently, his thoughts really on his wife.

Samantha felt his lack of interest, and she pursed her lips. It was a look that spelled trouble. "He's still sleeping," she said.

"Don't you wake him," Alexander admonished without looking up.

Samantha did not like to be given orders. Bored and feeling ignored, Samantha shrugged and everything on the table jumped.

Alexander caught his glass of orange juice before it fell over.

"Samantha!" This time he glanced up, but only briefly. Radiance had made the financial section of the *Excelsior*, and he was trying to read the article.

"I'm sorry!" the child said in a low, disgruntled tone. She sank back down on her chair, and then, forgetting the need to be still, she leaned forward on the table, tilting it.

Alexander looked up, and she guiltily lifted her elbows from the table too abruptly. The table straightened, sloshing juice and coffee.

Samantha would have done anything or said anything in that moment to get his attention. Suddenly her agile mind seized on the most disturbing topic she could think of, something she'd been bursting to tell for nearly a week. Before Alexander could return to his newspaper, Samantha spoke importantly. "If you leave tomorrow, I'll bet you'll be sorry. 'Cause you know what? If you leave, Mother's going to marry Uncle Jock."

This time he did look up, and he stared straight into her eyes with a fierce look.

"What? Where in the world did you get an idea like that?"

Samantha clammed up with fear. "Nowhere."

"Tell me what you're talking about this minute, young lady."

Samantha was momentarily too intimidated not to answer. "He was here again, and I saw him kissing Mother!"

Alexander's face darkened. "What do you mean?"

The words rushed from the little girl in a panic. "Uncle Jock came the morning after Juan burned Alex. You were still asleep, and Mother said I couldn't come upstairs till you woke up. That's how come I saw them kissing."

"Are you sure you didn't imagine this?"

"Why don't big people ever believe me?" Samantha cried, stung by his doubt. "I didn't imagine Juan in my bedroom, did I? And I didn't make up Uncle Jock kissing Mother either. Take us away, Daddy, please, before he comes back and kisses her again." Samantha jumped out of her chair and leaped into her father's steely arms. "I don't want Mother to kiss anybody ever again 'cept you, Daddy." She considered. "And me and Alex."

Alexander swallowed the bitter bile clogging his throat, his emotions raging in turmoil. Jock here. Liz kissing him when she knew how Alexander, her husband, felt about Jock? Was his wife such a skilled liar, such a skilled lover that she could go from one man to another? She had said Jock was not her lover, and like a fool, he had believed her. Liz had not mentioned Jock's visit.

He realized his anger was sweeping aside his ability to be fair-minded. Had Samantha misinterpreted what she had seen? Shouldn't he give Liz the benefit of the doubt and the chance to defend herself? But why should he? There were too many reasons for him to distrust her. She knew how he felt about Jock, and she had seen him anyway.

No, he would not confront her. That would only set her on guard. If he wanted to learn the ultimate truth about her character and the reasons behind her betrayal, he would have to ride her with a loose rein no matter how deeply she cut him with her treachery.

He set Samantha firmly on the floor. "Go outside and

play,'' he said, not wanting to inflict his grim mood on the child.

She ran from the room, and he sat back and stared unseeingly at the article about Radiance. The warm desire to see Liz had left him, and his heart felt hard and cold.

Alexander was still gripped in his abysmal mood an hour later when his older half brother, Paul, called from Paris. Paul skipped the amenities.

''A most unpleasant rumor has come to my attention, Mikki.''

''What, precisely?'' Alexander drawled, feeling irritated at the hysteria in his brother's voice.

''That the reason you have been gone so long is that you have found Liz and have reconciled with her.''

''What if I have?''

''It's the end of your career at Dazzle.''

''Why?'' Alexander's voice was low and dangerous.

''How can you ask the obvious, Mikki?'' Paul shrieked.

''She is my wife.''

''The board cannot forget she almost ruined the company.''

''That was never proven in a court of law,'' Alexander stated coldly, wondering cynically himself even as he did why he was bothering to defend Liz.

''We have evidence that one of the employees from your office visited our Swiss lab, supposedly on your orders, the night before the explosion. We're not sure yet if the purpose was to incriminate you or steal something vital.''

''I know. Michelle.''

''You know?''

''What does all this have to do with Liz?''

''We suspect Michelle is connected to Radiance. Liz is Roger Chartres's daughter and his chosen heir to Radiance. She sees Jock on a regular basis. But, of course, you cannot be ignorant of that fact. Jock was in Mexico visiting her not six days ago. Don't tell me he managed that without your knowledge? What is going on with you, Mikki, that you can lie to me about the reason you're in Mexico and then entertain Jock Rocheaux?''

''I did not entertain Jock.''

''Then it was your accommodating wife who welcomed him so warmly. There was a time when you would not have stood by—''

''Shut up, Paul, damn you.''

''Not before I give you some big-brotherly advice. Forget Liz. She's trouble. Disaster. You will not be able to keep the presidency of Dazzle unless you come back to London without her. For once, where she is concerned, do the smart thing.''

''And my children?''

''Get custody.''

''Liz won't give them up. Besides, they need her.''

''If you bring Liz home with you, no one here will trust you.''

''Not even you?''

There was a long silence before the line went dead, and Alexander had his answer.

So, at least part of Samantha's story about Jock having visited Liz had been confirmed. Did all of Europe know that his wife received Jock's attentions even when at the same time she made the most passionate love to her husband?

Alexander replaced the receiver and strode downstairs to the garage. He would take Liz's car and drive into Mexico City to wrap up a few business problems he'd planned to leave in the capable hands of his subordinates. Now that the last thing he wanted was to spend the day with Liz, he decided he would handle these matters himself.

Alexander was easing the car out of the garage when the soft sound of his name being called stopped him. Liz was in the drive, looking beautiful in a gauzy dress.

He braked, and she came to the car and leaned into the open window. The scent of her assailed him. The sight of her entranced him and made his stomach quiver with an odd pain despite the fresh evidence of her treachery. Alexander looked at her, his face twisting with conflicting emotions.

"Where are you going in such a hurry that you didn't even say good morning?" she asked in her husky, bedroom voice that stirred hot, sensual memories.

"I have something to do in Mexico City," he said curtly. His lonely, black despair had closed around him, smothering him, and he ruthlessly and deliberately shut her out.

"Oh." Her courage faltered, but still she managed to ask, "Alone?"

"Alone," he replied grimly.

"Be careful," was all she said in a tiny, forlorn tone as she retreated from the car.

"Your concern overwhelms me," he snarled, his voice harsh because his own pain was acute. He accelerated and the car whipped past her. Liz stared after him, stunned.

"Alexander," she murmured in bewilderment, chewing the edge of a nail as she watched the Fiat jolt around the bend in the rutted dirt road. She buried her face in her hands.

Had everything come to this? She'd tried so hard. She'd been kind, patient, even when he'd been rude and difficult, and slowly she'd sensed the beginnings of a change in him. Last night... Deliberately, she suppressed the glory of his lovemaking. It was too painful to think of now. She sobbed desperately. Was it all to come to nothing?

After a few moments, when she had managed to calm herself, she turned to go back into the hacienda. For the rest of the day she agonized over his departure. She couldn't understand why he had left so abruptly. Why had he deliberately wanted to hurt her, when this week he had begun to treat her at times with kindness and even tenderness? Now he was angrier at her than ever.

Chapter Eleven

Liz and Alexander ate dinner in the dining room that night. When she entered the room, he glanced at her warily. Liz's hesitant smile was soft and warm and beautiful, and Alexander was caught for a moment in the spell of it before he reminded himself she probably smiled just as warmly for Jock.

Liz's joy at seeing him was instantly dashed when his dark, brooding face hardened with contempt. When he returned from Mexico City late that afternoon he had not sought her out. She suspected he had avoided her all day because he regretted their closeness of the night before. Now his harshness confirmed her worst fears.

She wore a long black strapless gown. The dress was cut daringly low in the back, the tantalizing vee crisscrossed with silken black lacings. His eyes were hot and dark and ravaging, but his scowl only deepened. It mad-

dened him that he had only to look at her to feel bewitched by her beauty.

He bowed stiffly and helped her into her chair. As she
sat down, his eyes ran down the creamy length of her bare
back, the warm, smooth skin tempting his hand. He almost
touched her, but he managed to stop himself in time. He
balled his hands into fists and clenched them tightly until
the pain of his nails biting into his palms distracted him.

The *carne asada* might as well have been burned cardboard. They ate in awkward silence, but they were keenly
aware of each other. Liz felt the heat of his eyes frequently upon her, but when she glanced toward him, he
deliberately looked away. It was only when dessert was
served that Liz dared to speak.

"What time should I have the children ready tomorrow?" she ventured.

"As early as possible," came his terse reply.

"I'm looking forward to going home," she said shyly,
trying to make light conversation, thinking that perhaps
she had been wrong to humor him with silence.

He shot her an odd look, his heavy-lidded gaze cynical.
"Really? Why?"

"There are so many reasons."

"I'm sure there are." That cutting, sardonic edge she
hated had crept into his voice. He wondered if she was
thinking of Jock, who would be more accessible to her
when she was in London.

"For one thing, Alexander, I want to come home because of you—to try again."

"To try again." The words hung in the air between
them, husband and wife interpreting their meaning differently. She meant she wanted to try to save their marriage,
and he wondered if she meant she was determined to destroy him this time.

"To try what, my love?" He flashed her a look of deep bitterness.

"Alexander, I don't understand why you're so angry," she began uncertainly. "What have I done? Please, don't close me out like this. If you would only tell me."

"I will tell you nothing," he growled. "And I will take you with me only on one condition."

"What condition?"

"You are not to see or even to speak to Jock again. Nor do I want you to communicate with your father, at least for now."

'I see."

"But will you promise me?" he demanded.

"I promise," she said, agreeing only because she felt forced to do so. "But why, Alexander? What have I done?"

She started to push back her chair from the table, and he was beside her at once, helping her. When she stood up, he towered over her, his eyes studying the arresting beauty of her still face. The tenderness and pleading in her eyes moved him much more than he wanted them to. His gaze wandered to her upturned red lips, lips that taunted him with their sensuality.

She felt faint under the intensity of his dark stare.

"You ask what you have done?" his harsh voice mocked her gentle question as his hard brown hand moved beneath the curve of her chin and lifted it. His other hand caressed the smooth skin of her neck, but there was something threatening in his light touch. "What have you not done to destroy me would be a better question, my love. Once you nearly cost me my career. Are you such a witch that you demand my soul as well?"

"All I've ever wanted is your love."

"Then we are at cross purposes, my sweet. All I require

of you now is the pleasure of your voluptuous, talented body in my bed.'' His gaze roamed insultingly over her soft curves to where the bright sheen of black silk plunged between her breasts.

Shame scorched her. ''Alexander, please don't deliberately humiliate me,'' she begged quietly. ''I don't want to destroy you. I love you.''

Though he did not want them to, her velvet-soft words stirred him. He lifted his eyes and studied the becoming flush that tinted her ivory complexion with delicate color. She looked vulnerable and innocent. He watched her pink tongue nervously wet her lips, and he felt a wave of intense desire.

''My beautiful Liz,'' he whispered as he gathered her in his arms, despising himself for his weakness. Like the Sirens of mythology, whose song lured men to their destruction, she lured him. Nothing mattered but his need. He could almost forget that she probably offered herself just as shamelessly to Jock.

Liz was just as affected by him. She trembled from his embrace, from the heady nearness of him, the male scent of him hanging heavy in her nostrils. He crushed her to him fiercely, possessively, seeking to obliterate the image of her kissing Jock from that black corner of his mind where it lingered.

She slid her arms about his neck; she could feel his heart pounding against her breast. His powerful body was shaking as he leaned down, and his mouth closed over hers savagely in a forceful, demanding kiss. They clung together, each hoping for a clue to the other's heart.

Alexander kissed her long and deeply, his tongue plunging into her mouth before he lifted her into his arms and strode out of the dining room, across the patio, and inexorably bore her up the stairs to his bedroom. She held on to him, frightened yet eager, clinging, her mouth responsive beneath the suffocating pressure of his.

He laid her upon the bed and sank beside her, his fingers deftly unfastening the zipper of her gown and then the intricate network of lacings. The touch of his hands sent rivulets of fiery sensation radiating across her skin.

Black silk peeled, revealing the warm lush fruit of her opulent female flesh.

"Delicious," he murmured, sucking the nipple of her breast until it stood erect, pouting temptingly beneath his lips. He sucked its thrusting twin, and then let his tongue nibble the entire globe as though he were starved for the sweetness of her.

Sliding the dress downward until it fell in a pool at the foot of the bed, his hands wandered over her body, cupping her breasts, sliding over the curve of her belly, caressing her waist and hips, running the length of her slim legs and then returning to touch the velvet dampness of her womanhood with slow, gentle strokes. He lowered his head to kiss the soft folds of flesh.

She gasped and tried to push him away, but he subdued her easily, her puny efforts at resistance proving futile against his superior strength. With one hand he pinned her wrists to the bed and continued to have his way with her, returning to taste her tart nectar.

Much later his lips sought the pleasure of her trembling mouth again, and he kissed her long and insolently until she was weak and shaking from his hungry kisses.

"You are beautiful, my wanton, treacherous witch," he stated in a low voice before he left her briefly to shed his own clothes.

She watched him strip, his brown fingers jerking roughly at the knot of his tie, then ripping the loose, dangling ribbons from his neck, shrugging out of his suit jacket, unbuttoning his shirt. He ripped the shirt off, and with it came the last remnant of civilization. His bare chest and shoulders were bronzed and rippled with muscle. To Liz he seemed a primitive male, dangerously relentless and all-powerful.

Her senses clamored in response to the power of his pagan male appeal. Hurriedly he unsnapped his trousers and slid them down. When he came to her again, she gasped as he fused her body to his dark, virile length, the warm hardness of his naked flesh against her own, rocking her senses.

She longed for some shred of gentleness in his lovemaking, but he gave her none. He was determined to use her body and ask nothing from her soul and heart. Though his lips explored her with ruthless thoroughness, and her blood pounded in her veins, she felt the loss of something infinitely precious. She wanted love and tenderness and commitment, and he gave her only hedonistic sensuality.

She realized he was deliberately humiliating her. She hated that part of herself that reveled in his touch, and she began to struggle in the futile effort to save for herself some last remnant of pride.

"Don't do this to us," she begged. "Please, Alexander, you must stop this mad, destructive course you're determined to take. If you can't love me, let me go."

He laughed that soft, cynical laugh she hated, that low male sound that mocked them both. "How can you sound so naive when you don't want my love any more than I want yours, my tantalizing witch? All you want is this. Doubtless any man would do." He was thinking specifically of Jock.

He was about to lower his mouth to hers when she cried out in fury and lunged to slap him. He caught her hands in one swift movement and held them in his iron grip as he wrenched them behind her and lowered her back on the bed.

"I'm your wife," she murmured desperately, "the mother of your children. Have you lost all respect for me?"

"Respect?" He laughed at that. "I told you, you have only one thing I want now." He lowered his mouth and kissed the satin button tip of her pink breast, punctuating the point he was making with the whirl of his tongue against her nipple. "You are my wife in name only." His tongue licked again, leisurely, expertly, and a series of shivers radiated inward from the moist, sensitive surface of her skin. "I intend to use you as a mistress, nothing more. And that, my dear, is much much more than you deserve. I'm a fool not to throw you out."

She felt wretched with heartbreak. "Then I'll not let you," she said tonelessly. "Just because I love you, that doesn't mean I have to allow you to rob me of my self-respect."

"You can't stop me, love." His eyes were dark and merciless, but his hands were gentle on her body. He knew so well how to touch, how to caress, how to inflame. "You don't even want to stop yourself," he whispered. "Your own body betrays you."

Violently she kicked at him, and he laughed at her and she knew he enjoyed her struggles, the feel of her soft warm skin twisting erotically against his. When she jumped at him fiercely in one last burst of energy, he avoided her blow by twisting aside. His grip on her wrists slackened, and she jerked free and lunged toward the opposite side of the bed.

He caught her and pulled her back, rolling on top of her writhing body, pinning her arms beneath her, forcing his hot mouth on top of hers, kissing her again and again until her anger gave way to another, equally powerful emotion. Desire made her ache as his tongue thrust deeply inside, slowly, lingeringly and, in the end, gently.

At last he released her. "You belong to me," he murmured. "At least in bed. Tell me that you don't want me, and I'll let you go, Liz."

In the dim light his tanned skin seemed even darker, his hair even blacker than usual. There was a blazing wildness in his eyes. He looked like a primitive Indian or an ancient warlord, noble, proud and savage. He was shaking, and she knew that passion raged within him.

The will to stop him had left her. She stared up at him with a drowsy, voluptuous, yielding look. She existed only in a blurred world of sensation and carnal desire. He had won. She wanted him with such violent intensity that she could not deny her feelings even for the sake of her broken pride.

He lowered his lips and kissed her again. His hard mouth ground her lips against her teeth in a kiss that bespoke domination and mastery. She was his, hopelessly, desperately his. She was his for whatever casual, meaningless pleasure or use he wanted to make of her. It was useless to struggle or to ask for more than he was willing to give.

Wild pagan needs throbbed in her blood beneath his ruthless, expert caresses until she thought she would die without physical release. His fierce embraces gentled. He teased her with his languorous, slow lovemaking, withholding that which she craved with every fiber in her body as if to torture her as he was tortured by his own pulsating need of her.

She was quivering, begging him to take her even when some inner force screamed that she had lost all pride to allow herself to be so humbled by her love for him. But what good was pride, if she lost even this last glimmer of the fire that remained of their love? She loved him, and he wanted her. It was the one bond that still held him. If she denied him her body, he was lost to her forever.

For love of him she had no choice but to risk her heart, and soul, and pride.

Alexander's lips sought all the erotic places of her body, using his mouth to bring her the most exquisite sensual pleasure, until at last she moaned his name in ardent, mind-shattering surrender.

Her soft crooning made his passion rage out of control, the male in him satisfied that at least he could drive her as wild as she drove him, and he carried her with him to peaks of blazing ecstasy that left them dazzled by the volcanic glory of their union.

He took her again and again that night. He used her brutally, forcefully, and yet there was rapture in his fierce embrace, which ignited a mutual fire that devoured all save their desire one for the other.

When it was over, they lay on the soft mattress amid tangled sheets, plump pillows and scratchy sarapes, their moist bodies still touching, neither daring to speak.

He had conquered her, but in so doing she had conquered him. Neither was conscious of victory; each only of defeat.

Chapter Twelve

A gray slanting rain was falling when the Vorzenski jet touched down in London's Gatwick Airport. Alexander and Liz had flown to New York and spent the night there on their way to London so that Alexander could talk to Jon and Philippe, two of his cousins on the Dazzle board.

Liz felt weary and wrinkled from the flight. The children were tired and irritable. A customs official waited at the gate. Several journalists stood in an agitated cluster beside him, all of them jostling for a favorable position on the rain-slick concrete runway. There was a television crew with cameras.

At the sight of the crowd, Alexander swore to himself. Publicity was the last thing he needed; he had hoped to avoid it until he had made the board accept his reconciliation with Liz. Alexander stepped outside, his dark face a mask that revealed nothing of his misgivings as he smiled and invited the customs official on board.

When the press clamored to be admitted as well, he told them that he regretted there was not enough room to invite all of them inside the jet.

Once the passports and luggage had been cleared, Alexander called airport security to find out if his pilot could radio George, his chauffeur, to drive to the gate in order to avoid a scene with the press. Permission was granted, and when he saw the Vorzenski Rolls, Alexander helped Liz and the children disembark. They were instantly surrounded; microphones were thrust in front of their mouths. Flashbulbs popped in their faces as rapidly as the reporters' questions.

"I'm from the *London Times*. Prince Vorzenski, is it true that you have reconciled with your wife? That you have only recently discovered you are the father of twins?"

"Prince, do you consider that your marriage represents a conflict of interests? Will you continue as president of Dazzle when your wife is connected to Radiance? What do you have to say about your name being linked to the bombing at your Swiss lab?"

"Look this way, Princess, and give our readers a big smile!"

"Princess, do you plan a return to your career as a designer? Is it true that you have been manufacturing dolls in Mexico?"

To all these questions, Alexander replied curtly, "No comment, gentlemen." He whispered to Liz, "Smile, darling. Wolves bite harder if they think you're frightened of them."

The boldest journalist, an aging, obese man, jumped in front of Liz. He leered into her face. "Princess, why did you run away seven years ago? Is it true that you married the prince to steal Dazzle's formula? Isn't it a fact that you're still determined to ruin him?''

Liz's expression froze. An odd, frantic feeling built inside of her. Was this what everyone really thought of her? That she was a monster? She felt defiled by his insinuations, and she wanted to run, to be alone, to escape even Alexander.

Seeing the desperation in her face, Alexander realized how close she was to hysteria, and he felt intensely protective toward her. He stepped between Liz and the man, grabbing the burly fellow by the lapels. ''Leave my wife alone, do you hear? What kind of man are you to bully a woman?''

For an instant a breathless hush descended on the crowd as everyone reacted to the dangerous aura of Alexander. His tawny gold eyes had changed to fierce black glitter in his hard face. The powerful leashed force within him that he always fought to curb was barely held in check. Effortlessly, Alexander lifted the man onto his toes.

The man's eyes bulged with fear as Alexander set him down, but a hundred flashbulbs burst at once. Liz flinched as she realized that by trying to help her, Alexander had only worsened things for himself. The press would crucify him now.

To Liz, Alexander whispered reassuringly, ''It's almost over. Get in the car and let me handle this.'' He guided her gently toward the door.

She smiled at him gratefully, his touch and the proximity of his tall, muscular body imparting comfort and security.

The door of the silver Rolls swung open and Liz stepped thankfully inside, the wide-eyed twins and Alexander right behind her. The children climbed into the back seat and stared out the rear window, gaping at the journalists.

"I'm afraid that you made headlines when you grabbed that reporter," Liz said softly after Alexander shut the door. "And all because of me."

He regarded her pale, anxious face warily as he sank into the seat beside her. For an instant a strange feeling of excitement and happiness twisted his stomach before he reminded himself what a hypocrite she was. These were the hardest moments of all for him—when Liz pretended caring and concern.

"You're probably right," he replied in a low, tired tone. He was already angry with himself for the way he had acted. Normally he was cool in his dealings with the press, never showing any irritation even when he was furious. The trouble this afternoon was that he'd gone insane when that man had been bullying Liz and she'd looked so frightened and lost. Nothing had mattered to him in that moment except protecting Liz. When he thought of his behavior he considered it irrational, and himself a fool.

"It seems that I make things worse for you without even trying," she said in a small voice.

He laughed softly in his taunting way as he regarded her white, beautiful face again.

"I never..." She broke off, realizing the uselessness of defending herself.

"Always innocent, aren't you, my dear?" His gaze dropped insolently to her body. "When will you realize you can stop playing that part with me? It's not innocence I want from you." He looked away, but the gesture did nothing to rid her of the scorching shame of her humiliation. "I'm sure you realize, Liz that the scene at the airport was nothing compared to what will take place when I face the board tonight."

"Tonight?"

He nodded grimly. "My enemies are going to demand my head on a silver platter, and likely as not, they'll get it."

"Because of me?"

"You're one of the reasons."

She flinched. "Oh, I almost wish I hadn't come."

"But wasn't that why you came?" Glinting gold eyes swept her solemn face in cold amusement. "It's a pity you won't be there to witness my execution, love. You would enjoy it."

She gasped.

"What, love?" His voice was deliberately cruel. "Haven't you the stomach to see the blood you've spilled? I'm surprised."

How could he believe that? Her gaze dropped to her lap, and unconsciously she fingered the amethyst pendant she was wearing, feeling completely dejected by his coldness.

"Alexander," she murmured in a choked tone, "please, don't believe that about me." It took all her courage to lift her face and look at him.

He loomed closer beside her, dwarfing her, forcing her to tilt her bright head back to meet the angry glitter of his gaze.

Their eyes met, and the luminous concern in hers made him feel guilty for his hardness before he reminded himself that she was probably acting and that he would be a fool to trust any show of kindness from her. Unthinkingly, Liz reached for his hand, and his shook when she touched him.

"Alexander, please. It is so difficult for me to fight for us when even you are against me."

He was staring at her slim hand on top of his own,

which was still shaking. He was appalled that her slightest touch could make him tremble as though with a seizure. Good grief! He thought, despising himself. I want her love so desperately, I could take on the world if she truly cared. It wouldn't matter if I lost Dazzle, if I lost everything, if only I could have her. Without her, I will be nothing even if I win at everything else.

Aloud, he said deprecatingly, "There's no need for you to distress yourself, my love. I'm sure you're much closer to victory than you realize. Content yourself with the thought that your wantonness binds me to you and makes me capable of the most self-destructive behavior. There's scarcely a chance of you failing." His eyes stripped her, ravished her, branding her with the fire of his unwanted desire.

Her face turned ashen when she caught his meaning. Their bodies were close. Against her shoulders, she felt the heat of his curved arm stretched across the back of her seat. He moved slightly, and the granite-hard muscles of his thigh pressed against hers.

His thoughts plunged him into an utterly black mood, and he wrenched his hand from hers and forced his gaze to turn away. Never had London seemed more dismal to him, as the rain slashed against the hood of the speeding car. Much later he roused himself and began to point out the sights to the children when they reached the Chelsea Bridge and crossed the Thames, the limousine threading its way in the thick traffic of Chelsea Bridge Road and Sloan Street.

The noise of London was extinguished as the Rolls sped toward the townhouse that Alexander had leased in Belgravia for the past six years from Gerald Grosvenor, duke of Westminster, the richest landlord in London. The house was on a quiet back street a short distance from

Hyde Park and the gardens of Buckingham Palace. The residence would be convenient as well to Isobel's, Liz's shop in Knightsbridge.

Liz didn't care about the house, nor about the excitement of returning to London; she couldn't care about anything except surviving the next few hours and retaining the courage to go on.

She couldn't give up. But when she dared a glance at the immobile, dark figure of her husband, and felt so cut off from him, she was afraid. She was determined to find a way to save her marriage no matter how great the odds were against her success. She loved him. He'd been hurt because of what he considered her treachery, and she couldn't blame him for that. Wasn't she at least partially responsible because she hadn't told him that she was Roger Chartres's daughter? She'd been a fool to run away seven years ago. That had merely convinced everyone of her guilt. Now she was determined to fight no matter how much it hurt her. She had to do something, and quickly. If only he hadn't made her promise not to contact her father.

As the Rolls passed Belgrave Square, turned down a side street and pulled up in front of the house, Liz had her first clear view of Alexander's home. It was remarkably like its aristocratic neighbors on the street, enormous and grandiose with a classic stone exterior, like so many houses in London. The only difference was that a tangled wisteria vine ran up the grilled ironwork and the face of the stone building. The house was sedate and private, like the street, and Liz was thankful for that untamed vine, which lent rustic charm and a bit of wildness to the otherwise forbidding and austere building.

Alexander helped Liz from the car. As George unloaded the bags and the children scampered up and down the sidewalk, Alexander held Liz's arm. He didn't release her when he allowed the others to precede them into the house, and she was keenly aware of his towering presence. The scent of him made her conscious of a dull, unhappy ache inside her. If only...if only he would show some sign of affection outside the bedroom.

If only. Those two words said it all.

Inside the mansion, the rooms were grandly proportioned, with large windows to let in the sun when it chose to shine. The house was furnished with antiques, rare French rugs and paintings, the paintings belonging to the fabulous Vorzenski collection.

Samantha was jumping up and down in excitement, and then she whispered something devilish into Alex's ear. The boy let out a yowl of delight just as Mrs. Benchley, Alexander's portly, staid housekeeper, stepped into the hall to greet them.

"Whose children, Prince?" She gaped as Alex ran his toy car along the top of a polished table that had once graced a Scottish castle centuries ago, and Samantha watched, fascinated.

Doubtless the table had received worse treatment during the past two hundred years by rough Scots, but that was no comfort to Mrs. Benchley. She had a peculiar reverence for antiques, if not for children, and her round face couldn't have puckered with more horror if the twins had been a stampede of wild orangutans.

"The children are mine," came the deep, familiar baritone that brooked neither disapproval nor unwanted questions. "We will need to interview a governess. In the fall they will attend school, but they will still need to be supervised in the afternoons. You will see to that, won't you, Mrs. Benchley?"

"Of course, my lord." Mrs. Benchley's eyes widened

as she watched Samantha streak past a Rodin sculpture to yank Alex's hair because he had stolen her doll.

Alex screamed, but he dropped the doll. Not in time, though, to avoid Samantha's revenge. Another yowl erupted when she pinched him sharply on the arm.

"I don't believe you've met my housekeeper, Mrs. Benchley, Liz," Alexander began, introducing an embarrassed Liz in the midst of the hubbub while Liz tried in vain to subdue the children. Liz felt nervous, and Mrs. Benchely's disapproval only made her feel all the more so. Alexander's hand remained possessively on his wife's elbow as the two women exchanged courtesies, and somehow it gave Liz the courage to smile at the staid housekeeper, who was doubtless marveling at the necessity of introducing his wife of some seven years and his two six-year-old twins. An odd turn of events, to say the least.

Ana Lou, the upstairs maid, appeared on the stairs. "Why, what precious children, my lord."

The entire staff referred to their prince as "my lord" because he would not allow them to use his title.

Mrs. Benchley gaped at her maid. Ana Lou was the oldest sister from a family of seven, and she had a way with children.

"I can see they don't know what to do with themselves after a long day of travel," Ana Lou said with understanding. "You poor dears. It must have been terrible to be all cramped up for hours and hours." She came down the stairs, her young face warm and friendly. "How would you like some biscuits and milk, and I could tell you stories. Later we could explore the garden."

"In England biscuits are cookies," Alex said wisely.

"Oh, tell us stories," Samantha cried, unimpressed by her brother's attempt to show off. "About monsters and snakes."

Ana Lou laughed and took them each by the hand. "I know some giant stories," she began.

Neither child objected to giants, and Ana Lou led them away. At their departure, all was as silent and regally grand as before.

Liz wondered if it would be possible to fit herself and her two lively children into Alexander's elegant and well-ordered household. She was beginning to fear she had made a dreadful mistake returning with him. The housekeeper's next words did little to cheer her.

"Your brother, Mr. Paul Rocheaux, has been calling all afternoon, my lord," Mrs. Benchley said. "He says it's urgent that you return his call at once."

Liz felt Alexander's fingers tense on her arm. She raised her eyes uncertainly to his, but he deliberately avoided her gaze. She had known they would have no time together, no period of adjustment, but she hadn't really let herself believe it would begin the minute they stepped inside the house.

"Thank you, Mrs. Benchley." Alexander's level voice betrayed no emotion. "I will attend to that at once. Mrs. Benchley, will you show my wife to our room upstairs and send someone to assist her in unpacking?"

"Of course, my lord." She nodded and was gone. Orders were barked crisply and servants scurried, gathering pieces of luggage.

Alexander looked at Liz. "So you have survived your first encounter with the indomitable Mrs. Benchley. I advise you to take the upper hand with her from the first. Though she can be stubborn at times, she is an excellent woman. I would hate to dismiss her."

Liz realized he had remained at her side to help her during what he knew would be a difficult time for her. Not only that, but he was making it clear that the house was hers to run and that he would stand behind her. A little of her tension subsided. It was curious the way his protectiveness was at war with his determination to be cold and aloof. She never knew what to expect from him.

"I wish there were something I could do to help you, Alexander," Liz said impulsively in gratitude.

An arrogant brow arched in his aristocratic face to mock her. Once again his features hardened. She did not know that this happened because he wanted to mask the softness he felt. "Help me, my dear? Perhaps you would like to attend the board meeting tonight so you can wield the axe and gloat when my head rolls?"

She began to tremble, conscious of his searing eyes relentlessly fastened upon her. A startled cry of pain broke from her lips, and she whirled free of his grasp to mount the stairs and escape him.

"Liz—"

She ran even faster, and rather than make a scene, he watched her fleeing form disappear into the upper regions of the vast house before he turned and stalked down the hall to his study to call Paul. Alexander wanted to forget her, to immerse himself in the crisis at Dazzle. But he could not.

Seven years had not separated him from her even when he'd been determined to hate her. She had conquered even his fierce, stubborn will. There was no use running from her any longer. She was a part of him, albeit an unwanted part, and when he hurt her, he hurt himself. Damn it to hell! He loved her. He would have gone down on his knees and told her if he hadn't been sure that would only increase her contempt of him as well as her feeling of power over him. He wanted to forget her, but the vision of her stricken face remained with him long after he'd left the house and driven to Dazzle's offices.

Damn her. Damn himself for wanting her. Was that to be the perpetual circle of his thoughts?

Chapter Thirteen

The shades were drawn and the elegant silver room was
dark and silent except for the blare of the newscast. Liz
Vorzenski's ravished white face filled the screen before
the camera was jostled and Mikki Vorzenski's face
shielded her from view. Another camera caught the sce-
nario of the prince dramatically protecting his wife from
an overly zealous newsman.

The person on the brocade sofa in the dim room leaned
forward tensely, hands clasped on knees, brows furrowed
in determination to catch every word. When the newscast
ended, the set was switched off by gloved fingers that
shook with an overpowering emotion.

The sudden silence was startling, but the person in the
room did not note it.

Liz had come back. She didn't look as radiant as she
had as a bride seven years ago, so all was not patched up.
But there must obviously have been some sort of recon-

ciliation between Liz and Mikki, or Liz would not have returned with him. The twins were adorable, but that was something that didn't bear thinking about.

The person in the room felt like God. Hadn't the Vorzenskis suffered enough? Seven years? Should they now be allowed a normal lifetime of joys and sorrows?

The mere thought bit like the pain of a dagger in an unhealed wound and brought the stifling feelings of the old madness and hatred. The possibility of any happiness between Mikki Vorzenski and Liz was as unendurable as it had always been.

"Never! Never will I allow it."

Gloved fingers reached for the telephone and dialed.

The buzzing phone seemed as agitated as Liz's thoughts, but she did not answer it because she remembered that in Alexander's house the phone was always screened first by the staff.

Alexander's lavish suite included two bedrooms, two baths, two dressing rooms and a sitting room between the bedrooms. If Liz had not been so upset she would have thought the rooms beautiful. As it was, the subdued, elegant charm of the apartments scarcely made an impression. Bleakly she observed that her battered luggage had been placed on a pair of oak luggage racks, and a maid had hung her clothes in the massive closet that contained Alexander's.

Liz removed her heels and tiptoed across the soft Aubusson carpet to the dressing table with its gilt-framed, beveled mirrors. Her face was a stranger's face with haunted black eyes and a drooping mouth. Her red curls were a riotous, untamed mane. I look like an unhappy clown, she thought dismally, without my painted smile. She rummaged through her purse for a lipstick.

In the mirror she could see the bed, which was covered with a blue damask spread that matched the blue and gold brocade drapes. How long would she share Alexander's passion in that bed? She thought of the power of his bronzed body, the way he had clasped her so tightly to him only last night in New York. How long would she have even that? Desire without love to sustain it was bound to fade. She jerked her gaze from the bed, and her eyes flickered over the room and its furnishings.

A rich gold paper had been hung between lustrous wainscoting. In the bathroom there were fleecy towels monogrammed with golden, sloping Vs. Beside the fireplace in the sitting room were a white velvet sofa and two matching chairs. Everything down to the smallest detail was perfection, and Liz was reminded that Alexander was content only with the best.

This perfect suite for the not-so-perfect couple. How long would Alexander endure being half of a marriage that wasn't working?

The lipstick dropped from her shaking fingers and rolled across the dresser toward the wall, then tumbled over the edge noisily, so that it would be impossible to reach without summoning two men to move the heavy antique dresser from the wall. The lipstick hardly seemed worth that effort.

She paced restlessly. She didn't know what to do with herself in this grand, orderly house. Ana Lou had taken over the children, and for the present Liz was relieved about that. The flight had stretched her patience with Samantha's liveliness to its limit. But Liz would need something to do. In Mexico she had had the factory to run and the hacienda to manage.

She glanced at the phone beside the bed. After seven years she couldn't call old friends. They would be curious, and she wasn't ready for that. Her shop was closed for the rest of the weekend. She wondered if Ya Lee, who'd been managing the business, would resent her now that she had returned. She would have to tread warily there too.

Liz's thoughts returned to Alexander. An hour ago she had stood forlornly at the windows and watched the rain spatter his ebony hair and the expensive coat covering his broad shoulders, as he leaned down and stepped into the Rolls. He'd never looked up or given a thought for an affectionate caress or good-bye kiss from his wife. She'd burst into a frenzy of tears.

Why couldn't she accept their marriage for what it was? She was the wife of a powerful and wealthy man, a man who desired her, a man who was a conscientious father. Doubtless many wives had less. As she'd watched the Rolls disappear in the blur of rain and traffic, the truth had come to her. She might never be able to prove her innocence. Her life might be filled with such cold departures silently viewed from upper-story windows. Alexander might never stop hating and resenting her for what he believed she had done.

The gold walls and drapes closed in upon her as suffocatingly as a prison. She couldn't stand the feelings of hopelessness much longer. Alexander had said he would be crucified by his family and the Dazzle board tonight because of her. Was there nothing she could do to improve her situation? What if she went and pleaded with the board in his behalf?

What could it hurt? Perhaps someone on the board would believe her. Surely his own mother couldn't be utterly heartless.

A glance in the mirror told her that a bit of color had come back into her cheeks. Her black eyes blazed with new courage as she rummaged through her clothes in Alexander's vast closet for something appropriate to wear. Though she didn't know it, in the eyes of the conservative board members, anything she wore would be wildly inappropriate.

She was pulling out a satin jacquard skirt and a velvet bodice and bolero with its billowing sleeves, outlandish garments of her own design, when a knock on the door and Mrs. Benchley's muffled voice from the hall interrupted her thoughts.

Liz opened the door, and the sternly disapproving Mrs. Benchley said, "Mr. Jock Rocheaux is on the phone, madam. I told him I did not think the prince wished you to be disturbed."

The gossip surrounding the enmity between Jock and Alexander had not escaped the housekeeper's ears. Liz remembered her promise to Alexander and knew she should say sweetly that, of course, her husband was right, that she was resting and could not speak to anyone this evening. But the thought of Alexander exacting such an unreasonable promise still angered her.

"Nonsense, Mrs. Benchley," Liz said with a sharp note of defiance. "Of course I'm not too tired to talk to Jock."

The thin mouth sagged alarmingly as Liz's hand touched the receiver. For a minute Liz thought Mrs. Benchley was not going to allow her to speak.

"As you wish, madam," Mrs. Benchley replied stiffly, relenting. "May I ask if there is anything else you require?"

Liz extended an armful of rumpled velvet and satin. "Would you have these pressed. I'm going out—immediately."

When the door shut and the hall outside was silent, Liz lifted the phone. Her hand was shaking.

"Jock!"

"Hello, Liz."

"Jock, Alexander made me promise never to speak to you."

"Really?" Jock did not sound in the least worried about this pronouncement. "Don't you think that's carrying the jealousy bit a little too far, even for Mikki? I'm surprised you're willing to let him play dictator, *chérie*. After all, you were raised in England, and there are more uppity women on this insignificant island than anywhere else in the world."

"I don't exactly have a choice right now."

"You always have a choice, but I did not call to discuss Mikki. I must see you at once."

"Jock, I can't. Alexander would never forgive me."

"Mikki be damned! Your father wants to see you, Liz. He saw you on television, and he has asked me to bring you to Paris."

"Oh."

"Liz, the man's brokenhearted. He said you believe he is responsible for wrecking your marriage to Mikki. He wants to explain and to apologize for what happened."

"So he admits he's responsible?" Liz asked dully.

"Not in so many words. You know Roger is hardly the kind of man to lay his feelings out on the table for my perusal. But, yes, he feels responsible."

"Jock, I made up my mind a long time ago that I didn't want to have anything more to do with a man who destroyed the one thing in my life that mattered to me. Even if he is—" Her voice broke. "I can't see either of you because I promised Alexander I wouldn't."

"Liz—"

"Good-bye, Jock."

She sank down upon the bed, buried her face in her

hands and gave into a burst of frenzied anguish. She'd refused to see her father, and to what purpose? She did not have Alexander either.

Liz was already dressed and in the foyer waiting for a cab when the stony Mrs. Benchley came to her and told her that Jock was on the phone again.

'Please tell him I'm not at home.''

Mrs. Benchley opened her mouth to say something, but Liz had already run out the door, a flurry of bright hair, black velvet and opalescent satin.

Alexander sat at his desk, which was piled with mail, contracts and reports. Michelle, his secretary, was trying to explain the chaos.

Finally he stopped her in midsentence and snapped in his deep, thundering baritone, ''Save your breath, Michelle. You may need to explain this to the new president if I'm sacked tonight.''

''Surely they won't do that, Mr. Vorzenski.''

Michelle did not use his title because Alexander would not allow it.

Alexander glared at Michelle, wondering if in truth she worked for the competition. ''I'm not so sure.'' Slowly his hard expression softened, and he managed a smile, which deepened the wolfish slashes beside his mouth. ''Run along, and type that one report I asked for now, if you don't mind. I need to organize my thoughts before the meeting.''

Alexander lifted his gaze thoughtfully to the portrait of his grandfather. The painted eyes of Philippe Rocheaux, who had founded Dazzle Ltd. ninety years ago, met his. Alexander felt responsible for Dazzle, and he knew that the company was headed for certain disaster if he were ousted from the presidency. Ruefully Alexander thought of the company, of its history and the components that had made it a great fragrance company.

Dazzle was not as ancient as some French houses of perfume, but its name stood for excellence. Like his grandfather, Alexander was dedicated to the preservation of Dazzle's eminent reputation as well as to his company's financial well-being. The company's motto was that quality counts in everything—from the design of the stopper of a flacon to the perfection of an essence.

Alexander's grandfather had begun Dazzle in the nineteenth century. A chemist who'd grown bored with his soap and candle business in rural France, Philippe Rocheaux had sold everything and moved to Paris with the intention of developing delicate scents for ladies' soaps. Quickly he'd moved into perfume.

With the launch of his first scent, Empress, in 1906, and then Paradise in 1908, Philippe Rocheaux proved himself a giant, one of those rare talents in the perfume industry.

Within a decade, Philippe proved his undisputed right to be classed among the great perfumers, with Francois Coty, the creator of Guerlain's Shalimar; with Ernest Beaux, who did Chanel #5; and with the prodigious freelancer Edmond Roudnitska, author of Christian Dior's Eau Sauvage.

Philippe's business expanded into one of mammoth proportions. Dazzle had six Parisian shops as well as subsidiaries in eighty-five countries. In France and Switzerland alone there were four Dazzle factories. The major laboratory was in the Paris suburb of Colombes; another was in the Swiss Alps, where the explosion had occurred.

Paul Rocheaux was Dazzle's perfumer now, and he was the sole creator at the house of Dazzle. He was, like his grandfather before him, a genius.

Alexander found his brother Paul infuriatingly difficult to deal with. Paul could putter in his lab for three or four years, making hundreds of changes in one creation alone. Other perfume houses would launch one scent after the other while Alexander and everyone else on the Dazzle board waited for Paul.

During the years between creations, Dazzle had no new product to launch. Few perfume companies still operated in this old-fashioned way. Instead they relied on flavor and odor companies for new fragrances. That was why the stealing of Paul's formula seven years before had been such a disastrous occurrence. It had represented three years of perfectionism and arduous work.

Alexander chafed with impatience during the empty years between creations and their launches, but Paul, for all his slowness, had never created a flop. Paul gloried in explaining himself to the press during every launch. With an affected wave of scented sample papers, he would say, "I start with a basic note like a composer. I stay within a certain key signature, *messieurs*."

Alexander smiled to himself as he thought of his brother's ego at such times. Paul lived for those brief hours of glory, and when he spoke, he was always dramatic and metaphorical. He would wave his hands wildly with the pompous excitement of a conductor. "Then I blend scents, like the blending of notes into chords. I build harmonies and fugues of odors. Always I add and I subtract, changing the relative strengths on a delicate scale, until I realize the achievement of the ultimate scent I consider worthy of putting before the public."

In the shadows in the back of the room, away from the lights, the glitz and the clamor, Alexander, who always hired the best publicity people in the business to stage these media events, would watch and listen to his brother with great pride. It was in between these moments of dazzle and pomp that the brothers found it difficult to deal with one another.

The intercom sounded, and Michelle informed Alexander that Paul was outside.

"Send him in."

Paul Jacquard Rocheaux stomped angrily into the room. He was smoking one of his expensive Monte Cruz cigars, and the curling wisps of gray trailing his agitated motions increased the impression that he was spouting like a tea kettle ready to bubble over with rage. He came toward the desk and ground the stub of his cigar into the Wedgewood ashtray on his brother's gleaming rosewood desk.

"Hello, Paul," Alexander said blandly. "It's good to see you."

"Is that all you can say?"

"It seemed appropriate for starters," Alexander replied, still in the same imperturbable tone. "You've been so upset by my absence, I'm surprised you're not overjoyed to see I'm back."

"You come back to London less than two hours before this board meeting, and you're surprised I'm not overjoyed."

"Did you expect me to hurry back for my own hanging, Paul?" Alexander lounged indolently in his chair, but his eyes were alert.

"For a man about to be hanged, you don't look too upset, Mikki."

"As a matter of fact, I'm not—any longer. Thanks to you."

"And what is that supposed to mean?"

"All in good time, Paul." Alexander shrugged negligently.

Paul reached across Alexander's desk for the silver

lighter that stood beside a group of elaborately cut crystal flacons filled with exotically scented ambers and golds. Paul lit another cigar. The acrid scent of the cigar soon warred with the chaos of sweet odors, but neither of the hostile men, both famed for their sensitive noses, noticed it.

Paul sighed impotently. He hated fights; they overwhelmed his delicate nature. "Mikki, you picked one hell of a time to disappear."

"Ah, but I didn't pick it. It picked me. I would never have left if the circumstances had been anything other than extraordinary. Thank you, Paul, for filling in for me."

"Damned inconvenient for me and inconsiderate of you."

"I'm sorry, but you seem to have handled things. Besides that, I just read the report about your new fragrance. Frankly, I was overwhelmed with relief. Dazzle needs a new launch. It would give us the kind of positive publicity we must have."

"You can't mean that you intend to prepare for a launch at the same time we're having to contend with this police investigation in Switzerland! Your own name is being dragged into the mud. Who knows how long you'll even remain president? I thought in six months, when all this blows over, we could launch."

"I want to begin now. There are times when you've got to take aggressive action to turn the tide of events in your favor. I want a media campaign bigger than any we've ever had."

"Sometimes I think your enemies are right and you're nothing but a damned privateer who'll be the end of Dazzle."

"Everyone expects us to knuckle under and assume a

low profile, but that's exactly what we've done too long. I want to get out there and slug it out. Things couldn't have worked out better if I'd been home running the company myself.''

"I didn't come in here tonight for praise."

"I hardly thought you did. I know that look of bulldog purpose. What's on your mind?"

"I saw the evening papers. You brought Liz back with you."

"She is my wife."

"An unfortunate mistake that belongs in the past. Why don't you divorce her?"

A tiny line had formed between Alexander's dark brows. "Because I don't want to."

"Why are you so determined to make a fool of yourself over that woman a second time?"

"Because…" How could a man defend the pull of his heart and soul when he scarcely understood the intricacies of that process himself? "Because…Damn it, Paul! I don't have to explain my feelings for my wife to you or anyone else!" Alexander's hand slammed down on the desk, and then he dragged it wearily through his rumpled hair.

This exchange was followed by a silence just as lengthy and just as tension filled.

A pale gray light slanted against the rich paneled walls of Dazzle's executive suite. Alexander wore an expression of fierce determination and weary exasperation.

Though they resembled one another, Alexander was the bolder and more charismatic of the two. Paul had inherited his sensitivity from his father, who had been a concert pianist as well as the princess's second cousin, and his "nose" from their grandfather Philippe Rocheaux. Both brothers regarded one another gloomily, each knowing the futility of further argument.

The funereal atmosphere was broken when Michelle knocked and came into the room, announcing, "You told me to tell you when everyone was in the boardroom, Mr. Vorzenski."

Alexander smiled. "We'll be there in a minute, Michelle."

Michelle handed him the report.

"Ready?" Paul asked, rising.

"As ready as I'll ever be, I suppose." Alexander rose. "I met with Phillipe and Jon in New York yesterday, and not too successfully. Paul, you haven't told me whether you're for me or against me."

"You already know the answer, Mikki."

"I do?" Alexander was filled with doubt. Paul had never seemed more hostile.

"No matter my personal feelings over your stupidity regarding your wife, I am always for Dazzle. You're still the best man to run the company."

"Thank you, Paul."

"Don't thank me, Mikki. I don't really have a choice."

Alexander smiled genially despite Paul's barb. He realized Paul's attitude reflected the view of the board toward Liz. All Alexander had to do to win them over was to reassure everyone he would acquire a discreet divorce.

If he did that, the presidency was his, and his family would once more be on his side. If not...

Chapter Fourteen

The rain that had slanted in sheets in Belgravia gentled abruptly to a soft, weakening patter as Liz's taxi slowly threaded its way between red double-decker buses and black taxis onto Piccadilly. The Ritz Hotel was coming into view.

Wet asphalt and concrete glistened. The stone buildings loomed against a sky washed by the afternoon's showers to the palest of lavenders. Soft clouds stirred in the wet breezes, and a low orange sun painted their underbellies with a golden glow. It was a beautiful evening, had Liz been in the mood to enjoy it.

Instead she leaned forward on the edge of her shabbily upholstered seat and stared out the window at the familiar landmarks with dread. Through the open window a freshly rinsed London bombarded her. The smell of exhaust and diesel, the odor of fried food from a thousand restaurants, the scent of dogs, and cool, wet air. There were the hoarse shouts of street vendors, the whir of tires, the screeching of brakes, police whistles.

Everything was the same as it had been seven years ago—the plane trees in the parks with their enormous leaves that fell in the autumn to cover the earth with crackling gold, the row upon row of somber buildings, the traffic, the constant rush of people in their dark raincoats on the sidewalks beneath a roof of umbrellas, this eternal bustle that was London—yet she felt she no longer belonged.

Once England had meant Cornwall and Killigen Hall to Liz. Oh, the comforting antiquity of that house, that superb feeling of being part of a family that had endured for generations. Those illusions had been stripped from her by Ashley's death, but she still remembered her former home. She remembered cavorting on the sloping green lawns. Cornwall meant the rush of waves against cliffs, the scent of salt spray, the shrieks of gulls and ravens as they skimmed low above golden sands. She could almost smell the tang of cooking over furze fires on summer evenings when she and Ashley had camped out and lain beneath the stars, and he'd told her stories of knackers and tin miners.

In those years there had been Ashley and Mother. Her world had been filled with love and warm security. How fragile are the things we build our lives upon, Liz thought with a pang. But how precious. She was flooded with an aching nostalgia.

That peaceful world was gone forever. Funny, how she'd taken it for granted. She'd lost Ashley first. Then her mother had run off to France with her young man, in the futile search for her lost youth and beauty.

Liz swallowed the dry lump in her throat. Usually she never looked back because remembering brought too much pain. But she'd wanted to remember that time of love and security. She had the feeling that if she fought hard enough today, and if she could win Alexander's love, she might be able to give that kind of life to her own children and to Alexander. She longed to share that kind of deep happiness with Alexander, the kind of happiness that, for all his sophistication and success, he had never known.

Without his love, her future and that of her children were bleak and uncertain. What if she failed? She clenched her hands. She had to fight because she was fighting for her soul.

At the thought of braving the Dazzle board alone with Alexander against her, a wave of new terror made her stomach knot into a hard, queasy ball. What could she possibly say? How would Alexander react? And how would she even get into the building? She would have to lie smoothly and plausibly to get past the guard, and she wasn't a good liar under the best of circumstances. She could say that there was an emergency, that she had to see Alexander. It would have to have something to do with the children. The taxi driver braked sharply and began yelling to another driver to his left. The wall of taxis and buses in front of them had come to a standstill.

"What's going on up there?" the driver cried.

A dramatic shrug of hands and a violent curse from within the other taxi was the only answer.

When Liz realized that the traffic ahead where Regent Street and Piccadilly converged was impossibly jammed, she tapped on the glass behind the driver. "Let me off here," she said, handing him three pounds for the fare and tip. "I've decided to walk the rest of the way."

The damp air was refreshing after the stale cab. Liz walked past elegant boutiques and shops toward the gleaming white brick building that housed Dazzle's London offices. She saw little of her surroundings; she was only vaguely aware of the frustration and clamor of the stalled traffic.

In front of the Dazzle building a Volvo had crashed into a bus on Regent Street, and the bus had plowed into a building. The smashed car was abandoned. Water from a broken fire hydrant sprayed fifty feet into the air, and the streets and sidewalk were flooded. Liz had to tiptoe in her velvet shoes, and finally she was forced to step through deep puddles.

"Now isn't that a shame, lovey," a grandmotherly woman behind Liz said crisply. "You've ruined your shoes. I seen it happen, you know, the accident. Almost looked as if the man in the car did it on purpose, the way he ran into that bus. He ran off the minute it happened. Didn't stay around, not him that done it. A foreigner, if you ask me. Too many of them in the city these days, and not one in ten that knows how to drive proper like."

Liz nodded, and the woman began speaking to another pedestrian.

Bobbies ran about whistling and barking orders. Pedestrians crammed the streets between the blocked cars to view the wreckage and the impossible tangle of cars. A carnival atmosphere of excitement pervaded the area. Florid-faced men with wide smiles stood in the door of a pub across the street.

When Liz walked into the Dazzle building, no one was at the desk in front of the lift to question her. Everyone from security was down the hall in the office helping the police make telephone calls. Over the squishing of her wet shoes, she could hear the babble of voices. With her pulse racing for fear they would come out and discover her before she was safely inside the lift, she decided to take the stairs instead.

Once inside the stairwell, Liz sank against the wall in relief. She heard the sound of high heels skittering on the concrete stairs high above her, sharp, panicked beats like the pounding of her own heart. A door opened and closed, and then there was silence. Slowly Liz began to walk up. With every flight her stomach felt queasier than ever.

When she reached the top floor and stepped outside, the hall was abandoned. She was almost there. Almost. And it had been incredibly easy. Too easy, she would have realized had she not been so nervous.

She marched purposefully toward her husband's office. If she could only get into his office! She knew that it opened directly into the boardroom.

Her heart jumped jerkily when she turned the knob and let herself inside Michelle's office. The outer office was empty, but a cup of tea marred with a lipstick ring steamed on Michelle's desk, indicating this wouldn't be true long.

Liz opened the door to Alexander's office and stepped inside. The rich paneled walls were the same as she remembered, as were the wine-colored wool carpet, the long windows, the cathedral quiet, the sense of power and pampered luxury his office had always exuded.

On one wall hung the painting she had given Alexander so long ago. She went to the picture. She could not resist reaching up and touching the gilt frame. The wood was as smooth as polished gold beneath her fingertip. The painting depicted the granite cliffs of her former home plunging to caress golden sands and the wild surf of that Cornish sea. It had been her favorite view, and Ashley had commissioned a famous artist to paint it for her twelfth birthday.

On her wedding night, Liz had bestowed this greatest treasure of hers on Alexander. "A piece of my soul," she had whispered when he undid the wrappings. He had taken her in his arms, and they had not spoken for a long time.

Odd that he had kept it, that it still hung where they had placed it together. Her eyes misted, and Liz forced herself to look away from the painting in the vain hope of putting the past back where it belonged. But Alexander's office was too filled with other, unhappier memories for her to succeed.

This was where... The thought trailed off and then came back with renewed power. A pain as sharp and painful as a blow in the stomach hit her, and she leaned against the door for support. Seven years were swept aside, and she recalled that morning so long ago when she'd let herself inside this room in a state of joyous anticipation to tell Alexander she was pregnant.

She'd been wild with happiness. He was standing at the window looking down upon Regent Street, and he turned when she called to him from across the room. But instead of smiling as he always had before at the sight of her, his face had blackened with rage, and before she could say anything, he accused her of marrying him only to steal Paul's formula. Then she hadn't wanted to tell him about the baby. She thought she'd wait until the awful misunderstanding was cleared up.

The happiness they'd known had been destroyed within a half hour in the quarrel that erupted. He refused to listen to her. She'd run from him. There had been nowhere, no one to whom she could turn.

Despite the support of the door, she felt faint. For a moment she lost her courage. The memory of Alexander's anger and her own sorrow overpowered her present purpose. All she had to do was walk out the door and return to the house in Belgravia. Perhaps she could find some easier way to patch things up. Her backward footsteps toward the only avenue of escape were involuntary. Then a choked gasp from the darkened corner behind Alexander's desk snapped her rudely back into the present.

"How did you get in here?" Michelle asked in a shaken voice. The secretary stepped into the light. Something told Liz that usually the girl had a cool blond beauty when her blue eyes weren't wide with fear. Michelle clutched a sheaf of papers beneath her breasts as if her life depended on them.

Curiously, the girl's fear lessened Liz's. "I came to see my husband," Liz said, moving slowly toward the door of the boardroom. "I'm Mrs. Vorzenski."

"I know."

When she reached the door, Liz lifted the handle soundlessly.

"You can't do that!" Michelle cried. The papers she'd been so carefully holding spilled onto the floor.

"I just did," Liz said with a bold smile as she swept like a glorious butterfly into the room on opalescent wings of satin and black velvet, albeit a butterfly rooted to the earth with squishy shoes. Behind her Michelle's voice grew outraged.

"Mrs. Vorzenski, you can't—"

In a glance Liz noted the opulence of the boardroom, the long, polished conference table, the leather upholstery of the chairs. What struck her with potent force was the heavy atmosphere in the room.

She was one—against so many.

Princess Vorzenski, the family matriarch, had been speaking passionately in French, and she halted in midsentence, momentarily too stunned to continue. She was silver and elegant, and rigidly upright in her chair. In her well-ordered world things like this didn't happen. She looked unbendable.

Everyone in the room gaped at the woman in black velvet whose red hair cascaded in a shower of unruly ringlets, giving her the untamed, exotic charm of a gypsy.

Everyone except Alexander. He was seated at one end of the table. His dark face had been bored and impassive until Liz walked into the room with that wildness blazing in her eyes that could only spell trouble. He smelled danger, but her presence lit a fire within him that had nothing to do with danger. Paul and his mother sat on either side of him. Alexander stood up slowly, his eyes bland and guardedly amused, and yet everyone in the room was instantly aware of his power.

The same thought was in all their minds. Unwelcome or not, the woman was Mikki Vorzenski's wife.

Never had Alexander seemed taller nor more nobly majestic and beloved to Liz, and never had his tenderness and love seemed more hopelessly out of reach.

Alexander said smoothly, "Ladies and gentlemen, may I introduce you to the lady we've all been so avidly discussing. My wife, Liz." He pushed his chair back from the table.

"A pleasure," said Liz, filling the gap of awed silence with the musically flowing irony of her voice. Her French, as always, was atrociously structured, her genders and pronouns hopelessly scrambled, but for once it was to her advantage. Her American-British accent made her seem less French, less Roger Chartres's daughter, and there was a certain charm and ingenuous creativity in her horrendous constructions.

Several members of the board forgot themselves and smiled. Even Paul looked less sour when Liz flung out *"par usuel"* in an overconfident burst. Only the princess, who considered the French language sacred, stiffened and groaned, *"Comme, d'habitude."*

Satin rustled, velvet shoes squished, calling attention to the movement of Liz's slim wet feet as she strolled the length of the room. She knew she was leaving a trail of footprints on the expensive carpet like a swamp animal, but she couldn't stand still. Her courage would desert her completely if she did. She felt their eyes boring into her, assessing her, distrusting her, and she wanted to run.

Princess Vorzenski regained her tongue and attacked. "So this is your impossible wife, Mikki?"

"None other, Maman," he said in a tone of velvet steel.

Alexander came toward Liz, and when he reached her, his arms slid protectively about her waist. Liz could feel a hard tension in his grip that belied his negligent manner.

"How dare she come in here and break into our board meeting!" came the now-familiar high-pitched voice of the princess.

"Surely you would expect nothing less from such an arch criminal, Mama," Alexander said softly. "A woman with the courage to marry her father's enemy with the intention of ruining him can scarcely be expected to observe the proprieties, can she? Perhaps I should frisk her and see if she's carrying a gun."

This time it was Liz who shrieked. "No!"

Alexander bent his dark head to his wife so that only she could hear him. "Ah, love, delightful as frisking you would be, this is hardly the place." His hand, shaped against her waist, burned through the luxurious fabric of her gown. A hot flush stole across Liz's throat and cheeks. Aloud Alexander said, "Now that you're here, I'm glad you came, darling. The board couldn't have made an unbiased judgment of this matter without seeing you." His gaze left Liz and returned to his mother. "But, Mamam, would you and Paul chair the meeting for a few minutes without me? I would like to speak to Liz in private."

Before the princess could answer, Liz replied defiantly, resisting the pressure of her husband's hand, "Darling, that won't be necessary. You see, I didn't come to talk to you, but to the board. We can speak privately later."

"What are you doing?" Alexander demanded in an urgent whisper. "Just this once, surprise me and resist the impulse to be suicidal." His hand on her body held her so hard it hurt.

"Is this the wife you promised us you would hide in the country, Mikhail, while you smooth everything over?" the princess persisted. "The wife who would keep a low profile and avoid publicity? This creature who storms in here dressed so flamboyantly and who flagrantly disobeys you? Doubtless she feels she photographs well in that outrageous costume. I wouldn't be surprised if she's called every newspaper in town. I knew I was right and that you should be removed from the presidency until you recover your sanity where this woman is concerned. Maybe now everyone will listen to me. For one month you abandoned your responsibilities because of her. Liz Chartres, you tried to destroy my foolish son once. I'll not let you succeed a second time. You must leave this room at once so we can decide what to do about you."

"Won't anybody here listen to me?" Liz cried. "Are you so sure I'm guilty that you won't even let me speak?" She turned to Alexander. "So, you've been planning behind my back to bury me alive in some country house where I can do no harm. Well, that hardly surprises me, but you don't know me. I won't go to the country. You can't make me take up sewing and gardening or tennis or whatever innocuous pastime you have in mind. I won't be turned into a dull and suitable wife. I'd rather be dead than become the boring paragon you want—some whey-faced little seamstress that hasn't the sense to stand up for herself.''

It took Alexander an uncomfortably long time to banish his unbidden smile. He should have been furious, but he wasn't nearly so angry as he ought to have been. ''It never occurred to me I could turn you into a dull and suitable wife, my dear, nor—how did you put it?—a whey-faced little seamstress, though as a designer even you must admit you do have a few talents with the needle. Perhaps I should have considered that possibility.''

Was he trying to make a joke of it and thus render her harmless? Well, she would never never allow it. She flung off his grasp and whirled angrily on the princess and Paul.

''I know you're against me. I know you want Alexander to divorce me, but I love him. I never did anything deliberately to hurt him or you. It was reckless of me, I know that now, to marry him without telling him of my connection to Roger Chartres. But, you see, knowing who Alexander was, I didn't want to fall in love with him any more than he would have wanted to fall in love with me. I even tried to run away from him in France.''

''A shrewd gamble,'' the princess said scathingly, ''that a chase would only whet his appetite.''

''But I did fall in love with him, and then I was too afraid of losing him to tell him the truth. I came here today not, madame, because I wanted to be photographed by newsmen. Not because I want to make more trouble for any of you or Alexander, but because I wanted to tell you that I am innocent. And so is he. I know that some of you think you can't trust Alexander to remain president of Dazzle if I'm his wife. You hold him to blame for what I was accused of doing seven years ago. I came here because I couldn't stand by and let his career be ruined because of me without at least trying to—''

"Make sure you destroyed him?'' the princess finished. "If you're innocent, Liz Chartres, why didn't you come to the board seven years ago? Why did you run away?''

"Alexander told me he wanted me out of his life, and even though I was devastated, I tried, for his sake, to accept that. I was pregnant, and I thought if I stayed, there could be no clean break with Alexander. If I left him, maybe he would manage to save his career and return to his old life. I only wanted to help him. I thought he did not want...children from me, that he could not really love them.'' Her last sentence was a dying whisper. "But I was so very wrong...about everything.''

"Liz—'' Alexander's voice betrayed more warmth than he would have liked. Doubtless she was wielding the deathblow to his career, but it didn't seem to matter very much. All that mattered was Liz. He was losing the battle to suppress a startling tenderness that had crept through his expert guard.

"Don't try to stop me, Alexander,'' Liz said softly, speaking at last to him. "I'm going to find out for sure who stole Paul's formula and deliberately framed me, because I know you won't believe me unless I do. And, Princess Vorzenski if you have any feelings as a mother or grandmother, you would stand by your own instead of backing those who oppose him. You want to strip him of the presidency as a power play to make him divorce me.''

"A fine speech that I'm sure you've rehearsed, young woman, grammar mistakes and all,'' the princess said coldly. Her pale skin was mottled with rage. "How dare you accuse me of not being a good mother! By your own admission you trapped my son into this impossible marriage with a lie, while I've given him everything! All I want is for you to leave Mikki in peace. There can never be any happiness in a marriage like yours.''

"And is there in yours?"

A stillness came over the taut features of the princess. There was the fleeting glimpse of pain in her eyes, and then she said in low, measured words, ''Why do you cling to a man who has already begun to hate you?''

"Hate—"

That one word destroyed the noble fury that had driven Liz. To hear his mother say it made it loom as a horrible reality in her mind.

Alexander was pale from the exchange between his mother and wife. Liz looked stricken. He said gently, ''Liz, you should never have come here. You've made yourself ill. I'm going to take you home.'' To the others he said, ''I think that nothing more can be accomplished tonight. I'm sure everyone will agree we should resume this meeting in the morning.''

Liz swallowed. Had she ruined everything? No one believed her. Had she embarrassed her husband irreparably in the eyes of the board? Would they agree with the princess that he should lose the presidency because of his impossible wife? Or would he divorce her? The glimmer of tears brightened her eyes.

''I'm glad to see that you have at least some shred of conscience,'' the princess murmured. ''Give Mikhail up before you destroy him. Go back to Mexico and make your puppets again.''

Black misery filled Liz's heart, weighing it down like a heavy stone.

She said in a dull, tired voice, ''Princess Vorzenski, if you throw me out, you throw your grandchildren out as well. If I return to Mexico, I'll take them with me. Don't you have any curiosity about them? Not even a scrap of tenderness for them? Alex is very much like Alexander. He's six years old, and he was in a serious accident two weeks ago. He would love you so much. You couldn't help loving Samantha either if you would only give yourself the chance. She's so vital and irrepressible.''

For a moment the princess could think of nothing to say.

''If you want to see them, you will have to come to me,'' Liz said quietly.

After an infinite silence the reply came. ''I will never want to see any children of yours, Liz Chartres.''

Liz's eyelids fell. She stared fixedly at a patch of rug that she'd stained with her damp shoes.

''You've made your decision then, I see,'' Liz said in a strained, low tone. ''It's useless to talk further.''

''I made it seven years ago,'' the princess replied, ''and your coming here today has only confirmed that I was right.''

''What you want in a daughter-in-law is a speechless nonentity.''

''That would be infinitely preferable to what I have.''

Liz could bear no more. She spun on her heel and dashed into the hall. Behind her she heard the excited chorus of voices, and the princess's strident voice overrode them all.

A hammer pounded inside Liz's brain. She'd been wrong to come. There was no chance. No chance at all.

Liz pushed the button for the lift and waited, her feeling of hopelessness building. Alexander came out of the boardroom looking weary and drawn, and at the sight of him Liz felt a stab of fierce longing. Despite the shadows beneath his eyes, his dark, virile handsomeness compelled her more forcefully than ever. She devoured the lithe power of his body as he moved toward her with his long, easy strides. If only he would fold her into his arms and say that nothing that had been said in the boardroom mattered to him. If only he would kiss her gently, comfortingly.

But, of course, he did none of those things.

"You shouldn't have run off like that when I said I'd take you home," he said grimly.

"There's no need for you to trouble yourself about me," she replied, cut more deeply by his coldness than by his mother's attacks in the boardroom.

She did not know that her own voice sounded even harsher than his. When she looked at him like that, with her face closed against him, Alexander was tormented by thoughts of Jock. Again he wondered what had really happened between them when Jock had come to Mexico. He was angry suddenly that she shut him out while behind his back she had welcomed Jock into her arms.

"Damn it, Liz. I want to take you home," he insisted stubbornly.

His tone made her feel defiant, and she said stupidly, "So that I won't get into more trouble?"

"Don't you think you've done enough for one night's work? You've certainly stirred up a hornet's nest here."

"That's not what I intended."

"I won't ask you what you intended, then."

"Alexander, I'm sorry I came. I shouldn't have provoked your mother. I'm worried that now she'll find it hard to forgive me."

He laughed shortly. "Maman does not have a forgiving nature. I had hoped to bring you two together under different circumstances. I wanted to introduce her to the children first. As it is, you met. You collided. Now we must deal with the consequences."

"I thought only to—"

He was determined not to let her pretend she had had his interests at heart. "Liz. Don't. I'm taking you home."

She saw that he wouldn't believe in her, and a demon of recklessness possessed her. "Maybe I don't want to go home—with you."

He blanched, but she was too filled with her righteous fury to care. The doors of the lift opened, but when she was about to step inside, he leaned forward. His heavy arms circled her to prevent her escape. When she struggled, his grip merely tightened. The doors closed, leaving them alone once more.

"Where are you going, then?" he demanded. "To Jock?"

"What if I were?" She said this very nastily because she was afraid she might burst into tears. "You don't care about me. You said you only wanted me now for…for…"

"This," he rasped in a goaded undertone. He pulled her roughly against his hard, masculine body, his mouth crushing insolently down upon hers.

In that moment he did not care how he hurt and humiliated her. He was filled with resentment because she held him in thrall with silken threads of sensual bondage. She was in his blood. He needed to taste her, to feel her, to possess her, and these needs filled him with the savage desire to hurt her as well.

He forced her head back and pressed a ruthless kiss upon her upturned lips. She fought him, but she could not free herself. Her hands pushed in vain against his chest, but he was too strong and too brutally determined. Stubbornly, Alexander held her still and caressed her. His mouth moved upon her stiff lips and then moved lower.

A tongue of flame leaped from him to her like a charge of electricity, and Liz shivered. It was all she could do to restrain her arms from lifting to circle his neck. But even though a dizzying wildness tingled in her arteries, she denied her own desire in the futile attempt to thwart his.

Soon her passive submission was not enough to satisfy him. He forced her to return his kisses, parting her lips, filling her mouth with his thrusting tongue, slowly, lingeringly, killing her will to resist him until all too soon she felt dazed and hungry for much much more.

He forced her backward against the wall, his weight pinning her against the cool green tiles. The shape of his male body molded her curving slimness, and she felt his potent state of arousal. He was on fire, and so was she. She could feel the hammering of his heartbeats as crazily frenzied as her own, the disturbed unevenness of his breathing. He was no more immune to her sensually than she was to him, and this thought gave her a fleeting sensation of power until the ache in her heart reminded her of the lasting fulfillment she desired and could never have. She wanted his love.

Alexander's need was so grippingly elemental he was not troubled by rational arguments. He kissed her with ruthless passion; a wild, reckless abandon to prove his mastery over her drove him. Only when her body melted against his, and she trembled everywhere his lips and fingers played across her skin, did he release her.

Only then did he set her from him without uttering a word of apology. She was shaking with an overwhelming emotion that she wished fervently were unequivocable rage instead of the humiliating passion for him that it was.

"You are despicable," she cried. If only she believed that!

"So I've been told," he replied imperturbably, pleased to see she was as shaken as he. "Though not usually by a woman trembling from my embraces." The dark power that had driven him was once more leashed, though barely.

"Alexander, we can't go on like this, tearing each other to pieces one minute and the next minute making love."

"Do you dignify what just happened with the euphemism 'making love'?" he asked mercilessly.

On a sob she said, "Things only get worse between us every day."

"What do you suggest then?"

"I-I don't know anymore, Alexander. Look, I can't pretend that a while ago I didn't want…" She met the knowledge in his eyes with a shiver.

"Yes?" A black brow lifted sardonically.

She turned scarlet. "Why should I state the obvious, that I want you, that a minute ago I felt I'd die, I wanted you so much? Don't you know that you're killing me? I'm not cut out for the kind of marriage you want. I don't want to be a sex object you'll cast aside in a few months, when you tire of me."

"Is that all you really think you are to me?" he demanded quietly. "Don't you know—"

"All I know is that I can't go on with you like this, Alexander. And tonight I need to be alone, to try to think what to do. Please, let me leave, by myself."

"If you won't come home with me, at least let me see you safely inside a cab," he said wearily.

"Spare me your show of concern and gallantry. I can take care of myself, thank you. In case you don't remember, I've been doing it for seven years since you threw me out."

"Damn you, Liz. It's black as pitch outside. London's not as safe at night as it once was. For those same seven years you were taking care of yourself, I was crazy wondering if you were dead or alive. I'll put you into a cab if I have to carry you over my shoulders to do it.''

"I'm sure such caveman tactics are exactly the thing to appeal to a man of your baser instincts.''

This remark enraged him as she'd intended for it to. He was reaching for her when the doors of the lift opened. Only their mutual awareness of the man standing in the shadows inside it brought the situation between Liz and Alexander under control. Instead of seizing her, Alexander let her walk stiffly past him. He had every intention of following her, but when he glanced at the man who moved out of the rectangle of light toward the doors, Alexander recognized his cousin, Jock Rocheaux.

As Liz stumbled into Jock's waiting arms, both men stared at each other in stunned surprise. The doors began to close. Too late, Alexander lunged toward the lift as the twin sheets of stainless steel slid together. For an instant he felt paralyzed by the thought of Jock with Liz. Then he rushed blindly toward the stairwell.

Inside the lift, Liz pressed her shaking body against Jock.

"You've quarreled,'' Jock said gently with his old-world courtesy.

"Terribly. Oh, Jock, it was awful. I'm so ashamed of the things I said to his mother.''

"Don't be. Aunt Paulette deserves far more than you could possibly deliver.''

"And then in the hall just now, I was even worse. I deliberately wanted to hurt Alexander. I even let him believe I was going from him to you.''

"Dear me. You certainly wasted no time in throwing me to the most unpleasant wolf in the pack.'' He didn't look in the least worried. "And I thought you and I were friends.''

"Be serious, Jock. Please. I've made such a terrible muddle of my life. I've hurt everyone—even you."

"You can't be in love without hurting people. I should know. I'm an old hand at hurting. Here..." He handed her his handkerchief.

She dabbed at her eyes. "Then we must be deeply in love, because we're both hurting. Jock, I feel like I'm dying!"

"Take it from an expert, *chérie,* when you feel like that, that's the surest proof you're not. You're wretchedly in love, that's all. It was almost pleasant to see Mikki again. I've never seen him so miserably enraptured." His voice changed, and there was an element of something in it that would have alarmed her had she noted it. "But Liz, seriously, do you realize the jeopardy I'm in because of you? I snuck inside Dazzle tonight to see you. I would have broken the doors down if they hadn't been wide open, or assaulted the guards if they'd been on duty."

He was joking, and yet he was not. His face had never been graver.

"Why, Jock?"

"Liz, we have to talk—now." His golden face was more urgent than she'd ever seen it. "You've got to come to Paris with me."

The doors of the lift opened, and a powerful arm reached inside and wrenched Jock bodily from Liz.

"Paris! If you think for one minute I'm going to let you sail off into the sunset with my wife, Jock, you are deranged," Alexander snarled in a breathless burst. Breathless because he'd dashed headlong down the stairs. "And I'll thank you to keep your filthy hands off her."

"Unfortunately you've got things all wrong, Mikki. Liz won't have me. She foolishly prefers you."

Four uniformed men surrounded Jock and Alexander.

Jock eyed the five men about him. "Mikki," Jock stalled. "I came because I have to convince Liz to come to Paris. What I have to say can only be said privately—to her."

"I never doubted that for a minute. Say it to me, you bastard."

The four guards hustled Jock down the hall toward a small office. Liz realized there wasn't going to be a chance for her to talk to Jock now even if she stayed. Alexander would prevent it, and she wasn't up to any more quarrels tonight. Liz seized the opportunity to escape.

It was raining again as she plunged out into the street. The wreck had been cleared, and the traffic was flowing smoothly. She hailed a cab and slid inside.

Within the building Jock was the first to notice that Liz had not followed them into the office.

"Where's Liz?" he demanded, his voice urgent.

"I don't know."

"Mikki, you've got to find her. It's a—"

Alexander had already run out of the office and down the hall into the rain. He didn't hear the end of his cousin's harshly expelled sentence.

"It's a matter of life and death."

Chapter Fifteen

Liz was trembling with fatigue and nervous strain as she mounted the wide flight of steps of Alexander's house. The hour was late, the air cool and sweet from the rain. Ana Lou let her in and, to her anxious questions, gave assurances that the children were fine, having gone to sleep hours earlier.

"And my husband?"

There was the briefest hesitation.

"He has not come home, my lady." Ana Lou averted her gaze out of kindness, but the gesture of sympathy betrayed her suspicions more than anything she could have done.

Liz trudged up to her bedroom feeling a stifling sensation of aloneness. She should be glad that Alexander had not come home. At least she would not have to face him, but the tumult of her emotions had left her drained and yet at the same time too stimulated to sleep. Nor had her lonely dinner at the Savoy or her long cab ride eased her tension. Her mind was still a jumble of remorse over what she'd done.

She took a long bath, but that did not relax her. She had told Alexander she needed to be alone, but now that she was, that wasn't what she wanted. She found herself listening to every sound in the house. For a woman who did not wish her husband's return, why did she long for the heavy tread of his footfall on the stair?

She combed her hair, tugging her brush through the hopeless tangle of curls. She paused frequently, her brush suspended and still above the bright fall of hair, while she strained to listen. Much later she went to bed, but it seemed hours before she fell asleep.

The room was utterly black when she awoke, but she was aware of someone moving about.

In the darkness, Alexander's voice came to her. "Liz, are you awake?"

She pretended to be asleep though his vibrant baritone stirred every nerve in her body.

He began to undress. She heard the thud of a shoe falling upon the carpet, the sounds of a belt buckle and zipper. He went into the bathroom and closed the door.

The bathroom door opened again, and he strode across the room. The mattress dipped, and he pulled back the covers and slid inside. She smelled the fresh male scent that was his alone.

She felt his warmth even before he touched her.

"Liz?" This time her name was a low murmur.

She didn't answer.

"Aren't you awake?" The sheets rustled and he folded her stiff limbs against his body. "Yes, you are. I can tell." His hand gently smoothed her hair from her forehead. "I don't blame you for not wanting to talk."

She began to cry.

"I looked everywhere for you," he admitted, his voice as low and comforting as she had wished it to be earlier. "I came home on the chance that you were here."

"I had dinner at the Savoy," she mumbled through her tears.

He sounded relieved. "Why there?"

"Some nostalgic homing instinct, I guess. You took me there on our first date."

"I remember."

"Tonight it was so different."

"I can imagine that it was."

"We were so in love that night."

"Yes." He hesitated, stroking her hair. "We were."

"It seemed like such a long time ago. It made me even more unhappy to remember."

"Sometimes there's an odd enjoyment in stoking the embers of depression by indulging in sad memories. I imagine you were in that sort of mood."

"Tonight, when I went to Dazzle, I only wanted to help you, Alexander, and I ended up hurting you." More tears fell.

"I've been hurt before. I'll survive." His voice was infinitely gentle.

"I guess now it will be difficult for you to convince the board you can manage me."

"Quite difficult."

'I'm sorry. Can you believe me when I say that I didn't mean to make things harder for you?"

"Honestly?" His hand in her hair was still.

"Honestly," she said.

"I don't know."

"Alexander, how can we go on like this, when you have all these doubts?"

"Because not going on would be so much worse. I learned that much tonight when you ran out into the rain." Again his warm fingers moved on her, this time in a caress upon her shoulders beneath the heaviness of her hair.

A thrilling heat burned in the trail left by his fingertips.

"I'm the wrong woman for you."

"In all ways but one." His voice was huskier now. She heard the hint of a smile in it, the beginning of the warmth she so longed for.

He spanned her waist with his hands. His touch brought the familiar ripple of excitement. Slowly she turned in his arms and tilted her face for his kiss.

"I'm sorry," he said. "Not really for kissing you in the hall. I couldn't help that. But for everything else, I'm sorry."

"So am I."

"Even about Jock?" she insisted.

"Even about Jock." He had tensed, but his voice remained easy. "I was...I am...jealous."

"What happened between you two after I left?"

"I threw him out without finding out why he'd even come. I haven't the patience to deal with Jock." He didn't say, "Because I know he was with you in Mexico, and you didn't tell me."

Liz's hand slid lower over Alexander's flat belly, deliberately stirring him.

"You have nothing to be jealous about." Her tone had deepened suggestively.

To that he said nothing. He wanted to believe her.

A varnished fingertip dipped inside his navel, and it was a decidedly pleasant sensation.

"I hate to quarrel," she continued, still in the low bedroom voice that aroused him. "It makes me feel so lost. After I left you I was silly and frightened in London on my own. I'm afraid I didn't sort anything out. I just missed you and wished we hadn't quarreled."

His arms wrapped her body fiercely. "I missed you too. God, what an understatement! The last few hours have been a soul-searching hell." He'd never thought he'd confess that.

"For me too," she admitted.

He held her in silence for a long moment, his mood lightening.

"There's only one good thing about our quarreling, Liz."

"What's that?"

"Do you really have to ask?"

"I'm afraid I do."

"Making up, my darling."

"Oh, that?"

"Yes, that."

The one word spoke volumes. She moved so that her body slid erotically against his. "Making up, you say?" she teased. "Like this?" She moved against his thigh again. He gasped. Her leg brushed the length of his. "And this?"

"You catch on fast, my love. What in the hell are you doing with your toe?" She did it again, and his heart slammed against his rib cage. "Where in the world did you learn a trick like that? If you don't stop, my curiosity will have me insane with jealousy all over again."

She was laughing when he lifted her against his chest.

"Maybe it's time you showed me the one way you're right for me," he taunted.

"You mean a home demonstration?"

He chuckled. "Go right ahead and demonstrate, my love."

"My pleasure."

"No, love, mine."

Words became unnecessary. Within moments that powerful force that was outside them both had taken charge, making a mockery of their hatreds and distrust. In that timeless, white-hot moment of shattering passion they were one, all that was between them melting into nothingness in the deluge of their shattering fulfillment.

Then it was over, and he drew her into his arms. They didn't speak. Each felt slightly ashamed for that loss of self.

The next morning she felt shy toward him, and he was moodily silent. It was still dark when Alexander switched on a lamp. As Liz was slipping out of bed, he glimpsed a tantalizing curve of leg and thigh before she managed to pull on her silk robe. Because of his warm look, she smiled drowsily at him with love in her eyes. A quiver of unwanted desire darted through him, and he looked away. He remembered her sweetness and gentleness last night in his arms and her wantonness in his bed. The old torment gripped him, and he wondered how long he could endure the conflict of emotions she aroused. She was tearing him apart inside. One minute he hated her, the next he loved her. He got out of bed and dressed quickly, anxious to escape her and bury himself in his work.

Later, from the bath, she called to him in that husky tone that disturbed him because it turned his insides to mush, "Alexander, it's getting cold in here. I forgot to close the door. Would you please close it before you go?"

He moved warily across the room to oblige her, but at the sight of her naked reflection in the mirror on the bathroom door, his heart began to pound violently. She was provocatively immersed up to her pouting nipples in fragrant suds. Again the war of emotions began.

Unaware that he was standing outside the door, his

brown hand shaking on the knob, she leaned back lazily to soak, and he could not tear his gaze from the voluptuous sight of her body. His gaze lingered on her breasts, and he inhaled a swift, painful breath when she parted her legs and the washrag slid down them. Then, with a splash of water, she stood up and reached for a towel. His eyes were riveted to her narrow waist, the enticing swell of her hips.

"I'm freezing," she called, louder and more impatiently than before. "Alexander—"

"I'm here," he replied, his deep tone like velvet as he stepped into the bathroom, where she stood in shimmering wet splendor.

Startled doe eyes met the golden fire of his. At that moment it was impossible for him to imagine evil in her. Someone else had done what he had always believed her guilty of. He must find that person; as a husband he should protect her, not accuse her. He reached for the towel, his warm hands brushing her trembling fingers. She stood very still when he began caressing her satin skin with the soft terry.

"Alexander, I imagined you would be anxious to get down to the office," she said in a quiet voice as the towel gently massaged beneath the softness of her breasts. As always, any tenderness from him filled her with joy.

"I was," he murmured, tracing the curve of her belly before he pulled her damp body into his arms. His expression was both haunted and adoring. "But I'm not now."

"Oh—" Her one word was bold and breathless.

The towel dropped to the floor, but neither of them noticed. His palm cupped her face gently, and he kissed her tenderly.

The pressure of his mouth on hers destroyed her defenses. As always, there was a quality of arrogant mastery in his kiss that commanded her into submission. His tongue stole inside her mouth, exploring. Like a narcotic, a hot invasion of languorous sensation relaxed her rigid muscles so that his roaming hands could shape her pliant flesh to his body. When she offered not the slightest resistance, he lifted her into his arms and carried her to the bed.

The coldness was gone from his handsome face, and in its place was a hot wanting he did not bother to hide. There was another emotion as well, an emotion far more powerful and enduring than mere sensuality, but in her confusion, Liz did not note it though it evoked a subconscious pleasure in her that made her even more eagerly passionate than ever before.

As always the wonder of flesh upon flesh lifted them and shook them so that they forgot all in the blazing tide of fulfillment. In the aftermath of their lovemaking, a golden glow remained between them, and he pulled her on top of his chest, so that her hair spilled over his brown shoulders.

His fingertips caressed a strand of her hair, twirling a length of the flame wisps between his fingers. "You always smell like flowers. Jasmine and lavender." His drawl was soft and mesmerizing. "I hope you won't always prove so distracting in the mornings, or I'll never get to work."

The warm light in his eyes tinged her cheeks becomingly with a blush. She loved him; in that moment she would have given anything if he'd loved her too. Instead of telling him how she felt, her lips lowered and touched his in a brief, sweet kiss.

The phone began to ring.

"Oh, dear," Liz cried, jumping from the bed.

She had forgotten not to answer it.

His eyes followed her graceful movements, admiring the shapeliness of her body. He thought of other men, of Jock, and the desire her beauty would inevitably arouse in them. Jealousy jolted Alexander at the thought of another man possessing her, especially Jock. She was his, his alone, and he was determined to keep her no matter what the price.

"Hello," Liz whispered.

Princess Vorzenski's shrill voice exploded into the phone. "Let me speak to Mikhail."

Without a word, Liz handed Alexander the telephone.

As he listened to the princess, his expression darkened. When at last he hung up, he stared at his wife, and his eyes were as cold and hard as stones. Liz was filled with a sense of impending doom.

"Well?" she asked, unable to stand the suspense. "What did she say?"

'I'm sure you know already.''

"Tell me, Alexander."

"Paul's formula was stolen out of my safe in the Dazzle offices last night." In his voice there was a deadness that she had never heard before. "I have lost the presidency of Dazzle. Maman has temporarily filled the office herself."

"And you think I took the formula, don't you, Alexander?" He stared at her in silence. "Well, don't you?"

In his eyes she saw the unspoken accusation.

"Don't push me, Liz, about what I think."

She turned from him, unable to bear that look that killed her soul, that hopelessness in his eyes that destroyed the illusion that their relationship was salvageable.

Their marriage was as dead as ashes.

He got out of bed and dressed quickly, ripping clothes

from hangers, shirts from drawers. He was at the door when she called to him. "Please tell me where you're going, Alexander."

"Where do you think? To work, love. To see what, if anything, can be saved from this latest disaster. Get dressed. You're coming with me. I'm not leaving you alone and risk you running off to Jock and your father."

She turned her face to the wall so that he could not read her face. Those had been her precise intentions. If anyone knew what had happened to the formula, her father surely must. He had been against her marriage from the first, and she'd believed he was behind the theft of the formula even before Jock had practically confirmed it as the truth. Didn't logic point to his being guilty again? Fury consumed her that her own father could be so treacherous. No matter what she'd promised Alexander in Mexico about not seeing Roger, she had to go to her father and convince him once and forever to stay out of her life. But if she went, she risked losing Alexander.

"You realize," Alexander said grimly, "that if you run away now, to Paris or anywhere else, everyone will be convinced you had some part in this. Since I have brought you back and established you as my wife, I will be condemned a fool, if not worse. I want you to stand by me, no matter what happens. You made a promise to me in Mexico about your father and Jock. I want you to tell me—now—that you intend to honor it."

"I-I—" She couldn't utter a word. Did he really believe she would let Roger get away with this a second time? Even if it cost her her marriage, she wouldn't promise that she would stand by and do nothing while someone wrought utter destruction upon their lives.

"Liz—"

His eyes captured hers in a hard and relentless gaze

that stripped away her defenses, leaving her shatteringly vulnerable. Why did Alexander make her feel that she betrayed him, when all she wanted to do was help him?

"I was a fool to make such a promise to you," she admitted at last.

"I see," he said in a low, dead voice. "And I was a fool to think you possessed even an ounce of honor where I'm concerned. I should have left you in Mexico."

"No! You don't see at all! I—"

"Save your lies." Refusing to listen, Alexander pivoted sharply and stormed down the stairs. She heard him calling for George, talking to Mrs. Benchley, behaving toward the servants as if nothing out of the ordinary had occurred when in reality the fabric of their lives had just been ripped into shreds. The house was eerily silent when he went outside. Then she heard him climbing back up the stairs, and, realizing that she hadn't even started dressing, she went to the closet and pulled out a silk shift.

Alexander strode into the room and saw that she hadn't dressed. Her slowness further infuriated him. "Hurry up, or I'll strip you and dress you myself, love."

She started toward the bathroom, but he stopped her with a rough command. "Take off your clothes in here where I can make sure you're not being slow deliberately."

Her heart was near bursting with bitter pain, but she knew it was useless to cross him when he was in this kind of mood. Without a word she slid off the robe. She was aware of his dark gaze devouring her naked body as she fumbled to undo the buttons on the front of her dress so she could step into it.

The buttons would not come loose, and she turned scarlet with shame. He came to her and took the dress from her and undid the buttons himself. Next to her, he was so tall, so male. Her senses catapulted in alarm. When he had finished with the buttons, he handed her the garment. His brown hand cupped one breast in primitive possession.

"Do you have to be so hard, Alexander?" she asked. "I can imagine what you must be feeling, but…"

"Can you?" His mouth curled bitterly even as his hand upon her skin tantalized. "Maman tried to teach me something once. You've completed the lesson. She's always held that a man can have anything he wants—as long as he's willing to pay the price." His fingers caressed her warm satin skin. "Sweetheart, I wanted to watch you strip so I could remind myself of the charming body I'm paying such a damnably high price for."

Tears of humiliation stung her eyelids as she whirled away and pulled on her dress. Later they left the house without speaking, but they were each terribly aware of the other.

When Alexander and Liz reached Alexander's office, they found his mother, Paul, and their cousins, Jon and Philippe, waiting for them. The latest news was that Michelle had disappeared.

All eyes were riveted on Liz.

The princess was the first to speak. "Mikhail, why did you bring her?"

"Because Liz is as deeply involved as anyone else in this room," he replied tersely.

"But she stole the formula."

No one said anything, not even Liz.

"What is, is," the princess said at last, realizing she was forced to accept Liz's presence. "But I have a plan that just may save us from disaster. Gentlemen, why don't we sit down." The men complied, and the princess seated herself behind Alexander's desk. Liz moved to the window and looked down at the flowing traffic on Regent Street.

"I have given this matter a great deal of thought," the princess began. "No one outside the thief and those present in this room know the formula is missing, and I don't think we should release this information. The sort of publicity that would result if the theft were found out would do Dazzle no good. Furthermore, I feel we should go ahead with our launch."

'But the formula has been stolen. We risk competing with our own fragrance under a Radiance label," Philippe argued.

"We can use one of the formulas Paul discarded." At Paul's dark look, the princess said swiftly, "Oh, I know, darling, this is far from a perfect solution, but one of your discards is better than anyone else's creation. You're the best in the business. With your reputation, we can carry it off. You will be the only one to know the perfume is not up to your impeccable standards."

Paul was about to object, but Alexander cut in. "Maman's right, Paul. Her plan is audacious, but sometimes audacity—when you've got nothing else—carries the day."

"Exactly, Mikhail. And as for your marriage to Liz—"

"Maman, I've already heard your views on that score."

"No, darling, you haven't. Yesterday I was against your marriage, Mikhail, but today I'm reconciled to it as a reality. Since you've brought Liz back and established her as your wife, I now think it is very important for you to continue with your marriage. At the moment a divorce or a separation is most undesirable. Journalists would inevitably become curious, and there's no telling what they might unearth if they started digging into our affairs. I won't have anyone suspecting that the fragrance we're launching is not up to Paul's usual standards. What I suggest, Mikhail, is that you take Liz and the children to Sardinia and keep them out of sight for a while.''

"While you take my place as president of the company, Maman?''

"Temporary president, while you enjoy...a second honeymoon. You would not have to be idle. While you're in Italy, you could iron out the distribution problems we've been having in Rome.''

"I have no objections to taking Liz and the children to Sardinia,'' Alexander said, surprising everyone in the room, "if she'll come.'' He rose from his chair and joined his wife at the window. "What do you say, darling?''

She turned and met his gaze. The smoldering challenge in his eyes dared her to refuse him.

"And if I won't?'' she asked in a cool tone.

His gaze narrowed, his expression hardening.

"You're either with me, or against me, Liz. Come or stay. It's your choice. But if you bolt, to Paris, to Roger and Jock...''

He didn't finish the threat. He didn't have to. She knew that if she did, their marriage would be over.

"So, as always your terms are the only terms,'' Liz said in a quiet voice. "I am expected to go along with this cowardly cover-up and leave the person who keeps making trouble for us free to go on making trouble. Really, Alexander, you amaze me.''

"Did it ever occur to you, love, that my sole intention is to protect that trouble-prone individual?'' He stared at her hard and knowingly, but at the same time his eyes were brilliant with the emotion he always fought to conceal.

Liz saw the flicker of tenderness shining warm and true, and it drew her like a bright beacon. Suddenly she realized that for all his deliberate harshness, Alexander was deeply in love with her, so deeply he was ready to throw his career aside to protect her. For a moment a wild joy filled her.

Alexander loved her! Her joy quickly gave over to fresh pain. He was so in love he was willing to stay with her even when he still believed her guilty of having tried to destroy him, even when he thought she held some part in this new scheme.

She reached out and touched his hand, and his fingers curled possessively over hers, gripping hers, imparting warmth and strength and determination. She held on to him with equal fierceness.

It would be so easy, she thought, to go to Sardinia with him. They would be together. She could hold on to what she had with him. The nighttime passion. The wildness and ecstasy only he could give her. The children would have their father. All of that would be hers for the rest of their lives.

It was terribly tempting to do as he asked, but she was troubled. If she obeyed him and went with him to Sardinia, yes, she would have her marriage and Alexander's love, but forever Alexander would believe her guilty of this unspeakable treachery. It was thrilling that he loved her enough to make a life with her even when he was tortured by his doubts. But could she do that to him?

Over his shoulder she saw the painting of Cornwall she had once so lovingly given him. That time when they had loved each other completely and happily came back to her.

Suddenly she realized she couldn't do as he asked. As much as she loved him, she would give him up before she would subject him to a lifetime of a less than perfect marriage. He would never be really happy with her if he couldn't trust her. No, she was going to have to try to establish her innocence, Liz thought, even if it cost her the one thing most dear to her—Alexander. In the end, wouldn't he be better off without her if he couldn't believe in her? Wouldn't it be better if he married someone else whom he could trust, even though that would mean her own heartbreak? She squeezed her eyes shut against the agonizing image of losing him.

But if she went to Paris to see her father, might she not hurt Alexander just as terribly? Alexander would not understand. It would look as if she were running away because she had betrayed him and was guilty. He would be incriminated by her actions, and he might never regain the presidency of Dazzle. The press would lacerate him; his reputation and credibility would be destroyed. He would think that she didn't love him. Inevitably the children would suffer.

Her thoughts raced in painful chaos, and she jerked her hand from Alexander's and turned her back to him.

"Liz—"

"Don't ask me now to give you an answer," she mumbled in a low, choked tone. "Because I can't. I don't know what to do."

She lied. Oh, she knew. She knew. She was going to Paris to confront Roger.

"All right," he said.

There was death in his voice. She fought against the impulse to fling herself into his arms and promise everything he wanted.

At last he said, "If you go to Paris, I hope you understand it will be the end of...us."

Oh, she understood.

She met his deep, dark gaze. The vision of his too-dear features wavered. She turned blindly.

She knew Alexander was lost to her forever.

Chapter Sixteen

Liz's fingers curled around the steering wheel of her rental car as tightly as hawk's claws. The ugly suburbs of Paris swept past in a blur of tall houses with wrought-iron balconies and slatted shutters. Shabby little *tabacs* and bright café-bars edged narrow streets. A man stood on a corner selling lottery tickets.

At the thought of the way Alexander had looked when she'd run out of the Dazzle offices, Liz's stomach knotted as tautly as her clawed fists. His dark face had been a portrait of mute agony.

Well, she mustn't think about Alexander now, of the torment of losing him. She had to concentrate on Roger and what she would say to him. What did one say to a man as callous as Roger?

Once she had not thought her father callous. How differently she had felt that last time when she'd secretly flown to Paris to tell Roger of her marriage.

Shocked at first, Roger had pretended to understand. He'd gathered Liz into his arms, kissed her, acting as if he shared her joy. He had even gone as far as to say he hoped that this marriage could bring a reconciliation between himself and Alexander's family.

Oh, he'd fooled her completely. Liz had never suspected his ruthless intentions. They had lunched at her father's favorite restaurant, the Auberge du Vert Galant, on its summer sidewalk terrace beside the Seine. There Liz had poured out her heart, confessing the golden emotion that had overwhelmed her and made her go against her father's advice.

He had thrown back his silver head and laughed, and the sunlight that glinted on the river's surface shone in his eyes as well. He was very handsome for his age, romantically handsome.

"You speak so earnestly when you speak of him, Liz. I can almost remember what it was to be young and in love." The dark skin beneath his black eyes had crinkled. His expression was intense with the memory of that time.

"You have not forgotten what love is, Roger. You have Mimi."

"Ah, yes," he said. "Mimi." The intensity vanished. "I have Mimi to comfort me—in my old age."

Something in his voice had troubled Liz.

He patted her hand. "I'm very happy for you, my dear. Another glass of wine, Liz? This is from my own vineyard in Burgundy."

A week later it was discovered that Paul's formula had been stolen. Shortly afterward Radiance launched the pirated perfume under the name Liz, using publicity pictures that had been originally intended for another Radiance fragrance, pictures Roger had promised to destroy when he'd learned of her secret marriage.

After what Jock had said yesterday, Liz was convinced that what she'd always suspected was true, that her father had been behind the theft and launch because he wanted to break up her marriage. After all, hadn't he warned her when she first came to Paris that he considered Alexander his enemy?

When she'd left London for Mexico, she'd felt betrayed by both Jock and her father. A year later, when Jock found her in Mexico, he begged her to believe that he had had nothing to do with the theft of the formula. Jock even defended her father, saying that Roger had nearly fired him over it and that Roger had immediately withdrawn the perfume. In the end Liz had believed in Jock's innocence, if not in her father's. Dazzle had won damages in a lawsuit, even though Radiance had already taken the fragrance Liz off the market.

But why had her father done it? It had scarcely been a profitable venture. Only one reason that fit with his character came to mind.

Mimi, in one of her rare moments of candor, had told Liz once that Roger was possessive of everything he owned or loved, and Liz, remembering how forcefully he had come into her life and persuaded her she was his daughter, believed Mimi.

"He saw me, and he wanted me, and he brought me, *ma petite*," Mimi had said, tossing her golden head in that famous, sensual way of hers that made yellow silk ripple over tanned shoulders. "He owns the studios that make my pictures, the theaters where they are shown. I have nothing that is not his."

"And doesn't that bother you?"

"Very much." Mimi's smile scarcely curved her unpainted lips. Her voice was matter-of-fact.

"But why do you let him own you?"

"When you have had a life like mine, there is one thing you learn, *ma petite,* and that is that life, at its best, is a compromise. No one can have it all." Mimi's shadowed eyelids lowered enigmatically, and she pulled her lustrous sable jacket over her shoulders. "Yes, I have enough."

And yet Mimi had not looked satisfied.

Did Roger consider his daughter another possession he could dominate? Liz had wondered. Well, if so, Liz had decided to reject his brand of love. Unlike Mimi, she would not be owned, not after losing Alexander, not by the man who had betrayed her trust and destroyed her chance of happiness with such callous disregard for her feelings.

Still, it had been difficult in the beginning to believe her own father would betray her. He had convinced her during the three months she had spent in Paris that he genuinely loved her.

Liz hated remembering that time; it did not make the thought of seeing him easier. She shifted restlessly and rolled down the window and caught the familiar scents of Paris. The smell of wine, coffee, cats and damp air assaulted her. She switched on the radio, and the husky sensuality of French music filled the car. Oh, how she loved French music. It reminded her a little of Barbra Streisand. Almost, almost, she could forget the pain of the past and the ordeal of facing her father.

Half an hour later the car thrust its way down the confusion of the Rue Royal and then onto the great expanse of the Concorde where the Crillon was veiled with leafed-out chestnut trees.

Soon after that she reached her father's opulent flat, and Armande let her inside and showed her to her father's study. The shades were drawn, and the elegant silver room was as dark and silent as she remembered.

Liz paced before the long windows overlooking the Rue du Faubourg Saint-Honoré.

Armande returned. "Madame, I've reached your father's office. Monsieur Chartres is on the telephone."

Liz lifted the silver receiver. It was as cold as ice in her shaking fingers.

"Liz!" The deep, sensually accented baritone was warm with welcome.

For a moment, she was too shaken to answer. A treacherous fondness filled her. The horrible realization that she still loved him no matter what he'd done struck her. That was the reason she had run from him, the fear that her love would give him a ruthless control of her. How would she ever be able to stand up to him?

He went on easily, "Did Jock tell you I wanted to see you?"

"Yes."

"And is he with you now?"

"I'm alone, Father. I-I tried to call him before I left London, but he didn't answer."

"Odd." There was the faintest trace of alarm in his low voice, but when he spoke again, it was gone. "I've been unable to reach him myself. He was to have called me this morning."

"I did not come because of Jock or because of you, Father. I came to stop you from hurting Alexander again."

After a long pause, "I see," he said.

"Jock said you admitted having stolen Paul's formula seven years ago."

"In a way I do feel I am responsible. I—"

"Father, I would rather speak to you in person. When Paul's formula was removed from Alexander's safe last night, I'm sure you wanted me to be blamed. If you could come home—"

"Paul's formula? Last night?"

The line went dead.

"Father?"

There was no dial tone. Liz called for Armande, but he had disappeared. Upstairs a door opened and closed. Liz called out again for Armande. Her words sounded hollow and wavery. She felt alone and yet not alone. Again she was aware of that ridiculous sensation of danger she'd felt earlier.

A velvet reply rippled down the stairs, the French purr that was the most famous voice in all of France.

"Liz, I am so sorry I was asleep when you arrived. I sent Armande on an errand a few minutes ago when he told me you were here. He has gone out to buy a special wine for us to celebrate your return. I will be down in a minute."

A few minutes later Mimi swept into the room. Her lips were as red as blood. Her golden hair was caught in diamond clips. Despite the sophistication of pink silk clinging to her voluptuous figure, there was still a little-girl quality in her face. It was that mixture of innocence and worldliness that gave her such a sensual aura.

As always, Mimi acted warm and welcoming, and yet Liz did not feel welcomed. Mimi embraced Liz. Mimi's perfume was rich, and Liz felt she was being suffocated.

At last Mimi released her. "For seven years your father and I have worried about you. I saw pictures of your children in the papers. They are precious. Roger and I already love them. You may remember that I was never able to have children of my own. I went to every doctor in Europe." The famous blue eyes were sad.

"I remember."

"Life does not always give us what we want," Mimi

said. "But I try to be content. I have so much." Fingertips made sure the diamond clips were secure in her hair.

"Mimi, a while ago I was talking to Roger. The phone went dead before we had finished speaking."

"It happens. There is some construction in the area, I believe. It has been a nuisance lately, *chérie*. Let me check the other line for you and see if I can reach Roger."

Mimi left the room. She returned with an opened bottle of Burgundy in one hand and a glass of wine in the other. Liz remembered that Mimi's enthusiasm for wine was more than the usual French fondness of wine.

Mimi smiled. "Don't look so worried, Liz. I was able to reach Roger, and he wants to meet us at Charmont in an hour. An emergency has detained him at the office." Charmont was Roger's château not far from Paris.

"Charmont?" Liz felt even more deeply upset. "But I had hoped to see him sooner. I—"

"He works too hard, your father. I'm afraid I suggested Charmont. Paris is so hot in the summer. I'm sorry, Liz, I did not think to consult you. This is the wine I sent Armande after. He's gone down to get the car to drive us to Charmont." Mimi poured a glass of wine and handed it to Liz. "This will give us time to visit," Mimi said, "to talk girl talk."

Liz felt impatient. The last thing she wanted was to spend unnecessary time with Mimi. She was filled with dread at the prospect of seeing her father, and yet she wanted to get the interview over as quickly as possible. Mimi was acting as if this were to be an amicable reunion.

"Drink the wine, *chérie*. It will relax you," Mimi purred, pressuring.

For an instant Liz considered telling Mimi exactly how she felt. Then she reconsidered. That would be unforgivably rude. After all, no matter how Liz felt toward Mimi, Mimi was hardly responsible for her father's actions.

Liz lifted the glass and drank deeply. It had an odd, crispy sweet taste, and yet it was not unpleasant. The glass was soon drained, and Mimi coaxed her to take another.

"But I haven't eaten. Wine always affects me—"

"What then, *chérie*, is the point of wine? You need to relax before you see Roger." She poured the wine.

So, Mimi did realize how she dreaded seeing Roger. The wine was her way of being thoughtful. Liz felt a twinge of guilt for her negative feelings toward Mimi and did not have the heart to refuse her.

A horn sounded outside. It was Armande with the car.

With Armande at the wheel of Roger's Lincoln, the suburbs of Paris swept past in a blur. Mimi talked very little to Liz on the trip from Paris, and for that Liz was grateful. Although as always Mimi had taken great pains to be both pleasant and thoughtful, Liz felt even more ill at ease with her than ever. Perhaps it was the lapse of seven years. Perhaps it was the knowledge that Mimi was her father's mistress and no doubt condoned all that Roger had done. Perhaps it was only Liz's own dread of the coming visit with Roger.

There had always been a wall of reserve about Mimi. No matter how nice Mimi acted, Liz always had the impression that Mimi kept much of herself hidden. Jock had hinted that Mimi's upbringing had been a brutal one. Mimi was an actress, and Liz found herself wondering how much of the Mimi she knew was real. Mimi tried to appear warm and friendly, but somehow Liz never felt that Mimi was wholly sincere. Perhaps it was enough that at least Mimi always did make the effort to be nice.

For a while Liz lay back against the seat. Suddenly she felt woozy, unlike herself. She should never have drunk the wine on a empty stomach. The road seemed to be a perpetual zigzag, and Liz felt less and less well. It was only her nerves, of course, the wine, and the motion of the Lincoln. For a long time she lay with her eyes closed, but the dreadful feeling did not subside.

When she managed to open her eyes again, the car was roaring through prosperous, densely farmed country. On the right, through thickets of willow, the gleam of Charmont Lake showed itself through the trees. On the left, the countryside rolled until it blended with a line of fir in the purpling haze.

Mimi's head lay upon the back of the seat too; her eyes had been closed since they'd left Paris. She looked both exhausted and preoccupied, and Liz felt a pang of guilt when she remembered that she had interrupted Mimi's nap with her announced visit that evening. Liz remembered Jock saying that she had been hospitalized several times.

Liz rested her feverish forehead against the cool glass of the window as the Lincoln exploded through the somnolent village of Charmont, which lay at the base of the château. The car was climbing now. Trees lined the narrow streets. At the edge of the pavement in front of the shops were tubs of flowers—the last of the tulips and freesias and scarlet ranunculus. Vivid-eyed daffodils bobbed their brilliantly yellow heads beside clumps of purple pansies and a multitude of other flowers, crowded into their pots French-fashion. Liz shut her eyes as a wave of nausea swept her.

The car plunged into a thick fir forest, and then snaked upward on the hilly road. Liz's stomach tightened, and she was suddenly afraid she was going to be ill if they didn't reach Charmont soon. Her throat felt so dry she could scarcely swallow.

Great gray beeches rose from tangles of hawthorne. The Charmont Woods. Then Charmont itself burst into view, standing proud and high as a solitary sentinel on the crest of its hill as it had for centuries, the sweep of its lonely valley and wild forest beneath it. Near the road, oak and birch were wreathed with bright holly. The pale stone of the house stood out against the dark green of the forest. Polygonal towers, crowned by slate roofs shaped like witches' hats, defended every corner of the building. The last rays of the sun made the windows of the château gleam like scarlet foil.

The car shot through the tall, powerfully fortified gate. High, corbeled, rocket-shaped towers rose on either side of the entrance arch.

The tires bit gravel and Armande parked the Lincoln in front of the enormous south door. Armande came around to open the back door and help Mimi out. Liz felt so weak and shaky she almost fell when she tried to stand up.

"Madame, are you all right?" Armande asked.

Liz held on to the car for support. The ground wavered. She was too unsteady to answer.

"Liz, you're as white as a sheet," Mimi said with concern. "I feel a little sick myself. The road to Charmont is impossible. When we get inside I'll make you some hot chocolate before dinner." Mimi took her gently by the hand.

Without a word, Armande lifted the two suitcases from the trunk and led the way toward the château. Liz found herself leaning rather heavily on Mimi's arm the whole way.

Mimi was fumbling in her purse for the keys, chattering now, as she had not in the car, but Liz could make no sense of what she was saying. The house was still, so unlike the Charmont she remembered. Suddenly Liz had

the impression that something was wrong. She felt sick
and strange, and yet it was more than that. Charmont was
not as it had been seven years ago. The hedges were wild,
the garden untamed. No flowers graced the enormous
beds. Instead they were choked with weeds. Even the
house itself seemed forbidding.

The sun sank in a rim of fir as Armande opened the
great door and helped the women inside. He flicked on
the electric lights. The furniture was draped with dust
covers, making the house seem filled with silent, mis-
shapen ghosts. Liz stepped into the high-ceilinged hall of
the château. Long black shadows fell eerily across the
chilled white marble floor. At one end of the vast room
the staircase rose to the wide landing, which was shrouded
in darkness. The air was damp and musty as if the house
had been shut up for a long time. Something felt terribly
wrong.

Liz fought the strange impulse to dash back outside
where the evening was golden and smelled of fresh pine
and fir, but when she turned, she stumbled. Mimi's fingers
were tight on her wrist, and had they not been, Liz would
have fallen.

Mimi sensed her fears and said lightly, "I should have
warned you, Liz. This is the month we give the servants
their holiday. I'm afraid we'll have to do for ourselves
tonight. I don't mind, myself. I'm surrounded by people
so much of the time, I love to come to Charmont and be
alone. You'll find the kitchen well stocked. I was here last
weekend, and a lady from the village shopped for me this
week."

"I'm not even hungry," Liz mumbled. "Why isn't
Roger here?" Her voice sounded thin, like a frightened
child's. For the first time she thought of seeing her father
without dread.

"He is so terribly busy, *chérie*. He'll be here soon. Probably some business problem came up before he could get away. He and I come down often on the weekends."

Charmont did not look as if Roger Chartres came down on weekends.

The white shapes spun like whirling ghosts as a wave of dizziness hit Liz. "I need to lie down, Mimi," she murmured.

"Of course," Mimi replied. "I will show you to your room and then go down to the kitchen and bring you some warm chocolate milk. That will settle your stomach."

"You are so kind," Liz managed faintly. Her voice trailed off as if it were something that didn't belong to her. Vaguely Liz was aware of Mimi leading her up the stairs to the bedroom she had always used when she had come to Charmont with Roger. It seemed to her that the two of them floated weightlessly as they mounted an endless white staircase.

Once inside the bedroom, Liz sank down upon the elaborate bed. Her gaze skimmed the Louis XVI chairs, which were draped and upholstered in flowered chintz. The room began to spin. She shut her eyes, but the sickening feeling did not subside.

She lay there for a long time wishing Mimi would hurry. In all her life she'd never felt so sick. Then she heard the quick skittering of high heels on the uncarpeted marble stairs, tappings that sounded like sharp, panicked beats. The sound was somehow familiar.

Mimi opened the door and came inside. Her eyes were downcast, hidden. She said softly, "Drink this. It will make you feel better."

Liz obeyed, and the warm chocolate was soothing, or perhaps it was Mimi's concern that made her feel better. For once she was glad to be with Mimi.

A few minutes later Mimi said, "I'm beginning to
worry about you, *chérie*. You are too pale. I think I will
call the village doctor. Just in case."

"No, really…"

"I insist."

Liz shut her eyes, thankful that Mimi was there to take
care of her. She felt even dizzier and yet sleepier than
before. She heard the retreat of Mimi's footsteps on the
carpet and then the rapid, gunfire taps on the marble stairs.
Again the sound reminded her of something.

Mimi was going to call a doctor. How sweet of her.
How thoughtful. Liz opened her eyes and focused upon
the golden phone on the gilt table by the window.

There was a phone in the room!

Why hadn't Mimi used the phone in this room? Why
had she gone downstairs? A wild baffling panic possessed
Liz. Muddled as her mind was, somehow she knew something was wrong if Mimi had gone downstairs to use a
phone when there was one right there.

Liz rose and stumbled from the bed. She was so dizzy
she couldn't stand. She felt thickheaded. *Drugged.* She
had to crawl across the thick flowered carpet to reach the
phone. She pulled the cord and the telephone crashed onto
the floor. She lifted the receiver and held it against her
ear.

The phone was dead.

"Hello. Hello." She screamed into the phone, shaking
it.

Of course, there was no answer.

It came to her then. Mimi had not gone downstairs to
call the doctor. She had had some other reason.

Liz heard the Lincoln's engine roar in the drive downstairs. Armande was leaving! Mimi had gone downstairs
to send him away. Somehow Liz had to stop him.

Slowly Liz dragged herself to the window. Her fingers fumbled with the lock, and at last she managed to unfasten it. She threw the window open and screamed out into the purple twilight.

The Lincoln shot toward the tall, fortified gate. Armande had not heard.

But someone else had.

Mimi was standing in the drive staring up at her. Her pink gown billowed in the breeze. Her hair flew wildly. Even from the great distance, for the first time Liz was struck with the burning power of Mimi's true personality. It was a force as powerful as the roll of a surging surf in a violent storm; a force as feral and vicious as a tiger's fury.

Then Mimi raced inside, and Liz collapsed onto the floor. She heard the staccato tappings of the heels downstairs, and she knew where she had heard them before. In the stairwell at Dazzle's office building. Mimi had been there that night, the night the formula had been stolen.

The words of the woman in front of Dazzle's office building came back to Liz. "I seen it happen... Almost looked as if the man in the car did it on purpose... Didn't stay around, not him that done it."

That accident had not been an accident. Mimi had deliberately planned it as a distraction so that she could enter the Dazzle offices undetected.

It was Mimi. Not Roger. Mimi had wanted to destroy her marriage.

Suddenly Liz knew that Roger was not coming, that he had not been to Charmont in years. Mimi had brought her there because the château was the last place he would think to look for her.

Liz was alone in the vast house with Mimi, and Mimi had drugged her and brought her there to kill her.

Liz thought of Alexander. She longed for him. If only...

She called his name softly. He would never know how much she loved him.

Even as she screamed his name she tumbled like a madly hurtling bullet into a black and terrifying void.

Chapter Seventeen

In the hospital corridor outside Jock Rocheaux's room, Inspector Walters spoke to Alexander in hushed tones.

"I'll come to the point, sir. Last night your cousin was run down by an automobile shortly before midnight. Mr. Rocheaux is not expected to live. This was no accident. The driver turned around to come back and strike him again."

The inspector's suspicious gaze was both avid and assessing.

"How horrible," Alexander murmured.

"The only thing that stopped him was that three people ran out into the street to render aid to your cousin. It was so dark, no one could give us a clear description of the car."

"Have you been able to speak to Jock, Inspector?"

"Only briefly. He wasn't able to say much before he lapsed into unconsciousness. He mentioned your wife, and

then he asked me to find Mikki Vorzenski. That's why
we rang you. He said, 'Inspector, it's a matter of life and
death.' He kept repeating that phrase. 'A matter of life
and death.' His last words were, 'Find Mikki.' Do you
have any idea what he meant?''

"Not the slightest." Alexander's smooth voice did not
betray the sudden fear that gripped him. Liz was gone.
Someone had deliberately tried to kill Jock.

Attempted murder.

Suddenly Alexander realized that Liz was innocent, and
because she was, her life was in danger. She had not left
him because she was guilty but because she was innocent.
She had gone to confront the person she believed to be
guilty of the theft. That person would not stop at murder.
Jock had known, and he had come to warn Liz. Because
he had known, he lay near death.

The inspector was pursuing his own train of thought.
"I was informed you and your cousin quarreled earlier in
the evening, Prince Vorzenski."

"My cousin and I have not been close for many years."

"I understand he maintains a close relationship with
your wife."

Alexander realized the remark was a deliberate attempt
to inflame him, and it did. "What exactly do you mean,
Inspector?"

"I understand as well that there is some possibility,
remote at the moment, that you were involved in the explosion of your company's lab in Switzerland."

In a voice of steel Alexander replied, "Inspector, I was
not involved with what happened to Jock last night nor
with the explosion in Switzerland."

"Nevertheless, Prince Vorzenski, you must realize that
you are a prime suspect. I don't want you to leave Lon-

don. The charges that may be brought against you are very serious.''

The two men regarded one another grimly. Inside, Alexander went wild. Liz was in danger because he had bullheadedly distrusted her. By doing so he had forced her to run to France, straight to the person who wanted to destroy her.

And he could not leave England.

Liz awoke to the soft blur of sound in the room and the cloying fragrance of Mimi's perfume. In her confusion Liz mumbled. ''I don't know if I can wait for Father. I'm so sleepy.''

''You will never see your father again.'' These words rang, vibrating like a gong.

Liz remembered everything. For an instant she managed to focus on Mimi, whose golden face was naked with hatred.

''I put something in your wine and in your chocolate, Liz, so that your death will look like suicide. An overdose of sleeping pills. It will be easy to say that you were distraught because of your failed marriage.''

Mimi's words swam in a fog of sound. It was difficult for Liz to make her own lips move because they felt numb and stiff.

''But why, Mimi? What have I ever done to you?''

''Nothing.''

''You must be crazy.''

''Don't say that!'' The purr became a shrill, tormented burst. ''I have a reason.'' The purr was back and filled with bitter sadness. ''You see, my sister died of an overdose...many years ago. A tragic accident, the authorities said, but I always believed it was suicide.''

''W-what do I have to do with your sister?''

"Rochelle was my little sister, my innocent sister that I cared for like a baby, that I protected even when we were so poor in Marseilles. We were orphans. Everything I did, I did for her. For her I climbed from the gutter to stardom. No one knew we were sisters. Then in Deauville, because two playboys, Jock Rocheaux and Mikki Vorzenski, amused themselves and made a game of my sister's love, she died. She was so idealistic. After my wedding, she took pills because she was too excited to sleep. Or so they said. When she died, I wanted to die, but, of course, I went on living. Only my heart had died. It is not bad, Liz, to die. It is the living who are really dead that suffer. My last words were said to her in anger. You see, she did not approve of my marrying a count, simply because he was a count."

"Rochelle's death must have been no more than an unfortunate accident," Liz murmured. "It is wrong to blame—"

"Her death choked me with hatred. I had to have revenge. So I slept with Sasha Vorzenski, and then the night before one of his races, I told him that I was sleeping with his cousin Jock as well. Sasha was so jealous that he tried to kill Jock on the racetrack the next day, but he died himself."

"Mimi, how could you…so coldly…"

"Sasha's death did not matter to me. After Rochelle, nothing like that could ever matter to me. All that mattered was that Mikki Vorzenski suffered as I suffered."

"There is no profit in revenge. Mimi, you must…"

Mimi was not listening. Her eyes were glazed. "I became Roger's mistress to get close to Jock. I persuaded Michelle, my niece whom I supported, to go to work for Dazzle. Michelle rose in the company quickly, and we waited for an opportunity. Then you came to Paris. You were so young and beautiful, and, of course, Roger wanted you for Jock. I did not want to hurt you. I was by that time fond of Roger, but when Jock fell in love with you, I had no choice. Through you I could make Jock suffer. I took you down to Deauville so you could meet Mikki Vorzenski. It was fitting that you should fall in love in Deauville, don't you think?

"Your father told me of your secret marriage, you know. He thought he could trust me. I went to Michelle, and she said there was to be a Dazzle launch soon. So I had her steal the formula. She was sleeping with one of the chemists. It was really quite easy for her. I, too, had chemists who were loyal to me. Radiance was on the verge of a launch, so I was able to substitute the stolen formula at the last minute, and then I discovered that you had run away to Mexico. Jock was nearly ruined because he used your publicity pictures. You see, I had torn up Roger's orders not to use them. Mikki Vorzenski nearly lost his presidency. The only problem was that Roger found out what I had done. He took the perfume off the market. He was furious, but he still wanted me enough to forgive me. Men can be so stupid.

"Later I almost left Roger, but I was afraid that if I did, you and Mikki Vorzenski might somehow find each other again. So I let Jock find you. I tipped Mikki Vorzenski's detective agency so you could be found. I impersonated Michelle and planted the bomb in Dazzle's lab six weeks ago. You can imagine the rest. Michelle and I took the formula last night, and then I helped her run away. Jock is dying in a London hospital right now. Soon it will be discovered that Mikki Vorzenski's car ran Jock down. Mikki will lose you. He will be accused of murder. His career will be ruined.''

The words were a jumble in Liz's weary brain. One

thought remained with her. Alexander would be destroyed. She had to find a way to save Alexander. She had to stay awake. Her eyelids felt as heavy as lead weights, but she forced them open.

Sleep was death.

"W-what about my children? If I die, and you destroy Alexander, they will be orphans—like you and Rochelle were."

Mimi's resolve weakened. "It is always the children who suffer." She was clearly upset at this thought.

"You must help me—to save them," Liz said.

"I-I don't care about them. Don't you see. I *can't* care!" Mimi screamed wildly. Then she fled the room, turning a key in the lock, imprisoning Liz. High heels clattered on the stairs as Mimi flew down them.

For a moment, Liz thought Mimi might change her mind, but Mimi had vanquished the last remnants of her conscience. Her grief and hatred had warped her, and she'd left Liz to die.

A deep, inviting blackness seemed to swirl around Liz. It was so tempting to close her eyes, to go to sleep, but if she did not fight, she could not help Alexander. She thought of her children, and she knew she had to force herself to struggle.

Groggily she dragged herself to the window and pulled herself up so that she could see out. The night was dark and moonless. The cool air revived her as she leaned out. In the distance she saw white, darting lights on the Charmont road. Then they disappeared, blinked, and then disappeared again. Was someone coming up to the château?

Beneath the window was a ledge that was at least twelve inches wide. The windows of the bedrooms next to her had been thrown open earlier, doubtless by Mimi, who must have taken that bedroom for her own use. If

Liz could walk along that ledge the ten feet to the next window and crawl inside, perhaps she could get downstairs.

Liz stared down at the gravel drive fifty feet beneath. If she fell, she would die. But if she stayed...

The car lights twinkled on the road. The car was coming to the château. Liz pulled herself up onto the windowsill and swung her feet outside, sliding her body out the window until her toes touched the ledge. Shivering with fear, she told herself not to look down.

She could scarcely stand, but somehow she managed to lean back against the stone wall of the château, her arms spread wide to brace herself, her fingernails digging into the stone. Then she began to inch her way along the ribbonlike ledge to the other window.

The car was in the drive, and then it disappeared from view as it swerved toward the north entrance. A terrible blackness swamped Liz, and for a moment she thought she was going to pass out. Her knees became jelly. Her foot slid over the edge. Then, just in time, fear jerked her back to consciousness. She forced herself to keep moving toward the window. If she were going to faint, better that she fainted inside instead of out here where to do so was certain death. At last her hand curled over the windowsill. For a long moment she just gripped it, too weak to move. It took all her strength to pull herself inside, and when she did, she collapsed headlong onto the floor. A table lamp smashed beside her, and her last thought before she fainted was that Mimi had heard and would return to kill her.

Fighting her way back to consciousness, Liz sat up. The room was a blur. The blood in her head seemed to be a pounding force. Gathering her remaining strength, she half-crawled, half-staggered across the thick carpet toward the door. At last she reached it, and when she twisted the doorknob, it opened.

Deep baritone voices thundered from below. Liz crawled to the edge of the landing and pulled herself up. Leaning against the balustrade, Liz lurched toward that welcome sound of voices. When she reached the top of the stairs, she started down the dizzying spiral and felt faint. She could never make it down those stairs. She clung to the banister.

Alexander and Roger strode into the hall. Mimi was right behind then, trying to stop them.

Liz called out to them, but it was the terrible, soundless scream of nightmares. She clutched the newel-post so tightly that the pointed ears of the carved fox dug into her palm with sudden, rejuvenating pain. "Alexan—" Again no sound came.

Alexander and Roger were walking outside, out of the south entrance.

Liz heard Mimi say quite clearly. "No, I have not heard from Liz. I came down to Charmont to rest. You know how exhausted I've been, Roger. The film—"

"But to Charmont?"

The door banged as it was opened. They were leaving.

In her panic, Liz let go of the newel post and lost her balance. She screamed. The frail sound cut the air like the thinnest blade.

Alexander's voice rang out. "What was that?" He dashed toward the stairs and glanced up, his eyes filling with terror. He raced swiftly up the stairs, taking them two at a time, as Liz fell.

A violent stab of pain jolted her when she landed with a thud on a thick slab of marble. Too weak to catch herself, she rolled over and over until her soft body reached Alexander, who had climbed halfway up the stairs.

He wrapped her unconscious body in his arms and bent his black head very close to her face. He searched for her pulse, and when at last he felt the weak throb, he began to weep. It was the first time in his adult life he had ever cried.

He lifted her into his arms, his tears falling upon her face that was as cold and still as death.

But she was alive. There was a chance that he had not been too late. For the moment, that had to be enough.

Chapter Eighteen

The sound of music—Barbra Streisand—filled the sun splashed villa that hung from the sculptured edge of a cliff high above Sardinia's Porto Rotondo. Across a silver, mirrorlike sea, Porto Cervo was clearly visible.

A thousand bejeweled guests were crammed inside the villa or clustered upon the wide decks around the aqua expanse of the glistening pool. Scarlet and gold hot-air balloons hovered above the mansion. From the balloons, beautiful maidens cast perfumed silk petals down onto the villa so that the sky seemed filled with golden rain. Samantha and Alex were splashing in the pool. Alexander's Swan was anchored in the quiet harbor beneath.

From her balcony, a pale, thin Liz watched the milling crowd—executives from the highest echelons of both Dazzle and Radiance. Her red hair was braided with golden ribbons, and she wore a white flowing gown that made her look like a Roman princess.

Never had so many people been crushed into such a small space, and yet never had Liz felt so alone. Liz smiled as she watched Jock limp across the deck and join her father, who was standing beside the pool watching Samantha and Alex. Somewhere in the press of people was Jock's new wife, Sarah, the lovely English nurse he'd fallen in love with when he was recuperating.

So much had happened in the month since Alexander had driven to Charmont with Roger and saved her from certain death. Mimi had been institutionalized in Switzerland. Michelle was behind bars. Roger had confided that Mimi had been repeatedly hospitalized for psychiatric reasons over the past few years, but that he had not realized how dangerous she was. He said that in reality Mimi had blamed herself for Rochelle's death, but, unable to face her own guilt, she'd tried to convince herself Jock and Alexander were to blame.

The night Mimi drugged Liz, Roger and Alexander had forced Armande to tell them that Mimi had taken Liz to Charmont, which had been closed for over a year because Roger was planning to renovate it. The formula that had been stolen the night before Mimi tried to kill Liz had been a fake substituted by Alexander as a precautionary measure.

Liz had recovered after two nights in a Paris hospital. Roger told her that Alexander had hovered at her bedside until she was out of danger, but that when she had regained consciousness, he'd left Paris and returned to London.

"He loves you," Roger had confided at her bedside.

"Perhaps—in a way. But too much has happened between us. I suppose it is for the best that he has gone."

Brave words. The truth was that Alexander's leaving her had ripped her heart to pieces.

A letter from Alexander came to her in Paris. He offered her his villa in Sardinia to recover. When she accepted, in the hope of seeing him, he sent Ana Lou and the children to join her.

But he had not come himself.

Nor had he written again. The only letter that came from him was one he forwarded from Manuel, who wanted to buy the doll factory. She wrote Alexander and told him that she agreed to sell. She received no further communication.

Within a week, Liz had decided what she would do. She called Roger in Paris and invited him to Sardinia. The night Roger arrived, Liz picked him up at the airport in Olbia and took him to the Piazza San Marco. She ordered him a Bellini.

Roger lifted the frothy pale peach elixir of juice, sparkling white wine and ice to his lips. Across the café table he asked, "Why did you ask me to come?"

"I need your help. Because of me, Alexander has lost the presidency of Dazzle. I know that everything regarding the explosion has been resolved, that all charges against him have been dropped. But the news stories in the papers were so lurid, his career may never recover."

"Men like Mikki Vorzenski have a way of landing on their feet. Give him time, my child."

"But, don't you see, he's not fighting for himself. His mother will never give him a chance. And it's my fault."

"What do you want me to do?"

"Could you... Could we buy Dazzle?"

"And they call Mikki Vorzenski a pirate." Roger began to laugh, but his eyes were filled with love. "Order me another of these...these..."

"Bellinis."

"Alexander owns a great deal of stock in Dazzle, Father. So does Paul. Perhaps you could approach them?"

"Perhaps..." Roger folded her hand in his. "For you I will buy Dazzle. It will not be easy, but I will find a way."

"Then Alexander can be president of Dazzle again."

"You do realize you might be making a very grave mistake. Some men do not like to be bought by a woman."

The memory faded and the present came back with violent force, but Roger's words lingered.

Some men do not like to be bought by a woman.

The aqua pool glimmered; the sensual music made Liz shiver. Roger looked up from the deck and waved to her to join them.

This party was in celebration of the upcoming merger of two of the greatest names in the perfume world—Dazzle and Radiance. The financial papers had made much of it. Jock and Roger had been interviewed. Paul had spoken to the press. Only Alexander had declined to comment.

Suddenly a hush swept the party, and Liz saw a very tall black-headed man leading a silver-haired woman on his arm. They were Alexander and the princess. Roger extended his hand and Paulette took it. After a long while she knelt and leaned over the pool. She didn't seem to mind that the children splashed her when they swam near. Even from the great distance, Liz could see that the princess's smile was radiant.

Liz remembered something Alexander had told her once about his mother, that his mother was always on the side of the winner.

Liz was the winner. The princess had come to her.

As if drawn to a magnet, Liz's gaze melded with Alexander's. For a long moment he stared up at her. He was as still as a statue, and then he was running.

And so was she.

The staircase curled down the cliff's edge. High-heeled sandals scampered down red tile stairs. Liz flew into his arms. She was breathless, but not from running. He crushed her against his hard chest. He was kissing her, whirling her in his arms. Tears were falling, but they were tears of happiness.

After a long time he set her down and held her tightly against the white wall. Beneath them the cliff plunged a thousand feet to a sparkling sea.

"I love you," he said. "I don't know if you can ever forgive me for being so stupidly blind to the truth."

"I thought you were mad because I bought Dazzle."

"Mad?" He threw back his black head and laughed. "Mad? I thought it was one hell of a way to tell a guy you love him. It was insanely reckless, of course."

"I do love you, you know."

"I don't deserve you," he said. "I tried to be gallant and stay away, but, Liz, I can't live without you."

"Nor can I."

"So I'm to be president of your company?" he murmured.

"Our company."

"I bought you a gift," he said.

Her eyes flashed with excitement. "What?"

"Of course, it's not nearly so grand as the presidency of Dazzle and Radiance."

"I'm dying of curiosity."

"I went down to Cornwall and bought that crumbling antiquity you're so insane about."

"Killigen Hall?" She shrieked with joy when he nodded.

"Ghosts and all."

"How did you manage it?"

"By paying three times what it was worth."

"Whatever you paid, I'll make it worth it." Her voice was low and deliberately suggestive.

He lowered his mouth to hers. After a long time he said, "Do you remember that grotto where you taught me that an innocent can know more about love than a rake?"

She began to laugh as he lifted her into his arms. "Where are you taking me?"

"Somewhere private where you can start earning your keep."

"Why don't we go up to our bedroom and save the grotto for later—when our guests have gone?"

The husky voice of Barbra Streisand was a rush of sound. Slowly, hand in hand, they began to walk up the stairs to the sun-drenched terrace outside the master bedroom.

They kissed again, surrendering at last to the brilliant and fulfilling dazzle of their everlasting love.

* * * * *

MEANT TO BE

For Ted,
my beloved husband,
whose tender care has taught me
the meaning of love

One

Leslie Grant lifted the cup of steaming hot chocolate to her lips and sipped carefully. Through the floor-to-ceiling picture windows of the ski lodge she could see the falling snow, and she thought it looked like the gentle dusting of a giant powder puff. Inside, the ski lodge cafeteria was bustling with skiers, the buckles on their ski boots jingling like spurs as they moved about.

Leslie was beautiful. Her golden hair tumbled over the shoulders of her tightly fitting aqua sweater. Her white parka was draped carelessly across her lap. Her eyes were the deepest darkest shade of green; golden flecks danced in their depths. Had there not been a look of haunted loneliness, had she managed even the faintest of smiles, she would have been dazzling.

Laughter, shrieks of gaiety, and rock music pounding from the jukebox assailed her ears. Tables were piled high with mittens and knit hats and trays of serve-yourself lunches. The room was so crowded, Leslie had had difficulty finding a place to sit down.

It seemed to her that everyone in the room was with someone except her. She was alone—not that she hadn't grown used to that since her divorce eighteen months before. A tight smile twisted her beautiful mouth. She felt vaguely uncomfortable. If only she hadn't let Karen spend the whole day and the night with their next-door neighbor, Gini.

Instantly Leslie pushed that regret from her mind. If she were going to be independent, she couldn't cling to her seven-year-old daughter. Besides it wasn't fair. Karen needed her own friends, and Gini had been kind to invite her over to visit her children.

Every muscle in Leslie's body ached. Skiing was supposed to be fun, but she was beginning to have doubts that she'd ever be able to learn how to do it. She'd taken her third lesson this morning, and she'd fallen several times. Still, if she were going to live in Colorado she was at least going to give skiing a try. She had to. It symbolized what was almost a personal vendetta.

Her ex-husband Tim's shouted insults tore through her mind. "You never do anything different! Do you have any idea how dull being married to a woman like you is? You might as well be eighty years old!"

That had hurt, but there had been more than an element of truth in the accusation. She had realized suddenly that in eight years of married life she'd gotten into a dreadful rut. She'd cooked the same dishes, worn the same clothes, run around with the same friends. Of course she'd had good reasons. One had to simplify life when one had both a career and a child. She'd always been in such a rush, there just hadn't been time to be Tim's glamorous playmate.

Involuntarily she shivered. Even in her ski suit inside the warming house she was cold. Would she ever get used to the climate after living all her life in Austin, Texas? Had she been rash to accept a job in sales with R.B. Dexter Inc., a company that dealt in real estate and construction?

For eight years she'd been a teacher. By coming to Colorado and accepting such a job, she'd turned her back on everything familiar, on every link with her past. It was, she'd tried to tell herself when she'd been in one of her more positive moods, the beginning of a new life.

Never in all the months since Tim had walked out on her had Leslie felt lonelier than since she'd moved to Colorado two weeks ago. And this very minute she felt even lonelier than usual. Perhaps it was just that everyone else seemed to be with someone except her.

Her thickly lashed green eyes suddenly riveted to the most compelling man they'd ever beheld. The mug of hot chocolate—half-raised to her lips—sloshed into the saucer as, unconsciously, she set the cup down.

He was tall and dark and boldly handsome. His hair was black, as were his eyes. His skin was bronzed as though he spent a lot of time outdoors. A black ski suit with a slashing gold stripe molded his muscular frame.

Some quality made the man stand out from the crowd that buzzed on all sides of him, but Leslie was at a loss to define exactly what it was.

Was it his air of grim ruggedness that set him apart, making him seem more like a mountaineer than one of the brightly clad ski resort people? Or was it only that, in spite of his youthful aura, he was not as young as most of the crowd? There were laugh lines etched beneath his eyes and grooves slashed on either side of his mouth.

Leslie estimated the man's age to be at least ten years older than hers, and she was almost thirty.

A deep frown creased Leslie's brows. Surrounding the man were several teenage girls. One of the girls tossed her bright red hair and laughed up at him. For a moment the harsh lines of his face softened, and he smiled. His dark face was illuminated. Then carelessly he leaned over and whispered something in the girl's ear.

Why, he was old enough to be that child's father! A deep anger burned through Leslie, not justified by the stranger but by the hurt he had reminded her of.

Tim had left her because she made him feel old. When he'd hit forty, he'd suddenly bought himself a sports car. He'd changed his style of dress. And last of all he'd decided he needed a woman to fit his new, more youthful image.

Some people called it mid-life crisis. As Leslie gazed angrily at the compelling man across the room, she wondered if every man in the United States were going through it.

As though he felt her looking at him, the man turned and stared across the crowded room directly into her eyes. For a static moment it seemed that the very air that separated them was charged. A powerful emotion that she did not understand swept through her, stimulating every sense in her body.

He was a stranger, yet she had the oddest feeling that somehow, somewhere, they'd known each other before, and that they had been on the most intimate of terms. Yet they hadn't; she knew she could never have forgotten him.

To her horror she watched his smile fade into anger. He stared back at her fiercely with a look of profound shock carved into his handsome features.

The sounds in the warming house blurred into a loud

buzz as a feeling of weakness washed over her. Why did he stare as though he desired her even though he hated her utterly? The savage fire of his gaze made her tremble as though he held her and caressed her.

The man was a stranger! Again she asked herself, Why was he staring at her as though he not only knew her intimately but despised her? His sensual mouth twisted in contempt, and he leaned over and said something to the girls at his side.

Leslie's heart began to pound with alarming intensity. The man, his expression ruthless, was coming toward her!

Grabbing for her fur hat and gloves, Leslie raced clumsily from the room. Her ski boots cut into her ankles and prevented her from really running.

Blind instinct drove her on. Another man, a friend perhaps, seized the stranger's arm and prevented him from following her outside.

Later as she sat on the lift chair, Leslie's thoughts kept returning to the man she'd seen in the warming house. Why had he looked at her so fiercely? Did she remind him of someone? And why had she, a thirty-year-old woman, run from him as though she were no more than a frightened child?

Perhaps when he'd seen her staring at him, he'd been angered. A wood frame house at the end of the lift broke above the tree tops and came into view. Then the stranger was forgotten since she needed all her powers of concentration to get off the lift without falling down.

She made two more runs plus a trip to the warming house before she decided to take the higher lift to the very top of the mountain.

It was later in the afternoon, and the sun had long ago been lost in the dense thickness of clouds. Suddenly Leslie realized how cold she was. Her cheeks were cherry red;

her toes and fingers felt numb. As she began skiing, she felt increasingly uncoordinated. From time to time, she would stop and rest and enjoy the view. She could see miles and miles of snow-capped mountains fringed thickly with white-flocked fir and spruce.

She was concentrating so completely on trying to move her ankles correctly so that she could approximate parallel skiing and get out of the beginner's wedge, that she failed to notice the sign which indicated she'd wandered onto an expert slope. Suddenly beneath her the slope seemed to plunge straight down, and the yawning whiteness was pocked with huge moguls! True terror quivered through her. She could never ski down that! Hardly had this thought flicked through her brain, than her skis struck a patch of ice and went skidding out from under her. Groping wildly to regain her balance and failing, she felt herself tumbling down, down like an aqua and white ball, until she was buried in a deep drift of snow less than a foot from a tree.

When she opened her eyes and pushed her goggles from her forehead all was whiteness and silence. Ignoring a cutting pain in her ankle, she began digging through the snow trying to find the way out.

Then the deepest, most masculine of voices sliced through the silence. "Need some help?"

In spite of the instant relief the man's voice produced, irritation at the contempt in his tone trembled through her. Wasn't the answer to his question obvious?

"Yes," she managed in a weak, contrite voice.

Hard arms circled her, and she felt the man's hands roam over her body as he pulled her from the snow bank. Then she was staring into the blackest of eyes. A cold gust of air tousled the lock of raven hair that had escaped from his black knit hat.

"You!" He almost snarled the word, and as he stared down at her, the intensity of his forbidding gaze seemed to devour her. He was the very same man she'd seen in the warming house! The shock of recognition turned her face white and sent a faint tremor of exquisite apprehension racing through her.

Suddenly Leslie was terribly aware that she was alone on the still vastness of the mountain with this savage stranger, and a second tremor that had nothing to do with the zero-degree weather quaked through her. "Do we know each other?" Leslie asked, trying to remain calm.

For a long moment he studied her. His eyes roved the delicate oval of her face, her full parted lips, and downward over her curves revealed by her skintight ski suit. She reddened with embarrassment. Somehow his knowing gaze was too intimate to be that of a stranger.

His features were etched with the deepest bitterness. Then suddenly, to her surprise, the tension drained from his face. He almost smiled. "No, I guess we don't."

"Do I look like someone you..."

Harshly his voice cut her off. "I'm sorry if I was rude. It's not your fault..." His powerful anger of a moment before seemed to drain away. "But we have more important things to consider—like how we are going to get you down this mountain."

Leslie nodded.

"What were you trying to do—kill yourself?" he demanded.

"N-no..."

"You almost hit that tree," he said, indicating the thick spruce less than one foot away.

"I—I didn't realize..."

"This slope isn't easy for me, and I've been skiing all my life. A beginner has no business..."

"I made a mistake.... I..." Her voice trailed off. She felt strangely near tears. She was cold and tired, and this man was impossible.

As though he sensed her utter fatigue, he relented. "All right, I'll ski you down the mountain."

"My ankle hurts. I don't know if I can," she admitted weakly.

"If you can't, I can ski down and bring the ski patrol back up, but that would mean leaving you here alone."

"N-no..." Strangely, the thought of him leaving her was not at all welcome.

"I think you can make it," he said more gently as though he sensed her fear of him leaving her. "You're able to stand. If we go down very slowly, you'll be okay."

He was so sure that his confidence was contagious.

"By the way," he asked, "what's your name?"

"Leslie," she murmured, suddenly feeling strangely shy.

"Leslie..."

His deeply masculine voice seemed to caress her as he said her name. She had the oddest impression that he wanted to fit a different name to her face. In spite of the cold, and the throbbing pain in her ankle, she realized she was drawn to this man as she had been to no other. Not even Tim had attracted her to the extent that she felt his presence in every fiber of her body.

Why? As she stared up into his brooding countenance it occurred to her that he was suffering from some raw hurt just as she was. Though she didn't understand the reasons behind his bitterness, she knew too well what pain was. She understood the pride that made him want to mask his pain from the world.

"I know what we'll do," he said at last. "We'll ski through these trees. On the other side of them is a beginner slope. Just take it slow. I know it's steep, but remember, all you have to do is ski across the mountain, not straight down it. I'll be right behind you, in case you fall again.''

Somehow just knowing that he was there made everything easier for Leslie. Once she'd picked her way through the trees, she paused to rest, and he was there beside her. She felt the gentle pressure of his steadying touch at her elbow.

"You've done the hard part," he reassured her. His voice was oddly gentle, like his touch.

"That's good news," she murmured. She sensed that all the anger he'd felt toward her was gone—at least for the moment, and only his desire for her remained.

"I must say, skiing with you certainly improves the view." His warm black eyes that roved carelessly over her were alight with masculine interest.

For a moment his gaze left her breathless. Something was happening between them. Not only was there an intense awareness one for the other, an inexplicable closeness she felt toward him, but she sensed suddenly a building sexual tension. A tiny voice warned that her emotions were rushing her into something she might not be able to handle.

He towered over her, and she felt very small and feminine. It was a pleasant sensation. She realized suddenly how much she'd missed being close to a man.

Her divorce had shattered her self-image. In retaliation to all Tim's insults, she'd refashioned her appearance. She'd let her brownish blonde hair grow long, and she'd lightened it so that golden streaks gleamed. She'd lost ten pounds so that she was model slim and looked gorgeous in the glamorous clothes she took the time to select and wear. But though she looked glamorous on the outside, she was running scared. She didn't really fit her new image, though of course this man couldn't know that. And in that moment she determined he wouldn't know that. She was tired of being old-fashioned and out of date.

Jauntily she tossed him an inviting smile and allowed her eyes to linger on the hard curve of his sensual mouth. She strangled a sigh of the carnal pleasure that the thought of those lips on hers produced.

It was strange, but his admiring gaze and his compliment had done more to make her feel like an excitingly attractive woman than all her clothes or her new hairdo.

"From here on I'll take you down the easiest slopes on the mountain," he said.

"I—I'm sorry for all the trouble I've caused you," she said softly. "I can probably make it from here by myself."

" 'Probably' isn't good enough. I said I'd ski you down the mountain, and I meant it." The protective quality in his deep voice made Leslie feel warm and snug all over, and she looked up at him, her emerald eyes shining.

"You ready?" he asked roughly.

In answer she stabbed her poles into the soft snow and headed down the mountain. But she started too quickly and tumbled into the snow.

As his strong, hard hands circled her and lifted her to her feet, he pulled her unresisting against his own body for a long moment. "Well, not quite," she amended shakily, very aware of his arms about her. A tremulous smile curved her lips.

He looked down at her for a long time, his expression assessing. Their lips were so close that their steamy breaths mingled. She felt the corded muscles of his thighs, the flat hardness of his stomach, the broad expanse of his chest as she was pressed against him. And some part of her wanted him to go on holding her forever.

Suddenly he smiled, and a wild joy fluttered through her. It was the first time he'd actually smiled at her. "Take it easy from now on, Leslie," he commanded gently.

Every time she fell, he was there to help her. Once when he picked up her fur hat, he put it back on her head himself. As he tucked the shimmering strands of gold beneath the fur, she reveled in the intimate touch of this stranger.

What was happening to her? Had she been without a man so long that she was starved for one? She was sure that he was aware of her attraction for him; every time she looked at him, his intent, smoldering gaze met her own.

When they reached the bottom of the mountain she looked up into the dark, handsome face looming before her and said, "I don't know how to thank you.... I..." She was strangely at a loss for words. "Why, I don't even know your name."

"Boone," came his crisp reply.

"Thank you...Boone....I don't know what I would have done..."

"Don't mention it." His eyes flicked indolently past her. "Do you have your car here?"

"Why?"

"That's the last bus pulling out over there," he said, pointing over her shoulder.

"Oh..." Turning to look in the direction he'd pointed. Leslie's eyes trailed the bright blue bus as it disappeared around a steep curve. A tiny sigh of disappointment was emitted through lips tinged blue from the cold. It was a long long walk back to her condominium.

"Would you like me to drive you home?" There was

a sensual quality in his deep voice that warned he was probably offering her more than just a ride.

Leslie lifted her gaze to the warm, black eyes that were fixed on her soft features, and she flushed. "I couldn't ask you..."

"You're not." His hand went around her waist, and even through the layers of clothing she felt the strength of his fingers burning against her flesh. "I asked you."

All she had to do was say no. Ignoring the blatant message she read in the heated depths of his black eyes, she answered, "Yes, I do need a ride."

What was she doing? part of her mind screamed, accepting a ride with a strange man, letting him touch her in a familiar fashion, allowing herself to be picked up as though she thought nothing of it. Doubtless he thought nothing of it, and he certainly wasn't going to pass up such a willing female.

But was she willing? For eighteen months she'd scarcely had any contact with men other than at work. The few dates she'd accepted had been total failures. All any of the men had wanted was a quick one-night stand. Not one had asked her for a second date. Now for the first time she found herself attracted to a complete stranger, and the sensation was so intoxicating that she wanted to prolong it.

"I hope you're not in a hurry. I left my after-ski boots in a locker in the warming house," she said.

"So did I," he returned, guiding her toward the ski lodge.

As they walked together Leslie saw that Boone's striking looks caught admiring glances from several young women. But he seemed not to notice. Instead he focused all his attention on her. He helped her remove her skis, and then he carried them along with his own to the ski racks. When he pushed open the heavy double doors and waited for her to step inside the ski lodge, she reveled in the luxury of having a man do things for her. It had been so long, and she hadn't realized how much she'd missed all the little things one took for granted in a man-woman relationship.

He escorted her to her locker and told her he'd go on to his and then return.

Leslie snapped the second buckle on her boot, and pain shot through a numbed finger. "Ouch..."

Instantly a large warm brown hand covered her injured hand. A tingling thrill leaped through her as Boone slowly turned her hand in his. She hadn't heard him come back.

"It looks like you're going to have a blood blister," he said at last, gently rubbing the tip of her finger. He didn't release her hand, and his failure to do so filled her with a warm sweetness. "I'm beginning to think this isn't your sport. First you hurt your ankle and now your finger."

Deftly he knelt down, unbuckled her boots himself, and slipped them from her feet. "Which ankle did you hurt?"

"The left one."

He examined it carefully. His expertise reminded her of Tim, who'd been a surgeon, and prompted her to question, "Are you a doctor?"

"I nearly was, but I got married my last year in medical school and dropped out." He switched back to the present. "Your ankle doesn't seem to be broken. I think it'll be fine in a couple of days."

Married! Not for a minute had it occurred to her he might be married. An odd pain sliced through her.

"Your wife..." Leslie stumbled. "Is she..."

"She's dead," came the curt reply. Suddenly the warmth died in his black gaze, and all the shuttered bitterness was back in the harsh planes of his face.

"I'm sorry...." She broke off. The words sounded so hollow somehow. "I didn't realize..."

"It happened over a year ago," he explained tersely. "Her car stalled on a railroad crossing, and a train hit it. She died instantly."

That hot angry look was back in his face, and he regarded her intently as though she were somehow the cause of his pain. Leslie realized that he was used to guarding his privacy and hadn't wanted to share this with her. Yet he had.

"You ready?" he asked impatiently, and when she nodded, his arm slipped possessively around her and he drew her to her feet. Just his casual touch stimulated fiery sensations that made her feel strangely weak.

He picked up her ski boots as well as his own, and together they stepped outside into the whirling white snow.

As he lifted their skis from the rack onto his shoulders he spoke again.

"Don't ask me about my wife," he said. "She belongs to a chapter in my life that's closed forever."

Quietly she responded, "I think I understand."

"No, you don't!" He ground out the words with startling violence. "You couldn't possibly, and if we're to get on at all, don't even try."

Two

Through thick bristly lashes, Leslie glanced covertly at Boone, who was skillfully driving his truck over the snow-packed highway toward Winter Park. A winter wonderland whisked by, but she was aware only of the compelling, virile man beside her. One of his powerful arms was draped across the back of their seat so that every time she moved her tousled curls brushed against it.

Ever since the mention of his wife, Boone had been broodingly silent, and she hadn't been able to think of a word to say. Several more miles sped by before Boone made an attempt to bridge the awkward silence. Then she felt his fingers caress her hair, and she sensed he was suddenly more conscious of the woman beside him than the woman he'd once been married to.

"So, tell me about yourself," he said at last as though conversation were a deliberate effort. "Are you in Winter Park as a tourist?"

"I live here."

"Then how have I missed seeing you? With only four hundred locals it's sort of hard not to bump into one another rather frequently."

"I just moved here from Texas."

"And I've been away in Denver this past month. That explains it. Tell me, are you married?"

"Divorced."

"Isn't everybody?" A trace of the old bitterness was back in his cold tone. His cynical statement caught her off guard, and she didn't know how to reply. "I suppose marriage is too confining for people these days," he continued. "With women's lib and the sexual revolution, who wants to stay married to the same person for an entire lifetime?"

She had… His words, so close to Tim's beliefs, chilled her. "I suppose there's an element of truth in what you say," she admitted, feeling numb.

"More than an element," he snapped. "Why did you leave your own husband?"

Involuntarily she flinched. "Why did *you* leave…" He took it for granted that it was she who had walked out. The old hurt tore through her, but she covered it with anger.

"*That* is none of your business!" Her eyes felt hot, and she fought back the tears.

Through the shimmering haze of unfallen tears, she saw his swift dark glance in her direction.

Switching the topic to neutral ground, Boone's deep voice was devoid of emotion when he spoke again. "We're almost to town. You'll have to tell me where you live.…"

Carefully, in a tiny, choked voice she directed him to a modern stack of cedar condominiums clumped on the snowy side of a mountain beneath a cluster of towering lodgepole pines. When he braked to a stop in front of her garage, Leslie reached for the door handle and would have stumbled from the pickup, but Boone's hand closed warmly over hers.

"Don't go," he said thickly. "Not yet.... I've been damn near impossible ever since we met. And I shouldn't have asked such a personal question a while ago. I should know that better than anyone."

His dark face was grave. The genuine sincerity of his apology touched her heart. "It's all right," she whispered at last, letting her emerald gaze fuse with the liquid blackness of his own.

"It seems that the past is dangerous ground for us both," he murmured against her ear. His warm breath sent delicious shivers down her spine. This new intimacy was strangely comforting.

"Yes..." she whispered against the stiff collar of his parka.

"I find the present much much more interesting," he said huskily, pulling her into his arms.

For an instant he stared deeply into her eyes as though to drink in the sight of her. Then very slowly his dark head descended to her fair one. His hot moist mouth covered the lush softness of her lips, and a raw, naked hunger for his touch leaped through her. Tiny waves of liquid passion curled in her veins. She wrapped her arms around his neck and ran her fingers through his thick springy hair.

He felt her fiery response, the warmth of her desperate need for him.

"Oh, Leslie..." he rasped. "I knew the minute I saw you I was lost...."

Strange words.... Yet she'd felt the same way.

But she forgot everything as he crushed her slim body

against his own virile length. His breathing was harsh and uneven, his male scent touched her nostrils. She felt the powerful surge of his desire against her lower body, but the flaming onslaught of his savage passion only heightened her own burning ache. She returned his kisses with a wanton abandon, crushing her lips fervently to his. Her fingers reveled in the exploration of his magnificent physique, in the hard pressure of his lean, muscled frame tightly pressed to the tender softness of her own body.

"It's been too long...for both of us," he rasped. "We're like two starved..." He didn't finish as his mouth again nuzzled hers. She felt his tongue probe and enter and touch her own deliberately. His hands swept over the soft mounds of her breasts and downward to her rounded hips and molded her body even closer to his own.

From behind them a horn tooted impatiently. Slowly Boone dragged his lips from hers and studied her love-soft face with vision blurred from desire. "I'm going to have to move the truck," he said raggedly as the tiny foreign car bleated again.

As if in a dream, Leslie was aware of his deft movements as he slid his body away from hers and started the ignition of the truck. His thick black hair was rumpled from their loveplay; a trace of her lipstick lingered on his lips.

What was happening to her? Was this love at first sight? Or was it lust? Doubtless her response to this man had been heightened by the long months of despair and loneliness. But to find such rapture in the arms of a stranger was inexplicable.

Boone found a parking place directly in front of her condominium this time. When he cut off the ignition, he did not take her in his arms again. Instead he alighted from the truck and went around and opened her door.

Then he reached behind her and gathered up her ski boots. "I'll come back for your skis later," he explained as he followed her inside the building to her front door.

He took the key from her fingers and opened the door for her. For a long moment they stood in awkward silence as a furious mental debate raged in her mind. After those sizzling kisses, if she asked him in, he would take it as an open invitation to make love to her. And she wasn't sure she was ready for that, even though every fiber in her body clamored for his touch.

As though he read her mind, he said, "Leslie, I'm not going to ravish you if you ask me in."

"I didn't think you would," she said, flushing. "Of course, I want you to come in."

"Thank you." His amused smile had a devastating impact on her senses.

"Can I fix you something to drink?"

"I'd like a beer. But I can get it myself."

When she opened the refrigerator he was directly behind her. The two steaks she'd been too tired to broil last night for herself and Karen were in full view. She needed to cook them soon or they would spoil.

"Would you like to stay for dinner?" she asked, knowing but not caring that he thought she probably was inviting him to more than dinner.

His virile masculinity was like a fine wine that had gone to her head. She was enjoying his company too much to want him to leave, even though she sensed his continued presence meant danger.

"I thought you'd never ask," he murmured. His hand reached up and straightened a stray golden curl, but when she turned and gazed into his eyes, he let his hand fall quickly away. "If I touch you again, I won't be able to stop," he said in explanation. "And I'm sure after skiing all day you're as hungry as I am."

His eyes held hers, and when she said nothing she realized that her silence held a promise. The sensual tension between them was explosive, and a rippling excitement coursed through Leslie before she forced herself to look away.

"I'll start dinner," she said shakily.

"And I'll build a fire," he returned.

Then he lifted the beer can to his lips and deliberately moved away from her, breaking the spell that had bound them together.

The stainless blade flashed as Leslie rapidly sliced the head of lettuce into pale green strips that fluttered into the salad bowl on the kitchen counter. Covertly she observed Boone as he tossed another log onto the fire.

The mere sight of him—so overwhelmingly male—triggered a nervous yet pleasurable excitement in her. He looked up from the fire, and his eyes met hers.

At Boone's insistence she'd changed from her ski attire into "something more comfortable." She now wore a loosely flowing, emerald green caftan. The thick velour was trimmed with gilt. A rope sash cinched her tiny waist.

"Need any help with dinner?" he asked.

"No, just relax. It's almost ready."

Minutes later he helped her into her chair and then seated himself. "You've prepared a feast!" he said in admiration as he looked at the broiled steaks, the crisp, tossed salad, baked potatoes, creamy green beans garnished with mushrooms, and hot buttered rolls.

"Not without the help of my microwave," she admitted shyly.

His compliment warmed her. It had been a long time

since she'd cooked for a man. All Karen ever really liked was peanut butter and jelly. Leslie flashed him a warm, appreciative smile and murmured a trembling, "Thank you."

"I can see you're a very talented woman. You've done wonders with this place." His admiring gaze swept from her lovely face about the ultra-modern condominium, where cascading green plants and bold paintings accented the decor.

"Thank you...."

"It seems you're always saying thank you," he said, slicing into his thick steak.

"And do you live in Winter Park, Boone?" she asked, changing the subject from herself to him.

"Most of the time—for the past five years. Winter Park is a boom town, and I'm working on several projects here at the moment."

Before she could reply, something on the television arrested his attention, and he got up and turned up the volume.

"...and that's it folks," the newscaster blared. "We're in for a heavy snowfall throughout the evening and into tomorrow. So bundle up and stay inside...."

Boone switched off the set and strode restlessly to the expanse of glass beside the fireplace. Pulling back the drapes, he peered outside. Steady flurries of snow sifted in the pale stream of the electric light on her balcony. "Doesn't look too bad," he said. "At least not yet. Those newscasters are fond of melodrama."

At that moment a faint blast echoed through the mountains followed by a series of three more.

"What was that?" Leslie asked.

"The avalanche-control people are setting off dynamite charges in the mountains to cause small avalanches."

"Small avalanches?" A faint note of alarm crept into her voice.

He turned to her, his expression gentle. "It's nothing to worry about. In fact, it's because of those blasts that we don't have to worry. During a storm, when fresh snow falls onto old, it has to be constantly monitored and small avalanches triggered to prevent larger ones. Unfortunately, because of all the new development and expansion, we're becoming more vulnerable to the threat of avalanches."

Boone sat down once more and resumed eating.

"Do you live far from here?" Leslie asked, changing the subject.

"About half a mile," he returned. "But in a blizzard, it might as well be all the way to Denver."

They talked throughout the meal, and she was aware that, though he learned much about her, she learned practically nothing of him. She told him of Karen, her child, and how difficult quitting her teaching job and moving from Austin was for her.

"Sounds like you're determined to burn your bridges," he said at length, his eyes filled with understanding. "If I weren't so damned tied to Winter Park I would have left myself. But every cent I've got is tied up here, and I have no choice but to stay."

"You're probably as well off," she said softly. "I'm beginning to realize there are some things you can't run away from."

"How right you are." His sensual lips twisted into a hard line as he poured himself another glass of wine. "But sometimes, you can forget for a while." He caught her frightened glance and held it. The hungry brilliance of his black gaze startled her, and a delicate flush suffused her creamy skin before she quickly lowered her long-lashed eyes. He lifted the glass to his lips and then rose slowly from the table.

She felt his fingers roam beneath her heavy hair and caress her neck before they descended to the back of her chair. A prickle of desire flamed through her. "Let's enjoy the fire, shall we?" His deep voice had roughened slightly with emotion.

No more able to resist his invitation than a moth the brilliance of a flame, she allowed his arms to slide around her as she stood up. She was aware of her heart beating crazily. His dark intimate gaze made her feel oddly warm, as together they moved toward the fire.

Firelight made her hair gleam like tawny gold; her emerald eyes sparkled as she gazed up into his own dark eyes.

She was bewitchingly beautiful, and she only had the faintest idea of her power over him. As he moved his calloused hand from her throat down over her arm and back again in a slow stroking motion, he found her soft body as smooth as satin. He crushed his lips into her thick, flowing hair.

Ah, the scent of her.... She was delicious.

As he pulled her down beneath him on the deep plush carpet, he momentarily forgot the anguish that had tormented him every waking minute for a year. Her soft body offered oblivion, offered a surcease however brief from his pain.

For her his embrace assuaged the deep loneliness that had engulfed her since Tim had walked out. When Boone's mouth touched hers in a lengthy, searing kiss, she felt fused to him. The long, lonely months were swept away as his arms locked around her body, and she felt a hot passionate need licking through her.

The rounded sweetness of her body was pressed hard

against the lean, tough sweep of his own. Her lips quivered beneath his as he kissed her again and again.

In a daze of sexual desire she felt the warmth of his hands caress her throat, and then very carefully they slid the zipper of her gown downward, parting the velvety emerald softness so that the opulent fruit of her body was revealed to his heated gaze.

"Oh, God…Leslie…you're so beautiful.…"

Slowly he removed the gown, sliding it over the luscious curve of her hips until it lay, a velvety puddle, about her slender ankles. Her own fingers pushed his ski sweater upward, and deftly he shrugged out of it. Quickly he removed his trousers and he lay beside her. She caught her breath at the sight of so much exposed virile masculinity. Not an ounce of spare flesh marred his lean physique. He lay before her like some dark-skinned, princely savage—pagan and proud, latently ruthless.

Tenderly his fingers stroked her breasts, and then his lips followed where his hands had roamed. She felt his hard, sensual mouth, nibbling the tips of her breasts; she felt the moist sucking of his lips against her tender flesh. A tiny moan escaped her lips, as a spasm of exquisite pleasure shivered through her. She arched her body so that it fitted more tightly against his own. Her hands trailed through the thick darkness of his hair.

His fingertips moved lightly over her with the expertise of a skilled lover who knew where and how to touch a woman so that she reveled in dizzying sensual ecstasy. Again his mouth followed the path of his hands, reverently loving her, touching her in all the most intimate places, rousing her long-dormant sensuality until she was as wild with passion as he.

Then he was crushing her beneath him as though he couldn't contain his desire any longer.

"Marnie..." Boone whispered desperately into her hair. "Oh, Marnie...Marnie..."

Leslie froze in his arms. For a long moment his deep tortured utterance was the only sound in the room save for their mutual labored breathing. Then a log tumbled in the grate, and a shower of sparks popped.

Shivering and numbed, Leslie tried to draw away, but Boone caught her wrist and drew her slim body against his.

"That was a pretty bad slip, Leslie," he murmured against her earlobe. She lay like a stiff, wooden doll against him. "But that shouldn't spoil..."

"It did." The words were a tiny, strangled sound. She tried to choke back the hot pain that welled in her.

"I don't blame you if you're angry..." he continued huskily.

"I'm not angry, Boone," she said very quietly. "It's just that I see clearly that this..." Her fingers combed the matted hair of his chest. "That we were wrong..."

"Wrong?"

"Wrong to get so involved so quickly. We're making love for all the wrong reasons. I've been so lonely that I just...I couldn't say no to you even though I should have. And you wanted to pretend I was your wife...."

"Pretend *you* were my wife!" he rasped. Genuine shock laced his deep, cold tones as he pushed her from him in disgust and sat up. "If that's what you thought, you're very wrong!"

"Then what?"

"I thought I could forget," he muttered furiously. His saturnine glance swept the golden curves of her body gleaming in the soft light. "And maybe I still can..."

"Please, Boone..."

"I have to have you." In the flickering firelight

Boone's chiseled features were harsh and ruthlessly compelling. He looked like a bronzed pagan god. The message in his boldly hot black gaze was primitive and wild.

Fear pounded through Leslie's arteries as he dragged her into the electric warmth of his arms.

"Boone, don't…not now…I'm afraid."

"You don't need to be. All I'm going to do is make love to you."

Three

All I'm going to do is make love to you.... Boone's words thundered through Leslie as she tried to shrink away. But he moved faster than she and placed an elbow on either side of her shoulders, leaning over her so that she was imprisoned in his arms. Her golden hair spilled in tangled disarray over his hands; wispy tendrils of it were matted against her face. Green eyes glimmered like liquid jewels as she stared up into his darkly handsome visage.

Her heart beat with the delicate ferocity of a frightened rabbit's. Her breaths came in harsh, rapid gasps so that the tips of her breasts rose and fell against the bristly hairs that matted the hard warmth of his chest.

His muscles about her were like iron. She twisted in a vain attempt to free herself, but her every movement only brought her into more intimate contact with his virile body. Every time she touched him it was like an electric

shock wave rippling through her. She felt him shudder
and clasp her more tightly to him.

Slowly Boone lowered himself over her, so that it
seemed that every part of her felt the fierce raging heat
of his body against her own. In spite of her desperation
in the deepest part of her soul she registered the fleeting
sensation that this savage mating with this tall dark
stranger was meant to be.

His black head descended with deliberate slowness to
hers. Cruelly ravaging the lush softness of her lips, Boone
forced them open so that his tongue could plunder the
velvety depths of her mouth. She doubled her fists to beat
at him, but his long drugging kiss devoured her resistance.
Her hands that would have struck him fell away and lay
limply on the thick carpet. As the strength to fight him
slowly ebbed from her, the forcefulness of his assault gave
way to fierce tenderness.

In spite of herself, Leslie felt her body responding to
the gentle rain of kisses on her mouth, against her throat,
in her tumbling hair. His caressing hands moving over her
filled her body with a strange, flowing warmth until she
clung to him with breathless urgency. When he at last
drew away a tiny moan of disappointment escaped her
love-bruised lips.

"Tell me you want me," he commanded. His voice
against the softness of her skin was low and deep.

At first she did not comprehend, her senses spiraling in
a state of sensuous nirvana. He lowered his lips and kissed
her half-opened mouth again, his tongue plunging into its
satiny-warm interior. Leslie twined her arms around his
neck to hold him even closer, and his hot, demanding lips
brought forth a little cry of sheer, feminine rapture.

Lifting his head once more, he repeated his command.
"Say it! Tell me!"

Very gently Leslie breathed, "I want you. Oh, I do want you so.... Please...make love to me."

The grooves beside his mouth deepened as a faint smile curved his lips. When Boone took her in his arms again the lovers were both consumed by the savage fires of their desire. His heart pulsed in tempo with the wild drumbeat of her own as he drew her higher and higher in a soaring swirl of need.

For a timeless moment it seemed that they had always known one another, that each belonged only to the other. When he possessed her fully, she cried out his name in final surrender.

A draft of cool air stirred the tumbling masses of Leslie's hair, and drowsily she curled herself into a languid ball beneath the thermal blanket that had been carefully tucked about her. The click of the front door closing brought her instantly awake.

For an instant, in a dazed state of confusion, she stared about the room. Then her eyes fell on the rich jewel-green caftan swirled at her feet. She saw Boone's half-empty wineglass on the hearth, and a hot rush of color washed over her as everything came back to her.

Dreamily she recalled the passionate lovemaking that was the cause of her euphoric state. Where was Boone? Her hands groped for his warmth, and finding nothing but the cool thickness of the plush carpet, a terrible emptiness engulfed her.

He was gone. A spasm of pain like a sliver of glass cutting tender flesh sliced her heart.

Where was he? Again her eyes scanned the silent room, but he was not there. Then she remembered the clicking sound the door had made. He must have gone out. The

fire had burned low, and there was only one more log on
the hearth.

Languidly she lay back and thought over what had happened. She had given herself freely to a man she hardly
knew. And yet already she knew that this man was special
to her. From the moment she'd set eyes on him, he'd
compelled her deepest feelings. It was all very difficult
for her to understand because nothing like this had ever
happened to her.

With Tim her feelings had developed gradually; there
had not been this immediate yearning. Boone's touch, his
lovemaking, his ability to draw her out of herself with
such devastating completeness was out of the realm of her
experience. Even after eight years of marriage, she'd
never felt that she so totally belonged to a man.

She'd given a part of herself that irrevocably belonged
to him. It had been like fainting, like death itself, and she
knew that she would never be the same again.

Had she been stupid to give herself so completely—and
on the first night that she'd met him? She'd never done
anything like this before. Never had it even occurred to
her that she was capable of such powerful feelings for a
man she'd just met. Her good judgment told her it would
have been much more sensible to get to know him as a
person before letting him make love to her. And yet she
couldn't have stopped herself, and for some reason, she
didn't regret it. No matter what happened, their coming
together had been too beautiful for regret. Idly she wondered what Boone was thinking and feeling right now.

At the sound of a man's heavy tread on the stair outside, she started. The front door was shoved open and
quickly shut, as a gust of cold air seeped inside. Wildly
Leslie whirled, and her gaze locked with Boone's fierce
black one. A faint depression settled over her as she saw

that the haunted bitterness was back in the grim lines of his handsome face.

Snowflakes glistened in the thick tousled darkness of his hair. In his arms he held three snow-crusted logs.

"It's only me," came his deep, curt drawl. "I'm sorry I woke you up."

He was kneeling beside her and putting another log in the grate. "Looks like I'll be spending the night," he said offhandedly. "I shouldn't have left the truck out in this snowstorm. My snow tires are too worn for me to try to make it down the hill until the street's plowed in the morning."

He offered no words of endearment. He merely attended to the practical task of unloading the firewood.

An involuntary blush swept her when his knowing gaze roamed over her, lingering on the creamy flesh of her breast exposed where the blanket had fallen away. Suddenly her heart was beating too fast, and again she wondered what he was thinking. This night had been such a novel experience that she felt vaguely embarrassed.

In no time the fire was an enormous blaze, flooding the room with its warmth. When Boone finished, he knelt beside her and wrapped one of his arms around her. Gently he brushed the thick strands of her hair to one side so that it cascaded over her bare shoulders. "Did anyone ever tell you how beautiful you are...when you wake up after making love?" he murmured huskily.

Did he assume nights like this were commonplace to her? A strange uneasiness filled her.

"No," she replied softly. "You may not believe this, but you're the first man since my husband to..."

"I believe you. But just because it happened, I wouldn't read more into it than there is." There was a tense bitterness in his tone that made her feel unhappy.

"B-but…" The one word quivered in the air. "Are you saying that…that you spend nights like this with lots of women, that I meant nothing to you?"

Just the thought made her feel wretched. He saw the pain in her eyes.

"No." His negative reply was terse; his forbidding expression told her nothing.

"Then what do you mean?" For some reason it was very important to her to understand this man.

"I don't know why it's so difficult to figure out. What happened tonight…just happened. I don't know why. Nothing exactly like this has ever happened to me before. Look, I don't want to hurt your feelings by what I'm going to say…" He broke off, feeling uncomfortable. Her large green eyes never left his face. "I only know that I don't want to be involved with you or any other woman— not deeply anyway. Tonight didn't change that. It's not that I have anything against you personally."

"I see," she murmured quietly, very hurt by his attitude.

"Look, if you'll only try to see things from my point of view we'll get on fine," he continued. "There's no reason why we can't continue to enjoy dating one another. I just want you to understand I'm not interested in a serious relationship with anyone—not even you."

She was beginning to understand too well, and she didn't like what he was saying one bit.

"We'll get on fine…." she hurled back in a tight whisper. "How can you say that when you just said that what happened between us meant nothing?"

"You were good. I don't deny that," he stated coolly. His heated gaze raking her made her go hot with shame. "We were good together. I needed what you had to offer, but that's all I want from you…or any other woman—

ever. You're hardly an eighteen-year-old virgin. You're an adult with a life of your own, a child to raise, a bad marriage in your past. I doubt you're any more interested in entanglements than I am, and if you're honest, you won't try to pretend that you feel any differently than I do.''

''But I do...I do....'' she thought weakly, but pride kept this admission a silent one.

''What turned you against women?'' she asked softly.

His deep voice responded, and with every word she felt he killed a tiny fragment of her soul.

''A lifetime of observation and first-hand experience. I won't bore you by elaborating further.''

''I want to know,'' she demanded. ''If my entire sex is damned in your eyes I want to know why.''

''All right. You asked for it.'' She was startled by the raw anger in his voice. His eyes blazed as he looked down at her, but suddenly she had the oddest feeling it was no longer her he was seeing or thinking of, but someone else. ''The women I've known have only wanted to wreck any man they got close to. And are you really any different?'' His hand reached out and gently caressed the line of her throat. ''You're very lovely, but on the inside what are you like?'' Slowly he withdrew his hand and gave her a long searching look.

His eyes never left her face. His low voice continued, ''The minute I saw you I wanted you, and you knew it. I saw the hunger in your eyes. You looked lonely and vulnerable—beautiful and aloof. And yet with me tonight you were hot and passionate. You even seem sweet. But women are rarely what they seem, especially beautiful ones.''

She felt the pain in his voice, and she wanted to reach out to him, to make him understand somehow that even though he'd been hurt in the past, he shouldn't consider all women in such a biased light. Men could tear up lives as well as women. How well she knew.

His lips twisted cynically, and his voice was harsh. "Tell me, are you like the women I've known? Did you leave your husband broken-hearted when you got tired of marriage and wanted more excitement?"

"No!" she breathed. "It wasn't like that."

"Or were you—what is it all you women are doing these days—finding yourself? Is that why you left him?"

"No...." The word was a whisper which he didn't hear.

Suddenly it was no longer Leslie the person he was speaking to but Leslie as the physical embodiment of women in general. He wanted to hurt as he'd been hurt. "And what did you find in bed with me tonight?" he lashed.

"Oooo..." The wretched cry of anguish wrenched from the depths of her wounded heart was punctuated with the cracking sound her palm made against his tanned cheek. Her hand throbbed with pain. Where she'd struck him, there was a deep red mark.

He caught her wrist, and his eyes gleamed with anger. "Don't ever hit me again," he warned. Her violent action had at least served to bring him back to the present and made him aware of her as an individual once more.

She pulled her hand free from his grasp, shocked at what she'd done. Never had she hit anyone before.

"I—I'm sorry," she murmured. "But I'm not like what you said! I'm not! You don't know me!"

"Look, maybe I put things a little too brutally," he went on more gently, genuinely apologetic. "Sometimes I get a little carried away on that subject." He attempted a smile. "But I met someone once, someone you re-minded me of before, and she got inside me and destroyed..." His deep voice had become almost vengeful. "I'll never let another woman close again."

He was speaking of his wife, of course, Leslie thought. He'd loved her and her death had devastated him. No wonder.... Leslie's heart softened toward him in spite of everything he'd said.

His dark eyes held hers. "I wanted you even though I didn't want to," he admitted. "But that's all there'll ever be between us."

"No commitment," she sighed wearily. That's exactly what Tim had said he'd wanted. Was every man singing that same song?

"That's right," came his terse reply.

"That's just fine with me," she said shakily.

The last thing she wanted was to get involved with another man like Tim, no matter how compellingly attractive he was to her. In a way she should be grateful to Boone for telling her the way he felt right from the beginning. It had been a mistake to sleep with him before she understood him, of course. But it was a mistake she didn't have to compound by getting any more deeply involved. She'd learned a very bitter lesson.

He traced a fingertip along her shoulder blade, and she shivered as a molten tingle quivered through her. "I'm glad we understand each other," he said, not understanding her at all as he reached to pull her into his arms.

"Don't touch me," she cried, shrugging out of his embrace and ignoring the treacherous leap of her pulse at his touch.

"It's going to be a long, cold night, and I have no intention of sleeping alone," he said huskily, his dark mood vanishing as he thought of holding her in his arms once more.

She was very aware of his lean muscled frame stretching indolently beside hers.

"Well, I do."

"It's a little late in the day for virginal protestations," he said gruffly, letting his hand trail downward over the satiny skin on her arm.

"Nevertheless, you're sleeping on the couch," she insisted, trying to ignore the tiny ache the thought of not sleeping wrapped in the warmth of his arms produced.

"I guess you know this is the oldest trick in the book," he said, keeping his tone even.

"What?"

"Coming on hot and heavy and then acting like a coy miss. You think that after sampling the goods I'll do anything to have you again."

His insolence was suddenly unbearable.

"Oh, shut up," she snapped furiously. "I'm tired of you telling me what I'm like and what I think. If you'd listen to me for one minute I'd tell you myself what I'm like."

He infuriated her all the more by listening to her with a wicked gleam in his eye. A broad smile spread lazily across his tanned features as he noticed the way she trembled and the way her lips pursed in a provocative pout.

"You're even beautiful when you're mad," he whispered, deliberately baiting her.

"In the morning," she choked. She could scarcely look at him any longer she was so angry. "I want you to get out of my house and out of my life for good. I'm not interested in any sort of relationship with you because I've known men like you before myself. And I'm sick of them."

With that she gathered her caftan about her and stormed from the room.

Behind her she heard his mocking laughter. "Suit yourself, little spitfire. But if you change your mind, you know where to find me."

Even though it was still dark outside when Leslie woke, Boone was already gone. Wearily she straightened the condominium until there was no sign that he had ever been there. If only she could wipe him from her mind and heart as easily.

For a long moment her eyes lingered on the blanket strewn in front of the fireplace before she picked it up and folded it, replacing it in the closet. She'd certainly made a mess of things. Why, she'd made love to a man, and she didn't even know his name. If only... She caught herself. She had no time for *if only's*. With fierce determination she pushed last night and Boone from her mind.

A quick look at her calendar reminded her that Mr. Carson would be coming over at ten o'clock. He was a wealthy Texas oilman in Winter Park for a week-long ski vacation with his family. She'd shown him several pieces of property, and he'd called early yesterday morning to say he wanted to talk to her.

Dressing with special care to look attractive, she eyed herself critically in the full-length mirror of her bedroom. An extra layer of light makeup had been needed to erase the dark shadows that had lingered beneath her eyes because of her sleepless night. But other than that she was pleased with her appearance. It gave her a measure of pleasure to imagine Tim's response. He would have been shocked. Gone was the brown wren look she'd once affected. Instead she was a brightly garbed parrot; she was the glamour girl he'd taunted she could never be.

Her golden hair was caught in a flame-colored scarf that matched her flame silk blouse. A long, delicate, golden chain swung between the hollow of her full breasts, which were tantalyzingly revealed because several buttons of her blouse were undone. She wore a dark brown, tightly fitting wool skirt that had a long slit up the back. Every time she moved, shapely legs encased in nylon stockings were displayed. Over one arm she slung a matching jacket.

She experienced the oddest momentary sensation that the girl in the mirror wasn't really she herself at all. For all her exterior polish, inside she was still the same plain girl she'd always been. Then the doorbell buzzed, putting an end to her reflections.

Mr. Carson shifted his bifocals as he studied the blueprints of several condominiums laid out on Leslie's diningroom table. An untouched cup of coffee steamed beside him. Smoke curled from a crystal ashtray. "I can't make up my mind which plan to go with," he fumed.

"If you pick the D plan, you'll have four bedrooms and a view of the Continental Divide," Leslie inserted pleasantly.

He sighed. "That view certainly is spectacular. But my wife hates to walk upstairs."

"Then perhaps the B plan would be better. You'd be right over the garage and near the Jacuzzi..."

"This fellow you work for, R.B. Dexter, certainly is a quality builder. I think I'll buy the whole building," he decided. "That'll save me from having to make a decision."

"All four condominiums," she breathed. Excitement coursed through her. This would be her first real sale.

"One for myself and the other three as investments," Mr. Carson continued calmly. "It's hard to pass up below-market interest rates. What time tomorrow can I make an appointment at your office to sign an earnest money contract?''

''Why, any time, Mr. Carson,'' she beamed. ''Any time at all...''

At just that minute the doorbell buzzed. ''Now who could that be?'' she murmured distractedly. She didn't expect Karen until after lunch. ''Excuse me, Mr. Carson.'' She flashed him the warmest of smiles.

''Sure, honey....'' Absently he nodded his silver head.

As soon as she unbolted the lock, the door was pushed open by the tall dark man on the other side of it. The mere sight of him tore through her nervous system like a jagged pain.

''Boone!'' She paled even as she was aware of a tiny pulsebeat pounding in her throat.

His face was haggard and drawn. Fleetingly she wondered if he'd gotten as little sleep as she. He hadn't shaved yet, and the lines beneath his eyes were more deeply cut than they had been last night. But to her he was the most handsome sight in the world. He wore jeans and a sheepskin coat. The top two buttons of his flannel plaid shirt were unbuttoned, revealing the dark hairs that grew thickly on his tanned chest. In his arms he carried a dozen long-stemmed red roses.

''I—I didn't think you'd...'' Overwhelmed, she choked on her words. Had he come back because he cared more than he was capable of admitting?

His wandering gaze was dark with an indefinable emotion. His eyes slowly roamed over her, over the delicate features of her face, her exquisite long-lashed eyes, her lush, pearly lips, then down the column of her throat, lingering where her golden filigree chain plunged to the soft hollow between her breasts. The intensity of his gaze made her skin tingle with an odd warmth as if his mere look were a physical caress.

She hadn't known until this moment how much this man, a stranger, meant to her. She was weak with joy.

"Who'd you expect?" he demanded gruffly.

"I—I…"

"Certainly not me. That's for sure," he said dryly. "I would have called first, but I didn't know your last name. Can I come in?"

Behind her Mr. Carson rustled several papers with an air of impatience. "I, well…" she stammered. "I'm afraid I'm busy right now." She flushed deeply, feeling acutely uncomfortable for fear he would misinterpret the situation. "Perhaps…later…"

Boone's swift dark gaze took in at a glance Mr. Carson's coat strewn casually across a stuffed armchair. Thought he couldn't see the other man from where he stood, Boone caught the scent of tobacco that had not been in the condominium last night permeating the air.

"I see," he said curtly, not seeing at all. His dark face was harshly forbidding. "Like I said, I should have called first." He tossed the flowers into her shaking arms. "Keep these."

A thorn pricked her fingers, but she didn't notice. Wincing at the savage violence in his tone, at the fierce anger blazing in his eyes, she pleaded softly, "Boone…. It's not what you think. I…"

"You can save your explanations for the next poor fool that falls for you," he returned roughly.

"Boone…" But he ignored the soft sound of her voice falling after him as he stalked rapidly down the hall out into the white, winter day and was gone.

Slowly she closed the door.

"Boyfriend trouble?" Mr. Carson nodded sagely.

"You might call it that," she said wearily, depositing the scarlet bundle of flowers into the sink. Then she returned to the table and feigned a bright smile.

"Child, you've cut yourself," Mr. Carson said kindly, groping for his handkerchief, which he promptly located. "Here…"

She pressed the handkerchief to her bleeding hand. Mr. Carson's plump, kindly face swam before her. "Mr. Carson, I'm sorry," she said brokenly. "I…I can't go on."

"I understand. I think we've made all the important decisions today. I'll be at your office," he paused to check a tiny black notebook he was carrying, "at ten again tomorrow. Will that be all right with you?"

"Perfectly," she said gratefully as he rose and showed himself to the door.

When he had gone she sank into the plump cushions of her couch. Boone had come back, but nothing had changed between them. He'd leapt immediately to the wrong conclusion without giving her a chance to explain. It seemed he was determined to think poorly of her.

If she were smart she would forget him; she was certain that she had seen the last of him.

Four

Carefully Leslie studied the earnest money contract that she'd had the contract department draw up. Everything seemed to be in order, but she decided she'd better get Tad Wood to take a look, just in case she'd missed something. She rose from her desk and moved swiftly from her office into the hall and then knocked on Tad's office.

"Come in...."

She pushed the door open.

"Hello, beautiful," Tad gushed, laughingly. His blue eyes roamed her feminine curves clad in clinging blue silk. "If I'd known it was you I would have done a handspring over the desk to get that door open...."

Suddenly Leslie's warm laughter joined his. "I was wondering if you'd take a look at..."

"What the..." The unfinished question hung in the air like thunder before a storm. From behind her the deep, all-too-familiar voice sent shock waves rippling through

Leslie's nervous system. She whirled to meet Boone's savage, penetrating black stare that stripped her to the very depths of her soul. She gasped. The contract fluttered through her fingers to the floor, but she was unaware that it had done so.

As if in a dream she heard Tad's friendly, "R.B., when did you get back in town?"

"Friday night," came the deep, cold voice that chilled every nerve fiber in her being. His black gaze never left her face.

"R.B." Leslie's mind floundered. Were Boone and R.B. Dexter, her boss, one and the same person?

"I guess you haven't met Leslie Grant yet," Tad said, unaware of the seething undercurrents. "Les, this is R.B. Dexter. R.B., we were so short-handed since Roger quit and you were away that your mother hired Les to fill in while you were gone."

"Mother did what?"

"She hired Les."

"On whose authority? Everyone knows I do the hiring around here."

"But you weren't here, R.B.," Rose Mary Dexter interjected placidly in a softly cajoling voice from behind them. Silently she'd stepped from her own office to join the group in the hall. "Son, it's good to have you back," Rose Mary said, her vivacious black eyes sparkling. In her red and white dress she looked just like Mrs. Santa Claus and just as guileless. "Why didn't you call and let me know you were home?" Her cheeks dimpled as her face was illuminated by a cheery smile.

"I...er..." Boone's hot gaze lingered on Leslie.

"Something came up, Mother,...unexpectedly," he finished offhandedly. An involuntary blush stained Leslie's cheeks a deep red, and she forced herself to concentrate

on the chipped tip of a fingernail. "I want to speak to
Mrs. Grant alone," he continued smoothly, masking his
anger. "If you two don't mind?"

"Not at all," his mother demurred.

A trembling weakness spread through Leslie's body as
she scurried quickly behind Boone, who was heading rapidly down the hall toward his office. Once they were both
inside, he shut the door behind them.

Leslie was only dimly aware of rich dark paneling,
thick carpet, and a gleaming oak desk. Her eyes devoured
the sight of Boone as he towered before her—so ruthlessly
male, so formidably angry.

"I should have known the minute I saw you, this was
a setup." His face was dark with hostility.

"A what?" Astonishment widened her eyes.

"Don't pull that 'Little Miss Innocent' act on me
again!" he growled. "It nearly worked Saturday night,
but it won't work again!"

"Boone, I don't have the slightest idea what you're
talking about."

"Don't you? Then let me spell it out for you. You knew
who I was all along. You knew that when I took one look
at you I could scarcely ignore you. This is a deliberate
plot…"

"I don't know what you're talking about," she repeated.

"Don't worry. I intend to have a long talk with my
mother and get to the bottom of this."

"Boone, I…"

"You're fired. There's no way I want you working for
me. Do you understand?"

"But I signed a contract."

"It isn't worth the paper it's written on without my

signature." Though his voice was soft, it was laced with icy coldness.

"Boone, what is going on?" a deep frown creased her brow. "I'd never seen you before until Saturday at the ski slope. What makes you think…"

"For your information, this isn't the first time Mother's tried to find a woman for me. It seems she's determined to see me married again. You're not the first woman she's hired with this purpose in mind. I suppose she wants grandchildren. But this time she went too far." His voice was hard and filled with anger.

"Boone…" She was desperate to understand what he was talking about.

Suddenly he ripped his gaze from her lovely features and strode to the far side of his desk. Then he rummaged furiously in a drawer, searching for something. Long brown fingers closed over a gilt picture frame, and he pulled it from the drawer. Then he returned to Leslie's side and thrust it into her shaking fingers.

Slowly she glanced down at the photograph of a lovely blonde woman who so resembled herself that for a long moment she was shocked. Of course, on closer examination there were subtle differences. Leslie breathed in deeply. "Marnie?" she managed in a tremulous whisper.

"Yes."

"She's…beautiful.…"

"Yes," he snapped, grabbing the picture from her and placing it face down on the top of his desk. "Isn't she? As beautiful as poison. Now will you please get out and leave me alone."

The smoldering light in his eyes seared her to the marrow of her bones. The desperate pain she heard in his voice caught at her heart. "Boone, I'm sorry.… I—I didn't know.…"

"Get out!" he ordered, blind with emotion.

For one long moment her eyes tenderly roamed his handsome features searching for some sign of warmth, but she found none. He was very dear to her, but it was all too clear he cared nothing for her. Even so, she longed to help him, to ease his suffering, but in the end she realized that the only thing she could do to help was leave him. When she went out, the door clicked softly behind her.

As beautiful as poison.... Boone's savage utterance lingered in Leslie's mind as she quickly collected her personal belongings in her office. They were strange words from a man who'd been deeply in love with his wife. But then Leslie knew from her own experience after her parents had been killed when their light airplane crashed that anger was a part of grief.

"Leslie, I'd like to talk to you." Rose Mary's gentle voice interrupted.

Startled, Leslie looked up. She wasn't aware that the older woman had come in.

"Haven't you heard?" Leslie began unsteadily. "I've been fired! I'm to leave immediately."

"Not before we have a little talk," Rose Mary pleaded. "I need to explain...."

"Boone already has. He showed me a picture of Marnie. How could you do this without at least warning me?"

"Please..."

For the first time Leslie glanced up from her desk and looked at the older woman. Rose Mary's face was filled with warmth and concern as well as a silent plea that Leslie be understanding. In the two weeks that Leslie had known Rose Mary, she'd come to realize that, although Boone's mother could be quite forceful, she was basically a kind-hearted soul.

"All right," Leslie agreed softly. "Why don't you close the door and sit down."

Once seated opposite Leslie, Boone's mother began. "I should have told you from the first, but I was afraid you wouldn't take the job."

"I wouldn't have...."

"As soon as I saw your picture on the application I knew you were the right woman to snap Boone back to life."

"...because I looked like Marnie...."

"Not only that. There was a vulnerability about you that Marnie never had. Then when I met you in person I saw that you'd suffered yourself, so I thought you might understand what Boone's been going through. And, oh, Leslie, he's suffered so much! Ever since Marnie died...he's been different. It's been more than grief! He hasn't had anything to do with women. He seems to hate them all! He's done nothing except bury himself in his work. He's driven himself and the rest of us unmercifully. I've tried everything I knew to bring him out of it, but nothing's worked...."

"And hiring me was still another attempt on your part to help your son."

"Yes. But I was going to explain what I'd done as soon as I saw him."

"You had no way of knowing we would meet by accident."

"No."

"I suppose Boone was desperately in love with Marnie," Leslie coaxed.

"They were childhood sweethearts. They married young, and at first they were very happy. But later, I wasn't so sure. Boone wanted children, but Marnie didn't. And I think she found Winter Park a little confining, but perhaps that's no more than an old woman's imagination.... It was just that that last year she seemed so restless and temperamental. I never did seem to be able to stay on the right side of her. But then when she died, Boone carried on so. Yes, I think he loved her very much. That's the only way to explain the way he's been since her death...." Her voice trailed off.

"Rose Mary, I'm afraid your little scheme has backfired. Boone and I met, and...things ended disastrously."

"What happened?"

"Don't ask. Suffice it to say that he doesn't like me at all."

"I don't believe that," Rose Mary stated firmly. "He's angry. But he doesn't dislike you. In the year since Marnie died, I've never seen him show any emotion until I saw him this morning...with you. You've had an effect on him, no one else has. He cares..."

"Not in the right way."

"I'm not sure that's true. Don't leave Winter Park. I promise you that with your qualifications I can easily find you another job by this afternoon. I know you gave up your teaching position to come here. It's the least I could do."

"Rose Mary," Leslie gently refused, "I can't be a part of your scheme, however well-intentioned it may be."

"Well, dear, if you reconsider, you know where to find me."

Later that afternoon Leslie wondered if she'd been too hasty in rejecting Rose Mary's offer to find her another job. Tim's child-support check hadn't arrived yet, and her checking account balance was very low. A move back to Texas was more than she could afford. Besides that she'd signed a lease for her condominium, and she'd lose a substantial deposit.

At two o'clock Karen's teacher called and informed her that Karen was sick, so Leslie rushed up to the school to pick her up. Karen managed only a wan smile at the sight of her mother, and Leslie realized she must be quite sick. Usually Karen bubbled at everything. The child's blue eyes were lusterless, her chestnut curls matted damply to her forehead. When Leslie took Karen's hand to lead her to the car, it was limp and feverish.

Leslie drove at once to Dr. Rome's office, which was ten miles away in a neighboring town. The road was packed with snow, and she had to drive slowly.

Dr. Rome was one of the few doctors in a sixty-mile radius, and as a result his office was jammed. It was nearly six o'clock before she wearily led Karen up the stairs to their condominium. As she held on to Karen with one hand and fumbled in her purse with the other for her keys, she heard the phone inside ringing furiously.

When she at last got inside and rushed to answer it, she knew that the deep, angry tone could belong to only one man. The sound of Boone's voice vibrated through her. "Where the hell have you been?"

Leslie's nerves were stretched ragged with concern for Karen. She hadn't managed to get to the drugstore before it closed for the medicine Dr. Rome had prescribed, and she didn't know what she was going to do. Boone's anger was the final, unbearable assault on her nervous system, and she broke down.

"Mr. Dexter, you are one person I certainly don't have to answer to." With that she slammed the phone back on the receiver.

"Why were you so mean to Mr. Dexter, Mommy?" Karen managed in a tight voice.

"It's a long story, darling. Right now we need to get you into bed."

Ten minutes later Karen was tucked into her bed and Leslie was reading her a fairy tale. Karen's neatly brushed hair shone in the dim light. Beneath the frilly lace canopy of her bed she looked like a tiny princess herself. Just as the child began to nod sleepily, the doorbell buzzed.

Anxious to answer the door before the sound of it wakened Karen, Leslie quickly tiptoed from the room. Throwing the door open wide, she uttered a quick little cry of dismay.

"Boone!"

He stood before her like a bronzed giant—so close she could have reached out and touched him.

Dark chiseled male features filled her vision. His jaw was hard with suppressed anger, but she was more acutely aware of his virile masculinity than ever. In spite of herself some treacherous female part of her responded to him.

She would have forced the door shut once more, but he leaned against it. Using his powerful arm as a brace, he easily held it open.

"I seem to have used up my welcome," he jeered, smiling so that his even, white teeth were revealed. The thick sarcasm of his statement coiled about her.

She felt weak, unable to do battle with this powerful man. "You certainly have," she agreed. "Now will you go? I have better things to do than get into another argument with you."

"Do you?" His black eyes roved over the blue silk dress clinging provocatively to her female curves in slow stripping appraisal. "Like what—entertaining your latest conquest?" His deep voice dripped acid.

All the color drained from her face; her luminous eyes widened.

"Why won't you just leave me alone?" she cried wearily, backing away from the door so that he could follow her inside. "Haven't you done enough?"

The sight of her shoulders slumped in defeat made him feel vaguely uncomfortable, but he ignored the twinge of compassion that pierced the hardened shell surrounding his heart. "I need to talk to you," he said grimly.

"I can't talk now." Suddenly she felt very close to tears. She couldn't cope with Boone, not after all that had happened today. "My little girl's sick. And I wasn't able to get her medicine because the drugstore's closed. She's too sick to take out in this weather, and I can't leave her. I don't know what I'm going to do."

He caught the quiet desperation in her voice. "Did you take her to see Dr. Rome?" he asked more gently.

Surprised at the faint note of kindness in his voice, she lifted her shimmering eyes and held his deep, dark gaze. "Yes, but I couldn't get the medicine he prescribed."

"I'll get it for you," he said, deeply aroused by her vulnerability, yet not understanding what motivated him to want to help her.

A feeling of relief washed over her. Being a single parent was difficult, especially at a time like this. Shyly, Leslie flashed him a warm smile of gratitude.

Her tremulous mouth flooded him with an emotion that was inexplicably intense. "I'll need to use your phone," he said gruffly, tearing his gaze from her exquisite face.

All Leslie's attention was on his large, strong hands as he dialed the number—those same hands that had known her intimately and shown her heights of rapture she'd never experienced except in his arms. At the burning memory, she flushed, just as his knowing gaze met hers.

Quickly, too quickly, she looked away. His deep voice speaking into the receiver broke the awkward silence between them. "David, this is R.B. I need you to open up as a special favor. It's an emergency...."

When he hung up, he turned to her. "I'll need the prescription...."

She fumbled in her purse and found the crumpled scrap of paper. As she placed it in his hand, his touch burned her with his warmth.

"Leslie..." His voice was strangely gentle. "I'll bet you haven't eaten all day, have you?"

"N-no. But I'm all right. Don't bother about me. I'll fix something later."

"I'll bring you something," he stated.

When he was at the door, she said, "You don't need to ring the doorbell when you come back. It might wake Karen." Her eyes held his for an endless moment. "And...Boone...I do thank you. I don't know what I would have done..."

Very gently he lowered his lips and brushed her forehead briefly in a short, sweet kiss. His palm tenderly cupped her chin. For her the moment was one of breathless magic. Then he left, closing the door very softly behind him.

When he had gone Leslie rushed down the hall to see about Karen. The child lay limply against her pillows, her thick coverlet pushed aside. Her cheeks were bright, and when Leslie touched Karen's forehead, she realized the child was burning with fever. Carefully Leslie slipped a thermometer into Karen's mouth, and when she read it, her worst suspicions were confirmed—104 degrees.

Leslie had already given Karen as much children's aspirin as she could take for the next couple of hours so she decided that all she could do was give her a cool sponge bath.

Half an hour later she was still sponging Karen off when Boone strode silently into the room.

"How is she?"

"Oh, Boone, she's burning up. I've been doing this for nearly thirty minutes, and she's still as hot as a firecracker."

"You take a break," he commanded. "I'll take over. I brought you some fried chicken. You go eat."

"Boone, you don't have to do this…"

His hand closed firmly over hers, the one that held the sponge. She felt his other arm at her waist. "I know."

Meekly she obeyed him, and she did feel better after she'd eaten. When she'd finished and was walking down the hall to check on Karen again, she was surprised by the deep sound of masculine laughter mingling with Karen's curious, chirping voice.

"Gee, Mr. Dexter, you're so nice. Are you the same man my mommy was mean to on the phone?"

"The one and only. But don't be too hard on her. I had it coming." The easiness, the genuine friendliness in his voice didn't belong to the same Boone Dexter that Leslie knew. For a fleeting moment, Leslie felt a pang of something akin to jealousy—and toward her own seven-year-old daughter.

"Feeling better?" Leslie called brightly from the doorway.

"I just gave her her first dose of medicine," Boone said gravely. "I think she'll be like a new little girl in the morning. Now go to sleep, sweetheart."

"But I want you to tell me another story…."

"Not tonight. I'll come back when you're better and tell you one," he soothed.

"Promise?"

"I promise." Then he tucked the sheet gently about her.

In the livingroom Leslie said to him, "Earlier you said you needed to talk to me..."

There was a subtle hardening of his smooth, dark countenance, but he returned easily, "It'll keep till the morning." He opened the door. "You've been through enough for one day. Get some rest. I'll come back tomorrow...around nine."

The sunshine was brilliant on the newly fallen snow the next morning. The cloudless sky was a rich cobalt blue.

Leslie was again wearing her flame silk scarf and her flame silk blouse, accented with her delicate golden chain. Only this time she'd dressed more casually in skintight designer jeans that showed her figure off to enticing perfection.

Apprehensively she searched for things around the house to do to keep her occupied before Boone's arrival. But in a small condominium that was already immaculate, she found herself repeating the same tasks. She was adjusting the coffee table for the third time when she heard Boone's footsteps on the stairs outside. After his crisp knock she forced herself to wait at least half a minute before answering it.

The ruggedly handsome man who stood in the doorway was the same embittered person who'd resoundingly fired her yesterday, and he was again a dark and forbidding stranger. She was acutely aware of his black gaze traveling over her and lingering where her golden chain dangled between her breasts, of his jaw tightening slightly as though something about her appearance disturbed him.

"Come in," she said weakly, wishing she could will her fluttering heartbeats to settle down, wishing he didn't have this strangely powerful pull over her emotions. "Would you like some coffee? I made it especially because you..."

His terse words interrupted her. "I've had some."

"Oh." His coldness hurt, but she determined that she would conceal her feelings from him. "Then you don't mind if I pour myself a cup?" she said coolly.

"Not at all." With studied politeness he used her same turn of phrase. "And *you don't mind* if I sit down?"

"Make yourself comfortable," she tossed, "and I'll join you in a minute."

From the kitchen bar she achingly observed the indolent movements of his hard, male frame as he seated himself, sprawling with a casual air across the couch. Because she was thus distracted she spilled some boiling coffee onto her shaking fingers.

"Ouch!" She jerked her hand to her lips, and the cup clattered precariously in its saucer.

"You all right?" Boone called sharply, leaning forward, his great body tense.

For the briefest instant she saw concern flicker in the black depths of his eyes.

"Yes."

Once more his gaze was cool and hard, his tone indifferent. "I'm beginning to think you're accident prone."

After running cool tap water over her fingers, she joined him on the couch. Attempting to regain her composure, she said, "Karen's much better. I want to thank you again."

"Don't bother. Anyone else would have done the same thing." Casually he dismissed his kindness of the night before. "Let's get down to the business at hand."

"By all means." Her voice was as cool as his own. "And what might that be?"

"Yesterday you left me in a damned awkward position, as I'm sure you know."

"I left you? You fired me, remember?"

"You failed to mention your contract with Mr. Carson. When you didn't show up for your appointment..."

His cold, steely look made her tremble slightly, but she managed frigidly, "I had no choice in the matter."

"You could have said something. Instead Mr. Carson arrived and you weren't there. He was very upset, needless to say, that you weren't. It took us a while to locate the earnest money contract on the four condominium units he wants to buy. He's also interested in another piece of property. But he kept demanding to know why you weren't there yourself. He said he wouldn't consider using another agent on the deal."

"I'm sorry that Mr. Carson's involved, of course," she retorted icily. "But, Boone, I can't see how any of this is my problem. It's yours. Now I have other things to do that are more important than..."

She would have risen, but his brown hand clamped around her tiny wrist like a vise, forcing her to remain where she was. She gasped at his casual touch. A low, unwanted fire simmered in her veins.

"Than a million-dollar deal. I can't imagine what they might be," he said sarcastically.

Neither could she, but she wasn't about to admit this truth. She pulled her fingers free from his.

"Besides," he continued. "It's your sale. You deserve the commission."

She wanted to hurl back the words that she didn't need his money, but that simply wasn't true. She desperately needed it. Having spent all her reserve cash to make this move to Colorado, she needed a lot more than one commission. Tim's late child-support check made her realize more strongly than ever that she was completely on her own. She'd taken the job with his company in good faith. How could she have known that Mrs. Dexter didn't have the authority to hire for the family-run business?

Karen's illness underscored the fact to Leslie that she was a single parent with a child to support. She had too much at stake to allow herself to be treated unfairly. And for whatever reasons, Boone Dexter had fired her unfairly.

"As I understand it," she began slowly, feeling her way, "even though I'm still fired, you want me to come back and handle Mr. Carson's sale. I take my commission and then it's goodbye."

"That's it," he said blandly, superbly confident that no one in their right mind would pass up such a juicy commission.

"Well, I won't do it!" She took intense satisfaction in the look of stunned shock that swept the placid look from his features.

"You what?" he muttered fiercely.

"You heard me! I won't do it! I don't work for you anymore. I never did. As you so bluntly put it yesterday, my contract with R.B. Dexter isn't worth the paper it's written on without your signature. And if you're thinking of patching up your deal with Mr. Carson, I think I'll give him a call at his hotel and cry on his shoulder. He has a daughter my age who's divorced and struggling to support three children. He won't think too highly of your professional ethics, Mr. Dexter."

"'Mr. Dexter!' You and I are too intimately acquainted to address one another with last names. And I don't give a damn about professional ethics," he lashed out at her.

"I'd be the first one to agree with you on that score," she managed to retort sweetly.

"What do you want—revenge? More money?"

"Neither of those. The answer's much simpler than that. I want my job. That's all! Your signature on my contract!"

A falling feather could have been heard in the thick, hostile silence.

"That's blackmail!" he uttered savagely.

"Call it what you like," came her faint, yet defiant whisper. "Those are my terms. Take them or leave them."

Trembling, she rose, taking her coffee cup with her and heading for the bar for a refill. But he was right behind her. The coffee cup was wrenched from her fingers and set on the bar. Then he pulled her into his arms, against the muscular sweep of his heated length.

"You little fool! There's no way we can work together!"

Her heart beat against her ribs like a caged, wild thing as she struggled to break free. She felt the rippling muscles of his arms tightly wrapped around her. He held her so fiercely that she could scarcely catch her breath. Blackness whirled around her, and all the hot, angry words that had gone before were momentarily forgotten. She was aware only of the hard contours of his masculinity molded against her yielding curves.

Suddenly something melted in both of them. The sweet, fragile scent of her, the feel of her soft flesh crushed against himself thawed the raging heat of his anger. Vengeance no longer drove him. In its place was raw, hungry desire. And for her, as always, his touch was wonderful madness. Sensual longing flared through them—more intense than ever before—because they'd already had each other once and knew what rapture each could give the other. In spite of everything he'd said to deny it, when he held her in his arms his body told her what he could not admit—that their coming together was the mating of two souls each of whom had spent a lifetime searching for the other.

When his lips claimed hers with bruising pressure she surrendered herself to the mastery of his embrace. Boone drew her onto her tiptoe and bent his head to fervently nuzzle the warm hollow between her breasts. "That damned chain," he muttered thickly, tickling her sensitive flesh with his lips as his mouth traveled over the delicate strand of gold that lay against her breasts. "It's been driving me wild ever since I got here. Did you wear it just to torment me?" There was a time of silence as they kissed one another passionately. "How am I ever going to get you out of my system," he groaned at last as though in pain.

His words made her feel very unwanted, and she was reminded of his true feelings. He didn't really want her. And no matter how she felt, she wasn't going to make the same mistake she had Saturday night. Wrenching herself free, she stumbled blindly away and ran behind the kitchen bar, feeling safer only when something substantial was between them. She stared dazedly out the window at a patch of brilliant snow because she couldn't risk looking at him. She was too vulnerable to his rawly virile, handsome charm. Hugging her arms tightly about her to assuage the empty ache in her heart, she drew a quick, shallow breath.

"Leslie..."

"What was that?" She forced a sharpness into her voice that she didn't feel. "Your brand of sexual harassment? If we're going to work together, you'll have to keep your distance."

His jawline hardened, and she knew that her barb had

found its mark. "And that's exactly why you and I can never work together," he hurled back.

"Surely, Mr. Dexter, you have some self-control."

"Not where you're concerned. What does it take to convince you? This?"

He moved toward her with the swift fluid grace of a panther lunging for its prey and pulled her once more into his arms. There was a savage glint in his black flashing eyes, a cruel twist to his sensual mouth, and she quivered with fear. She didn't know this tall dark stranger who held her with such force against his powerful body that she could scarcely draw a breath.

She panted an infuriated, "Let me go," and vainly attempted to struggle free. He caught her by the wrists and pinned them behind her back so that her breasts were mashed flat against his chest. The edge of the bar cut painfully into her hips.

"You see what you do to me," he muttered brutally.

Of course this was just an underhanded trick to make her change her mind, she tried to tell herself. He was deliberately humiliating her. Still she couldn't stop the single tear that spilled over her long lashes and glistened on her cheek.

"Boone, you're hurting me," she gasped. "Surely you don't intend to use force to convince me that we can't work together?" she pleaded.

Cursing softly, he pushed her from him. Suddenly from the hall came Karen's sleepy voice. "I thought I heard voices. Is Mommy being mean to you again, Mr. Dexter?"

Boone turned toward the child in the fluffy white nightgown. For a long moment he hesitated. Then Karen spoke again, filling the uneasy silence with her lilting voice.

"I'm sorry Mommy doesn't like you, but she's really very nice once you get to know her."

A faint gentle smile curved his lips. "I'm glad to see you're feeling better, Karen."

"Did you come back to read me a story?"

"Not this time, sweetheart. But I haven't forgotten. Right now I've got to go to work."

He left without once glancing in Leslie's direction, but an hour later when the phone rang Leslie sensed it would be him even before she lifted the receiver from the hook.

"I just signed your contract," he said. "Be in the office by eight tomorrow." He spoke in low measured tones. "But I'm warning you, keep out of my way."

"That will be my pleasure," she returned pertly. A tiny smile of triumph lifted the edges of her lovely mouth as she hung up the phone. She had the impression that rarely did anyone get the best of Boone Dexter and that this was doubtless a unique experience for him.

But her feeling of triumph was fleeting. At the thought of tomorrow a curious dread began to build in her. She'd won the first battle. Nevertheless, she couldn't help wondering who would win the war.

Five

The next morning Leslie dressed carefully in a soft, sheer, sea green dress. Every time she moved, the dress swirled and clung to the voluptuous curves of her body. Around her neck hung the delicate strand of gold that had so tantalized Boone the day before. Only today it lay gleaming against the bodice of her silken dress instead of against her own creamy flesh. For the sake of practicality she wrapped herself in a thick silvery hooded fur coat. It was, of course, a synthetic, but it was such an exquisite facsimile that most people assumed it was mink.

There was a hushed stillness when she opened the outer office door. Leslie registered at once that Boone hadn't told anyone she would be coming back to work. Rose Mary and Tad greeted her warmly after they recovered from their surprise, but Boone's door was closed. Leslie was about to walk past it and go into her own office, when she thought better of the idea. It would never do to take

Boone's word that he'd signed the contract. She'd better collect it from him herself before doing anything else.

With a boldness she was far from feeling, she knocked on his door.

"Come in," came the deep, masculine voice that was so achingly familiar. Just the sound of it made her toes curl in the impractical, sexy high heels she'd worn. Drawing a quick, shaky breath she forced herself to march briskly inside.

Excitement at the prospect of seeing Boone brought a rosy blush to her cheeks. Her silvery hood had fallen away, and her thick mass of golden tresses framed her face enchantingly. For the briefest moment his eyes flickered over her lovely features, and they were avid with a hungry emotion he at once sought to suppress.

A tiny thrill of feminine triumph coursed through Leslie. At least he was no more immune to her efforts to look attractive than she was to his compelling virility.

"You!" He muttered a savage oath which she only half heard. "I thought I told you to stay out of my way." He slammed the ledger he'd been working on closed.

"So you did," she whispered silkily across the distance that separated them. "But before I go to work, I'd like a copy of my contract—the one with your signature on it. I want to take it to a lawyer..."

"A lawyer! Damn! I told you, you have your job back. I have no intention of going back on my word." His glittering black eyes were darkly menacing, the cold, tight line of his mouth ruthless.

"But I can't be sure of that, can I?" she managed to retort, intimidated by his harsh expression.

The contract was under his fingertips, and he lifted it from his desk. "Come and get it then, if you want it," he jeered in a coldly slicing voice. When she reached for it, his hands closed around her wrist. "Not so fast." Anger and some other emotion vibrated in his thick tone. The savage passion she had so effortlessly provoked told her plainly how deeply her mere presence could upset him. "I've given you what you wanted. Now it's up to you to uphold your part of the bargain. Stay out of my way!"

"All right, Boone, I will," she said quietly. "I would never have forced you to give me my job back if I didn't need it desperately. Working around you won't be any easier for me than it is for you."

He released her abruptly, but not before she saw an odd look of pain scrawled across his handsome features.

What she'd said was true. Her feelings for him had been inexplicably intense from the first moment she'd seen him. Where he was concerned she couldn't seem to help herself. She was hopelessly involved with a man who cared nothing for her.

In the weeks that followed Leslie saw little of Boone even though they worked in the same branch office. He was frequently away in Denver or in meetings with the City Council. She wondered if these numerous absences were a deliberate effort on his part to avoid her. As it was too cold for construction, he spent his time planning and coordinating future projects.

Leslie spent her time showing properties. Many of her clients were Mexicans and Texans. Her fluent command of the Spanish language helped her make several sales, and the fact that she was originally from Texas established an instant rapport with the many Texans who loved to vacation in Colorado.

Boone's continued coldness made Leslie nervous, and she was less patient with Karen during the evenings. One night Karen lashed out, "I wish you were still married to my daddy! You never screamed at me then!" After that Leslie struggled to be more even-tempered with her child, but she was not always successful.

During the Thanksgiving holidays Karen flew to Austin to be with her father, and Leslie spent a lonely four days mostly by herself. Since her divorce, holidays had been especially difficult. Leslie ate turkey dinner with her next-door neighbor, Gini, and her family. Tad and his girlfriend Lucy took her skiing Saturday afternoon. The rest of the long weekend she was alone, and never had solitude weighed more heavily on her hands. She thought of Boone and wished that they could start over. But, of course, that was impossible.

Tim was to have Karen again during the Christmas holidays. The evening before Karen was to leave for Texas, Boone called. Thinking it might be her father, Karen answered the phone. Leslie heard Karen's voice piping exuberantly. "Wow, you didn't forget after all, Mr. Dexter. No, tomorrow I'm going to see my daddy for two weeks. You'll have to come tonight. Sure…come over any time you like."

A tiny shiver of excitement coursed through Leslie. Boone was coming to see her. Why?

When that question was put to Karen, the child's answer was instantaneous. "To tell *me* a story like he promised when I was sick!"

Both females went to their respective rooms to ready themselves for Boone's imminent arrival. Long cascading curls gleamed as their hair fell over their shoulders. Both wore jeans and velour tops.

When he knocked, Karen ran to the door and threw it open. "Mr. Dexter, come in."

Boone stepped inside, filling the small living room with

his masculine presence. A wild shock of pure pleasure ran
through Leslie's body at the sight of him. He was so tall
and commanding. He wore a navy western shirt that was
unbuttoned at the throat. Blue jeans molded his narrow
hips. She caught the intoxicating scent of his aftershave.
His aura of male virility was so powerful that he completely dominated his surroundings, not only Leslie but
also the tiny female reaching gaily up for the red berib-
boned package he was holding.

Leslie's senses swam, and she sank weakly against the
back of a nearby chair for support. Boone raked his eyes
over her with a lingering intensity that shattered the remnants of her composure. Just the way he looked at her was
dangerous; he could strip away her defenses until her very
soul was bared.

"You feeling all right?" he asked her in the way of a
greeting as Karen ripped into the package he'd brought
her. "You look a little pale."

Those were the first words he'd spoken to her in nearly
two weeks—twelve days to be exact. Leslie's throat went
dry, and she ran her tongue across the pearly layer of
lipstick, unaware of the erotic message she was sending.

"I'm fine," she murmured shakily. "Karen's so excited
that you remembered your promise. It was thoughtful of
you to bring her a Christmas present."

"It was the least I could do after waiting so long to
keep my promise, wasn't it, sweetheart?"

It didn't make Leslie particularly happy to know that
all of his kindness was for the sake of her daughter and
not for her.

"A new doll," Karen squealed. "And two dresses! Oh,
thank you, Mr. Dexter. And now will you come to my
room and tell me that story?"

"Of course."

For at least an hour Boone sat on the edge of Karen's bed telling her stories. From time to time Leslie heard his deep rich laughter blend with the softer tones of her daughter's voice.

The volume of the television was a low drone, and Leslie was restlessly thumbing through a fashion magazine when Boone at last left Karen alone as she finally dozed off. To Leslie's surprise he did not go at once to the door. Instead he sank into the chair beside her. She noticed that his long muscular frame barely fit the chair. She was startled by the way his dark eyes observed her intently. His nearness was deeply unsettling, and she tossed her magazine onto the coffee table.

"I'm afraid Karen's fallen asleep fully dressed," he said, smiling.

Leslie warmed to the friendliness in his manner. Karen certainly brought out the best in his nature.

"That's all right," Leslie began unsteadily. There was a latent sensuality about him that she found disturbing. Just his nearness made her feel slightly breathless. "I know it meant a lot to Karen that you came over."

"I made her a promise, and I had to keep it." His black eyes lazily touched her mouth. Unnerved, she curled her bottom lip inward and caught it with her teeth, moistening it. Little did she realize how provocative this gesture was.

"Can I get you something?" she asked awkwardly, remembering her role as hostess.

"No, stay where you are." His avid gaze seemed to burn through her. "I haven't told you how pleased I've been with your work," he said. "For a beginner you've done a first-class job of selling."

"Why, thank you." His praise made her unaccountably happy.

"I was wrong to have fired you without even giving

you a chance, in spite of the fact that I knew why Mother had hired you.''

The lingering dark force of his gaze held her spell-bound. Or was it just his apology that made her turn all soft and quivery inside? It took a big man to admit he was wrong.

''Boone, I—I think I understand why you did what you did,'' she said gently.

''I'm not sure you do.'' His hot intense stare seemed to strip her bare of the clothes she was wearing, leaving her completely exposed to his ravishing gaze. ''It hasn't worked—our avoiding each other. I still want you as much as ever.''

Restlessly he moved toward her as though he couldn't bear to be so near her without touching her. The springs of the couch groaned as it received his weight, and she was enfolded in the hard circle of his arms. The warmth of his body against her own, and the fresh clean scent of him working on her reeling senses made it difficult for her to control her tumultuous emotions. She tried to twist away, but he held her to him with gentle force.

''And I still want you,'' a tiny voice in the depths of her mind cried silently. ''Wanting...without caring is not enough for me, Boone,'' she said aloud. ''It never will be. Maybe I'm old-fashioned...''

''I hardly call a woman who goes to bed with a man the first day she meets him old-fashioned,'' he commented bitterly.

''How long will it take,'' she flared, ''for me to live down that one mistake?''

''A long long time,'' he muttered huskily. His mouth was so near hers that she felt his warm breath fan her lips. ''Some mistakes are worth repeating,'' he murmured in-vitingly.

"Not that one," she rasped. Edging away from him, she replied stiffly, "I think you'd better be going."

"I'm in no mood to spend another night alone, knowing that you're over here alone too."

Had he been as lonely as she? Had he spent his nights thinking of her as she had of him? "Then what are you in the mood for?" she retorted, realizing at once what a slip that question was.

"I'd rather show you than tell you," he replied lazily, crushing her back against the soft couch.

"No, no," she whispered fearfully, trying to get up, but she was pinned beneath him. Every movement brought her into even more disturbing contact with his body. He ignored her words. He kissed her full on the lips, very tenderly; he felt her trembling response as her arms circled his neck.

A hot rush of feeling swept through her like a raging undertow pulling her out into the dangerous depths of his desire. Then she caught herself and fought against the whirling passion that was consuming her. "Let me go," she murmured pleadingly. But he did not obey her. "Please, let me go," she cried softly, weakly struggling against him even though she couldn't control the awakening desires his lovemaking aroused.

"No."

A deep flush bathed her face with glowing heat. His lips gently kissed the warmth of her creamy flesh there before wandering once more to her mouth and claiming it fully in a long, breathless kiss.

"You must!" Leslie gasped, dragging the swollen softness of her mouth from his. "Karen! She's in the other room!"

"She's asleep." His warm mouth was hungrily nuzzling downward into the curve of her throat as he molded her body to his own.

"She could wake up and come in here," Leslie forced herself to insist.

"All right," he said wearily, relenting, removing his mouth from her sensitive skin. "But she's leaving tomorrow night. What excuse will you have then?"

His smoldering gaze locked with her own unwilling one, devastating her self-control, compelling her to need him. Surely, if he touched her again, she would be lost. His eyes, black and deep like the darkest depths of the ocean, lured her to follow him into the raging lovetide of his desire.

"Boone, please don't force me into the kind of relationship I can't handle," she begged softly. "No matter what you think, sex isn't just an appetite with me. It entails love, respect…friendship…"

"Love," he spat contemptuously. "Respect…. Women don't understand the meaning of those words."

His harshness was like a quick savage pain, wounding her soul.

"I can see I'll never be anything to you except a body who can give you physical release when you need it," she began weakly. "Well, that's not enough for me. Just because I went to bed with you the first time I met you, I'll never have your respect. Well, maybe you're right! Maybe I don't deserve it."

Unshed tears moistened her thick, long lashes. Seeing them, his mood softened.

"Leslie, you want too much—more than I have to give," he returned with quiet firmness. "You're complicating what should be a perfectly simple situation between a mature man and woman. All I want is sex. You're a beautiful woman, and I need you…physically. I can't deny that, but I don't need love or friendship from any woman. I've a mother and sister to love me as well as the necessary men friends I can hunt and fish with when the mood hits me. You're just like all the rest of your sex. You think that because I desire you, you should have total control over me. That's all love and marriage represent to women—control. Power. Well, I've been controlled and used by the last woman.''

"No stereotype could fit every woman in the world,'' she said, attempting to appeal to his logic.

"In this case it does.''

"So you have decided to use women—to satisfy you and nothing more?'' Her voice was as smooth and soft as silk.

"Bluntly put…''

"But true,'' she sighed.

"Yes.''

"I want more…''

Brutally his rough voice interrupted her. "Like every other woman, you want to do the using.''

His fierce black eyes ravaged her lovely pale features.

"All I know is that what you're offering isn't enough,'' she admitted unsteadily. "I couldn't live that way and live with myself.''

Boone exhaled a long, deep breath of exasperation, showing her clearly that he believed her statement a pose and not the truth. "Have it your own way, but if you have a change of heart…''

"I won't.''

"Then I'd better be going,'' he told her levelly. If he couldn't have her on his terms, he didn't want her at all. The harsh planes of his face seemed chiseled from some dark stone. His eyes were flat and hard.

Though Leslie was deeply hurt by his rejection, she tried not to show it.

"Well, then I'll see you at work tomorrow," she said tightly, rising to show him the door.

"Not if I can help it," he muttered savagely, and then he was gone.

It was all too obvious she was of no interest to him as a person. She was only a sexual object.

Throughout the night her thoughts whirled around Boone. As she lay in her bed aching and alone, she remembered everything he had said.

He was right about one thing. She wanted him as much as he wanted her. They had already been to bed once, and she knew what sexual ecstasy he could rouse her to. No other man had ever appealed to her as he did. In some indefinable way he was special, even though she wasn't to him.

Life was short. Why should she pass up an experience that could be so pleasurable, not only for him but for her as well? Yet, she would be swimming in deeper waters than he; she cared, and he didn't. She loved him. Perhaps she had from the first minute that she saw him. But she'd already suffered once from her first unwise love. And she had Karen's happiness to consider. She had no intention of rushing blindly into a second disastrous love relationship with no thoughts of the consequences.

Fleetingly Leslie thought back over the past. She and Tim had fallen in love and dated when she was in college and he in his first year of surgery residency. When she'd graduated, they'd married, and she'd helped him in the long years of his residency. They'd loved each other intensely when they were young, but somehow other things had come between them. The disintegration of their marriage had happened slowly. The constant pressure of

Tim's training, acute financial worries, and an early pregnancy had all taken their toll. They'd both worked very hard, and suddenly when Tim was an established surgeon and they were on the brink of success, Tim had realized that he'd spent his youth in school and he'd never been young. So in the exuberant company of a bevy of younger women, he'd left Leslie in search of his youth.

Odd, but thinking of Tim brought no pain tonight. There was only one man now capable of hurting her, and that was Boone.

As she lay beneath the thick covers of her bed, she determined that no matter what, she wasn't going to let herself become more deeply involved with Boone than she already was. As tempting as a sexual relationship with him might be, it held more danger and ultimate pain than pleasure, if Boone could never grow to love her. She'd been too hurt in the past by Tim to take the risk of sleeping with Boone again in the hopes that the union of their bodies could bring about the ultimate union of their souls. She knew that if it didn't, and he left her, a part of her would die forever.

And so with her decision firmly made, she fell into a deep long sleep and dreamed of a man who was tall and dark and handsome, the only man whose touch inflamed her, the only man who compelled her love, but a man who refused to make a place for her in his heart.

Six

Two days later Leslie was sorting through a stack of papers on her desk. She'd been so busy lately that she hadn't had a chance to do any routine filing or other office work.

"Looks like you're digging out," Tad said warmly from the doorway. "When you finish, why don't you come next door and give me a hand?"

"Hi, Tad. How's it been going?" Leslie smiled at him, tossing her golden hair as she looked up at the handsome young man who'd become a casual friend.

"Not too hot. Lucy's gone home to spend the holidays with her parents, and I'm feeling pretty lonely. She won't be back until New Year's Eve. We have a date for the Devil's Brand Ranch annual party that night."

"Well, at least you have something to look forward to. I've been feeling pretty lonely myself the last couple of days. Karen's gone too."

"You coming to the office party tonight?"

"I—I hadn't given it a thought," she replied casually, toying with the end of a pencil. That wasn't exactly true. She felt nervous at the idea of driving in snow at night alone, and she hadn't been to a party since her divorce. Boone had been out of the office for the last two days, but Rose Mary had told her he was planning to come to the Christmas party.

"Well, if you decide you want to come, I'd be glad to drive you," he offered gallantly.

"Why, Tad, if you don't mind, I'll accept your offer. The idea of sitting home alone tonight definitely doesn't appeal to me."

"I'll pick you up at seven."

That evening Leslie was darkening her eyebrows with a deft stroke of a pencil when the telephone rang. Picking it up on the third ring, she instantly recognized her ex-husband's languid Texan drawl. Fearing the worst, her heart lodged in her throat.

"Tim, is…is…Karen… Is everything all right?"

"She's fine. I mean it's nothing serious."

Leslie sagged with relief against the bar stool.

"What is it then?" she asked.

"She's very upset about our divorce. She wants us to get back together again, or at least to talk to each other."

Leslie gasped. "It's been eighteen months. She's never said anything to me."

"She didn't say anything during Thanksgiving, but last night she cried for hours. She kept saying you'd been fussing at her all the time, and she knows it's because I left you. She said all she wants for Christmas is for me to come up to Colorado and visit you so you'll feel better. She won't even look at any of the Christmas presents I've bought her. I think she secretly hopes that if we see each other again we'll be able to patch things up."

"It's definitely too late for that," Leslie sighed wearily, thinking of all the scars and months of hurt that made a reconciliation impossible.

"I know. But she's only seven. She can't understand. I've decided to fly her back up there myself on the thirty-first. Maybe you could think of some place we could go out New Year's Eve...for Karen's sake...unless you have other plans."

This was the last thing she needed, but as she thought back over how nervous she'd been with Karen lately, she realized her behavior must have threatened Karen's security. If Tim made the effort to come to Colorado and she refused, Karen might grow resentful toward her.

"I definitely don't have other plans, and I guess if this is important to Karen..."

"Good, it's a date. I'll see you on the thirty-first."

"Oh, Tim, what will our going out accomplish?"

"Karen and I'll get a good night's sleep tonight for one thing. Here, I'll let you tell Karen you've agreed to it."

As soon as she hung up, Leslie dialed the Devil's Brand Ranch and made reservations for two for their annual New Year's Eve dance. It would feel strange going out with Tim again; she wasn't looking forward to an evening with him at all. Once she would have given anything for just such an invitation, but now another man claimed her love.

A brief flicker of annoyance at Tim for letting Karen maneuver them into an evening together passed through Leslie's thoughts. Tim had always been lax with Karen, and now that he rarely saw her, he spoiled her totally when he did have her. If he had tried, he could have found a suitable explanation that would have soothed Karen, and they wouldn't be faced with having to spend an evening together.

Slender fingers curled tightly into Tad's coat sleeve as Leslie's long-lashed gaze swept the crowded room and found Boone at once. A swift pain stabbed her heart at the sight of him so elegantly dressed, yet so ruggedly handsome—and at the same time so totally unconcerned whether she appeared tonight or not.

His well-cut gray suit fit his lean body to perfection. Every movement of his powerful frame was as lithe and fluid as a jungle cat's. In spite of his debonair attire, there was a quality of danger about him, of latent virility, that enhanced his attraction to the female sex. Women fluttered around him, laughing and chattering.

Leslie drew a small, shaky breath. Her dry throat ached. Suddenly she realized how much she'd missed just seeing him these past two days.

The pair of striking, look-alike redheads at Boone's side were the second people in the room to catch Leslie's attention. The younger girl was the same one Leslie had seen him with at the warming house the first day she'd met him. It was obvious that they were on intimate terms, and Leslie felt her heart was as thoroughly green as her eyes.

As Tad bent to help Leslie from her coat, Boone's black gaze swung to her. The instant he saw her, his features hardened. The heat of his anger seemed to shrivel all the happiness in her heart.

Why had she come? Seeing him like this and having him indicate so clearly how much he disliked her was even more painful than having to work in the same office with him. At least during the day she had her work to distract her.

Rock music filled the air as Boone devoured her with his eyes. His lingering gaze swept with possessive force over her body, which was alluringly clad in a long-sleeved, low-cut black gown that hugged her supple curves like an outer silken skin. At her pale throat white sapphires sparkled. The necklace was a gift from her grandmother.

"Would you like a drink?" Tad offered.

"Y-yes, that would be nice." She flashed him an artificially bright smile.

On no account must she ruin Tad's evening because of the way she felt. She was determined to make an attempt, however difficult, to have fun. And she was more successful than she would have dreamed possible. She was constantly the center of a lively crowd when she was not being stolen away to dance. If she laughed a little too frequently or drank a little too much, well, no one seemed to notice.

No one except Boone. His sharp gaze twisted knots in her stomach every time she chanced to look at him.

Josh, a salesman from another branch office, was dancing with her, holding her closer than she would have liked, when a steely voice from over her shoulder demanded rather than asked, "Can I cut in?" A fiery thrill shot down her spine at the sound of those deep, masculine tones.

"Sure, R.B."

Leslie's heart pounded in her throat; startled green eyes met the hard blackness of his compelling gaze as Boone's arms slid possessively around her. She felt the hot pressure of his fingers against the naked flesh of her back, and a delicious shiver traced through her as she allowed her body to melt against his. Three glasses of wine on an empty stomach had gone to her head, and even though she knew she was playing with fire, she deliberately sought to arouse him, to make him ache for her as she ached for him.

Her lips were pressed against his stiff dress shirt; her

warm breath seeped through the fabric and made contact
with his own hot flesh.

"Have you been dancing with all the men like this?"
his hoarse voice demanded against her earlobe.

"No, only you," she murmured, twining her fingers
into the thickness of his raven hair that curled over the
edge of his starched collar.

She felt his lips in her hair, nuzzling the sensitive flesh
near her temple. She went strangely warm.

"Oh, Boone," she sighed.

"There ought to be a law against this," he murmured
huskily.

When the music stopped, they remained locked in one
another's arms for a long moment as though spellbound.
Neither were aware of Rose Mary watching them from
afar, a broad, complacent smile dimpling her plump features.

Tad came up to them and said, "Sorry to interrupt...."
An angry flush darkened Boone's face, hardening his expression. "I just wanted to tell Les that my brother called
me, and I've got to go now. Josh has agreed to drive
Leslie home tonight."

"You can tell Josh I'll drive her myself," Boone con-
tradicted in such a fierce tone that all the tenderness she'd
felt while dancing with him was destroyed.

Tad, sensing trouble, quickly excused himself.

"I'd rather go with Josh," Leslie inserted stiffly, afraid
of her own emotions and not trusting herself to be alone
with Boone.

"You don't have any choice," came Boone's firm reply as he tightened his grip about her waist.

Leslie was deeply offended by his high-handed manner.
"I said I'd rather..."

"You little fool!" Boone snapped angrily. "Josh has

been drinking. It's been snowing all day, and the roads are as slick as glass.''

"He looks all right to me," Leslie tossed defiantly and would have moved away had Boone's hard arms not imprisoned her.

To her stunned amazement he rasped, "Marnie died on a night like this. I let her go—in spite of the fact that she'd been drinking."

Boone drove slowly, skillfully maneuvering the Cadillac through the thickly falling snow. The roads were packed with snow; deep drifts were piled on either side of the highway. Boone had insisted on driving Josh home himself, thus, the roads they followed were unfamiliar to her.

When he headed into the garage of a three-story mansion nestled in a thick grove of spruce, she said, "Boone, this isn't where I live..."

"I know. It's where I live."

Before she could reply, he was already outside, going around the front of the car to let her out. "You didn't even ask me if I wanted to come here."

"I knew you'd say no."

She let him help her from the car. What was the use of opposing him at this point? It was obvious he had no intention of taking no for an answer.

The interior of his home was as beautiful as the exterior. Sheets of glass spanned one wall. In a glance she saw how completely masculine his house was—unfinished slanting cedar on the walls, burnished gold carpeting, heavy leather furnishings, Indian paintings. Nowhere was there evidence of a woman's softening touch. The house was as completely masculine as the man himself.

He helped her from her coat. Where his fingers grazed the naked warmth of her flesh, excitement tingled faintly.

"That's some dress," he said, his gaze roaming over her from head to toe, taking in the feathery curls falling lightly over her shoulders, her brilliant eyes, their color intensified because of the heavier evening makeup she was wearing. But his gaze continued downward to the firm swell of her breasts visible above the decolletage neckline of her gown.

A becoming blush heightened her color. Just the way he looked at her made her feel slightly breathless. Then the carved planes of his face hardened.

"What were you trying to do?" he drawled thickly. "Move in on Tad while Lucy's gone? Or did you just want to make a spectacle of yourself? You had ever man at the party drooling after you."

"How dare you accuse me of trying to come between Tad and Lucy! And as for this dress—why every other woman there was wearing a cocktail gown." Leslie hurled the statement at him indignantly, stung by his harsh words.

"You hardly looked like every other woman there. Every man at the party outdid himself on your behalf."

"Who are you to be talking? You spent most of your time with that beautiful redhead. Why, she's young enough to be your daughter!"

"She practically is," he returned, smiling suddenly as his mood unaccountably lightened. "She's my niece. Were you jealous?"

Painfully.... But that was scarcely an admission she relished making. Nevertheless, his intent gaze made a lie impossible. "I—I..." She looked away, thoroughly disconcerted. "Oh, you're impossibly conceited!"

"I'm willing to admit I didn't like seeing you with Tad." His voice, low and well-modulated, wrapped her in its warmth.

The thought that he actually might care for her more deeply than he chose to admit and was extremely jealous penetrated her senses with the force of lightning, melting away her anger. Vainly she tried to fight off the emotions that he would so effortlessly arouse by adopting a kind manner. She had to keep her wits about her for she was very alone with a man who'd made his intentions terribly clear on more than one occasion.

"He just drove me to the party," she replied coolly. "Tad and I are friends. That's all."

Boone had moved behind the bar and was splashing expensive Scotch over an ice cube in a crystal glass. She watched as he opened the brand of diet cola she always drank at work for her.

"The other night you said that was something you wanted from a man—friendship," Boone persisted, lifting his black eyes to her face.

Her cheeks burned, and she quickly tore her gaze from his. How could his mere look be so disturbing?

"I suppose it is—one of the things," she said tightly.

He moved toward her, his every step one of fluid grace. Again she was intensely aware of his sexuality, of his potent virility. His nearness was so intoxicating that it swept away her fear of the danger.

Her fingers wrapped gratefully around the cola he offered her. For no reason at all her throat suddenly felt very dry. "Thank you," she murmured softly.

His raven hair glinted in the overhead track lights like polished ebony. His dark features seemed to be carved from teak. Her gaze drifted to the sensual curve of his mouth and lingered for a breathless instant. He was unnervingly handsome! She struggled to fight back the erotic memories of that first night when he'd made love to her.

Black fire flamed in his eyes, and she quickly swept

her lashes downward, not wishing to read their sensual message. But not before a hot blush painted her cheeks a telling crimson. It was obvious that he was remembering that first night too.

"It's been hell these last two days—without you, Leslie," Boone muttered hoarsely.

"Boone, if you brought me up here because you thought I'd change my mind, you were wrong. I may have had several glasses of wine too many, but I still know what I'm doing."

"I brought you up here because you were so stunningly beautiful tonight I wanted a few minutes alone with you." His gaze touched the golden tumble of hair, the exquisite loveliness of her face.

As her eyes met his, she felt the will to resist him draining from her. If he didn't take her home soon, she would be lost.

"Boone..."

"Leslie, I want you enough to try things your way."

Leslie sensed that this was the closest he'd ever come to humbling himself for a woman.

His voice was low and husky, his sincere dark gaze caressed her, eliciting a multitude of confusing emotions. A wild feeling of elation rippled through her. There was an odd catch in her throat as she looked at him. Then she was immediately besieged by doubts. Was this a play to salve her conscience and thereby get her into his bed? No, she knew him well enough from having worked with him that he meant what he said.

"What do you have in mind?" she asked tremulously.

"Could I take you skiing tomorrow? On Saturday the slopes are crowded and with the sub-zero weather and all the clothes we'll be wearing, that should make it easier to keep things on a…'friendship' basis.'' She caught the bite of harsh self-mockery in his voice.

"You know I don't know how to ski very well,'' she replied humbly.

His intent gaze ignited a liquid fire that flowed through her arteries. ''All you need is practice,'' he said suavely. ''I could give you a few pointers. Besides skiing isn't what matters—it's our getting to know each other that's important.''

''Boone…I…'' She was suddenly at a loss for words.

''I want you with me Leslie—even without sex.'' He strode to the television set and flicked it on. ''How do you feel about a late movie?''

''W-why that would be nice,'' she said, totally surprised at this suggestion. When she would have sat in a nearby chair, his arm came around her waist.

''Sit with me on the couch.'' His heady male smile made her heart turn a somersault. His coal-black eyes lingered on her moist lips. The sensual impact of his nearness made Leslie try to pull away, but he caught her to him. ''Don't be afraid.''

''I'm not afraid,'' she denied, but even her words trembled.

''Liar,'' he whispered gently into her hair. ''But you're not the only one.…'' His statement caused her to remember his fierce determination not to ever let any woman close to him again.

He led her to the couch and pulled her down beside him. His arms wrapped around her, and he held her close against him as if she were very dear. But his embrace was affectionate, not sexual.

The nerve ends in her shoulder tingled where it came into contact with his body. Then she forced herself to concentrate on the movie, a comedy, and soon her shaky giggle blended with his own rich, deep laughter.

An hour passed. He held her snuggled against him on the soft couch, his dark brown hands interlocked with her smaller ones. There was an easiness between them that had never existed before.

When the movie was over, Boone switched it off and freshened their drinks. "Perhaps it's time we got to know each other as people," he said, a faintly sardonic expression hardening his chiseled features. "Tell me about yourself."

"Well, you already know that I'm just another 'desperate' divorcee with a child to raise...."

She told him of her childhood and school days, revealing everything except the details about her marriage and divorce. "And now," she said, "it's your turn to tell me about yourself."

"There's not much to tell."

"You're older than I am, and I talked for fifteen minutes," she teased.

"It's the same old story of poor boy makes good."

"No two stories like that are ever the same," she said gently. "Yours is uniquely your own."

"My dad died when I was just a kid. After that I always worked—summers, holidays, even during school. You name it, and I've done it. All my life I wanted to be a doctor, and my last year in college I was lucky enough to get a scholarship. I worked constantly at odd jobs because the scholarship money wasn't nearly enough. Mother had to have several operations during that time, and we never had enough money. We both went without so that I could stay in school. And then I started dating Marnie again. We'd gone together in high school, but this was different..." A shuttered look darkened his features as he remembered.

A tiny twinge of jealousy ripped through Leslie that was quickly followed by guilt.

Boone's deep voice continued. "I spent so much time with Marnie my grades fell. I never had enough time to study because she and I were constantly together. It wasn't really her fault. When she got pregnant, I dropped out of school and married her. A month later she lost the child, and although for a few years I talked of going back to school, I never did. I had a wife to support, and Mother needed my help. So I determined to make it any way I could. Somehow I ended up in construction and real estate. You can guess the rest."

Leslie caught the thread of fierce determination and struggle that lay behind his success. He was a man who stopped at nothing to get what he wanted, a man who could turn failure into success.

He'd told her about himself, but she was sure that there were great gaps in his story. She was no closer to understanding the reasons that lay behind his distrust and bitterness toward women than ever.

Boone did not touch her in any intimate manner during the evening until he drove her home and they stood beneath a shower of golden light in front of the half-opened door to her condominium. Ignoring the tiny quiver of anticipation that shivered through her, she would have darted inside, but he caught her wrist and gently drew her into the hard warmth of his arms.

"Surely friendship isn't all you want from our relationship, Leslie," he mocked, a bold, sardonic grin slashing his features.

"No, Boone, it isn't," she admitted hesitantly.

She felt especially close to him this evening because

he'd made such an effort to relate to her as a person instead of someone he merely desired. Even before he leaned down she was stretching onto her tiptoe to meet the deliberate descent of his mouth. The instant flesh met flesh, a moan of pure pleasure escaped her lips.

At the touch of his mouth—hard and firm, yet featherlight against her own—a warm wonderful feeling spread through her, making her pulse trip crazily, making her draw short, irregular breaths. Her fingers, spread like open fans against his shoulders, twined around his neck. Her mouth parted at the insistent pressure of his, and his tongue slid inside and explored the moist, intimate depths of her mouth. She felt his fingers trace a tingly path down the slender column of her throat to the place where her breast swelled above her low-cut gown. Yet he did not hold her close to his body.

With consummate skill, his lips continued their slow method of arousal until Leslie's need grew into a terrible ache that only he could cure. In everything he did—every movement, every gesture—it was apparent that he was experienced at the art of making love. Even though he vowed he was bitter toward all women, he was an expert when it came to sexual intimacy with them. But Leslie was too consumed with wondrous, passionate feelings to ponder how a man who could give a woman so much pleasure could swear he hated them.

As always his virile magnetism affected her. Hot molten desire surged through her. She felt weak with longing, aflame with wanton, carnal impulses; the thought of him going home to his own bed, of both of them sleeping alone struck her as distinctly depressing. She clung to him, desperately seeking to prolong this treasured moment of shared closeness.

His breathing was as harshly uneven as her own. She

felt the pounding of his heart beneath her lips when she kissed the warm flesh of his throat. They were both sensually hungry for more than mere kisses could satisfy. His mouth tugged at the bottom of her earlobe, and she shuddered. She had only to invite him to stay....

Yet she knew that she couldn't sleep with him again when there was no commitment between them, when he thought no more of her than any woman he would use for his pleasure.

He was the first to pull away. A tiny cry was wrenched from her throat. But as she gazed up into the dark handsomeness of his face, the words, "Don't go," didn't come.

A callused finger reached up and gently fondled a mussed strand of gold that had fallen into her eyes. Her eyes met his own, which were deep and dark with desire. Her lips still trembled from his kisses.

"Good night, Leslie." His low voice was rough with controlled emotion. "I hope you get more sleep than I will."

"I'll see you in the morning, Boone," she said huskily.

As she closed the door softly behind her, a tiny rapturous smile illuminated her features until she was truly beautiful as she anticipated the day that was to follow.

Seven

A tiny quiver of disappointment caught in Leslie's throat as Boone's words penetrated her senses.

"I hope you don't mind if Dina and Tess go with us?" Easily he slid Leslie's skis onto his broad shoulders. His white smile made her go weak with happiness, dispelling her doubts.

"Dina and Tess?" she questioned tentatively.

"Those two beautiful redheads I was paying so much attention to last night." A devilish glint danced in his black eyes.

His deep chuckle intensified her warm happy feeling. It was so good to be with him again that she didn't care if she had to share him with his sister and niece.

As soon as they reached the Cadillac, Boone helped Leslie into the plush leather interior of the front seat and made the necessary introductions. Dina was the elder of the two; Tess was the vivacious beauty Leslie had first seen him with. Dina was friendly at once, but Tess barely managed a sulky smile in Leslie's direction.

Snow crunched under the tires as Boone maneuvered the car onto the main road. As they sped to the ski slope, conversation flowed around Leslie. Boone was a different person with his sister and niece. He was no longer dark and forbidding. Leslie marveled at how changed he was, and as she listened to the light banter between brother and sister, she learned things about him she could never have learned otherwise. Dina was as chatty and open as he could be secretive. Tess, however, entered the conversation only when courtesy compelled her to, and Leslie grew apprehensive that she might somehow be the cause of Tess's bad mood.

Conditions for skiing were perfect. The deep snow-packed slopes were topped with ten inches of soft powder. Boone chose Leslie to be his partner riding the lifts, and as they were whisked over the snow-covered trees, they looked in wonder at the silent, agile dance of the skiers as they whisked by beneath them.

The day was gloriously beautiful. Or perhaps Leslie only thought so because she was with Boone and for once there was a rare sense of harmony between them. Deep blue skies against gleaming white mountains stretched into the distance for as far as they could see. The frigid air stung her cheeks, and she snuggled close to Boone.

Boone pointed toward a ragged mountain. "That's Snowpeak over there. This spring I'll begin developing it into another ski area. We'll start by clearing some runs and building the lifts as well as a base lodge and a second lodge halfway up the mountain."

"Sounds exciting," Leslie murmured contentedly, reveling in the joy of simply being with him.

"I've got a lot of my own money tied up in that project," he continued.

"But are there enough hotel rooms and condos in Winter Park to house more skiers?" she asked.

"No. But then that's the kind of problem a builder likes." His bold smile devastated her senses, and for a moment she completely lost track of what he was saying and concentrated on the sensual line of his lips. "For the past week I've been with my architect going over plans for several more condominium units."

Boone continued talking and Leslie listened. She was aware of his arm wrapped lightly around her possessively, of his body pressed close to hers. This time of sharing, of talking to one another was intensely precious to her. She could almost forget the hostility that had come between them. For Boone, being with her, telling her of his plans and his dreams, was stimulating. He hadn't enjoyed himself so much in months, no, years.

The hours passed too swiftly because they were both so happy. The day was one of deep contentment for both of them. Leslie found herself enjoying riding the lifts with Boone far more than she did the sport of skiing itself; only then did she have him all to herself.

It was nearly four o'clock. Leslie's cheeks were bright from the cold. Her fingers felt numb in her thick gloves, and she clapped them together as one of her instructors had advised to improve the circulation. Leslie, Boone, and the two redheads were at the top of the mountain when Dina said to Boone, "Tess said she'd ski down with Leslie if you wanted to race me down a couple of Black Slopes."

Boone's eyes flashed with enthusiasm, and Leslie knew that he wanted to accept his sister's challenge to go down the Black Slopes, which were the expert runs. They'd

grown up skiing the mountains, and they both relished the
thought of a quick run to the bottom.

"Go ahead, Boone," Leslie said softly. "I'll be all
right."

"You're sure?"

The genuine concern for her that lit the black depths of
his eyes made the sacrifice of his company more than
worth it.

"Yes."

Her face was radiant as he bent his lips and brushed
her forehead gently. Both were unaware of Tess observing
them, hostility etched into the downward droop of her
mouth and a deep frown ravaging the loveliness of her
young face.

From behind them came Dina's exuberant, "On your
mark, get set, go!"

Reluctantly, Boone dragged his lips from Leslie's
smooth skin. But his eyes lingered caressingly on her for
a long moment.

"You'd better hurry," she chided gently, not wanting
him to go at all.

"I always give her a minute head start," he explained.
"This time I'll give her two minutes."

But all too soon two minutes were up and he was gone.
She was left alone on the vast stillness of the mountain
with only the sullen Tess for company.

Leslie turned and saw that Tess was glaring at her with
a look of utter hatred contorting her expression. Leslie
asked the younger girl lightly, in a vain attempt to dispel
her dark mood, "Do you want to go first, or should I?"

"Suit yourself," Tess said in a seething, low tone.

Such blatant hostility could not be ignored.

"Have I done something to make you mad?" Leslie

asked gently. "If I did, I'm sorry. Maybe if you'd tell me…"

Hazel eyes glimmered darkly with rage. "You're just like *she* was!" Tess lashed savagely, spoiling the beautiful moment that had passed between Leslie and Boone a moment before. The harshness of her tone shattered Leslie's euphoria completely. "You may have Boone fooled. But not me! I can see right through you. You don't care for him—not really!"

"I do care for him. I'm sorry if…"

"Well, he doesn't care for you! And he never will! It's her! Only her! He wants her, but she's dead! He's only interested in you because you remind him of her! Can't you see that?"

All the blood seemed to drain out of Leslie's features as though the blow she had received were physical rather than emotional. Pain clogged her throat. She could scarcely speak. "That's not true!" she managed in a tight whisper. "That's not true!" But even as she denied it, the doubt had been solidly planted in her heart.

Tess turned then and said, "I suppose you should ski first. I promised Boone I'd see you down the mountain."

Woodenly Leslie turned her skis so that they pointed straight downward. The tears that formed in her eyes but did not fall blurred her vision, but she sped down the mountain recklessly.

She was nearly to the bottom before she recovered herself at all. Only when she saw Boone scanning the mountain side for her did she slow her pace. He would be upset if she took risks; if she fell he would blame himself for not having skied with her.

Leslie paused on the sheer side of the slope. Boone would think she was resting. But she was really trying to compose herself before she skied to the bottom so that

she could face him without him immediately realizing that
something was wrong.

Tess skied past her, her long skis slicing into the snow
like sabers, a shower of powder flying on either side of
her graceful form. Leslie watched her without malice even
though Tess had deliberately lashed out at her to upset
her.

The younger girl clearly loved Boone very much, and
everything she'd said had been to protect him. All the
females in his life certainly took it upon themselves to
look after Boone's best interests, Leslie thought ruefully.
First Rose Mary had hired her because she looked like
Marnie. And now his niece had attacked her for the very
same reason.

Leslie wasn't ready to ask Boone what the basis of his
attraction was for her. The bond between them was too
tenuous. Leslie knew too well that Marnie was a dangerous subject. The first day he'd met Leslie he'd warned
her not to ask him about his wife, that she belonged to a
closed chapter in his life. Later when he'd been making
love to her, he'd called out her name. What did it all
mean? Was she really only a look-alike substitute for his
wife? Or was he beginning to care something for her?

But these questions would have to remain unanswered
for the time being because she sensed it was more important to develop her own relationship with Boone. No
matter how desperately she wanted answers, she would
have to wait until the time was right.

Boone and Leslie were in the warming house drinking
hot tea. Dina and Tess had excused themselves to go
down to the locker room.

"Something's wrong," Boone said astutely, his knowing eyes examining her pale features. "What happened up there on the mountain? Did you get scared?"

"You might say that," she hedged. "But I'm all right. I'm just a little cold. That's all."

"Here." Boone nestled her more closely against his side. "Drink your tea."

When Tess and Dina returned, Leslie caught the flicker of irritation that flared in Tess's tawny eyes at the sight of Boone holding her tightly, and all her doubts returned, obliterating whatever joy his nearness produced.

That night when he invited her out to dinner she pleaded a headache, and he reluctantly acceded to her wishes. Then she was alone with only her doubts for company.

Boone was away for the whole of the next day, and her only contact with him was a phone call late in the afternoon at which time he invited her for dinner the following evening. Readily she accepted.

The doorbell buzzed twice the next night before Leslie rushed, hair brush in hand, to answer it. Breathlessly she flung the door open wide, and her face instantly lit with pleasure at the sight of Boone towering before her, strong and masterful as though he were a granite statue instead of the vital man he was. Then he smiled down at her, and as always she felt devastated by his sensual power, by the sheer force of his male charisma.

"I'm sorry it took me so long to get to the door," she said.

"It was worth the wait," his deep voice admired. His gaze roamed her curves lusciously displayed in clinging red silk. The warmth in his eyes took her breath away and caused her heart to flutter wildly. When he deliberately sought to charm, he was overpoweringly able to do so.

"I'm not quite ready," she said, stating the obvious. Her stockinged feet were bare of shoes. Her golden hair tumbled in becoming disorder. "Come inside while I finish dressing."

"You don't have to on my account," his amused voice teased.

Something in his tone made her knees go traitorously weak. Her stomach felt jittery.

"Let me help you with that zipper," he offered.

She'd forgotten completely that she'd only managed to zip it halfway up her back. Before she could slip from his grasp, she quivered with shock as his cold hands brushed the warmth of her flesh.

"Boone," she struggled, wanting to escape him for fear he would sense how much even his casual touch could arouse her, "your hands are cold..."

"You know what they say. 'Cold hands, warm heart,'" his low, husky voice mocked. "And tonight that old cliche definitely rings true." She tried to ignore the disturbing effect his words had on her, but was not wholly successful. "Leslie, it's only been a day, but I've missed you," he murmured.

His hands moved through her hair in a caressing motion, lifting up the heavy, billowing tresses. She felt the hot, moist pressure of his lips graze a tender place at the nape of her neck, and she shivered. "I missed you too, Boone."

If they were going to make it to dinner they'd better leave quickly, she thought, sensing that he had an intense desire for her tonight and realizing that she felt the same way. Her only chance was to remove herself to her room and get ready, thereby escaping the magnetic range of his personality that overpowered her will to resist him.

Twisting free from his embrace, she asked, "Could I fix you a drink?"

"If I can't have you, I guess I'll have to settle for one." His warm gaze and sexual innuendo made her heart beat more quickly. "But I can make it myself. You go on and get ready before I forget why in the hell we're going out...when staying in makes so much more sense...."

Boone drove her to a French restaurant tucked against the side of a mountain that commanded a magnificent view of a moonlit valley. After the haughty maitre d' seated them beside a window that looked out upon the wintry fairyland beneath, he struck a match, and candlelight glimmered from a crystal and silver hurricane lamp in the center of an elegantly set table. Fine bone China shone on white linen.

Leslie was unaware of how lovely she was. In the soft golden light her hair shone like cornsilk; her smooth skin glowed. She felt the warmth of Boone's gaze drifting over her, intimately touching the straight, delicate bone structure of her nose, the moistened curve of her lips, and the pale column of her throat. For a long moment his eyes lingered where the upward tilt of her breasts thrust against the red silk.

A rush of warmth brought a rosy hue to Leslie's cheeks as a stiff cardboard menu was placed between her trembling fingers, and she dragged her eyes from his own boldly dark ones. Vainly she tried to concentrate on the menu in an attempt to still the confusing sensations his look aroused.

He was seducing her with his eyes, yet little did she know how she affected him. The drowsy, voluptuous, yielding expression on her own face inflamed him. The gentle smile of her full red lips invited him to plunder their softness. Her involuntary blush told him that she read the sensual message of his own magnificent dark eyes and responded to it.

He reached across the table and took her slender hand in his own large dark one. His calloused thumb stroked her soft palm in a slow, circular motion that was acutely disturbing. Her eyes met his for an endless moment, and the blazing passion she saw in their ebony depths jolted through her, kindling a similar emotion in her that she sought desperately to suppress.

Wildfire raced through her arteries as a primitive pagan song quickened the tempo of her pulse. Wanton memories of the rapture she'd known when he'd made love to her assailed her. She wanted him again—desperately. Her hand squeezed his very tightly in an unconscious effort to fuse her flesh to his.

Then, quickly as though burned, she drew her hand from his to escape the heady erotic stimulation of his flesh moving in a slow, stroking motion against hers.

Nervously, she bit her bottom lip, hoping the pain of this action would bring her to her senses.

"You shouldn't have brought me to such an expensive place," she said unsteadily, trying to break the sexual tension between them.

"How do you know it's expensive?" His low tone flowed around her like sensual music. "There aren't any prices on the menu." There was a smile in his deep voice. Again his heated gaze slid over her, causing a strange warmth to course through her.

Violins began to play softly, and the romantic melody only served to increase Leslie's vulnerability to the potent charisma of the virile man who sat opposite her.

Dinner was superb; onion soup gratinée, watercress and tomato salad, sliced filet mignon with marrow and truffles, ratatouille, and macedoine of fruit. Every luscious bite seemed to melt in Leslie's mouth, and she forced herself to eat slowly, to prolong the meal.

"You've toyed with that last strawberry for at least fifteen minutes," Boone drawled pleasantly as he sipped his brandy from a crystal liqueur glass. "If you aren't going to eat it, feed it to me."

There was something almost sexual in his husky invitation. Her long lashes fluttered in confusion as she stabbed the strawberry with her fork and proceeded to do as he had asked. All evening she'd avoided looking at him, but now her gaze swept hesitantly to the bronzed handsomeness of his face. For no reason at all her heart beat in an oddly pained rush and her fingers trembled. Carefully she inserted the berry between his lips. When she removed the fork, he munched into the juicy fruit.

"That was good." His black eyes held hers. "Your hand is shaking," he said at last. "Why?"

"B-because..."

"Cold?" he murmured.

"A little," she lied.

"Then why don't we dance." Already he was rising from his chair and coming around to help her from hers.

His arms wrapped around her, and he drew her body close against his. The swaying motion of their bodies undulating rhythmically together to the soft sensuous violin music stimulated every sense in her body. She was aware of every place he touched her; of the light pressure of his hand at her waist, of his other hand curling her fingers against the hard warmth of his shoulder, of his lips buried in the masses of her hair, of his breath fanning the wayward tendrils of gold at her temple.

All the strength drained from her, and she melted against him, clinging to his hard strength for support. His every movement was expert, and as they slowly swirled in one another's arms all of her remaining will to resist him flowed out of her.

Being with him was the most natural thing in the world; it seemed to her that her loving him was preordained.

From somewhere in the depths of Leslie's mind, Tess's words returned to haunt her. "He doesn't care for you...and he never will! It's her! Only her! He wants her, but she's dead! He's only interested in you because you remind him of her...."

Perhaps that was true in the beginning, another part of her cried silently. Perhaps it was still true. But she couldn't blame him for whatever he felt. If she didn't—perhaps in time it would be her that he really wanted instead of Marnie. Leslie knew that she was rationalizing, but she couldn't stop herself. She loved him, and she wanted him so desperately that she no longer had the self-control to follow the dictates of her rational mind.

They danced again and again. Their bodies flowed so smoothly together it seemed they were made for each other. The hours of the evening wore quickly away, and it was late when Boone suggested that they leave.

This time when Boone turned off the highway Leslie recognized the road that twisted up the mountain drive to Boone's house.

"Boone, I really think that you should take me home," she forced herself to insist.

"That's exactly what I'm doing," he said, deliberately misunderstanding her. The sensual line of his mouth quirked in tender amusement, as his hand moved to caress her shoulder.

"That's not what I meant," she whispered.

"I know. But it's what you want," came his husky reply. "Admit it."

It was all too true. "I don't seem to be able to be smart

where you're concerned," she said softly. "I went to bed with you the first night I met you. I should have learned my lesson."

"I'm tired of smart women," he said quietly, his low voice strangely cool as he removed his hands from her shoulders.

She'd said something wrong, but she didn't know what. Had she somehow reminded him of Marnie? At the mere thought of his wife her chest ached as though a tight band had been drawn around it.

"You know I'm right," she insisted, testing. "I'm not just talking about us. If a woman goes to bed with a man right off, he can't ever really care for her. She should wait..."

"Until she's got her hooks so deeply into him, he can't get away," Boone muttered savagely more to himself than to her. Then he drew a deep breath as though to control his anger.

Dimly she was aware of Boone flicking the button on his visor and of the garage door opening. Abruptly Boone braked the car and pressed the button once more. The door shut silently, and Boone switched off the ignition. They were wrapped in total darkness. She shifted uneasily, but he caught her against his hard strength.

"I'm too old for all those games, Leslie. Maybe they make sense for teenagers. I hope so, because all those rules drive you crazy as hell when you're young. All I know is I want you more than I've ever wanted any woman. Why should I do without you when I know you feel the same way?"

He'd said he wanted her more than he'd ever wanted any woman. For a brief moment happiness filled her. Did he include Marnie? And then her joy faded as doubt reasserted itself. Or was it just that he thought of her as Marnie—in a physical sense?

"Things aren't that simple, Boone," she said gently.

"They are if you'll let them be."

"But, I can't..."

"Sure you can. I'm going to show you how... tonight...."

"Boone..." she protested weakly.

She felt the imprint of his finger against her lips, gently shushing her.

"You talk too much. You know that don't you?" he whispered into the soft swirling darkness as he pulled her into his arms.

She was about to answer his question when his mouth closed over hers, forcing back her reply as he explored the velvety softness of her lips. She felt limp as a strange yielding weakness enveloped her and yet more alive than she'd ever felt before. Every sense seemed more acute.

She felt the roughness of his cheek graze her own, satiny smooth face. He tasted deliciously of brandy. She caught the scent of him—his heady, clean, male fragrance mingling with his aftershave. After a long kiss that made her reel in a world that contained nothing except whirling darkness and her fevered awareness of him, he drew his lips away. He inhaled a deep, long breath.

She was so hot, she felt she glowed. Her voluptuous curves trembled against the lean, hard contours of his body.

"Kiss me again," she begged softly.

Lightly his lips gave her nose a chaste peck, and she emitted a tiny, disappointed sigh.

"Not like that," she murmured huskily.

"If we're going to stop," he said, "it'd better be now. Do you still want me to drive you home?"

Slowly, all evening he'd sought to awaken her to the sensual needs she fought to conquer. Desire burned through her as hot as a raging conflagration.

"Love me...." she surrendered weakly.

Eight

"Love me...." Leslie's softly spoken words lingered in the black silence.

"I thought you've never ask," Boone murmured silkily, gathering her warm body into his arms.

Dreamily she let him lead her inside up a circular staircase to a vast, utterly masculine bedroom. She scarcely noticed the brass kingsize bed, the tans and golds, the leather furniture. A great brown bear rug stretched across the dark wood floor, and she saw it just as he pulled her down onto the thick fur.

He lay sprawled across the fur beneath her while she sat beside him, her hips lightly touching his waist. From beneath the hooded sweep of thick lashes she stared deeply into the shimmering darkness of his eyes.

He reached up and traced a finger from her chin over her soft throat to the edge of her red silk dress. Long brown fingers played with the tiny silken bow at her neckline, loosening it so that her dress fell open, exposing creamy breasts encased in delicate white lace. He tugged at the string once more, and the edge of her dress fell a tantalizing inch further, baring her shoulder. He ran a roughened fingertip across the shadowed hollow between the fullness of her breasts. At his touch she sighed, shivering. She was drowning in a sea of exquisite sensations. As he pulled her down against him, she abandoned herself to the extravagant, languorous sexual pleasure only he could give her.

Slowly their clothes were removed, and as she lay on top of him his eyes skimmed her satiny body downward over her breasts that gently rose and fell with each breath, the flat smoothness of her belly, down to her well-turned hips. He thought her unutterably lovely. Her yellow hair, casually disheveled from his loveplay, gleamed like liquid gold in the pale light.

She stared down at him lovingly. He lay sprawled with indolent grace across the rug. Her arms wrapped around him, and he pulled her down against his great hard-muscled chest and hungrily plundered her lips. Then he caressed her body with his warm hands, trailing his fingers down the curve of her spine and over her hips. Lightly he explored her thighs and the sensitive flesh between her legs.

His intimate touch, his wild kisses, his possessive words of endearment muttered hoarsely against her ear drew her deeper and deeper into a hot, wondrous world of desire. Her emerald eyes glowed with fire; her skin burned with feverish need.

When he pulled her even closer and pressed his hard lean body against the yielding softness of her own, she cried out, a gentle, muted cry of ecstasy. A faint tremor of emotion rippled through her like a tiny wave. This new feeling grew, surging through her, until she surrendered herself to him completely, clinging to him with a desperate need.

The fierce blaze of their love was like a splendid, soaring flame against an ink-black sky—brilliant and beautiful, primitive and wild.

After that they lay together for a long time, shuddering, and then they were still. A warm brown hand gently stroked through the golden disorder of her hair. He stared deeply into her eyes, and in that moment she believed that she meant more to him than he could say.

He made love to her again and again that night, wanting her to need him as he needed her, wanting her to cry out for him, demanding that she do so. Leslie gave herself to him with a total completeness that was even greater than the first night he'd possessed her. She loved him hopelessly, shamelessly, as he awakened her body again and again to new and wanton pleasures.

At last they fell asleep wrapped in one another's arms, the warmth of his breath against the softness of her breast, the gentle beat of her heart beneath his ear.

Outside it was gray dark when Boone's lips nuzzling against Leslie's throat awakened her.

A faint golden glow tinged the mountain top, hinting that it would soon be daylight.

Gently Boone's hand roamed over her belly. Drowsy yet from the long night of love, her emerald eyes opened slowly and lifted to his. She smiled a slow sweet smile, the smile of a woman sated from her lover's caresses, and he returned her smile with a tender one of his own.

The passionate tenderness of his gaze warmed her through. All the months of loneliness were washed away, and she felt that she had at last found a man with whom she could share her life, to whom she could give her heart and her soul. Without love, life had seemed unbearably empty. She hadn't realized until this moment of sharing, just how empty.

"Lazy bones," he gently teased. "We're going to have to get up if we're to get to work on time."

"Slave driver," she accused lightly, sitting up. The sheet fell away, exposing the voluptuous curve of creamy breasts for his keen, masculine appraisal.

His lips descended to kiss a nipple. Then he rose and strode before it was too late across the room to the bathroom. She heard his deep voice as he sang in the shower, and impulsively she scampered lightly across the cool oak floor and flung open the shower door.

"Mind if I join you?" Her impish smile illuminated her delicate features.

Dark, gleaming eyes roved over her. In answer, a bronzed arm wrapped around her narrow waist and pulled her inside. His hard male body crushed her against the steaming tiles as the warm spray of water flowed over them.

"Boone, my hair..." she protested softly.

His body moved against her, communicating his rising need.

"You should have thought about that before you came in here," he muttered fiercely. "To hell with your hair...."

Thus began the first day of a week of such glorious days and nights. Every free moment that they could steal away from the pressures of work, they spent together, reveling in the exquisite sensual pleasure each could give the other. Though Boone never told her he loved her, he showed her in a hundred small ways that he cared.

Twice when he had to drive into Denver he arranged

for her to go with him, as though he couldn't bear to be parted from her any longer than he had to be. When he couldn't take her with him, he called frequently.

Every afternoon they lunched together at some new and charmingly different restaurant. He took her ski touring all over Snowpeak, explaining all his plans for its development, sharing his dreams. Every day she sensed his trust in her growing a little more. But still he never told her about Marnie. Nor did he make any explanations for his bitterness toward women. Leslie knew he was still bitter, even though he tried very hard to conceal this from her.

She thought he was trying to find happiness in their present, that he deliberately sought to disregard their future because he was too cynical to believe that what they had together could last. For the time being, Leslie was content to do as he did.

Some part of Leslie warned her that she was foolish to take so much joy in the present without considering the future, without forcing a commitment. But she couldn't stop herself. She was committed irrevocably. She loved Boone and needed him too much to deny him anything. If he needed time, she would give him time. Whenever they were together her doubts would drain away, and she would wonder how anything could go wrong when they were so blissfully happy.

This euphoric state was abruptly shattered late one afternoon. Leslie was fumbling in her handbag for her keys outside her front door when the telephone inside her condominium began to ring. Thinking it might be Boone, she made a special effort to catch it. In the middle of the fifth ring, she breathlessly lifted it to her ear.

"Hello," she gasped.

"Hi, Les, it's me," came the all-too-familiar, Texas drawl of her "ex."

"Tim...." A chill swept through Leslie, and she clutched the receiver more tightly. She'd been so wrapped up in Boone she'd scarcely given Karen or her imminent return a thought.

"From that husky voice of yours it sounds like you were expecting someone else—someone more exciting," he jeered lightly.

A wave of irritation washed through her. He knew her too well.

"That's certainly none of your business anymore!" she snapped.

Ignoring her burst of temper his bland drawl continued. "I was just giving you a call to let you know about my plans for tomorrow, the thirty-first."

She'd completely forgotten about her date with Tim for New Year's Eve. Her throat was suddenly dry at the thought of having to explain this ticklish situation to Boone.

Tim's voice continued, and she had to force herself to concentrate on what he was saying. "Karen and I'll get to Denver around twelve. I have to rent a car. I guess that'll put us in Winter Park around three in the afternoon."

Fear rippled through her at the thought of telling Boone. What was she going to do? Instantly she knew she had no choice but to talk Tim out of going out with her.

"Tim, I—I can't go out with you...I'm dating someone else...someone special...."

"So am I."

"But he won't like...me going out with you."

"Look, you and I made a date two weeks go, and if you're set on breaking it at the last minute you can tell Karen yourself." There was a hard edge to his voice. "I'm going to put Karen on the phone right now."

"Tim..."

"Hi, Mommy."

"Karen, darling....I was just trying to tell your daddy that it's really silly for he and I to go out now that we're divorced."

The long hushed silence grew increasingly awkward between them.

"Karen, are you there?" Desperately, she pressed on. "Karen?" A bitter sob was clearly audible on the other end of the line, but the child made no other response. "Karen?"

"You promised," Karen finally choked. "You promised you'd be nice to Daddy. If you break your promise, I'll never believe anything you say again!"

With that the line went dead.

For a long moment Leslie sat in numbed silence. She couldn't go back on her word to Karen. That was very clear to her. She would have to find a way to make Boone understand.

Tomorrow night she had a date with her ex-husband! This unpleasant thought throbbed through her mind over and over again. How could she have forgotten that this was coming up? It was just that she'd been so absorbed in Boone that all the realities had blurred. All week when she'd forgotten appointments or slept through her alarm, she'd laughed indulgently at herself, knowing the reason for her absent-mindedness. But now she couldn't laugh.

She'd completely forgotten about New Year's Eve. Boone had never mentioned the evening, and she just hadn't thought....

She would have to tell him at once, even though she instinctively knew he wasn't going to like it. He was so fiercely possessive.

Glancing down at her delicate gold wristwatch, she realized she would be seeing him soon since he was planning to bring steaks over and cook them at her place at seven. Before Tim's call, she'd looked forward to the evening. But now a vague apprehension coursed through her as she tried to think of a way to tell him about Tim. The afternoon passed all too quickly.

That night when she opened her door to greet Boone, tension trembled through her as his possessive gaze roamed over her, lingering where her bare nipples pushed against sheer, cream silk. A bright flush tinged her cheeks as she remembered she was braless. She'd omitted the lacy undergarment at his own request. What had he whispered this morning in the privacy of his office? "Don't wear anything under your clothes tonight. We're not going out. It'll make it less trouble to undress you...."

He was looking at her warmly, as though she were his alone. How was she going to tell him she planned to spend the next evening with another man? The mere thought made her flinch.

As always the sheer male size of him overwhelmed her, and she gasped. He was breathtakingly handsome. A pale blue western shirt was stretched tautly across his massive chest; faded jeans molded his lean hips. Slung over one shoulder was his familiar sheepskin coat.

He extended a brown grocery sack which contained two steaks, and she took it, leaving him briefly at the door while she took them to the refrigerator. He was still lounging indolently against the door frame when she returned. She realized with a blush that he'd been watching her intently. His eyes traveled upward from the gentle swaying movements of her hips to the faint bouncing of her full breasts beneath sheer silk. His avid stare was all male. A tiny thrill that she, by simply walking across a room, could arouse him, overcame her.

Golden light glinted in his jet-dark hair as he stepped lithely inside. His black eyes roved over her, the heat of his gaze stripping away her clothes as his hands had so often done recently. She flushed again prettily. She noticed for the first time that his tanned features were more harshly drawn than of late, and she remembered he'd had an important meeting with the County Planning Commission about Snowpeak this afternoon. In spite of her anxiety, the mere sight of him stirred her pulse, and she slipped her hand into his.

"How did things go this afternoon?" she asked as he led her toward the bar.

"Bad." He ground out the word as he remembered. "I've got a real fight on my hands with the County Planning Commission over zoning."

"Oh…" She watched worriedly as he poured himself a double Scotch on the rocks and then mixed a shot of Scotch with water for her.

"I'll probably have to waste valuable time fighting, but I'm sure I'll get what I want in the end. I've been through this sort of thing before." He smiled grimly down at her, and her exquisite loveliness caused his expression to soften. "But I didn't come over here to worry about all that. What I want to do is relax—with you. I've had enough problems thrown at me for one day."

There was a fierce, dark element in his voice that struck a note of foreboding in her heart, increasing her anxiety as she remembered she had planned to tell him about Tim tonight.

Drawing her down onto the couch beside him, he set his drink on the end table. His black eyes slid over her. Then his lips quirked in a slanting smile that disturbed her emotional equilibrium.

"I know something that'll do me a lot more good than that drink," he murmured, gazing deeply into her eyes.

"What?"

"You." His low tone vibrated through her, tingling every nerve end in her body.

Before she could reply he lowered his dark face toward hers, and she felt the bruising pressure of his mouth, forcing her lips open so that his hot moist tongue could enter and probe. Moving one of his hands through her golden curls, he tilted her head backward so that he could more intimately explore the soft voluptuous curve of her lips. His other hand unbuttoned the tiny fastenings of her silk blouse, and as the blouse slid down her creamy shoulders, his hand moved over her bare breasts, cupping them before his mouth descended to ravish their love-swollen tips.

"Leslie, you drive me wild," he muttered thickly, his warm breath tickling the bare flesh beneath her breast. "I can't wait...tonight...I have to have you...now...."

The raw urgency in his deep voice shivered through her. Even though she sensed that her body was like the double Scotch he'd poured himself—a means of forgetting his problems—she ached for him.

His lips sent searing waves trembling through her nervous system until she was as wildly delirious for him as he was for her. As he nuzzled her, caressing the ripe fullness of her breast with his large hands, nibbling at a nipple with his mouth, a low, erotic fire began to burn in the depths of her being. She moaned softly, arching her body so that his raven head was buried in the opulent lushness of her breasts, so that he could continue to explore their soft fullness.

He shifted his body. The hard muscular strength of his arms imprisoned her against the massive wall of his chest. She was very aware of the blistering heat of his skin burning her through the coarse fabric of his western shirt. She felt the hard imprint of his male desire against her lower body.

The compelling force of his passion shuddered through him, as he held her tightly against him. She felt the wild pace of his heart; she heard the ragged intake of his breaths.

Leslie could do nothing but surrender to the powerful force of his desire. He needed her. He ached for her, and she reveled, she gloried in her feminine power over this virile man.

Need as fierce as his own drove her as her shaking fingers unsnapped his shirt, ripping it apart so that a strip of lean brown flesh was exposed. For a while her lips roamed over him. Then her slender hands explored lower, undressing him completely.

She wanted him to know how much she loved him, how completely she was his, how completely she wanted him to be hers. And there seemed to be only one way of showing him.

Slowly, in a mindless love trance, she lowered her lips to his skin and kissed the hard, warm flesh—tentatively at first and then more confidently, reveling in his complete and total masculinity, wanting to know him more intimately than she'd ever known any man. She caught the faint tang of his male scent and was inflamed by the intensity of his response to her.

He groaned beneath the steady onslaught of her exploring mouth. "Leslie..." he rasped her name. She felt his hands, heavy in the cascading masses of her golden hair as she made love to him in a way that she'd never done before. She told him with the exquisite wet softness of her lips what she couldn't yet tell him with words—that for her there would never be another man but him.

All that she did roused her own desire, but her need was not as important to her as his. And when he lost himself completely in wave upon wave of sensation, she at last lay upon him for a long time, savoring the wonder of her rapturous feeling for him. She felt the heat of his languid gaze scanning her face as though to memorize the loveliness of her features, and at the memory of what she had just done, she flushed bright crimson.

"Leslie..." His deep voice was hoarse from emotion; the mere sound of it was a sensual caress.

Then his mouth lowered to hers, crushing her unsuspecting lips in a kiss that obliterated all shame, everything save the hard feel of his mouth plundering hers. The force of his kiss wiped away all, leaving only an aching awareness of him. Liquid fire raced through her arteries as he ignited a passion that only he could quench.

He released her mouth only to pick her up in his arms, cradling her soft voluptuous curves against his hard, masculine body. Then with long strides, he carried her toward her bedroom.

"Boone, what are you doing?" she murmured weakly.

"I want to give you as much pleasure as you just gave me," he said gently into her flowing hair, as he lay her down between crisp, laundry-fresh sheets upon the vast softness of her bed.

Shyly, "You don't have to..."

Her words trailed away into a haze of sexual oblivion as his mouth sought her source of passion, and a tiny quiver of pulsating wildness shivered through her. She knew no shame at the intimacy of his embrace. She had no thought of resisting him, no will to do so. Instead she melted against the heat of his expert lips and hands that knew where and how to touch a woman to produce the most exquisite sensations until she was aching with de-

lightful torment. As his mouth brought her to new peaks
of shuddering ecstasy, she cried out his name again and
again, clutching him to her as she savored the wanton
splendor of passionate release.

Making love to her thus had aroused his own fierce
ardor once more. After allowing her a brief rest he made
love to her again—his touch, his lips stirring her once
more so that she was consumed with the wildly pagan
need for his love. Their fierce lovemaking bound them
together in love's wanton dance for a timeless time. When
it was over she lay on top of him, using his great warm
body as a bed, the vast expanse of his chest as her pillow.
His arms were draped over her in careless, familiar possession.

Much later, as they lay satiated in one another's arms,
she stirred drowsily and nipped the bottom edge of his
ear before murmuring into it. "You've been here for
hours, and we still haven't eaten those steaks."

"Somehow I haven't given that a thought." His lips
quirked in dry amusement.

"We're going to have to get up before too long and
cook."

"I'm not sure I have the strength," he teased gently,
drawing her closer.

"I'm not sure I do either," she whispered, nibbling at
his earlobe again.

"And I don't have the strength for that either," he
smiled.

But she did not heed him. Instead her lips continued
their seductive exploration, and in a very short time she
proved him wrong.

"Vixen..." The words was a husky endearment, lingering on his lips as his black gaze caressed her. "You're

the only good thing that happened today."

"Thank you," she returned softly.

"You never did tell me about your afternoon," he murmured. "Was it as bad as mine?"

The unexpected question caused her to remember what had happened, and the memory of Tim's phone call jolted through her. She blanched slightly.

"Something wrong?" he asked, noting that she'd suddenly gone pale.

The drowsy passionate languor in his eyes matched her own feelings of a moment before. If she told him about Tim now, the mood would be radically changed.

Still now was the time to tell him about Tim, she told herself wildly. But as she stared into his deep dark eyes, the words wouldn't come. She rationalized her desire to procrastinate by telling herself he'd had such a hard day she couldn't burden him with this...just yet. Not now, when he'd finally managed to put the cares of the day behind him. Besides she knew telling him would spoil the marvelous spell their lovemaking had cast over them. And she couldn't bear to do that.

But as she gazed into the blackened depths of his eyes, she quivered. She saw the unrelenting hardness and strength in his implacable features, and she remembered when he'd been cold and hard to her. She couldn't bear it if he turned against her again. What if he did that when she told him?

How was she ever going to summon the courage to tell him? When? A tiny pulsebeat pounded in her head. She knew that it had to be soon.

After dinner...she promised herself desperately. She would tell him after dinner. She would procrastinate until after he'd eaten.

Boone lifted the last bite of steak to his lips, and Leslie watched with an utterly feminine satisfaction that this man had devoured with such relish the meal she had prepared for him.

When he finished eating he said, "I should have asked you about this sooner, but to tell you the truth I've been so preoccupied both with Snowpeak and with...you," his husky voice wrapped her with a sensual warmth that made her heart flutter happily, "that I completely forgot about New Year's Eve until Rose Mary reminded me that Yvonne, my cousin, was coming down and that we all ought to go somewhere. Anyway, this afternoon I bought tickets for the dance at the Devil's Brand Ranch."

This announcement was as unexpected as it was upsetting. A tiny quiver of dread began to pound in Leslie's throat. Suddenly her throat felt dry and parched as though she were dying of thirst in a desert. Inadvertently she lifted her wineglass and drained it.

"Is something wrong, Leslie? You're as white as a sheet!" His black, intent gaze bored through her.

"Boone...I..."

"What is it?"

"Karen's coming home tomorrow. I..."

"I'd forgotten about that. But, if you'd like, we could include her in our plans. The dance is a family affair and they have activities for children; however, if you'd prefer for the three of us to spend a quiet evening together, I can return the tickets. Mother would understand."

"Boone, I can't go out with you." Her tongue felt like a huge dry thing that she could scarcely move between her lips.

A new hardness shone in his dark gaze that terrified her. But when he spoke, his voice betrayed no emotion. "Why not?" he asked.

"B-because Tim's coming too," she said softly.

"What does that have to do with us?" There was a vague coldness in his deep tone that chilled her.

"N-nothing...except..." She broke off. Why was he making this so difficult?

"Except what?" he demanded.

"I made a foolish promise..."

"Go on..."

She could no longer meet his level gaze.

"To go out with him."

His expression darkened, the sudden blazing passion in his eyes searing her heart with an odd pain. Vaguely she was aware of the fierce pressure of his fingers gripping her shoulders. She felt herself floundering helplessly like a swimmer washed overboard in the furious storm of his wrath.

"What?" His single word thundered through her.

"I'm going out with Tim tomorrow night," she said desperately. The dark shuttered look that she remembered so well and hated masked all of his emotion. "I don't want to. I don't! Oh, please! Boone! Don't look at me like that! Don't shut me out!"

But even as she begged him to believe her, he shrugged her from him and strode toward the glass door that opened onto her balcony. He stared broodingly out onto the glistening snowy landscape.

Quickly she followed him, but when she reached out to him, he said curtly, "Stay away from me...Leslie. The last thing I want right now is for you to touch me."

She heard the coldness in his voice that told her more clearly than anything he could have said that he didn't believe her, that he couldn't trust her, that he again saw her as the kind of woman he hated. And something very precious deep in her heart shattered.

"What was I?" he asked at last, his wintry eyes piercing her soul, "A passionate diversion, while you waited for him.... A delightful interlude to keep your boredom at bay...." His deep self-mockery coiled around her, strangling her emotionally.

"No... Boone, you know that's not the way it is between us."

"No, Leslie, I don't," he said very quietly. "I thought I knew you. But now I see that I don't know you at all. And I'm not even sure I want to."

At the cold finality in his tone, she shivered. As she stared past him out the window, her heart seemed as bleak and empty as the snowy vastness of the valley outside.

Nine

"Please, Boone, try to understand," she pleaded.

"I am trying, Leslie. But it's damned difficult when I think of you planning to go out with the man you were once married to."

"It doesn't mean anything, Boone."

"Maybe not to you. But what about him? And me? Have you given it any thought what it does to a man when a woman strings him along?"

"I'm not stringing either of you along. I told him how I feel, and I've told you the truth about tomorrow night."

The blistering heat of his gaze told her that he wanted to believe her, but some demon from his past prevented it. He couldn't trust her.

"Where are you two going…tomorrow night?" he asked in an even, dead tone, as though he no longer really cared.

"I have a date with him to the Devil's Brand Ranch."

"That figures!"

"Oh, Boone, I don't want to go out with him. I really don't! I told him I would two weeks ago...before... us...."

"Then break your date!" he snapped.

"I tried to this afternoon. But I couldn't."

"You could if you wanted to."

"It's not that simple."

"Of course it is. Leslie, there's no point in arguing over this. I have a long day tomorrow."

"Will you please listen to me while I try to explain."

"That's what I thought I've been doing. You were telling me that you couldn't break your date."

"It's because of Karen," she said weakly.

"What in the hell does Karen have to do with any of this?"

"I'm going out with Tim because of her."

"Leslie, I don't believe that for one minute. You're an adult. Don't blame your desire to go out with Tim on your child."

"It's the truth."

"Just what in the hell kind of woman are you anyway?" he rasped. Suddenly his arms were around her like hard, tight bands, imprisoning her against him. His black eyes glittered as they swept over her, devouring her fragile loveliness. "When you made love to me a while ago I thought you gave yourself to me completely, and all the time you were planning...this. It's obvious you don't give a damn about either of us. But I suppose that dangling two men from some emotional string satisfies some basic need in your ego. The thing that really gets me is that for the life of me, I don't understand myself. How could I have been so taken in...the second time around."

Abruptly he released her and strode briskly across the

living room. He was lifting his sheepskin coat from the armchair by the door and swinging it across his broad shoulder. He was leaving her, and she knew that this time he wouldn't be coming back.

"Boone, don't go. Please..."

Quickly she followed him to the door. Her slender hand reached out and gripped his arm. The minute she touched him, he recoiled as though burned. Then he swept her once more into his arms, and stared savagely down at her, with a look of utter disgust stamped into his hard, angry profile.

"How can anyone as beautiful as you are be the way you are?" he demanded roughly.

"I'm not like what you think, Boone," she pleaded desperately. "I'm not..."

He felt his anger melting. Her frantic sincerity almost penetrated the shell of his defenses. Her eyes were overly large like great shimmering liquid emeralds. Tears spilled over her long lashes and down the creamy softness of her cheeks.

At the sight of her so desperately vulnerable, he stiffened, rejecting the impulse to relent. She looked exactly like a wounded animal, and the powerful urge to cradle her against him and protect her rose up in him.

But he forced himself to loosen his grip on her slender shoulders and set her from him. He shot her a cold, hard look of farewell. As she gazed for the last time on his beloved, chiseled features, little did she know how close he'd come to giving in to the message of his heart.

When Boone had gone, Leslie lay on the couch in a daze. Tears streamed over her face, but she was scarcely aware that they did. Her whole body shook as she remembered his savage rejection.

He'd left her, and he wasn't coming back! This thought made her heart pound like a heavy gong of doom. How could she have known two weeks ago when she'd told Tim she'd go out with him that things could have changed between herself and Boone? And now after nearly two weeks of utter happiness, losing him was like death itself.

What was she going to do? She couldn't bear to lose him. And all because of a stupid, idiotic misunderstanding that was somehow tied to his past distrust of women. Something had happened to him that had scarred him so deeply, that he wouldn't even try to believe her. Instead he was associating her with the woman in his past who'd hurt him.

It wasn't fair! her heart protested. She could scarcely breathe. The bitter pain in her chest was suffocating her. And yet as the night wore into the early hours of the morning, the intensity of her pain lessened until she felt nothing except a curious numbness.

The next morning black shadows were etched like tiny black moons beneath her eyes; her complexion was utterly colorless. Because of the holiday, she didn't have to work. Otherwise she would have had to call in sick. She simply couldn't face anyone—not yet when she was totally devastated emotionally.

After she'd cleaned up the apartment and washed and rolled her hair, she sank onto her bed in a state of sheer exhaustion and fell sound asleep only to awaken later to the insistent ring of the telephone on her bedside table.

Hope that it was Boone made her heart flutter madly, and then at the sound of Tim's flat drawl, it seemed to stop completely.

She drew a slow agonized breath.

"Les, Karen and I are running a little late. Our plane

just got to Denver. We won't get up to Winter Park until around five.''

"I'll be here," she replied dully before they hung up.

An hour before Tim was to arrive she rose listlessly and began to dress for the evening. A white stick of makeup erased the remnants of the shadows beneath her eyes. Her perfumed hair tumbled over her shoulders, glistening. As she expertly made up her face, she never gave Tim or how he might react to her now that she dressed so glamorously a thought. Once she would have given anything for an evening with him, to prove that she was the attractive woman he'd said she could never be.

But now...tonight...nothing mattered except Boone.

Leslie had time to read the Winter Park newspaper. She was shocked to read that a skier who'd missed the last bus to town had tried hitchhiking and had been picked up by two men who raped her.

Crime was supposed to be nonexistent in Winter Park! As the doorbell buzzed Leslie refolded the paper. She felt shaken. How many times had she driven out that way and shown property all by herself late in the afternoon without ever giving her personal safety a thought?

As Leslie opened the door Karen dashed into the livingroom and into her mother's arms, heedlessly crushing the low-cut rose silk gown that Leslie was wearing. Karen's exuberant greeting washed a little of Leslie's pain concerning Boone away, and as Leslie lifted her lovely eyes to Tim's, her smile was artlessly radiant.

Blue eyes gleamed with a strange light as Tim stared uncomprehendingly down at the exquisite woman he'd so rashly divorced. She had changed so that he hardly recognized her.

As Leslie stood up slowly, still clasping Karen's hand tightly in her own, she thought Tim no different than he'd ever been. The only difference was her own reaction to his Nordic, blond handsomeness. Once she'd loved him, and now she was amazed that he inspired no more than a cool friendliness.

She was completely indifferent to him as a man. For the first time she was glad that he'd insisted on coming because she was at last free from him, from all the hurt he'd caused her when he'd walked out. If he hadn't come, she might never have known how completely she was over him.

Why was he looking at her like that, as if he were seeing her for the first time, when they'd been married for eight years? The bright light in his eyes made her feel slightly uncomfortable as she extended her hand to welcome him into her home.

After the amenities had been exchanged, she was the first to draw her hand away from the clinging warmth of his grasp.

"Do we have time for a guided tour of Winter Park?" Tim asked lightly. "Before it gets dark."

"Yes, of course," Leslie replied mechanically. "And while we're out we can check you into a motel room."

"I thought Daddy would be staying here," Karen inserted.

"I made a reservation at a motel just down the way, Karen dear," Leslie replied firmly.

"But Mom..."

"Karen, your father and I are divorced. We have been for a very long time, and I think it's time you accepted it. I promised you I'd go out with him tonight, but that's as far as it goes."

Karen's dark brows creased together in a petulant frown, and she fought against the brimming tears as she headed sulkily toward her room.

"Leslie, was that really necessary?" Tim chided, a husky note that made her feel uneasy creeping into his voice. "I feel damned awkward not staying with my daughter and wife."

"I'm sorry for that, Tim," she returned sincerely, lifting her lovely emerald eyes to his. "But one thing you made very clear eighteen months ago was that you no longer wanted me for your wife."

His blue gaze slid over her. "Somehow seeing you...now...I still think of you as my wife."

"I'm sorry for you then," she returned quietly. "Because I no longer think of you as my husband."

Karen went next door to see Gini and her children, and Leslie suspected that this was a ruse to allow her parents some time alone together. Leslie used that time to drive Tim around Winter Park. She pointed out Karen's school, the ski slopes, and other points of local interest. Last of all they stopped at his motel, which happened to be directly across the highway from one of Boone's construction sites. Though he'd stopped building condominiums because of the weather, Boone frequently stopped by to check on them. She breathed a sigh of relief when she saw that the site was abandoned.

When she would have waited outside while Tim went into the motel, he insisted she come inside.

"You're being ridiculous, you know," Tim admonished with mock severity. "You could freeze to death out here while I take a shower."

"I suppose you're right," she said at last, remembering that Tim took notoriously long showers.

"Besides you should know me well enough to know I've never yet taken advantage of an unwilling woman."

His smile was infectious, and to her surprise she found

herself returning it. The thought of cool, debonair Tim resorting to violence of any kind struck her as humorous.

An hour later Tim and she emerged from his motel suite. She'd read several articles in a news magazine he'd given her while he had unpacked and showered.

As Tim helped her into the passenger side of her car and slipped behind the wheel himself, she noticed Boone's truck parked on the opposite side of the highway. Just as Tim pulled out onto the highway, Boone strode from around the back of the project out into the golden sunlight.

His black hair was ruffled and tossed with golden highlights. His tanned features were harshly set. Never had she been so aware of anyone as she was of him in that moment. For a moment the dark outline of his hard male form blurred, and she fought back the burning tears that just the sight of him produced.

Then she felt his black, searing gaze touch her, before he quickly looked away as though she were the last person on earth he wanted to see or think of. Never had she felt so totally rejected.

As Tim sped toward her condominium over snow-packed roads, fleetingly she wondered how long Boone had been there. Had he seen her car at the motel? Had he only stopped to see how long she stayed at Tim's motel room? Did he think that she and Tim...

Suddenly she sensed with absolute certainty that Boone thought her fully capable of sleeping with Tim even though yesterday she'd tried to show him the depth of her feelings for him. Couldn't he understand that for her he was the only man in all the world? That not even Tim had ever meant to her what he did?

It was all too obvious the answer was no.

Karen had gone to spend the night with Gini and her children. Again, though Karen's manipulations made Leslie feel uncomfortable, Leslie could only admire her child's determination to provide the proper setting for her parents' reunion.

"And so," Tim was saying as he maneuvered her car down the road toward Devil's Brand Ranch, his smooth drawl self-deprecatory, "we have the whole night... together."

"Not quite," Leslie responded dryly.

"That's only because you insist," he persisted, braking the car in front of the sprawling dude ranch house.

"Tim, I wish you would quit... teasing me."

"Leslie, I think you know me well enough to know I'm not teasing."

Leslie sighed heavily and burrowed more deeply into her silver fur as he got out and walked briskly around the front of the car to her door.

It was going to be a very long evening if Tim kept this up, and in her battered emotional state she wasn't sure she was up to coping with him.

Apparently the Devil's Brand Ranch party was the most widely attended New Year's Eve party within a sixty-mile radius. Both locals and skiers packed the rambling ranch house. The band played a lively mixture of country-western music and rock.

In spite of herself, Leslie found some of her tension abating as Tim and she chatted with the other guests. Now that she no longer desired Tim, now that all the old hurts he'd inflicted seemed to belong to the past, there was a new easiness growing between them, a brother-sister easiness that can only exist between a man and a woman who know each other very well.

As the evening wore on, Leslie found herself occasionally laughing. She danced often with the men who sat at their table, just as Tim danced often with the women.

They'd been at the party for nearly two hours and she and Tim were dancing together when Tim whispered into her ear, "Don't look now but that arrogant black-haired bastard who just walked in is staring holes through us."

A shiver of apprehension raced through Leslie, and missing a step, she clung more tightly to Tim for support.

She could not stop her gaze from slanting to the tall dark man who had just entered the room. Her misting eyes met the angry blackness of his for a long moment before she looked away. His gaze swept knowingly over her, stripping away her clothes in such a boldly insolent fashion that Leslie turned a deep shade of rose that matched her dress.

Grasping the sleeve of Boone's dinner jacket was a beautiful girl who was much younger than he. Glossy black ringlets framed the delicate oval of her face. She was petite and didn't even come up to his shoulder.

Tim winced, feeling the cutting edge of Leslie's long finger nails through the heavy fabric of his suit as, unconsciously, Leslie tightened her grip.

"So that's him," Tim stated baldly, with the maddening perception only an ex-husband could have.

"Who?"

"The man you're dating...who you said was special."

"Y-yes...."

"That girl he's with is...quite something."

"Y-yes. Isn't she?" Leslie's voice was strangely faint, and once again she missed a step.

"Who is she?" Tim persisted.

"I don't know. Maybe it's his cousin. He said something about an out-of-town cousin."

"For your sake I hope so," he mocked gently before he swept her down the length of the dance floor until they were out of range of Boone's vision.

Some time later Tim was pouring Leslie some punch.

"I'm sorry I came," he apologized, looking gently down at her with genuine affection.

"What do you mean?"

"Well, it's obvious you two are really in love. *He* can't take his eyes off you."

"He hates me now."

"I agree that he's very angry. Why didn't you explain that we planned this evening because of Karen."

"I tried to."

"But he's the possessive-macho type…"

"There's more to it than that, Tim, though I don't know exactly what."

"Well, since I've split you up, I'm going to do my best to help you get back together."

Some element in his voice startled her.

"Tim, what are you going to do?"

He nodded his blond head in the direction of the small, beautiful girl Boone had brought with him. Boone had left her by herself momentarily to get her a drink.

"I'm going to ask his date to dance. And that'll give you two a chance to make up."

"No, Tim, stay out of it," Leslie hissed. "He won't like it, and you'll just make matters worse!"

"Sorry, Les. I never was any good at taking orders…especially from you. Besides, this won't be a total act of charity. Other than you she's the best-looking woman at the dance. If she's really his cousin… Who knows? Maybe she goes for tall, dashing blondes. You know what they say—opposites attract."

"Tim!" she cried desperately after him, but he ignored her completely and moved with confident ease toward Boone's date.

"Just what in the hell does your husband think he's doing?" The hot anger in Boone's voice sliced through Leslie, and she whirled to face the tall, dark giant of a man who stood directly behind her.

Her luminous gaze met his fierce black one and held it. Tonight there was a bold recklessness about him, an element of sensual danger that heightened her feminine awareness of him, mesmerizing her.

"I don't really know," she replied uneasily.

"I believe you do," Boone insisted. "And I want an answer."

"I think he feels responsible for you being angry, and he thought he'd help by asking your date to dance," Leslie replied tightly.

"The poor bastard..." She caught the genuine pity in his deep voice, as well as the condemning light in his dark look. "He's so ensnared by you that he'll demean himself by helping you make up with your lover."

Leslie tried to avert her gaze from the cold contempt in his deep black eyes, but brown fingers moved quickly and cupped her chin so that he could stare into her eyes. She felt like an unjustly accused prisoner. Even so, his mere touch sent a sensuous ripple tingling along her nerve ends. Shivering she backed away, but he relentlessly pursued her until he'd cornered her against a wall.

"Or perhaps he's indifferent to me as a woman and wants to help me...with you," Leslie reasoned. "He and I have been divorced a year and a half. If he was so wild about me, we wouldn't have separated."

"It never occurred to me that he had any choice in the matter," Boone's deep, cold voice accused her.

"Then perhaps it should," she pleaded quietly. "He left me because he wanted to date younger women. He said I made him feel...old...."

A black brow cocked in surprise. "I don't believe you," Boone said, very softly.

"What can I say then? I didn't believe it myself at first. I'd never looked at any other man. I thought my marriage would last forever, and then suddenly Tim announces that he's bored."

"He what?"

"I know you think that only women can get tired of a relationship and walk out. But men can do the same thing. It happened to me."

"Somehow I don't think he's tired of you any more," Boone persisted. "I'll bet he'd take you back now...in a minute. I don't believe you make him feel old any longer."

Leslie paled momentarily at Boone's perception. At last she murmured, "If Tim's changed his mind, I can't be responsible for that. I couldn't have known. Boone...I only care about you..."

The word "you" died in her throat at the brutal hardening of Boone's expression.

"And tell me..." he lashed out at her, "do you want your husband back? Or have you already taken him back...this afternoon in his motel room?"

Involuntarily Leslie's hand went to her throat and she drew a deep long breath. The atmosphere seemed suddenly dense and suffocating. A country-western tune whined loudly about a cheating woman and her hard-hearted lover. The pulsating beat of the song throbbed through Leslie. The acrid scent of cigarette smoke curled around her.

"Boone...I..." She broke off, so deeply hurt she was

unable to deny what he accused her of. The harshness in his tone, the deep bitterness in his gaze betrayed how little he trusted her. Tears glazed her eyes, and she trembled.

"Did you?" His voice was low and deadly, and his hands closed over her wrist in a tight grip so that she couldn't escape.

Leslie's golden hair framed her pale features. Her green eyes were luminous as she stared desperately up at him.

Suddenly she saw that nothing she could say or do would make any difference to him. Boone had set his mind against her from the beginning. She remembered that first night when she'd made love to him and he'd turned against her, accusing her of being capable of only an empty, meaningless relationship. Suddenly she felt very tired. She saw the utter hopelessness of trying to make him believe in her.

"Boone, I don't have to tell you anything," she said weakly. "And I'm not going to. There's no use in my even trying to defend myself. I'm tired of trying to make you believe in me. Think the worst. And now…if you'll let go of me, I'd like to look for Tim. I'm tired, and I want to go home."

"Leslie…"

"There's nothing more I have to say to you, Boone. You and I are finished. I see that…now…as clearly as you do. I'm not going to try to explain myself to you any more. I've given up."

His dark face swam in her blurred vision for the briefest instant, and she blinked hard to hold back the tears.

"All right," he said at last. His roughly hewn profile appeared chiseled from granite. There was a new hardness about him, a roughness in his voice. "Have it your way. I think I knew all along you were no different than all the other women I've known…"

"No good," she finished for him, her voice quiet with defeat.

"You said it," he accused. "I didn't. But for the first time tonight we're in agreement. Go back to your husband...if he'll have you. I hold no claim on you."

Then he turned and stalked away. Out of her life, she knew, forever.

Ten

Tim left first thing the morning of the first, but not before he had a long talk with Karen. He tried to explain to their daughter that although Leslie and he were still her parents, they were divorced. There would never be a reconciliation. Karen listened to him and seemed to accept what he said.

Business was especially brisk at R.B. Dexter Inc. after the week-long holiday season. Leslie forced herself to work very hard, showing more property than normal in a vain attempt to keep from thinking about Boone.

A Mr. Ryan who owned Ryan Real Estate Company invited her to lunch on Friday. Leslie couldn't have been more surprised when he offered her a job.

"And so you see, Mrs. Grant," Mr. Ryan began, beaming at her from across the table after having explained his job offer, "we're willing to make it worth your while to move from Winter Park to Vail if you'll sell our property."

"You certainly are," she smiled, flipping through the sheaf of papers he'd handed her. "I'll have to go over these numbers and give your offer my careful consideration. Of course, I have a little girl, and I'd begun to think of Winter Park as home. I don't think she'll want to move."

"I think you'd like Vail." He flashed her a broad smile. "There's a lot more for a single person like yourself to do there. Why don't you come over this weekend and see the office? You could meet some of our personnel."

"I'd like that."

"Can you come Sunday?"

Thinking of Boone and the recent tension and hopelessness of their relationship, she replied, "All right."

Snow fell heavily all afternoon as it had for the past several days. Dynamite charges blasted through the mountains at regular half-hour intervals.

It was nearly four o'clock when Leslie returned from dropping Karen off at Gini's house to the office to pick up a set of keys to a custom-built house Boone had on the market. She was rustling through a drawer in Boone's office for the keys to the house when she heard his door open and close softly.

Leslie looked up straight into Boone's black eyes. His chiseled, rugged handsomeness affected her far more then she would have liked, and the bright glowing smile of welcome she tossed him was spontaneous. Why did she have to be so vulnerable to his masculine appeal? His black hair was mussed from the wind; tiny flecks of snow clung to its dark thickness. Her eyes drifted yearningly over the wide stretch of his broad, muscular shoulders. He moved easily across the room toward her with the lithe grace that was a characteristic of his. Her smile faded almost at once at his own grim expression. The planes of his handsome face were set in harsh, implacable lines. The air in the room seemed suddenly to crackle with the rippling tension between them.

"I thought you were still in Denver," she said in a carefully light tone.

"Obviously." His one word was terse and sarcastic.

"What is that supposed to mean?" she asked quietly. "I was just looking for a key to the house at Hunter's Creek."

"What I meant was you would never have been in my office if you expected me," he explained. "You've been deliberately avoiding me all week."

"I thought that's what you wanted."

She felt the heat of his gaze flick indolently over the loveliness of her upturned face. For the briefest moment some emotion she didn't understand came and went in his dark eyes before he succeeded in repressing it. He tore his gaze from her beautiful face as though the mere sight of her affected him in a way he didn't like. "So it is," he returned coldly, leaning over his desk and picking up several files that had lain on top of it. His complete indifference to her caused an odd tight pain to compress her heart.

Leslie's fingers closed over the cool metal of the keys to the house, and she slipped the drawer shut. Straightening to her full height, she said coolly, "Then you'll be happy to learn that Sunday I'm driving over to Vail to look into the possibility of moving there."

For an instant his cool indifference was gone. "You're what?" His deep voice was hoarse.

"I received another job offer today that's so good I'm going to consider it."

What was she hoping for so desperately? That he'd say don't go, that he'd say their past differences didn't matter, that he'd say he understood why she'd had to go out with Tim? She should have realized the futility of such a hope.

"You and I have a contract." The menace in his cold tone wrapped around her as he moved nearer. No words of personal endearment, of wanting her for himself, softened his statement.

He towered over her; he was so close she caught the spiced tangy scent of his aftershave. She hated the quivering response of her traitorous body that made her intensely aware of him as a man, more so now that he was indifferent to her.

"I—I seem to remember you weren't too enthusiastic about signing it," she managed to say, forcing herself to meet his level gaze. "I'll need a job when that contract runs out, and it suddenly occurred to me that I would be foolish to wait until the last second to look for one, especially if one just falls into my lap."

"Your contract doesn't run out for nine more months. And when it does, I have every intention of offering you another one—with better terms."

Startled by his words, she lifted her gaze again to his. His face was a cool, dark mask, but she sensed a coiled tension about him. Did he dislike her so? Swallowing against the dryness in her throat, she suddenly realized she felt very nervous herself.

"I—I thought that under the circumstances…you'd prefer that I left," she said. "I made you sign that contract. You didn't want to. And now…this job offer could release us both from a difficult situation. Working with someone you've been personally involved with can pose problems...as you yourself once pointed out in the past.''

''How eminently sensible you sound, Mrs. Grant,'' he taunted sarcastically. ''What you say is...true. But as we're no longer personally involved, and we won't be in the future, I see no reason why we can't work together.'' He snapped the files he'd been holding shut and set them once more on his desk.

''Boone...I thought you'd be happy if I left.''

His hard gaze raked over her softly vulnerable features, but if he liked what he saw he gave no indication of it. ''Please don't confuse my motives for wanting to keep you on with my personal feelings for you,'' he said in a voice of steel. ''My motives for wanting to keep you here are strictly related to business. You've proved you're damned good at selling real estate. I need good agents...whether or not I personally like them.''

His compliment cut her more deeply than any insult, and she winced.

''Well, in that case,'' she began unsteadily, ''I'd better get to work so that I can continue to deserve your approval. I'm supposed to show the Hunter's Creek house in fifteen minutes, and it's more than a ten-minute drive...''

''You're not planning to show that house tonight....''

''I most certainly am,'' she returned defiantly.

''Where's your client?''

''He called me on the phone and said he'd meet me there at five.''

''And you went along with that?'' he demanded.

''Of course.''

''I've told you in the past I don't want my women agents going out at night to meet clients they've never even seen.''

"It's not night."

"It will be by the time you get out there. Besides, Hunter's Creek is very remote, and they've had some trouble out there. You know that's not far from where that girl got raped. There's several tumbling down rental houses that Carl Jacobs doesn't mind leasing to drifters. I don't want you up there on that lonely road in that little car of yours, especially when you're wearing next to nothing."

"Next to nothing..."

"That sweater clings to every curve—as you well know. If one of those men sees such a delectable piece of womanhood drive by on such a desolate stretch of road, who knows what he'll decide to do? I'm not sure you know how men think when they see a woman driving alone. It brings out their predatory instinct."

The unmistakable male interest in his black gaze that lingered insolently upon the swell of her breasts sent a swift hot current through her. Then his gaze slid boldly downward, stripping her. She felt embarrassed, and suddenly she was blushing furiously.

"I don't have to ask how you have come by your understanding of the masculine predatory instinct," she said with mock sweetness, wanting to insult him as his bold gaze insulted her.

His lips curved slightly with cynical humor. "Besides that danger, haven't you noticed that the weather's been steadily worsening all day? Look outside!" Glancing briefly out the window, she saw that snowflakes were blitzing downward in whirling fury. "You can hardly see through that stuff, much less drive in it. I'll bet you don't even have chains on your tires!"

"Yes, I do."

"Well, they're hardly fool-proof insurance in conditions like these. The snow control experts have been blasting to prevent avalanches all day! A woman shouldn't be out in such hazardous weather with or without chains. Call your client and cancel," he commanded. "That's an order."

"Boone..."

"You heard me. I don't want to be responsible for you up there at this hour."

Rage at what she considered an unreasonable, masculine, high-handed attitude surged through her as she marched briskly out of Boone's office and into her own. Quickly she searched through her appointment book for the telephone number of her client.

It wasn't that she wanted to drive up that mountain road alone; it was that she'd decided when Tim left her that if she were going to be a single woman on her own she couldn't let fear stop her from doing her job. She'd told herself she had to take care of herself like a man did. Just because she no longer had a husband to protect her didn't have to mean that she couldn't get out. She had a living to make for herself and her little girl. As a real estate agent she couldn't always show property during the day.

She rang the number twice, but there was no answer. Glancing at her watch, she realized she just had time to make the appointment if she disregarded Boone's order and left immediately.

Slipping behind the steering wheel of her car, she paused for a long moment to consider the wisdom of going against a direct command from Boone. It wasn't as if she were blatantly disregarding her boss's wishes. She'd tried to call her client and hadn't been able to reach him. Besides, she'd shown that house before, and nothing had happened. Boone was overreacting to the danger. Her client had the money to make this purchase if he decided to, and she hated the idea of standing him up. If she did that, it was highly likely he would find himself another agent and she would lose a sale.

Five minutes later all these well thought-out reasons for disobeying Boone seemed a little less sensible as the sun, concealed by the thickly falling snow, sank behind the mountains. The long, sweeping shadows made the forest on either side of the twisting mountain road eerie and gray. Since she'd left the outskirts of Winter Park, she hadn't passed a single car.

The snowbanks along the narrow, winding road were only knee-deep at first, but as she inched onward they gradually grew higher.

Slowly she drove past the row of shabby, tar-paper houses Boone had warned her of. A rusted pickup partially covered with a blanket of snow was parked in the road, but no one was in sight. She breathed a deep breath of relief.

The road twisted, and she could no longer see the houses in her rear-view mirror. She was nearly to her destination at Hunter's Creek when the snow began shooting down like white bullets, almost obliterating the road. For the first time she noticed that the snowbanks beside the road were deeper than the car was high. A newly posted sign almost buried in snow read "Hunter's Slide Area—No stopping or standing." In the silence she was aware of her pounding heartbeats. Never had she felt so alone.

The road was slick with ice and fresh snow. The snowbanks beside the road were so high now, she almost felt that she was driving through a white-walled tunnel. She was beginning to realize that Boone had been right; she had no business in such a remote area with darkness approaching in a snowstorm.

A blast of wind raced through the trees, swirling the

flakes and vibrating against the car. Her heart began hammering with rapid, jerky beats. Quickly she stifled the nervous impulse that made her toe press more firmly against the accelerator. The road was packed with snow; she couldn't drive any faster or she would lose control of her car and drive into a snowbank. On such a desolate road, she might be out all night.

Suddenly she rounded the last curve. In the semidarkness the mansion she was to show loomed from out of the trees. It was boldly modern. Normally she would have marveled at the beautiful simplicity of its design and how wondrously it blended with its setting. But not tonight. The wind whistled through the trees, shaking snow loose from the heavily laden branches and swirling it and fluffing it into such dense clouds that Leslie could scarcely see.

Squinting, her eyes straining, she peered at the road. No car tracks marred the smooth whiteness of the snowy road. Nor was any car parked in front, which meant that her client was not here yet. Where was he? she asked herself nervously. Was he going to stand her up?

Fumbling in her purse for the keys to the house, she alighted from her car and made her way carefully up the icy sidewalk. She clutched her silvery fur close around her cheeks and body to keep out the intense frigid gusts of air and snow.

Where was her client? She felt so terribly alone all by herself. Why hadn't she listened to Boone? He'd known what he was talking about, and she'd been so stubbornly set on doing as she'd planned that she'd ignored the wisdom of his advice.

Fleetingly she wondered if she should drive on back to town without even waiting for her client. But she instantly decided that since she was already here, it wouldn't hurt to wait a few more minutes. Suddenly her feet slid on the glassy surface and she almost fell. Gasping, she drew a long, deep breath and decided she must be more careful.

Her body shook violently from the cold, and she'd only been out in it less than a minute. Why hadn't she worn something warmer? But when she'd dressed this morning she hadn't realized it would turn so much colder, nor had she expected to be out like this.

She brushed the crusts of ice from the doorknob. Shaking fingers unlocked the door, and she let herself inside. For one long moment she leaned heavily against the door.

The house was as cold and silent as a vast tomb. At least she was out of the wind, but as she stood shivering beside the door, she realized the temperature inside the house was below freezing. The electricity was turned off, and the house was eerie and uninviting.

Leslie went to a window and looked out, hoping to see the headlights of her client's car. But outside all was darkness, and furious flurries of snow were blowing and drifting. Snow lay a foot deep on the window sill, almost obscuring her view. Snowflakes angrily lashed the window panes, bouncing off and flying away. Wind whipped around the house, and somewhere a loose board banged against a wall.

What was she going to do? How long should she wait? Nervously she chewed on a mittened hand and then decided.

The storm seemed to be growing stronger. If her client wasn't coming, then her best bet was to go on and head down the mountain before it grew any later. She had hoped he would come and that she would be able to trail him down the road. But with every minute that passed it was darkening, and she felt that if he were going to come he would have done so by now.

An explosion—a sound like the mountain itself ripping apart—jarred the house. Then Leslie heard a distant rumbling. She stood very still, as alert as a frightened wild thing as she peered out the window and listened, wondering what had made that noise.

Outside all was as it had been—darkness and thickly falling snow. But the strange thunderous sound had increased her anxiety, and she decided she'd leave at once before anything else happened.

Hastily she pulled the door closed. She was so upset that she didn't realize she hadn't locked it. Then she picked her way across the icy walk through snow—a foot and a half deep by now—to her car. Her ankles felt frozen by the time she slipped inside her car.

Starting the engine, she carefully turned the car around and headed back down the twisting road.

Leslie's emerald eyes widened as she leaned forward over the steering wheel, struggling to see through the blinding whiteness. It was almost impossible.

Suddenly ahead of her she saw snow piled deeply across the road and fallen trees scattered about as though they were matches that had tumbled haphazardly out of their box.

The road was blocked! She remembered the explosion she'd heard and suddenly knew that it had been an avalanche. For a long moment, she stared as though paralyzed at the mass of trees and snow and ice the size of box cars that cut off the road.

If she'd left for Winter Park any sooner, she would have been crushed.... Her face was white with tension; her heart was pounding fiercely.

Instead of relief she felt terror; there was no way back to Winter Park but down that road. She was trapped!

Her expression was bleak and lost. Without the proper

clothes and food she would surely freeze to death. She knew nothing about survival in the snow.

Her mind raced, and thinking of the house she'd left behind, she decided that it was probably well insulated and offered more protection from the elements than her car. She would go back there and wait. And hope....

A vision of Karen, her blue eyes brilliant with their customary excitement, her thick chestnut curls framing the delicate beauty of her angelic face, her bright smile.... Then instantly the dearly beloved dark visage of Boone sprang into her mind, and Leslie had to fight back tears. She wanted to be with them so desperately.

Fear that she would never see the two people she loved most in all the world was a savage emotion that made her feel close to hysteria. This couldn't be happening! It was a nightmare and she was going to wake up!

But it was no nightmare. It was reality turned into a nightmare, and she had to get a grip on herself if she were going to survive. Her whole body was shaking with fright.

At last she managed to force herself to calm down. Cautiously she attempted to turn the car around, but to her horror she backed too far into the drifts along the side of the road, and the back tires began to spin helplessly. She was hopelessly stuck.

This had happened to her before when driving in the snow around Winter Park, but always there had been someone nearby to help push her out. Now there was no one.

Shifting to neutral, she got out of the car and tried to push, but she was not strong enough. The car didn't budge, even when she was breathless from her exertions.

The mountain trembled beneath her feet, and Leslie held her breath. Another avalanche! Oh, dear God... She prayed silently that she would not be swept down the mountain like another piece of rubble.

She heard a furious rumbling and panicking, she began to run down the road back toward the house. Her lungs felt clogged, and she was gasping for breath. But still she ran. Snow was drifting like shallow waves over the road; snow, knee deep, was sliding over the road bed and down the side of the mountain.

She was caught in the fringe of the avalanche. But she struggled against the tide of powdery cold swirling up to her knees; she struggled against her own exhaustion.

She fell down several times, cutting her legs on the icy road and ripping her nylon hose. But each time she got up and forced herself to walk back toward the house. Her feet and legs felt numb. Her breaths came in harsh burning gasps. Every part of her felt frozen, but she ignored her pain and fear. She was intent on one thing only—getting back to the house.

Finally the snow stopped moving. It lay across the road in deep drifts, but she was able to stumble through it more easily until finally she reached the house.

Fortunately she hadn't driven too far down the road. Wearily she dragged herself up the door, and when she pushed it, it opened. She practically fell inside.

Stepping into the kitchen she opened the pantry. It was a small airless room, but because it was so tiny perhaps her body heat—if she still had any—would warm it. Taking off her coat, she pulled the door until it was almost shut and huddled beneath her soft fur, rubbing her frozen legs and forcing her toes to move in a vain attempt to warm herself.

Oh, please, please let someone find her before...it was too late.

Waves of darkness seemed to curl over her, and she

fought desperately to stay conscious. Never had she felt so tired, as though she wanted to sink into the deepest of sleeps.

"Boone...Boone." She said his name over and over again in a breathless sigh of despair. He would come for her. He had to.

It seemed that she lay in the cold dark airless space for hours. Her muscles were cramped, her throat dry, her legs cut and bleeding. She drifted in and out of consciousness.

Sometime during the night she thought a light flashed, but when she opened the pantry door and looked out, the house was shrouded in darkness. Once more she fell asleep, awakening again a short time later because of a faint purring sound.

Terror brought her instantly awake. Was it another avalanche? But as she strained to hear, the only sounds were the faint stirrings of the wind. She realized the intensity of the storm had lessened.

Every part of her ached with cold, and she stretched beneath her fur coat. Somewhere outside she heard scraping sounds as though someone were tramping through the snow. A man's voice... Her name... Leslie's heart leapt with excitement before she wondered dismally if she were hallucinating.

Something heavy thudded against the house. The front door was thrown open, and the most wonderful sound Leslie had ever heard filled the house—Boone's voice calling her name.

"Leslie!" The deep sound echoed through the empty house.

"Boone...over here." Her own voice was weak and faint. When she tried to stand up, a dizzying nauseous feeling swept through her and she collapsed, her limp body spilling onto the cold tile floor of the kitchen.

When her lashes fluttered open a minute later she was wrapped in Boone's arms, thick blankets bundled over her legs and body. A propane lamp gleamed from the kitchen cabinet.

Boone's dark face was gentle as he gazed down at her. A cut above his dark eyebrow was open and oozed a faint trail of blood down the side of his face.

She was struggling to sit upright, and he helped her. Relief that he was really here, that he'd come in time fought against her rising hysteria. She'd been truly terrified. Suddenly she began to shake, and Boone cradled her against the broad warmth of his chest. It felt so good—his holding her close. Never had any sensation been more comforting. Her head rested against his shoulder; her golden hair streamed over his arms.

She felt his fingers smoothing back her tangled hair, his touch as gentle as a caress. She clung to him and sobbed quietly, feeling that if he ever let go of her she'd never feel safe again. Tears spilled over her long lashes, staining her cheeks with mascara. She wondered if she'd ever be able to stop crying.

Only vaguely was she aware of him gently drying her tears on a monogrammed handkerchief he pulled from his coat pocket, of him lifting her to her feet. He tucked her silver fur coat more closely around her shoulders. Then he folded his arms protectively around her.

"Leslie, are you all right?" His strong brown hand cupped her chin gently. "I saw your car upside down on the side of the mountain."

"I—I had gotten out of it...in time...." Her voice broke, and she blinked against a new surge of tears. She felt shattered inside.

"Thank God," he murmured, staring deeply into her eyes as though she were very precious to him. "If anything had happened to you...I don't think I would have ever forgiven myself." He paused. "I'm going to fly you home."

"Fly..."

"I got the federal rangers to fly me up here in their helicopter."

"Oh, Boone, you're hurt." A sob caught in her throat at the sight of his bruised and bleeding hands. With her fingertips she wiped at the blood smeared on his cheek. "What happened?"

"It's nothing. Cut myself jumping out of the helicopter."

"And it's my fault. If I'd listened to you in the first place..."

"Hush.... It's okay." His hand wrapped around her fingers that were lightly brushing his cheek. "I understand why you did what you did. You couldn't have known what would happen."

He was being so infinitely gentle, so completely kind. Her heart was filled with love and gratitude as she smiled weakly up at him.

Leaning heavily on his arm, Leslie was guided outside into the brisk cold then down the road to a clearing where the helicopter hovered like a giant dark bumblebee.

Boone lifted Leslie into the waiting arms of one of the rangers and then jumped inside the helicopter himself. The pilot rose abruptly at a sharp angle and flew toward Winter Park.

The warmth from the heater blasted around Leslie, but in spite of that she snuggled against Boone.

Above the vibration and noise of the helicopter Leslie yelled, "I kept thinking my client would show up. But he never did. I wonder what happened to him?"

"He called right after you left," Boone said. "I was

still in the office, and I took his call. When he said he'd been out and you couldn't have reached him, I wondered if you might not come on up to the house. I decided I'd better check.''

"I'm glad you did," she murmured gratefully. "I should have listened to you."

"In the future I'll expect you to obey me unconditionally," he teased, patting her hair. "When I tried to drive up I found the road was blocked, so I went back to Winter Park and talked Kelly here into risking his neck and flying me up here."

Kelly winked over his shoulder and then turned all his attention back to flying the helicopter.

A comfortable silence lapsed between Boone and Leslie. Leslie felt that she was at last thawing out. She could feel her toes tingling. Her teeth were no longer chattering.

As she lay in Boone's arms, she reflected that only in Boone's presence could she feel this snug, wonderful sense of security.

Half an hour later when he had escorted her safely inside her condominium they began to talk again.

"Where's Karen?" he asked. "Gini's?"

"Yes." Leslie sank wearily onto the couch, nervous exhaustion sweeping her. She didn't feel up to facing her lively child just yet.

"That's a good place for her for the time being," Boone said, sensing how she felt. "I'll give Gini a call and explain."

"Would you?" she asked gratefully. "I—I don't feel up to any…explanations…tonight."

He made the call and arranged for Karen to stay overnight with Gini. Then he strode to the bar and poured two glasses of Scotch over ice. Returning to Leslie's side,

Boone handed her a glass and then lifted his own, swirled the liquid and ice cubes in one quick motion, lifted it to his lips, and drained it.

When she sipped hers slowly, the strong liquor scalded her throat. Sputtering, she would have set the glass on the table beside the couch, but Boone's brown hand arrested hers. A faint, warming tingle shivered through her at his touch.

"Drink it," he commanded. "All of it. It will not only warm you up but it'll help you to relax."

"I haven't eaten. I—I'm not used to such a strong drink," she protested. "It makes me feel…funny."

His handsome face was set in hard, stubborn lines. "Drink it."

Only when she obediently brought the glass to the pouting curve of her lips once more did the tension drain from his hard features. She drank almost all of it before she set the glass down and coughed. "I need some water," she choked, starting to rise. "I really do."

"Stay where you are. I'll get it."

Gratefully she reached for the glass of tap water he brought her from the kitchen. When she'd finished drinking it, he knelt down in front of her.

His hands separated the edges of her fur coat, and she felt the warmth of his touch move slowly over her as though he were examining her like a doctor. Slowly his hands explored downward over her legs, her feet and toes.

Involuntarily she cringed away from him as his hands touched a bruised place on her bare leg. "Don't… Boone," she murmured, trying to push his hands away. "Please…" A bright flush suffused her cheeks at the intimacy of his gesture.

"Leslie, I want to see if you're hurt," he insisted. His deep voice was gentle with concern and yet firm.

"I—I'm all right," she said. "Really.... You don't have to..." A strange shyness was sweeping her, a ridiculous modesty, and she clutched her coat together and tried to curl her legs underneath her.

"If you won't let me, I'll have to call Dr. Rome."

"No....I don't need a doctor. I'll be all right. I've been through enough tonight."

"Leslie, I know you're tired, but I have no intention of leaving you tonight without either examining you myself or calling Dr. Rome. Exposure can have very serious consequences. Frostbite..."

"Boone..."

"You're not going to change my mind," he stated emphatically. His steadfast black gaze held her own, and she knew that he meant what he said.

When she sat defiantly before him for a long moment, Boone shifted his weight to get up, and she knew that he intended to call Dr. Rome.

There was absolutely no point in calling the doctor out in the middle of the night. Instantly she made up her mind. "Wait," she whispered as she reached hesitantly for his hands and led them slowly back to her body. "All right."

His eyes glowed like dark fires as he registered her meaning. A tender smile curved the harsh line of his mouth as he looked down at her. She placed his hands on the bare curve of her legs. The intimacy of his touch caused a strange warm current to ripple through her that wasn't at all unpleasant.

"I'll try not to hurt you, Leslie." His low voice was oddly rough, his expression gentle.

He removed her coat so that it slipped over her shoulders. He carefully stripped away her torn stockings and shoes. Skillfully his hands moved over her, and when she moaned slightly with pain he asked her all the appropriate questions and listened for her answers.

She remembered that he'd once studied to be a doctor and that he'd had to drop out of medical school because of his wife. Boone's concern for her was obvious in every movement, in every question that he asked. In that moment Leslie realized what a good doctor he would have been and what a shame it was that he hadn't been able to continue his studies. His heart had been in medicine, not real estate.

Abruptly she thought of Tim and how important his own medical career had been to him. Had he been unable to complete his training to be a doctor, he would never had made the successful adjustment to another career that Boone had made. Boone had an inner strength, a depth of character that most of the men she'd known had lacked.

"I think you're all right—other than a few bruises and surface cuts," he said at last, interrupting her thoughts. "Take a nice long bath and relax…. But if you have any pain tonight I want you to promise me you'll call Dr. Rome. And I want you to go in and see him tomorrow."

"Okay, I will."

"Then, if you're settled for the night, I'll be going."

He was rising to his feet; he towered over her like a magnificent dark giant. She realized with a frightened start that he was leaving.

"Boone…" Her voice was a tiny quavering sound that reached out and touched him.

He was slipping his sheepskin coat over his broad shoulders. "Ummm," he replied absently, looking down at her.

"Boone, I—I'm scared. I don't want you to go."

The black fire of his gaze went over her quizzically,

and she felt warmed through by the tenderness of his expression. Quickly she jumped to her feet and reached for one of his hands. The sudden movement caused her coat to slide the rest of the way down her shoulders so that she stood before him with her clinging sweater revealing the shape of her breasts. Her tattered skirt hung about her legs in strips. But as her hand made contact with his, she flushed as he looked down at her, desire suddenly scrawled across his handsome features.

Boone forced himself to look away as though the sight of her semi-clad body disturbed him uncontrollably. Even though he wasn't looking at her, Leslie realized that he was keenly aware of her beauty, of her golden hair falling softly over her breasts and shoulders, of the delicate golden-toned loveliness of her flesh, of her diminutive femininity. She roused him, and he sought to reject this reality.

"I need to talk to Kelly," he said grimly, pulling the keys to his truck from his pocket. "You're safe now. There's no reason for me to stay." When she clung to his hand stubbornly, he said, "I'll call you later...and make sure you're all right."

He stepped toward the door, but she held onto his hand, pulling him back.

"Please, stay with me...tonight," she pleaded. Then she wrapped her arms around him tightly as though to bodily prevent him from leaving. Her breasts were crushed against the massive heat of his chest, her lovely face was tilted upward so that she could stare deeply into his eyes. "Please...don't go.... I know it sounds stupid, but I need you. I was so afraid up there...all alone. I don't want to be alone tonight."

She was acutely aware of everywhere that his body touched hers. She felt his muscles stiffen, and when he spoke his voice was harsh. "Leslie, do you have any idea what you're doing to me? You're touching me...so that I can feel the heat of you, your softness against me.... You want me to spend the night...to keep you company and make you feel safe. But I don't know if I can. I know what you went through up there on the mountain, and in spite of that, I want you. But you're in no condition..."

His words trailed off, yet in the pregnant silence that lapsed between them she was aware of an intense emotional tension growing between them.

"I don't blame you for how you feel," she said softly. "If you'll only stay—I'll leave you alone. I'll get dressed in something that buttons up to my chin, and I won't get any nearer than across the room to you."

His lips twisted sardonically. "Perhaps that's carrying things a bit far," he mused dryly. "If you'd just put some clothes on I'd probably be able to put the lid on those...er...predatory masculine instincts you so aptly accused me of understanding earlier. Here, wrap up in your coat for starters."

He reached down and pulled her coat over her slim shoulders so that she was completely swathed in silver fur.

"I know that we're not interested in being...personally involved with each other...any longer," she murmured shyly. "And I'm not expecting that. I don't even want it. I just want you to stay tonight. You can sleep in the guest bedroom. I won't come near you."

An odd light flickered in the depths of his black eyes, and for a minute she wondered if she'd thoughtlessly said the wrong thing and hurt him. Then his face was a smooth dark mask once more, his taut expression unreadable. She thought she must have imagined that quick look of hurt.

He heard the desperation in her voice; he sensed her

irrational terror. Understanding the reason behind her fear, he couldn't stop himself from wanting to help her.

"All right. You talked me into it." There was a smile in his deep voice. Her own face was wreathed in radiant happiness as she looked up at him.

"It's a good thing I wasn't born a woman," he said, attempting a lightness as he shrugged out of his coat again and tossed it onto the chair. His keys jingled faintly as he set them on the coffee table. "Because I never have had the strength of character to say no even when I know I should to a woman as beautiful as you."

Eleven

Although Boone spent the rest of the night with her, even in her small condominium, he managed to avoid having personal contact with her. First he insisted that she go back to her room and take a long bath.

When she came out of her bath dressed in her thick emerald corduroy robe, he was sitting at the dining room table, his brief case open and files scattered about. He looked up disinterestedly from his papers, saying pleasantly, "I hope I won't be in your way here. I had these contracts and blueprints in my truck because I was planning to work late at home. Since it's late and I'm going to spend the night, I might as well get down to work here."

"No.... You won't be in my way," she replied weakly, fighting back a twinge of disappointment that he so obviously preferred working to talking with her.

He bent his black head and began scribbling something

rapidly on several sheets of paper. She realized he'd completely forgotten she was there.

Slowly she moved into the kitchen and began rummaging furiously through her pantry. Only when he glanced up impatiently in her direction did she stop and realize she was acting like a child. She wanted him to pay attention to her, and he clearly had no intention of doing so. She bit a nail in frustration and forced herself to move more quietly.

Taking a tray filled with crackers and cheeses into the dining room, she set it beside him. "I thought you might be hungry," she offered.

"Why thank you, Leslie," he replied absently, never looking up from his work. "But you don't need to worry about me. I can find whatever I need. You go on to bed and get some sleep. I'll probably be at this the rest of the night."

Never had she felt so completely rejected. But what had she thought would happen? He hadn't wanted to stay with her. He'd done so only because she'd insisted. Suddenly she saw with a new clarity that although he found her physically attractive, he was totally indifferent to her as a person. He no longer wanted any personal involvement with her.

He'd rescued her as he would have saved any woman in the same situation. She meant nothing special to him other than the fact that she was a valuable employee. He'd told her that himself that afternoon in his office. What was it going to take before she realized that their relationship was over?

Nothing else, she vowed silently as she pressed out the light beneath the Chinese silk lampshade beside her bed.

"Nothing." Faintly she murmured the word. He was lost to her...forever.... Perhaps he always had been. He had said from the beginning that he wanted no involvement with any woman, that he'd been badly burned in the past. He hadn't been able to believe that her feelings for him were deep, that her going out with Tim had meant nothing. And if he couldn't trust her, if they couldn't communicate, their relationship never had had a chance. If only...

Darkness swirled around her. The effects of the double Scotch never had worn off. The emotional trauma she'd endured had exhausted her more than she realized. And because she knew that Boone was in the other room, and that she was utterly safe, she fell into a deep and soundless sleep.

The events of the day affected her even in her sleep. Several hours later she awoke in the pitch blackness of her bedroom. She was cold with sweat, and she sobbed incoherently.

She was back at Hunter's Creek again in the dark, swirling snowstorm. Again she was plunging through snow, only with every step the snow seemed to grow deeper, and she was sinking into it as though it were an icy quick sand, sucking her under and down the mountain. The harder she fought, the deeper she sank. She was aware of her complete helplessness. Her heart was near bursting as it pounded against her ribcage. Then she began screaming—that terrible soundless scream of nightmares. Then her own voice, high-pitched and desperate, broke through the black silence.

"Help! Oh, please...please help...Boone!"

Suddenly Boone was leaning over her, and without a word he drew her into his arms as though she were a child and held her close against his hard muscular chest, his low voice soothing away her fears until her sobbing ceased.

"Oh, Boone, I was back at Hunter's Creek. In the storm. I…I was sinking into the snow. I—it was like drowning… I—I…"

"Hush, darling," he murmured. His warm breath quivered over her bare flesh, scalding her into a pleasant awareness of him. "It was only a dream."

"But it seemed so real."

"You're safe now. Nothing like that will ever happen to you again."

He pulled her onto his lap and cradled her gently against him for a long while. One of his hands stroked through the tumbling masses of her hair. The other gently rubbed the bare flesh of her back as he pressed her close against himself. Her face rested against the prickly black hair covering his bare chest, and she could hear the quick, uneven pounding of his heart.

Slowly new sensations stirred through her. The steady motion of his hand through her hair sent a fiery tingle of shock waves through her. She was intently aware of the hard pressure of his thighs against her own. It had been so long since he'd made love to her, and she loved him so desperately that suddenly, unexpectedly, she wanted him beyond reason. She was a woman with a woman's needs. And he was the man she loved.

Because she was still drowsy with sleep she was no longer so aware of the barriers that separated them. Forgotten for the moment was the fact that Boone had rejected her. She wanted him, and the hard pressure of his body told her that he wanted her.

She wasn't exactly sure when or how it happened, but Boone's embrace changed from being comforting to being sexual. His hands moved languorously over her with their sure, expert knowledge of how to awaken her desire. Her pulse was racing, and she was aware that his raced no less intensely.

Her filmy nightgown was tangled about her creamy thighs. The sheet he'd wrapped around himself when he'd heard her screams had fallen away, and she could no longer ignore the fact that he was naked beneath it. The length of his hot bronzed flesh was crushed tightly against her female form, and when her curves were molded to the hard contours of his masculinity, Boone's low groan of arousal vibrated thrillingly through her.

With a complete and shattering mastery his lips sought hers, claiming them in a fiercely passionate kiss. Her lips parted for the intimate invasion of his tongue. She felt his hands moving over her, seeking out the softness of her breasts, as though he wanted and needed to feel her flesh completely against his own. Her filmy nightgown prevented his body from having total contact with her. And the raw urgency of his passion drove him to rip at the gauzy fabric. Leslie made a feeble attempt to stop him, but her own passion swept her away. And Boone's strong hands shredded her nightgown.

More of her bare flesh touched his, and she felt hotly alive, flaming with desire. He shifted her in his arms so that she lay beneath him, so that his teak-brown torso lay on top of her soft breasts, so that her hips fitted his. His lips moved from her mouth, downward over her throat, their teasing and nibbling wreaking erotic havoc with her senses.

In the burning darkness she was aware only of him, only of the bruising, demanding feel of his mouth on her bare skin, of his aroused body crushed tightly to her.

As he intimately explored her voluptuous curves with his mouth and tongue and hands, she lay against the soft mattress lost in the thick swirling passion of his embrace.

She loved him, and she didn't care about anything in all the world except being with him. This moment of supreme, glorious, sensuality obliterated everything except her intense awareness of the present and the man who made love to her.

He drew her deeper and deeper into a dark world of passion where she experienced wild thrilling feelings such as she had never known before—blinding happiness, exquisite terror, flaming excitement. She surrendered herself completely to this man who took her with bruising force, mastering her, dominating her, loving her with devastating totality. In the thick enveloping darkness she was aware only of hard arms circling her, of the intense heat of his body everywhere his touched hers, of the hot, traitorous need flooding through her veins.

For one intensely shattering moment they merged completely—body and soul. When he would have withdrawn from her, she clung to him, weeping soundlessly, her tears falling onto his chest and dampening his hot flesh. Finally she fell asleep, wrapped in the hard, protective warmth of his arms.

A pattern of bright sunlight played against the white curtain in Leslie's bedroom the next morning when she yawned widely, awakening.

"Boone," she murmured drowsily, reaching across the bed for him. Her long lashes fluttered indolently and she opened her eyes.

An odd little pain stabbed her. He was gone, and had it not been for the shredded nightgown on the floor and the rumpled pillow on the other side of the bed, she would never have been sure the night of passion she was remembering was not a wild figment of her imagination. As her green gaze focused on the filmy strips of her nightgown on the beige carpet, she blushed deep crimson. Last night the fierceness of his desire had been beyond anything in her experience, and her own need had risen to match his.

She lay contentedly back against her pillow, a tiny smile playing with the edges of her mouth as she remembered the rapturous ecstasy of her surrender to the only man she could ever love.

Boone loved her! He had said it in that final moment when they had been joined together. No matter what had ever been between them in the past, she was sure that she meant more to him than he'd ever been willing to admit. A man didn't lie...at a time like that...did he?

Yet later when he called that morning, she wondered.

His crisp voice was emotionally remote, and she clutched the receiver more tightly, a strange chill shivering through her.

"Leslie, Kelly and another federal ranger want to talk to you. I'll drive you to his office and then to see Dr. Rome in an hour...if you can be ready," he stated curtly.

There was not one word of endearment for her, no mention of last night and that it had meant anything special to him. Suddenly she was shaking uncontrollably because of his coldness. Something was dreadfully wrong!

"Boone...last night," she began unsteadily, "when you came to my room...I thought..."

Savagely he cut her off. "Last night was a mistake," he said coldly. "I take full responsibility for what happened, and I'm sorry."

"But Boone..."

"I knew that I had no business staying overnight with you. Believe me, I regret what happened as deeply as you do."

Leslie's heart pounded dully. Each pulsebeat produced

a tiny constricting pain. He continued talking, but she
scarcely listened.

He didn't love her! He was sorry for what had happened between them! It was all too obvious he wanted no
involvement with her! And she'd thought, she'd truly believed that he loved her! What a love-sick fool she was—
grasping at straws, hoping against hope that he cared
something for her.

"Leslie, I want you to take that job in Vail," he was
saying, still in that same cold tone that was freezing her
emotions. "I think it's for the best. In fact I'll drive you
over there tomorrow myself so you can look into it. I
won't hold you to your contract with me if you want out,
and I'll pay your moving expenses."

Oh, Boone, no, no, no! she wanted to cry out, but pride
kept her silent. He didn't want her; he wanted her gone.
She'd tried everything she could think of to save their
relationship, and she realized with awful finality that it
was time to give up. But last night and the new closeness
she felt for him made this more difficult than ever for her
to bear. She gasped at the intensity of sheer, raw, aching
sensation that ripped brutally through her.

"Thank you, Boone, for everything," she heard herself
mouth mechanically. "I appreciate all that you're doing.
You couldn't be more generous."

The next two weeks passed in a dismal blur. Boone had
helped her buy a new car and driven her to Vail as he'd
offered, and when he'd heard the terms of the new job
offer, he insisted that she take it. In no way could he have
been kinder or more helpful.

But every act of kindness, every way that he helped her
only proved to Leslie how deeply anxious he was to be
rid of her. She realized that she no longer had any choice

about leaving. If he were this desperate to have her gone, she must go. If she loved him at all, she would do as he wanted and leave him.

Leslie was snapping the last of her suitcases shut. Boxes, packed to the brim, teetered in precarious stacks about the living room. The movers wouldn't be arriving for several days, but she was leaving today in her car for Vail. All she had left to do now was pick up Karen at school....

For a long moment her eyes wandered around the familiar room. A hot tear pricked from behind her lashes but didn't fall as she stared at the place in front of the fireplace where Boone had first made love to her.

She hadn't lived in Winter Park very long, but she had a heart full of memories that would have to last her a lifetime. Well, there was no point in dwelling on them now. She would never be able to leave if she did.

Slowly she stooped to pick up the leather handles of her purse. Then she headed toward the front door to go down to the garage and finish loading her car.

Just as she was about to swing the door open, a brisk knock sounded from the other side. Then the doorbell buzzed once and then again.

She flung open the door, and a little gasp of amazement and joy escaped her lips as her eyes met Boone's black gaze. He looked haggard and gaunt. He hadn't shaved, and his broad shoulders drooped slightly as though he were either despondent or exhausted. But as always, to her he was the most handsome of men, the most welcome sight in all the world.

"Boone." There was a strange lilting sound in her husky voice as she welcomed him; she'd thought she would never see him again. Her beautiful face was illuminated with joy as she stared up at him.

His own expression was utterly bleak. He looked like a man who'd lost whatever it was he prized most in life, a man who'd reached the bottom of despair.

Reading his emotion, she cried out, suddenly stricken with concern. "Boone, what is it? What's wrong?"

Her slender hand reached out and seized his, and he drew back as if burned. She was reminded of his distaste for her, and yet if something were wrong, if he needed help.... She had to know if there was some way she could help him.

"Boone, why did you come over? Tell me!"

"I...I came by to tell you goodbye," he said slowly. "I wanted to see if you had anything heavy to lift...if you needed any help...."

So he'd only come by to help her leave—or to make sure that she left.

If only he hadn't, she could have kept her fragile control. But the sight of him, the hot sensation of his hand in hers, was suddenly too much for her. And the tears that hadn't fallen streamed down her cheeks. She sobbed brokenly and hated herself for doing so.

"You shouldn't have come by," she cried out desperately, wrenching her hand free from his. "I didn't want you to. Why couldn't you just let me go?"

"Leslie..." His deep voice was hoarse with passion and pain.

Then his hard strong arms were circling her in a vain attempt to comfort her. For a fraction of a second she melted in his arms, but then she realized what was happening to her. She balled her hands into fists and pounded at his broad chest frantically. She couldn't bear for him to hold her when he felt nothing for her.

"Let me go, Boone. Don't you know what you do to

me when you hold me? Don't you understand that it's torture—your touching me?''

Her quivering voice seemed to pierce him like a quick, savage blade, and abruptly he let her go. Shaking, she collapsed against the chair. To her surprise she saw that his own dark face was ashen as though he were suffering as intensely as she.

''I'm sorry, Leslie, but I had to see you again—one last time.''

The terrible finality in his ragged tone slashed through her, and she sagged with defeat.

Nothing had changed between them. He didn't care. He never would.

Twelve

"I wouldn't have come, Leslie, if I'd known how much it would upset you. But I want you to know that I don't blame you for feeling the way you do. I've hated myself, despised myself for what I did to you.''

''What you did to me?'' she repeated quietly. The anguished pain in his low voice caught at a corner of her heart. Never had she felt more vulnerable to his virile appeal. She didn't understand what he was driving at.

''In spite of what happened...two weeks ago...when I spent the night here, I never meant to hurt you. My God... You'd been hurt—nearly killed up at Hunter's Creek that evening. And then that very same night I ripped your nightgown to shreds and forced myself on you...after you'd told me you didn't ever want to be personally involved with me again. I know you only let me make love to you because I'd rescued you, and you felt grateful,''

She stared wonderingly up at him.. Was that really what

he had believed? Had he really been so deeply stricken with guilt because he thought he'd hurt her? She saw the deep lines of suffering etched into his face, and suddenly she knew that he had.

"You didn't hurt me, Boone," she began very softly, her eyes shining with her love for him. New hope fluttered in her chest as her heart began to beat jerkily. "Not that night...not ever. I wanted you as much as you wanted me."

There was disbelief in his swift dark glance that met her own shimmering one.

"Boone, I mean what I'm saying. You've always thought you understood me, even when you didn't. But it's very important to me that you know you have nothing to feel guilty about for that night. That—well, it was the most beautiful experience in my life," she admitted brokenly. "The only way you hurt me is that after being with you again, after thinking that we'd found each other again, I can hardly bear to leave you, even though I know it's for the best."

His black eyes gleamed fiercely as he stared with burning intensity at her exquisite features. "It's for the best... Whose best?"

"Because it's what you want," she whispered.

"The hell it is," he muttered fiercely, dragging her into the hard force of his arms and holding her closely against himself for a wondrously long moment.

"Boone, what are you saying. I—I don't understand."

Unexpected contact with his masculine body made her tremble slightly.

"I want you back, Leslie." His hand moved through her hair in a slow, caressing motion. "If you really meant what you said, I want you back. But I don't want to force myself on you. The only reason I was helping you move was because I thought you wanted to go—to get away from me. I didn't want to stand in your way.''

"Oh, Boone, I can't believe it.''

"I love you, Leslie,'' he murmured huskily, his hot breath stirring the silken tendrils at her temple. ''I think I have from the moment I saw you that day at the ski slope. You were beautiful like Marnie, and yet there was a sweetness, a softness to you that she never had. I'd loved her for so long, or at least I thought I did. And then I hated her when I found out what she was really like. I blamed myself for her death because there was a part of me that had wanted her dead.''

"Are you sure that it's me you want...and not her?'' Leslie whispered anxiously, remembering Tess's words on the mountain.

"The minute I saw you I was struck with the resemblance between you and her. My feelings for Marnie were powerful even after she died. I thought her beautiful, I wanted her physically, and yet she used her power over me. She never loved me. I'd wanted to be a doctor all my life, but when I got her pregnant, I dropped out of medical school and married her because she mattered more to me than anything else. Years later I found out that she aborted our child deliberately. I couldn't forgive her for that. She began drinking. There were other men, but still my feelings for her ran so deep I couldn't divorce her. We had a terrible quarrel the night she died. She was drunk, and I was so angry I let her go out anyway.... When she died...I blamed myself.''

"It wasn't your fault,'' Leslie said softly, seeking to comfort him.

"Then I met you. I think I saw almost at once that your resemblance to Marnie was only superficial. But I wouldn't trust my instincts. You had that same power over me that she had had, only it was even more intense. When I found out Mother had deliberately hired you, I was convinced for a while you were as conniving as Marnie was. Then when I was around you on a day-to-day basis, I was sure you weren't. You looked like her, but you weren't like her. Still, I kept remembering what she'd done, how she'd twisted my life around…my very soul. My feelings for you were so intense that I was afraid you would have the same power over me and use it as she had to destroy me. I couldn't trust you because of her. Even when I wanted to.''

''Oh, Boone, if only you'd told me all this sooner. I would have understood. I know what it's like to be hurt by the one person you trust. That's what happened to me when Tim walked out. I think I sensed how deeply you'd been hurt that first day you helped me ski down the mountain.''

His black head lowered to her golden one, and his mouth claimed hers in a tenderly fierce kiss that inflamed every sense in her body. She quivered from his touch.

''Why didn't you go back to Tim?'' he asked very quietly.

''You big lug,'' she whispered passionately. Then she smiled tenderly. ''Do I have to spell it out for you? Because I loved you…and only you… I tried to tell you that I went out with him because of Karen and not because I wanted to. I didn't sleep with him. Since the moment I met you, you've been the only man in my life.''

The fierce dark light in his eyes seared her as they searched her soul and saw that she was telling the truth. Then his lips smothered hers again. The hot, moist contact of his possessive mouth sent a wildly glorious fire racing through her veins, and she clung to him, pressing her body against him.

She was breathless when he dragged his lips from hers, and the feeling remained when he lowered his mouth to her earlobe and burned a trail of tingling fire along the sensitive skin of her throat.

Suddenly she felt his great body shaking against her, and a wild tremor shuddered through her as she realized that he was as aroused as she.

"There's one question I haven't asked you," he said hoarsely against her love-swollen lips.

"What's that, Boone?" she murmured impatiently, wanting him to kiss her and hold her and make love to her more than anything else.

"Will you marry me?"

The deep passion in his voice vibrated through her.

"Oh, Boone…" she sighed, blissfully happy. Never had she been so happy. And then when her lips met his again in passionate surrender, she communicated the answer to his question without words.

Vaguely she was aware of him kicking the door shut with his boot. Until that moment she hadn't even realized that it was still open. He lifted her into his arms and strode with her toward the bedroom. Gently he placed her on the bed and lowered himself on top of her.

And as he drew her into the hot swirling world of their desire, she knew that from the first their love was meant to be.

* * * * *

BEYOND LOVE

One

It was a typical frozen November afternoon in Napa Valley, but it was one Dinah Kirsten would never forget. Not that she had the slightest premonition of disaster when she slammed out of the house, her sixteen-year-old heart pounding with the stifling resentment she always fought to conceal from everyone, especially her grandfather.

The cold roared up the hill and stung her cheeks. After bundling her long black hair into her hood, she stood on the porch and zipped her yellow Windbreaker. Then she raced toward the barn, impatient to get away from her grandfather and the house.

The ground was sodden beneath her feet, and the mist hovered between the hills. Kirsten Vineyards was as bleak as one of the fading photographs of a World War I battlefield in Grandfather's album. The remnants of grape leaves that were scattered on the dirt beneath the gnarled vines were a dull brown; the sky, gun-metal gray. Beneath her grandfather's white Victorian mansion that crowned a hill overlooking the Napa River, black and brittle vines marched away with the somber orderliness of tombstones in a military graveyard.

Oddly, the cheerless day made Dinah feel better. As always she felt a kinship with nature and the vineyard. She loved the valley, and she yearned to feel she truly belonged—as Holly belonged. If only it were Holly who was adopted and not she! Holly, who didn't care about having Grandfather's love, Holly, who found the vineyards and winery dull.

Instantly Dinah's better nature forced the ugly thought from her mind. She must not think things like that. Usually she didn't dwell on Holly, but today a letter had come from her older sister, who had apparently run short of funds. Nevertheless, Grandfather had been thrilled because if was the first letter in two months, and he'd read it aloud over lunch. Dinah had been filled with that all-too-familiar jealousy she'd thought she'd put behind her when Holly had left for Berkeley in September. She'd been forced to listen when he spoke of Holly and how he missed her. When he had said wistfully it sounded like Holly was missing them a little too, Dinah had bitten her lips to refrain from hurting her grandfather by saying that was just his wishful thinking. Holly never wrote unless she wanted something.

His delight in receiving the letter had been a stake in Dinah's heart because Dinah wanted him to love her as he loved Holly. Ironically, Holly had always been indifferent to his affection. It was Dinah who had toddled after him as a child in the vineyards, Dinah who had followed him into the winery while Holly had stood at the door, puckered her nose, and complained of the sour smell of fermenting grapes.

As she'd grown older, Dinah had done everything she could to please her grandfather. She could drive a narrow tractor through the vine rows as well as a man. She could taste a grape for sugar content when it was almost time for the crush and know when it should be harvested. She could prune better than anyone at the vineyard except her grandfather. All these skills she had learned to earn her grandfather's love, but no matter what she did, it was never enough. It was Holly he loved, and Dinah who felt like an outsider. Sometimes, like today, she almost felt like running away. But that would be stupid because the only place she wanted to be was here.

But how could he not prefer Holly? Holly was his own grandchild, a feminine version of the son he'd loved and tragically lost along with his daughter-in-law in an airplane crash. Holly had not been left on the doorstep in a wicker basket as Dinah had. It was Holly's parents who had adopted Dinah, after all. Not Grandfather. Her adopted parents had been dead so long Dinah couldn't even remember them. Perhaps Grandfather hadn't wanted her then, and now he felt he was stuck with her. Not that Grandfather was ever deliberately unkind to her. For he was not.

Holly was blond like all the Kirstens. Unlike them, she was languid and easily bored. Her teachers had put this defect more bluntly and said she was lazy. They warned her grandfather that he was spoiling her, but Holly had known how to get around him when he tried to reform her. It was as if even when she'd been a child she'd known that her beauty and charm would get her what Dinah's industriousness would never obtain. Oh, how Dinah wished she were as beautiful as Holly, who had golden, shoulder-length curls, gray blue eyes fringed with long lashes, and a figure that was willowy and graceful.

Dinah was everything Holly was not. Worst of all, with her Indian-straight, black hair, she looked nothing like the Kirstens, and her petite figure was so embarrassingly curved she had to be careful how she dressed. A T-shirt made her look like she was all breasts. Boys had made her very self-conscious about these unwanted assets.

Dinah considered her eyes her best feature. Dark and sparkling when she was happy, they flashed when she was angry. Edouard from the neighboring vineyard said they betrayed her as a girl who would grow into a passionate woman. But then Edouard was French and lived most of the year in a château in Bordeaux, coming to the Napa Valley only in the summers, and Grandfather said such remarks from a French boy were not to be taken seriously.

The differences between the sisters went deeper than their appearances. Where Holly was laxily unambitious, Dinah had the restless energy of one who must constantly prove herself.

Dinah had slowed her pace in the vineyard. She was breathing hard, and the cold air burned her throat. From the help house came laughter and male voices in a mixture of Spanish and broken English. An ancient, rusting Cadillac with enormous tailfins was parked in front of the house. As usual on Saturdays, the Silva brothers were entertaining their friends from other vineyards. Later they would be off to a dance.

Dinah avoided the help house as well as the winery and stables where she kept her mare Chardonnay. Instead she went directly to the barn her grandfather used to store his tractors and farming equipment. She was not in the mood to see anyone, especially not anyone as depressingly cheerful as Enrique Silva and his brother.

She seized a pair of pruning shears and stalked out of the barn, having decided to tromp down to a remote section of the vineyard that was a favorite childhood haunt of hers. There was scarcely ever any traffic on the country lane down there where it skirted the deserted winery that stood crumbling on the edge of her grandfather's land, and she was sure no one would bother her.

To distract herself from her jealousy of Holly, Dinah thought of the old winery and its history. She loved that old stone building and the stories her grandfather told of the Sauvignanios, the Italian family who had owned it and nearly been wiped out by the terrible phylloxera in the late nineteenth century. The final blow to the Sauvignanios had been dealt by Prohibition, and it was then that her grandfather had bought the estate for a pittance on the gamble that Prohibition could not last forever. He'd told his granddaughters that there had been bats in the attic of the house then and rats in the cellars. The vineyard had been choked with weeds as tall as a man.

An hour later Dinah was pruning a block of zinfandel near the old winery when she heard the roar of a car on the lane. Suddenly there was a loud thud and the splintering of vine stakes. Something had been thrown hard and slammed onto the ground.

Startled, Dinah peeked over the top of her vines and saw that a boy of about eighteen in grimy jeans and a thin shirt had been ejected from the speeding car. His lean body spun gracelessly across the mud. When he stopped rolling, he gave a deep groan and sat up, running his hand gingerly down his left leg.

Thinking at first he'd been thrown accidentally from the car, Dinah was about to go to him.

He caught sight of her, and she paused uncertainly. Fierce blue eyes blazed from beneath a thatch of tumbled black hair. "Get back," he growled. She didn't move. "Hide, I said."

It was obvious he was a very unpleasant sort.

"But you're hurt," Dinah insisted stubbornly.

"Do as I say," he hissed. "I jumped out of that car 'cause I wanted to. I can take care of myself."

Dinah saw that in one of his hands he clenched a thick wad of money. He looked awfully unkempt. Was he a dangerous bank robber on the run? Or something worse? Just as wild thoughts of murder and drug running flickered in her teenage imagination, the car squealed to a stop and began backing up.

"Oh, Lord," Dinah muttered, shrinking lower, glad she was several rows from the hurt boy. Two bank robbers!

The driver, a burly, defiant-looking fellow, burst in an explosion of anger from the driver's side. "Morgan, what did you go do a damn fool thing like that for?"

The thin boy with the money stood up slowly. He was as white as paper and looked dangerously close to collapsing. Only some fierce inner strength drove him to try to stand. Mud clung to his jeans, and he favored his left leg. He was surprisingly tall, and there was an awesome maleness about him that even in her innocence Dinah registered. He was shivering from the chill wind, but his voice was smooth and firm, curiously adult. "You weren't listening, Jack. I want out. I don't want your money."

"You earned it! You're in this as deep as me."

"Maybe. Or maybe you're trying to suck me into this thing as deeply as you are. I didn't know what you were doing, did I? I thought you went into that drugstore to buy cigarettes."

"You can't prove that! Once the authorities find out who you are, who would believe you? Look! You weren't such a goody-goody back at Lawton's. We have to get money from somewhere. We haven't eaten in two days, and we're out of gas again. It wasn't so wrong, what I did.''

"You know it was wrong as hell. Keep your money!'' Morgan angrily jammed the money into the larger boy's hand. Several bills fell onto the ground. "Go without me. I'm splitting.''

"So you can call your rich man in L.A. and let me take the heat for stealing your car,'' Jack said on a sneer. With a look of dark violence he swaggered toward Morgan.

"I'm through with L.A., and my mother and I lost interest in each other the day I was born,'' Morgan said in his bitter, adult voice. "The car is yours.''

There was something unnameable about this Morgan that drew Dinah to him despite the damning circumstances. She knew too well that terrible motherless feeling. The walls of her chest tightened until she could scarcely breathe, and she realized she was afraid for this boy she didn't even know. Morgan, however, was unafraid. Stupidly unafraid, she thought as she glanced toward the scowling giant who was his adversary.

Morgan's eyes were vivid blue, chillingly intense with determination as he stared at Jack with disgust.

Don't look at him like that! Dinah wanted to cry out loud to Morgan. If Morgan saw he was angering Jack, he obviously did not care, and Dinah grudgingly gave him her admiration for his raw, mindless courage.

Then Morgan did the most stupid thing of all. He turned his back on Jack and began to limp down the lane, his every dragging step more painful than the last. From the look on Jack's face, Dinah thought it far wiser to turn her back on a spitting bull.

"Morgan, you can't walk out on me!'' Jack hollered.

Morgan turned and gave Jack another of his intense

blue stares. "I just did," he said in a low voice filled with
disdain. Then he turned his back and resumed walking.

Jack's face contorted with rage. With one swift gesture
he leaned down and picked up a large rock. He threw it
hard after Morgan's dark, retreating head. He picked up
another.

Dinah screamed as the first stone hurtled toward its target. "No!" Then she ran out of the vineyard, waving her
shears angrily at Jack. Because she had screamed, Morgan
managed to duck just enough so that the rock only
glanced the side of his head. He staggered and because
of his injured leg, fell. A thin stream of blood trickled the
length of his pale cheek.

"You might have killed him, you maniac," Dinah
cried, forgetting her own fears.

His foxy eyes narrowed, Jack took a step toward her
and growled in inarticulate rage. "Where did you come
from?"

"Don't you dare come near me," Dinah said. "And if
you don't get off my grandfather's property right now,
you'll be sorry."

Morgan stumbled to his feet, blood streaming down his
face. "Do what she says. It's two to one, Jack. You never
were one to fight with the odds against you."

"And who says they're against me?" He leered at Dinah.

It was the purr of an approaching car in the distance
on the lane that decided Jack.

"Bastards!" Jack grumbled as he raced for his car. He
revved the engine, and the car roared down the road.

When he was gone Dinah ran into the lane to try to
flag down the approaching car. The car weaved dangerously toward her, and Morgan, despite his leg, lunged into
the street and yanked her hard against his body, lifting

her out of the road. The blue Buick zoomed past with inches to spare as Dinah clung to Morgan.

Her fear ebbing, Dinah slowly grew conscious of strong, warm hands trapping her against a male physique laced with tough muscle. The softness of her breasts was mashed intimately against his chest. For one so thin, he was very strong. Her pulse fluttered wildly, but that was only because she'd been so frightened a moment ago, she told herself firmly. Not because of any excitement he aroused. Still, she was quite breathless as she twisted free of Morgan's embrace, and the memory of his hard body made her flush with acute embarrassment.

"That old woman must be as blind as a bat," Morgan muttered angrily. "She damn near ran over us both."

"That was Mrs. Donague. I didn't recognize her car till it was nearly too late. She told me once she'd memorized the vision part of the driver's license test so she could keep passing it."

"Then why did you step out in front of her like that?"

"To get help for you, of course," Dinah snapped.

"Help for me—" Dinah awkwardly faced Morgan, stunned at the anger in his voice and hard face.

"I told you I didn't want your help." His blue eyes, which swept over her from raven head to mud-spattered toes, blazed. "That was pretty stupid of you, too, taking Jack on like you did a while ago. Jack might have..." He broke off with a look of sheer contempt.

She felt the heat of his gaze sliding over her too voluptuous figure, and her cheeks flamed with fresh embarrassment.

"Don't look at me like that," she cried.

"I would expect a girl built like you would have gotten used to guys looking at her," he said roughly.

"I hate it, though."

At the sudden sound of choked tears in her voice he averted his gaze. The hot look went out of his eyes. "Jack would have done more than look," he said quietly, almost gently.

For the first time she realized how dangerously beautiful his voice was. She dragged the toe of her shoe in the gravel shoulder. "Some thanks I get for saving your life," she grumbled, still embarrassed and desperate to change the subject.

"Who saved who?"

"I would have jumped out of Mrs. Donague's way," she returned tartly. "That rock Jack threw would have flattened your skull."

"I'm sure most people wouldn't think you deserved any thanks for saving me. You see, people never have liked me much."

"If you're always this charming, I see why."

"I'm not always this charming. Usually I'm worse."

"I believe you." She smiled. "At least you can be honest."

He stared at her hard, assessing her, and finally his expression softened. "You're almost pretty when you smile. You look soft and innocent, but you're not afraid of anything, not even a no-good like Jack or…me. I don't think I ever knew a girl like you before."

"Almost pretty." Her smile faded. "Thanks a lot."

"You were the one who said I was honest."

"You carry your one virtue to an extreme."

"Perhaps." He shrugged.

"And I'm not so innocent either." It was important that he not think her entirely stupid.

"Really?" There was definitely the suggestion of amusement in his low voice.

"Really," she replied.

He almost smiled, and the effect was devastating. He really was quite handsome when the bitterness left his face. Her pulse quickened. She remembered the firm warmth of his hands on her body, the way his chest had felt hard with muscle. She was aware of him physically as she had never been aware of any of the nice boys her own age who clumsily flirted with her at school dances.

"You don't look a day over sixteen—to be so experienced, that is," he said.

The male knowledge in his sharp blue gaze made him seem wickedly exciting. Dinah laughed huskily. She didn't know that her eyes were dark and sparkling. She only knew his alert stare now held masculine admiration. For the first time in her life she felt pretty. Recklessly, she tossed her head free of its hood, and her long hair swung across her shoulders. With her fingers, she caressed a strand.

"What's your name?" he asked.. His eyes watched her wind and unwind the length of gleaming black hair.

"Why do you want to know?"

"You saved my life."

"Dinah," she whispered shyly.

"Thank you, Dinah," he said in a formal, grave tone. "In spite of what I said, I do appreciate what you did."

"What's your name?" she asked.

"Morgan...Smith." He looked uncomfortable, and she guessed he was lying. "I'd better be going before I wear out my welcome." His eyes were on her lips and then quickly on the ground when she licked them nervously. He turned swiftly and limped out onto the road.

"You can't go," she cried. "You're hurt, and you haven't eaten in two days. You're dirty. Most people would be afraid to help you, even if they wanted to. Why, I thought you were a bank robber at first."

"A bank robber!" He threw back his black head and laughed. It was a deep, pleasant sound. "And you're not—afraid of me?" he murmured, looking down at her. "That figures." She had run after him and was standing right beside him. With one hand he lifted her face and stared deeply into her eyes.

It was a delicious feeling, the way he towered over her, the way his fingers brushed her chin.

"No," she managed. "I'm not afraid."

"Perhaps you should be." His voice was gentle.

"If you can walk up to the house, there's food. Grandfather will get you a doctor for that cut on your face and your leg."

"I don't want your charity or your grandfather's," he said, suddenly fierce again. "And a girl like you shouldn't have anything to do with a guy like me." He dropped his hand from her face, but the gentleness of his touch lingered in her mind.

She wondered if he had to be fierce, to tear himself away. It was almost as if he felt the same invisible force she felt pulling them together.

"It wouldn't be charity."

"I can take care of myself," he muttered.

"Like you did when you turned your back on Jack."

"Yeah," he managed. "Like that." He attempted a smile, but his lips thinned in pain when he moved his left leg. He managed only a few dozen steps before he stumbled and pitched forward onto the ground.

Instantly Dinah ran and knelt beside him in the road. "Stupid and stubbornly proud," she whispered, "and I'm sure those are the least of your faults." She remembered her own jealousy and her own insecurities. She was scarcely perfect herself.

Tentatively she touched his thin shoulder. Beneath the

flimsy material of his shirt his body was lean and hard and warm. Too warm, she thought, realizing he was feverish. She ripped off her Windbreaker and wrapped it around him and then sat down and cradled his head in her lap. She was afraid to leave him and go for help. If he regained consciousness, he would leave, and he was in no condition to fend for himself.

The freezing wind whipped her, and shivering, she pulled him closer. She had never held a boy, never felt a boy's hard body against her own, but oddly, it was nice, being this close to someone. No one had held her in years. Her adopted mother and father had died when she was a baby, and Grandfather wasn't the demonstrative sort.

The gash on Morgan's cheek was caked with blood. She stared helplessly at him, wishing there was something she could do. At last she dared to smooth a thick lock of dark hair from his brow. It was very pleasant, touching him. Dangerously pleasant.

He had a wide forehead, a straight nose, and a carved jawline. It was a strong face. Very male, and very handsome beneath the smudges of dirt and blood. Unconscious, with the bitterness smoothed from his face, his sultry appeal was more evident. He was too thin, but she didn't mind. To her horror, her gaze lingered on his sensual lips, and the overpowering urge to touch them possessed her. The thought came—he would never know if she did.

Trembling fingers traced his face, exploring him with the curiosity of a child, and yet it was the woman in her and not the child that was drawn to do it. Her fingers hovered for a tantalizing moment above his lips. Then she dared what she never could have dared had he been conscious. She touched his mouth, and the feel of his soft, warm lips beneath her fingers caused a strange thrill in her abdomen. He stirred in her arms, and she jerked her hand away.

What was happening to her? This rough boy was a stranger and of the most dubious background, but none of that mattered. She had to help him. He was alone and hurt, and she could identify with that because she felt that in the deepest part of her soul she'd always been as alone as he was.

She heard the whir of tires, and was terrified lest it be Jack, but to her profound relief, it was the Silvas' Cadillac with the long tailfins. Gently she laid Morgan on the ground and stood up to flag them down.

Enrique Silva and his brother were filled with questions as they lifted Morgan onto their shabbily upholstered backseat.

"I found him on the road," she said. "He's hurt."

Enrique leaned over and picked up a glittering object from the dirt where Morgan had lain. "You lost your necklace, Dinah," he said, handing it to her.

It was a school name tag on a broken chain. She glanced at it, and her gaze turned to one of blank shock. The name on the tag was not Smith, but a name she recognized at once, a name that he and his world-famous mother had made even more notorious less than a year ago.

He was not a poor boy in need of help, and he was the last sort of person she would have done anything for, had she known who he was.

Everything changed at Kirsten Vineyards after Morgan came. Dinah had thought that as soon as he was able to be up and about, Morgan would demand to leave, and she told herself this was why there was no need to tell her grandfather who Morgan really was.

Though Dinah avoided Morgan, she couldn't help being aware of him. Clean and freshly shaven, he was devastatingly handsome in the new clothes Grandfather had bought him. He was tall and lean and ever alert. There was a wild recklessness about him, an aura of dashing male self-confidence. When his hot blue eyes chanced on her, she felt like a woman instead of an untried sixteen-year-old girl, and she resented his power over her. When he tried to be friendly, she rebuffed him. She wanted him to leave quickly before…before it was too late.

Slowly she began to recognize the danger of him. Instead of being bored, Morgan was thoroughly enjoying himself at Kirsten Vineyards. He basked in the attention he was receiving, and after the first few days of being initially hostile toward everyone, he went out of the way to make himself charming—especially to her and her grandfather.

There was something so overwhelming about Morgan's personality that the entire household quickly came to revolve around him. Her grandfather spent an hour every evening at Morgan's bedside the first two weeks of his convalescence. Grandfather would bring a bottle of wine upstairs and educate Morgan about its unique qualities. They would taste together, and as Dinah did her homework in her own bedroom next to Morgan's, she gritted her teeth at Morgan's sly pretense of interest. How she writhed inwardly when she heard the frequent sound of her grandfather's laughter. Grandfather had not laughed like that since Holly had gone away.

Swamped by her old feelings of jealousy and insecurity, Dinah listened, unable to study as she chewed her pencil. This was even worse than when Holly had been home, because Holly had never encouraged her grandfather as Morgan did, and Grandfather had inevitably turned to her for companionship.

Dinah was filled with new fears. The more time her grandfather spent with Morgan, the more he wanted to spend. Though it was bad enough that Morgan's presence threatened the delicate balance of her own relationship with her grandfather, her deepest fear was that he might somehow hurt her grandfather.

It was annoying, too, the way Graciela Silva, the housekeeper, doted on Morgan. She scurried back and forth from the kitchen with delicious things for him to eat.

"He is so thin, Señorita Dinah," Graciela explained one day. "Tonight I cook for him a big roast and a platter of vegetables. I told him already about the roast, and he smiled." Graciela beamed. "It was the first time he smiled at me, senorita."

Plump, middle-aged Graciela was bewitched by the thin, sick boy who liked her cooking. Not that Dinah would have wanted him to starve, but did he have to ensnare everyone so completely? After all, it was not as if he would be staying indefinitely.

Yet every afternoon when she returned from school, Dinah discovered that Morgan was more firmly ensconced in the household than before. For the first week he'd lain in his bed in Holly's old room recuperating from a concussion and broken ankle, too weak and feverish to be particularly troublesome other than to complain about the pink flounced spread and curtains. But, by the second week, he was hobbling downstairs against doctor's orders to read in her grandfather's library about wines and vineyards. He even pretended an interest in the pruning of the vineyard. He would go out and watch the Silvas making their deft strokes shaping the vines with the cuts that would determine the crop each vine would bear. He asked countless questions. As if a vagrant like him could genuinely interested.

At dinner near the end of the second week after Morgan's arrival, her grandfather said, "Morgan has a fine mind, Dinah."

Dinah glanced at her grandfather. In the candlelight Bruce Kirsten looked twenty years younger than his actual age. His white hair and brows were thick, his gray eyes alert, his skin glowing bronze. He was smiling fondly at her. She picked up her water glass and twisted her wrist, making the water swirl.

"But he has such resentment toward life," she said, her eyes on the water, which looked like curling fire in her glass.

"That's understandable. He told me a little about his life the other night. His parents are dead..."

"Dead!" she choked. "Is that what he told you?"

"I think if he had a chance, he could amount to something."

If you only knew! she thought. Aloud she said, "He's been in trouble too long to know how to stay out of it."

"Perhaps. You've always been so good yourself, it's hard for you to understand someone like Morgan. There's an intolerance in you, Dinah," Bruce said with regret. "Do you know who he reminds me of?" he asked quietly.

Dinah couldn't imagine. "Who?"

"Myself at his age."

"I don't believe you."

"It's true. At his age I had to leave Germany because I'd gotten myself into a spot of trouble. I made a new beginning here. There's no reason why Morgan couldn't do the same. I've invited him to stay here with us. He's tough and young and smart, just the sort for an outdoor life. Dinah, I need him. As a man grows older he feels the loss of a son more intensely."

Dinah's heart went out to him. All her life Dinah had

tried to be the son her grandfather didn't have. Never had she seen with such clarity how miserably she'd failed. Her jealousy toward this interloper overpowered her. "Y-you can't be serious about Morgan staying here."

"I've never been more serious."

In her mind she was screaming at the impossibility of this, but her voice was cool and controlled. "He only wants to use you, Grandfather. What makes you think he can change?"

"Because he says he wants to, Dinah. Tonight he told me he can't make promises, but he'll stay and give it a try."

Dinah was shaking as she stood up. "The biggest mistake I ever made was not to leave him on the road," she cried, flinging herself toward the door. But to her horror, Morgan was leaning there on his crutches, blocking her way.

There was no escaping his piercing blue gaze. "I *do* want to change," came that cynical, adult, but oh-so-beautiful voice. "Is that so difficult to believe, Dinah?"

She looked him straight in the eyes.

"Impossible!" she ground out before she swept past him and fled to her own room.

Six weeks passed, six weeks in which Morgan insinuated himself more deeply into the life of the vineyard, until Bruce and he were inseparable. Because Dinah was determined to avoid Morgan, she saw little of her grandfather, and this saddened her. Bruce had said more than once that she was sulking like a child. He couldn't understand that she didn't trust Morgan, and that she was afraid Morgan would do him some harm. Still, for some unfathomable reason, she didn't tell Bruce what she knew.

One frosty Sunday afternoon, Dinah was outside walking alone by the river, thinking of Morgan and how different everything was since he had come. The vines were laden with a mantle of ice, and they glittered in the sun. The trees beside the river had lost their leaves, and their branches were black talons, as gnarled and ice-laden as the vines.

Despite the biting chill, Dinah was in no mood to return to the house. There she would be reminded of Morgan and the conflict in her own heart. She walked a mile farther, until suddenly she looked up and saw Morgan ahead, threading his way slowly through a row of vines with his cane. As usual, he was studying the vineyard. She frowned as she watched his tall form lean over a vine to inspect it. He was studying the cuts healing under the brown pruning seal. She knew it was unfair, but even this diligent effort Morgan constantly made to learn was suspect to her because she couldn't believe his interest was sincere. She tried to duck before he saw her.

His reasonant voice stopped her. "Dinah—"

She paused, clenching her hands as she waited for him.

"I've been wanting to talk to you, Dinah, for a long time."

He was standing beside her, the clean scent of his aftershave permeating the air. Dark slacks molded his hips and thighs. Her grandfather's leather jacket, which was much too large for him, swung from his broad shoulders. She looked everywhere but at him, but as always she was too aware of how tall he was, how male.

"You've been avoiding me, Dinah."

"I have my reasons," she mumbled.

"And I want to know what they are." His beautiful voice was soft and gentle.

"Because I don't want you to stay here. That's all." Still she could not look at him.

"Why not? Am I hurting you in some way I don't understand?"

"Eventually you will hurt someone if you don't leave."

"Why do you say that?" Again there was that soft, beguiling gentleness in his low tone. "Is it because…"

With one hand he brushed a strand of her long black hair out of her eyes. The light caress of his fingertips against her skin tingled, and the treacherous flicker of warmth she felt toward him terrified her. She was not used to such feelings and she tried to push his hand away, but he caught her wrist and brought it to his lips. After that she couldn't have moved if her life had depended on it.

"Dinah…Dinah…" he murmured.

No one had taught her that a boy's touch and sweet words could sweep reason aside. His mouth nibbling sensitive skin, the music of his voice against her ear compelled her, and all her carefully erected defenses crumbled. Hungrily he drew her into his arms and ran his fingers through her hair, smoothing it against her slim neck. Then his fingertips glided along her throat in sensual, circular strokes, and she was flooded with hot, wild feelings she'd never felt before.

"Dinah, I've been crazy to touch you like this, to hold you," he said in a broken, wondrous tone. "But I didn't mean to. Not today. I only thought we would talk."

If only he would stop holding her, stop whispering to her, she could think. But she didn't want to think; she wanted to be held and caressed. All her life she'd craved such things. His lips were warm magic in her hair. Somehow she'd guessed that love would be this wonderful if she could ever get past the terrible emotion of feeling shut out. The world seemed to spin, and she clung to Morgan in glorying bewilderment, wanting him, yet thinking herself awful because she did.

He tilted her face, and through half-closed lashes, Dinah glanced breathlessly up at him. "D-don't," she managed faintly. "We mustn't."

"I was wrong that day when I said you were 'almost pretty.' You're beautiful, Dinah. You're the most beautiful girl I've ever known. Shy as a new kitten, yet brave as a lion. That's how I always think of you. I'll never forget the way you stood up to Jack. You're too young for me—in more than years, and I didn't want you to know how I felt. I wanted to wait, to be friends first, but you run whenever I come near. I think you sense what I feel, and that's why you want me to go. It's only natural to be afraid at sixteen. You're not ready for this, but neither am I. I never thought I could feel..." He broke off. "I can't stop myself wanting you, but, Dinah, after today, I promise you I won't touch you again, not even if it kills me. I had to hold you this once to tell you how I feel, to show you, you don't have to be afraid. Not of me, Dinah. Never of me."

She gazed helplessly as his face blurred and his mouth crushed down upon hers. His kiss seeped through her like molten magic, igniting the passionate core of her body, spreading its fire through every fiber of her being. A thousand stars exploded behind her closed eyelids. She was swimming in a sea of flame; she was soaring. She kissed him back as she had never kissed anyone before. Her hands moved over his body, learning the broadness of his shoulders, the lean contours of his back, until finally her fingers crept up his neck and held him tightly.

His hunger was almost insatiable as his hands shaped her body to the hard length of his. Dinah's heart pounded like violent thunder.

With driving mastery, Morgan parted her lips to taste the sweet depths of her mouth, drawing a moan of ecstasy from the deepest part of her soul. The white-hot fire of their passion seared them both, and Dinah knew that the trembling ache in the lower part of her body was desire. She was a child no longer. She wanted him completely, and this desperate need for total intimacy both frightened and shamed her.

"Morgan, we've got to stop," she managed in a hoarse, low voice that didn't sound like her own. "We must."

"I know. I know," he murmured tenderly.

But he couldn't stop. His arms tightened, and pulling her onto her tiptoe, he held her more fiercely than ever, his arrogant sureness conquering her weak attempt to protest. She sobbed when he kissed her ardently again, and then melted against him in complete surrender. Finally he dragged his mouth slowly from hers and pressed her head against his chest, holding her possessively against him. She felt the wild frenzied pace of his heart. With one hand she reached up and gently traced the carved lines of his face. A wild peace enveloped them as they clung to each other. It was a rapturous moment that neither wanted to break. The wind roared in the trees, and made ripples on the river. It was a sparkling time that Dinah would remember all her life.

At last his ragged breathing stilled, and he eased her from his chest reluctantly though his hands still gripped her arms. She looked up into his smoldering blue gaze.

"Isn't this why you want me to go, Dinah? Why you avoid me? Because there's this wanting between us, and you're no more ready than I for this kind of thing?"

She stared at him in blank confusion. Was it? A moment ago she'd been mindlessly, irresponsibly wanton. She'd never even kissed a boy before, and to give herself so shamelessly to Morgan... But now sanity was slowly seeping back into her. She remembered who he was and what he had done. Besides, he had lied to her grandfather. Wasn't he tricking her with his expert kisses and talk of love? Why would he be interested in a raw girl like herself except to use her? Surely he was capable of any deceit if it would get him what he thought he wanted, and for some bizarre reason he wanted to stay at Kirsten Vineyards.

She pushed him away. "No." Her voice quivered. "That's not the reason."

"But…"

"I know who you really are," she blurted. "I have your school name tag, Morgan. I—I don't know why I let you kiss me, but I don't want you to ever touch me again. There's no way I can ever trust you."

She felt his muscles go rigid as he released her. It was like a knife wound to her own heart.

His face was as hard and gray as a stone. "I see." She looked up at him. The wind was in his tumbling black hair. His eyes were bleak, frozen. Yet his face was more fiercely handsome than ever, and something in his expression made her hurt inside with the deepest regret in her life. "Why haven't you told Bruce?"

"Because… Oh, I don't know," she whispered desperately. "I thought at first you would leave without my having to."

"But I won't. You will have to tell Bruce, or I won't go."

"Oh, why can't you just leave?"

"Because of you."

"Don't lie to me! I can stand anything but that!"

"I'm not lying. Dinah, I want to start over. But I can't stay if Bruce knows. I couldn't live with him thinking that I…it will be hard enough, knowing you know."

"I could never trust you. I would never know what you might do."

"So you believe what my mother said about me too,"
he said roughly, passionately. "You think I'm some sort
of uncontrollable maniac. Well, it wasn't like that, Dinah!
But what could you know of the kind of life I was brought
up to? Of a person like my mother?"

"Only what was in all the papers."

"I never touched her! I would never hurt any woman,
especially not my own mother."

"After the tragedy she committed you to that school,
Lawton's. For your own good, she said, and because she
was afraid of you."

"Yes. That posh jail for the disturbed youth of the rich
and famous." He laughed bitterly. "They tried to reha-
bilitate me." His voice was thick and mocking. "I can't
go back there."

"Maybe it's where you belong."

He pulled her hard against his body, and she trembled
at the leashed violence she felt in him. "No decent human
being belongs there."

"And can you become a decent human being?"

"Maybe I've always been one. Is that so difficult for
you to believe? Maybe it was the crime against decency
that drove me to do what I did. I want to change. I'll try
very hard even though I don't know if I can. There has
always been so much anger in me. I've lashed out at everything and everyone I've ever known until these last
few weeks. Your grandfather had made me see that I don't
have to keep making the same mistakes."

For a long time he was silent. There was only the lull-
ing sound of the river. His eyes swept Kirsten Vineyards,
and she felt the intensity of his longing to stay. At last he
said, "The vineyards are beautiful, even in winter. I want
to see the vines when they're lush and laden with grapes.
I wonder if there is any more beautiful place on earth.

There's something healing about nature and working outside, your grandfather says. It's odd, I've been here such a short time, but this is the only place in my life I've ever felt I belonged.''

"You can't ever belong. Not here," she cried. She was being unkind, but she felt she had to be, as much for her grandfather's sake as her own.

"Do you—belong?" His voice was rough. "I know all about you, Dinah Kirsten, the urchin left on the doorstep in a basket, the real granddaughter away at the university. Do you belong any more than I? Is that why my presence troubles you? I've watched you. I've seen your smothering possessive love for Bruce, the way you look when he speaks of Holly, when he spends time with me. You want to chain people with love.''

The old pain welled in Dinah. How could Morgan know these secret hurts? How could he be so cruel? Yet how could *he* be otherwise? She would have run from the pain and from him, had his hands not gripped her so tightly. He pulled her into his arms and held her against his body. She thrashed wildly, but he was too strong, and at last she quieted.

"Dinah, I didn't say those things to hurt you. I understand you because in a way we are alike. Only the circumstances of our lives are different. We're both outcasts. I've felt unwanted all my life, just as you have. That's what made me so mad I could do the wild, stupid things I did. You saved my life, but if you send me back to Lawton's, or to my mother, you'll take it. My only chance is to stay here and try to start over. Let me stay. I'm begging you, and I've never begged anyone for anything before. Your grandfather says he needs me. I know I need him. Please, Dinah.''

She broke free and ran stumbling toward the house, and

as she ran she kept remembering the haunted pain in Morgan's eyes when he'd humbled himself and begged her. If she refused him, he would be lost, but if she let him stay, she would remain what she'd always been. The outsider.

Two

Dinah could not bring herself to tell her grandfather the truth about Morgan.

Morgan came to her just once, his beautiful voice low and soft. "Thank you, Dinah. You won't be sorry. I promise you."

Oh, but he was so wrong. She already was.

Morgan stayed, throwing himself wholeheartedly into the task of learning viticulture and the art of winemaking. Because he stayed, Kirsten Vineyards was never the same.

Dinah could not help bearing Morgan a vague resentment. She had made a great personal sacrifice, but if he was grateful, after that one time he did not overtly show it. He seemed to accept it as his due. Worse, he usurped her place with her grandfather. He did all the things with Bruce that once she had done, only Bruce seemed to enjoy doing them with Morgan more than he had ever enjoyed doing them with her.

Once when she'd lashed out at him in a pique of jealousy, Morgan had said gently, ''I thought I'd release you. Now that I'm here, there's no need for you to be tied to the vineyard. You can do all the things other girls your age do. I want you to be happy.''

As if that could be possible as long as he remained. He took over the work she loved, did it better than she, and had the gall to tell her he was doing her a favor. But how could she complain to her grandfather, who was obviously so besotted with Morgan? Bruce was constantly singing his praises.

Dinah wanted to ignore Morgan completely, but Morgan was a bold presence who could not be ignored. He worked intolerably long hours; he worked as if he were driven by his own set of personal demons. When he played, he played equally hard. There were rumors of girls in his life, but he never brought any to the vineyard. Nevertheless, to her dismay, Dinah found herself secretly wondering about those women, wondering what kind of woman Morgan would find interesting. She remembered the one time he had played on her feminine emotions when he had kissed her and begged her to let him stay. The memory of her response was doubly humiliating since he now no longer indicated the slightest interest in her as a woman. She supposed he saw her as a stupid, silly little fool, easily managed by someone as clever at lovemaking as he. Whatever his thoughts, he was friendly and unfailingly polite and respectful to her.

Four years came and went, four years in which Dinah graduated from high school and became a woman and Morgan a man, and never did Morgan speak again of wanting her. Recently though, in the past year, she had grown aware of him watching her with the same intense look as when he watched the grapes ripen in summer, and she wondered what he was thinking.

During his four years in the valley, Morgan had concentrated so single-mindedly on the vineyard that Dinah felt he would be a ruthlessly ambitious man. Sometimes she heard him arguing with her grandfather. He wanted to know if he had a future at the vineyard. What money Morgan earned, he saved. He had even bought a few acres that he had planted with vines. His supreme interest was in the winery and Bruce's vineyards. Because of Morgan, different grape varieties were planted on his own land and even in Bruce's vineyards. He experimented with new wines in the winery. He began to win international prizes. He had great talent, Bruce said, and great energy. Bruce did not want him to leave, but he made Morgan no promises about his future. Thus, there was a growing restlessness in Morgan. Bruce was pensive, as if on the verge of a momentous decision.

As for Dinah, she had done all the things high school girls do. After graduation she'd halfheartedly enrolled in the local college. She was popular and she'd had boyfriends, though none of them serious. Her most loyal had been Edouard de Landaux, now twenty-one and in his first year at a French university. He came every summer from his château in France and stayed at his father's neighboring vineyard and champagne winery.

Edouard was the son of the Comte de Landaux of Bordeaux, a world-class *vigneron* of premier wines and champagnes. Edouard had been brought up in the wine business, and it was expected that he would inherit not only his father's title but his eminent position in the wine world. The de Landaux owned vineyards and wineries in Champagne and Bordeaux as well as in Napa Valley.

It was the spring of Dinah's twentieth year. Bruce

wanted her to continue with college, but she wanted to
stay with him at the vineyard and work at the winery.
Why couldn't he understand?

"Because you need to learn that there's more in the
world than Kirsten Vineyards," Bruce argued. "Later, if
you want to come back, I'll find a place for you here."

"College didn't help Holly!" Dinah blurted and then
she was instantly sorry when she saw pain flash in Bruce's
eyes.

Dinah knew that it had been a bitter disappointment to
her grandfather when Holly had dropped out of school
two years ago and had gone to live in San Francisco,
where she'd gone from job to job and was so extravagant
that she rarely made enough to live on. Bruce supported
her, of course, no matter how much money she wasted.

Spring at the vineyard was always a time of waiting,
but this season was even a more restless time than usual
for Morgan, Dinah, and Bruce. Though Dinah still had to
finish school, she needed to decide what to do with her
life. Morgan wanted to determine if his future lay at Kirsten Vineyards, and Bruce, who never made snap decisions on important matters, was irritable because he had
choices to make that would affect them all.

The week before her twenty-first birthday, the most terrible quarrel of all erupted between Bruce and Morgan.
Dinah could have heard their shouts from the library anywhere in the house, but she hovered on the landing above
the library.

"Then if you can't make up your mind, I've made up
mine," Morgan said. "I've worked hard for the past four
years."

"Four years, boy? Are you forgetting who owns this
place? I've been here fifty-six years. I brought my first
scrap of land in 1933 during Prohibition when no one

knew if that insane law would last another decade. I was only eighteen. I worked like a slave to make this place what it is.''

"I'm not discounting what you did for this place or for me, Bruce. But if there's nothing for me here, I'm moving on."

"Who said there would be nothing for you?"

"You've never said anything."

"Don't rush me, Morgan. I can't make up my mind in a hurry the way you do."

"And I can't wait any longer."

The library door slammed, and Dinah leaped toward the wall so that Morgan wouldn't see her as he stormed down the hall and out of the house. Dinah's heart felt like a leaden weight imprisoned within the walls of her chest. She should have been jubilant that he was leaving, but instead she felt terrified and lost.

What was happening to her? Why did she feel so empty? As if a warm, glowing light had gone out in her heart? All these years she'd been so jealous of Morgan, so determined to dislike him. Suddenly she realized that she hadn't thought badly of him in a long time. It was just a childish habit, a stubborn determination to believe the worst in him because then she could feel superior. Always her own insecurity and jealousy got in the way of her seeing the truth about people.

Hadn't he long ago redeemed himself in her eyes? He worked so hard. He'd never been unkind to her nor to anyone else at the vineyard. She'd thought he was bad because of what she'd read in the papers when she was sixteen years old. Whatever he'd done to his mother or because of his mother, he must have had a good reason, because the Morgan she knew was a fine man. Now he was leaving, and she'd never told him or shown him that she really admired him.

At the sound of his pickup, she rushed down the stairs and ran outside to the drive. The night air was cold, but there was no time to grab a sweater. Her long hair came tumbling out of its pins. The glare of his headlights flashed upon her as she raced like a wild creature toward him. He stopped the truck beside her.

"Morgan—" She was too breathless to say more.

He leaned across the seat and opened the door. As always, his voice was gentle when he spoke to her.

"Dinah, what's wrong?"

"I heard you quarreling with Grandfather."

"I'm sure we could be heard clear to Calistoga."

She climbed in beside him, and suddenly she felt nervous to be alone in the dark truck with him. He must think her a fool. This was not the unkempt, uncertain boy she had saved and regretted saving. That angry boy had vanished years ago. This was Morgan the man, Morgan whose skin was now a permanent bronze, whose tall, lean body had filled out with muscle and hard flesh, Morgan who knew what he wanted and how to get it, Morgan whose ambition would not be denied. This Morgan was a stranger to her.

"Are you ever coming back?" she managed at last.

There was silence and then his voice. "Would you care?"

Before his direct gaze, her own fell in confusion.

"I think I've finally gotten used to you," she conceded.

At that he laughed, and his laughter eased some of the tension between them. "Well, I'll be damned. So, you've gotten used to me?" He leaned back against the seat and drew his pack of cigarettes from his pocket. He shook one out and lit it. "You sure know how to flatter a man."

"As if you need flattering from a woman."

"And have you become a woman?"

Something different and excitingly intimate had come into his low drawl, and suddenly she did not know how to answer him. She was still a virgin. He was watching her with that old intensity that used to make her so nervous. Blood pounded in her head like a thousand Indian war drums crying danger. She felt vulnerable and wary of him.

"I don't know what you mean," she said in a low voice.

"Are you a woman?"

Before she thought, her answer tumbled from her lips. "I've been with a man, if that's what you're asking." She blushed. Oh, why had she admitted that? Why, her clumsy words almost sounded like an invitation.

He laughed softly, and she sighed in frustration.

"Don't laugh at me, Morgan. I don't know what you want me to say."

"Oh, you said what I wanted you to, and I'm not laughing at you," he murmured dryly. "I was just thinking. You didn't like me very much four years ago."

"No."

"I've always wanted you to like me, Dinah. I'd almost given up. When you started dating Edouard, and you were so cold to me, I thought you were in love with him. All those letters from France." He did not go on, and she wondered if she imagined the passion and jealousy in his voice. He ground out his cigarette.

She trembled, and because the car windows were down he thought she was cold. She watched him shrug out of his jacket and place it around her slim shoulders. For years she'd lived in the same house with him, slept in the room next to his. She should feel toward him as one felt toward an older brother, but that wasn't how she felt at all. Never before had she been more conscious of any man as a man, of the breadth of his wide shoulders, of the clean scent he exuded, of his dark, virile handsomeness. It was dangerously pleasant to be like this with him. When his hands accidentally brushed her shoulders, she felt the old, treacherous fire in her veins.

"I haven't always been very nice to you," she murmured.

He was staring at her, and something in his eyes mesmerized her. "In a way that's true, Dinah. But in other ways you were nicer to me than anyone, and much nicer than I deserved at the time. You risked your life—to save mine. And you let me stay though you didn't want to. I've never forgotten that, Dinah. I owe you everything."

"Maybe I would have been nicer if you had talked to me like this and said how you felt before."

"How could I? You didn't want me near you. And maybe it was for the best."

"Why?"

"I told you once," he said.

Was he referring to the time he'd kissed her? "Morgan, I...I wanted to tell you, I'll miss you."

Before he could react, she flung herself into his arms and hugged him. Tears were streaming down her cheeks. "I was mean to you because I was so jealous—of you and Grandfather."

He held her shaking body close against himself. She felt his hands tenderly smoothing her hair. "I know, honey. I know. You don't have to be sorry for being yourself. Not to me."

"And now that you're going, I don't want you to."

His mouth brushed her cheek in a sweet, brotherly caress that ended much too soon. She fumbled with the door handle so long he had to reach across her and open the door himself.

"Take care," he said.

"You too." Her face was stricken with remorse.

Then he was gone, and the swift, hot tears spilled down her cheeks as she flew into the house to her room. She cried as if her heart was breaking, and suddenly she realized that was exactly what was happening.

She loved him, and not as a brother. Perhaps she'd always loved him. Only she hadn't realized it until it was too late. Oh, why had she treated him so terribly? If only he would come back, she would find a way to show him how much she loved him.

The first week Morgan was away, a great gloom descended upon the vineyard and winery. It was as if someone had died. Grandfather shut himself up in his room for long periods every night. The employees were downcast, especially Graciela, whose greatest pleasure had been spoiling Morgan with her cooking.

Dinah was desolate, but despite her own unhappiness she was even more worried about Bruce. It seemed he had aged ten years. He passed his days listlessly, not even bothering to go out to the vineyard to check for signs of bud break. It was as if he no longer cared. She wished something, anything would happen to pull her grandfather out of his lethargy.

She was almost glad when the phone call came from Holly. Dinah knew her sister was in some sort of trouble, because Bruce left immediately for San Francisco. But at least he looked vital again, even if there was a grim fury in his vitality. For the first time when he raced to Holly's aid, Dinah felt none of her usual jealousy.

The day Bruce drove into the city, Dinah rode the bus

home that afternoon. As she stepped off the bus, she was too preoccupied to notice the startling beauty of the day. Endless wild mustard blooms waved in the fields between the vine rows like a golden froth above a sea of new grass. A solitary red-tailed hawk skimmed low before billowing white clouds.

She heard her name, and the husky male sound was the most beautiful music she could have imagined. She looked up, the sad stillness in her face gone, her eyes suddenly sparkling.

From the opposite side of the road the sound came again. "Dinah. Over here."

As if in a dream, she turned and saw him. She blushed with pleasure. Across the highway Morgan's truck was parked on the shoulder. He was leaning in that careless, nonchalant way of his against his pickup, obviously waiting for her. Never had he looked more handsome, with the sunlight gleaming in his black hair, his pose indolently rakish. A crisp white shirt and jeans molded his muscular body. The day was cool, but a disturbing warmth stole through her at the sight of him, so lean, and tall, and virile. She raced across the highway, her sudden smile as dazzling and spontaneous as his.

"I thought you'd left for good," she cried as he took her books from her and put them inside the truck. His fingertips brushed hers.

"So did I," he murmured.

"But you came back."

"Only because I couldn't stay away, Dinah."

"And why was that?" she asked.

"I think you know," came his soft, tantalizing voice. "If I spell it out, it'll only make you more conceited."

She had always been starved for love. "Make me conceited," she whispered as he folded her into his arms.

"What I want to do—is to make you my woman." He caught her frightened glance and held it.

It was what she wanted too.

His large hands spanned her narrow waist, and she felt their imprint burning through the light material of her blouse. He lifted her into the truck and climbed in beside her.

"Morgan, I've never been so unhappy as I was with you gone."

"Nor I."

"I missed you," she admitted.

A callused finger tilted her chin upward, forcing her to look at him, and her heart skipped crazily at the lazy warmth in his dark carved face.

"And I missed you...and the vineyards. When I cooled off, I realized I didn't want to leave Bruce either... especially now."

It hurt somehow that Morgan could mention anything other than his passion for her, even though she knew how dedicated to his work he had always been. She almost felt jealous of the vineyard as he stared past her at the vines in their fields of gold. The pruned vines, still in their dormancy, looked lissome and almost ready to spring into growth, like row upon row of dancers poised at the barre.

His gaze turned back to Dinah. "It's your birthday, honey. You're twenty-one. You've grown up—at last."

With his thumb Morgan traced the outline of her lips. Lightly he explored every curve of her mouth before his thumb probed her lips apart, and her thoughts turned from her jealousy to Morgan who was touching her so exquisitely. It was suddenly very difficult for her to breathe because of the erotic stimulation of his caresses.

"It was selfish of me to even think of leaving Bruce this time of year, no matter how I felt," he murmured.

His voice was absent, as if even he found it difficult to think of the vineyard when she was in his arms. "Hell, maybe that's why I left—the spring tension."

Hazily, she knew what he meant. Spring was an especially tense time at a vineyard. Every season this time of waiting between winter and spring brought the same sense of terrible expectancy. For with bud break would come the constant fear of nightly frosts, the constant vigilance. Yet with the winter pruning done, and winter gone, there was a restlessness to get on with the wine season, no matter how hard the work would be.

He drew her into his arms. Afraid to move, Dinah felt the quickening beats of his pulse as well as her own.

"You're not being very romantic—to think of the vineyard at a time like this," she teased.

"Jealous—even of a vineyard?" He smiled tenderly. His lips hovered within inches of hers. "Someday, when you truly grow up, Dinah, you'll know that you don't have to feel jealousy. You're very special to your grandfather and to me. You don't have to fight for our love. You've always had it."

"Have I, Morgan?"

"Since that first day I saw you."

"But all these years, you never said anything. You worked so hard."

"I worked to keep my sanity. You were sixteen, and I loved you even when you hated me. I had to wait until you grew up."

"You dated other girls."

"They were never important. Only you…"

Conversation stopped abruptly.

A tremulous silence hung between them. Reaching out, he caught her shoulders and pulled her toward him, her body trembling under the pressure of his hands. Then he kissed her mouth, gently at first and then with ever deep-ening passion. Her arms slid around his shoulders, her fingertips brushing his soft black hair, lightly, tentatively. She was quivering like a frightened animal even as she responded to the flaming delight of his lovemaking.

"You'll never know the hell it was loving a sixteen-year-old," he murmured thickly, kissing her again and again. "I think you were the most heartless girl that ever lived. You have a lot to make up for."

"I can imagine."

There was no question that Morgan could have taken her the first day that he came home, but he did not. He said they had the rest of their lives for the fulfillment of their physical love, but only this brief time of mutual, innocent loving before. He wanted her to be very sure.

During those golden, glorious days she went to school, and he worked hard at the vineyard. There were last-minute equipment repairs to be made before the rush of the coming season was upon them. Bruce remained in San Francisco, and certain tasks at the vineyard had been ne-glected in Morgan's absence. Despite their full schedules, Dinah had never felt more alive, more expectant. She lived to be with Morgan. In the afternoons when she came in from her classes, he quit working early and courted her.

They did all the things tourists do in Napa Valley. Mor-gan took her up in a hot-air balloon. The balloon was brought alive in the parking lot of Vintage 1870, a re-stored winery filled with shops and restaurants. Slowly it sprang into a breathtaking inverted teardrop with rainbow stripes. Dinah clung to Morgan tightly as they rose above ground-hugging mists, gently floating with the wind over Napa Valley.

The higher it rose the more tightly Dinah held on to Morgan. By nine o'clock they could feel a Mediterranean

sun on their arms. Below them Dinah recognized a cen-
tury-old frame winery and cried with delight.

"Look, Morgan. There's the old Eshcol cellars. It's
now the Trefethen Vineyards, you know."

"I know." He did not look down. He was too distracted
by the beauty of the woman in his arms.

The balloon lifted to three thousand feet, and they could
see almost the entire thirty-five-mile valley, a lush strip
from one to five miles wide. To the north loomed the
truncated cone of Mount St. Helena, the extinct volcano
that guarded the valley like a fortress. Below the mountain, vineyards flowed like golden lava, encircling the
small towns of Calistoga and St. Helena.

Another afternoon Morgan drove her to Sterling Vineyards Winery in the northern part of the valley. Situated
on a prominent hill, the gleaming white buildings with
their rounded belfries looked like a Grecian monastery
from an Aegean isle. Hand in hand, Morgan and Dinah
sat together in the steel basket of the aerial tramway that
carried them to the summit of the hill. Then they strolled
through the winery, seeing little of the romantic setting,
having eyes only for each other.

In the waning sunlight the vineyard beneath was fiery
gold. The wild mustard weed had not yet been plowed
into the earth.

"Have I ever told you the legend about why we have
the mustard weed?" Dinah asked lightheartedly, leaning
against a white wall. The warmth of Morgan's body
pressed against hers.

"I don't think you have," he whispered as he lifted her
hair and kissed the nape of her neck.

"Well, legend has it that when Father Altimira first
visited the Napa Valley in 1823, he carried with him a

bag of mustard seed that intentionally had a small hole in it.''

"That's very interesting," he said absently. He seemed to be concentrating solely on the movement of her lips.

She could scarcely speak. "You're not even listening."

"Oh, yes I am," he murmured with a smile.

"Well, the bag of seed was mounted on one of Father Altimira's burros so that the movement of the animal allowed a thin trickle of seeds to drop. When the father retraced his steps a few months later it was easy—he simply followed the ribbon of growing gold that marked his previous trail."

Morgan laughed, glad that her story was over because suddenly he wanted to kiss. "I never heard that. All I know is it's a valuable cover crop and provides aquifiers and green fertilizer."

"That's the sort of thing you would know."

"There's not much romance to farming, Dinah. And that's what I am—a farmer."

"A very romantic farmer," she purred as he kissed her.

That was the last thing either of them said for a very long time until they remembered they were in a public place.

He was crushing her against his body. "I want to be alone with you."

Mutely she nodded, and then she kissed him one last time before they descended to take the tramway. She was as anxious for his hungry kisses as he was to give them.

Another evening he took her to eat at the lovely dining room at Domaine Chandon, the vineyard owned by the French Champagne firm. Over an elegant meal of salmon and champagne they talked, holding hands, their voices soft and hushed as they made new discoveries about each other.

She poured out her heart, telling him anew of all the insecurities and jealousies that had plagued her as a child.

"I wonder if childhood is easy for anyone," he said at last.

His expression was dark, and she knew he was thinking of his own childhood, which had culminated in the wild recklessness of his youth.

"You've never told me about yours," she probed softly.

"Someday...maybe I can. I still can't talk about that time. All I can do is try to bury it."

"Morgan—"

"It's called survival, Dinah. I can't spill my guts like some soap opera character. I can tell you only one thing."

"What?"

"While I was gone this past week, I went to Los Angeles. I saw my mother."

She didn't know what to say. There was something so forbidding in his eyes that she could do nothing but grip his hand more tightly beneath the table.

His low voice continued. "I thought I never wanted to see her again, you know. I thought she was dead to me. I wanted her to be! I wish now I'd never gone back! But there is someone, a former neighbor of ours who tried to help me once before the situation got too intolerable, that I call from time to time. She told me my mother was very ill, and I went to see her. It was horrible. She's so ravaged by her alcoholism, she scarcely knows what's going on, but when she finally recognized me, she went wild. She hates me that much. She's made herself believe her own lies. She kept asking me, 'Why do you have to look like him?' I didn't know what she meant by that."

For a long time they did not talk. They just held on to each other, but after that night when he tried to talk about his past, there was a new closeness between Morgan and Dinah. She had learned something vital about him. For all his aura of self-confidence, he was still haunted by his past.

That Friday evening after they finished dinner and Graciela was clearing the table Morgan whispered, "You don't have school for two days, and Bruce called and said he won't be home until Tuesday. Why don't we go away tonight? I have in mind a very romantic place." His hot dark eyes held hers. Suddenly the sensual tension in the room was electric. Her heart began to pound. His low voice went on. "When I was in L.A. my old friend offered her family ranch in Marin county to me when I told her I needed to go somewhere to think about my future. Instead of going there, I came back here—to you. We could drive to her ranch tonight."

Her answer was a passionate kiss that took his breath away.

The ranch house that crowned tall cliffs plunging to the Pacific was as grand as a Moorish castle. Morgan and Dinah walked from room to room. Each room was more lavish than the one before, and all of them had views of the ocean.

"Morgan, who does this belong to?"

"I told you. A friend."

"She must be very rich."

"As well as famous, my curious darling," he added, smiling. "She's an actress."

"Like...your mother."

"Like my mother once was." His voice had grown grim. "Dinah, I don't want to talk about her."

Suddenly neither did she. The topic was dangerous, and Dinah was in the mood for a different kind of danger.

"My friend keeps horses. Blooded Arabians," Morgan

said. "I asked her man Joe to saddle two. He said he had a mare gentle enough for you."

Morgan wanted to ride horses in the middle of the night when she wanted nothing but to be in his arms! Her acute disappointment made her angry.

"Give me a stallion! I can ride as well as you!" she snapped indignantly.

"My kitten is now my lioness."

"Morgan, I do ride as well as you!"

"Not quite as well, surely darling," he teased. "I'm beginning to see how inexperienced you are with me. It would be wise if you at least let me think that I'm a little better at things and more knowledgeable than you."

She did not see the twinkling in his eyes.

"Those ideas are old-fashioned."

"They have a certain charm, and tonight, you are going to ride the mare. I have no intention of letting you get trampled before...I make love to you."

"I refuse to be bossed by a man."

"Then our lives will never be dull," he replied, unperturbed, "for I have no intention of being bossed by a woman."

His hand curved along her slender throat, turning her face toward his. For an instant she stopped breathing. Then his mouth closed over her parted lips, and she could taste the faint traces of tobacco on his breath. The fierce pressure of his hand near the small of her back arched her soft body against his.

"Open your mouth, Dinah," he instructed in a hoarse whisper.

She complied, and he kissed her softly at first and then more deeply, his tongue entering her lips in sensual exploration. Wildfire flamed in her veins as he stroked and caressed her, his fingers sliding over her body, touching her in places where he'd never touched her before.

A knock sounded at the door, and slowly they drew apart, their bodies on fire with their need. It was Joe, saying that the horses were ready.

Morgan sighed. "Ah, yes. The horses. Thank you, Joe."

Hoofbeats pounded on wet sand. The beach stretched before the two riders like a pale silver ribbon. The waves were wet, white flame exploding against black headlands.

Dinah raced ahead of Morgan, her mare lighter and swifter. Behind her, Dinah could hear the thunder of the stallion's hooves. She leaned forward in the saddle, rising on the stirrups, her head low, the wind whipping her long hair against the mare's neck.

"Dinah, wait up," Morgan shouted from behind her. "You win."

She laughed, because she had defeated him so easily. The narrow beach was long, at least a mile of sand they could have raced. She knew he was thinking of the horses when he had called to her. He had not wanted to risk ruining an animal simply to win a race. Gently she began to rein in her mare. Morgan came up beside her, his stallion falling into stride beside her mount, the two horses moving together as if in some timeless rhythm, like the dark glittering ocean caressing the rocks beyond.

At last they stopped, and Morgan slid from the stallion, took the reins of both horses, and with his free arm, gathered Dinah from the saddle. He kissed her, and even as her whole body responded, she caught the taste of salt on his lips, the tangy flavor of that wild, wind-tossed sea. A wave of pleasure filled her, her desire so intense it was almost painful.

This breathless promise of passion between them was

something quite beyond love. As he held her in the moon-lit darkness she knew that she was irrevocably committed to this man, that she could love no other. All her life this moment would remain to haunt her with its brief, sparkling magic, this hour that would bind her to him for all time.

He kissed her again and again, and she thought it was true what all the books and half-remembered songs had promised of love. The coming together of a man and woman could be this wild splendor that was fierce and savage and yet infinitely tender.

Slowly she drew away from him, laughing, happy, supremely confident that nothing could ever come between them. His hand swept the tangled mass of her dark hair aside. He lifted her into his arms and carried her to a small protected cover where a eucalyptus grove grew close to the beach. Beneath the trees he spread a blanket and pulled her down beside him.

He touched her hair again. He traced the curve of her jawline. She had never felt so free, so alive. The sensation was intoxicating, both sharp and sweet. Their eyes met, his gaze touching her soul.

Wordlessly he began unbuttoning her blouse.

Skillful in the intricacies of buttons, hooks, and zippers, he unfastened her clothes and removed them. He took off her lace bra. She shivered as her breasts swung free, and his hands roamed over them. She'd always felt ashamed of her breasts, thinking them vulgar because of the un-wanted male attention they evoked. But now she felt shy pleasure that she was so lushly endowed because there was nothing vulgar in the beauty of Morgan's lovemak-ing. He was obviously aroused by her figure and pleased she was designed so voluptuously. When his devouring gaze slid the length of her opulent body, which gleamed

like ivory in the moonlight, she hadn't the slightest wish
to cover herself.

He whispered into her hair, "You're beautiful, Dinah,
even more beautiful than I imagined."

And she felt beautiful as Morgan bent and kissed her
softly, opening her mouth under the expert pressure of his
lips. His hands slid over her body, gently kneading her
breasts until her nipples tautened, stroking bare thighs until at last his fingertips discovered and touched her womanhood.

She gasped, feeling embarrassed at her warm wetness
as his fingers explored there, yet her pulse quickened because of this intimacy. Despite her uncertainty, she did
not deny him access to her tingling flesh. Against her
earlobe he murmured reassuring endearments. Then his
mouth trailed along the hollow of her throat. Her body
grew hot from his skilled, stroking caresses. Soon these
strange, new intimacies with him were too desirable and
pleasurable to be embarrassing, and she kissed him as
deeply and passionately as he kissed her, even though she
could not yet bring herself to touch him as he touched
her.

At last he stopped caressing her and stripped out of his
clothes. She watched, finding pleasure in the male beauty
of his dark, muscled length. He gathered her warm body
in his arms once more, and she quivered at the contact of
her naked skin sliding erotically against the heat of his.
Timidly her hands moved over his broad shoulders and
then lower, closing around his waist tightly, as if she
wanted to press herself into him forever.

"Easy, honey," he groaned. "Oh, Dinah, love—"

He lowered his body on top of hers and very gently
buried himself inside the incredible warmth of her softest
flesh. His body felt as hard and tough as a shaft of steel.

Dinah cried out softly, quivering, and he held himself still for a long time deep within her. She felt his lips on her closed eyelids, his hands caressing her cheek. A trembling weakness spread throughout Dinah's body.

"Did I hurt you?" he murmured, concern in his low voice.

For fear that he might leave her, she replied huskily, "No," as she clung to him, her hands laced around his powerful body.

Her arms crept around his neck and down his shoulders to touch and feel the hard muscles of his back, which were damp with perspiration. He kissed her, and her lips and tongue responded to his with wild abandonment.

She stirred restlessly, and this movement aroused him even further. He could remain still no longer. Slowly he began to move inside her in a rhythm that gradually roused in her a deep female satisfaction.

It pleased her the way his hands gripped her, the way he murmured in broken, unintelligible whispers. The slight pain she had felt earlier was gone and waves of delight began to build. Slowly her body responded to the sensual pleasure of his deliberately controlled lovemaking, and her guilt and shyness were swept away in the ecstasy of fulfillment. She clasped him tightly, her newly awakened body hungrily restless.

Suddenly it was as if a force outside herself and yet deep within her took over, lifting her to unbelievable crescendos of emotion, shattering her, consuming her. She cried his name again and again. Then she began to sob softly at the beautiful poetry of it. At last it was over, this wild magic between them, this volcanic tide of emotion that had swept them, but afterward there was an indescribable sweetness as he continued to hold her fast against his body.

Slowly she grew aware of the world outside Morgan, of the pungent odor of eucalyptus trees in the cool, humid air, of the whinnies of horses, and of the hollow boom of the surf crashing upon the distant rocks.

Wrapped in his arms and the thick folds of blanket with her head against Morgan's broad chest, Dinah fell asleep beneath a canopy of stars and moonlight. His hands gently stroked her dark hair. Very softly she murmured before she slept, "I love you."

"Forever, my love," came his low, beautiful drawl.

It was raining Sunday night when Morgan and Dinah returned to Kirsten Vineyards. Thick clouds sifted over the tops of the wooded hills, and wisps of fog lay in the valley. In the pickup the lovers touched. His arm was draped over her shoulders. Her hand rested on the warm denim that encased his thigh. They talked quietly, their voices husky, their hearts filled with the wanton memories of newly discovered sensual joys.

When the automatic garage door lifted, they saw the sleek, white Corvette already parked in Morgan's space, and abruptly there was silence.

"Why, that's Holly's car," Dinah choked, unable to keep her old jealousies from settling unhappily upon her.

"So the prodigal granddaughter has returned. I wonder if Bruce will serve fatted calf for dinner tomorrow night?" The cynicism in Morgan's low voice made Dinah stiffen. She tried to relax when she felt his hands smoothing her hair, but his warm lips on her forehead felt alien. He was staring at her, reading her misery all too accurately. "Try to be generous, darling. You have so much, and the Holly's of the world have so little. I should know."

His words chilled Dinah. He hadn't even met Holly, but already he was defending her.

Three

Dinah awoke to the sounds of Holly's silvery laughter mingling with Morgan's.

"This was my old room, you know," Holly was saying from the hall. "My, but you've made it so masculine. What's happened to my pink organza curtains and bedspread?"

"I'm afraid they weren't quite my style."

"So I see." There was female admiration in Holly's low tone.

"If you want your old room back, I can move downstairs."

"I wouldn't dream of it. I like the idea of your sleeping—in my room," came the huskily flirtatious reply.

Dinah sagged limply against the door, her heart filling with anguish and fear. There was no mistaking Holly's predatory interest in Morgan. Why did Holly always want whatever Dinah loved? Feeling wooden and dead inside, Dinah opened her door.

"Why, Dinah," Holly cooed pleasantly, "don't you look all grown up." Only her lips smiled. There was a definite coolness in those beautiful slate blue eyes.

Holly's words deliberately emphasized that she still saw Dinah as a child, and Dinah could not stop herself from frowning. Then she was aware of Morgan watching her, a look of warning in his dark face, and she remembered he'd told her she should try to be generous toward Holly. That was going to be very, very difficult. "Welcome home, Holly," Dinah managed stiffly.

"Why, how sweet of you, little sister. It's good to be back. If I'd known there was someone this interesting at home, I might have come back a long, long time ago." Holly batted long, fringed lashes at Morgan, who was smiling down at her.

Dinah cringed, desperation building inside her. What was she going to do? Never had Dinah felt more jealous of her older sister, nor more keenly aware of Holly's beauty.

Holly was a vision of loveliness in frothy, ice blue chiffon. Her pale hair fell in curling waves past her shoulders, framing her exquisitely made-up face. Dinah had never been able to compete with Holly, and suddenly she felt terrified and unsure of Morgan's love. How could he want her, if Holly offered herself to him?

"While you're in class, Dinah dear, Morgan's promised to show me the vineyard and the winery," Holly said.

"Has he?" Dinah murmured faintly, feeling too sick even to look at Morgan. She could only retreat into the privacy of her own room to numbly dress for school. She tried not to listen to Morgan and Holly through the door, but it was impossible to ignore the horrible sound of

Holly's skillful, flirtatious banter. All her old, terrible feelings swamped Dinah, and she felt as lost and shut out as she'd always felt as a child.

Later, when Holly had gone downstairs to dress, Morgan knocked quietly on Dinah's door. "Dinah — " His voice was gentle.

She felt too miserable to face him. "Go away."

"Dinah, please—"

"I said go away."

"I want to talk to you."

"Talk to Holly, if you want to talk to someone. She obviously finds you fascinating."

"Dammit, Dinah!"

"Oh, just leave me alone," Dinah cried miserably.

"If that's the way you feel, I damn sure will."

She heard the clatter of his boots as he stormed down the stairs, and heartsick, terrified of what she'd done, Dinah opened the door to cry after him.

Holly's lilting voice from below stopped her.

"Morgan, I thought you were going to drive Dinah to class."

"Well, I'm not."

"Then would you mind showing me the winery now?"

There was a moment's hesitation before he answered.

"Why the hell not?" came that beautiful male voice that Dinah loved more than any on earth.

Tears blinding her, Dinah stumbled to her window and lifted the curtains just in time to watch them leave the house together. Holly was folding her arm possessively through his as Morgan bent his black head to her silver one to catch something she was saying.

They made a beautiful couple, and Dinah realized that if she was not very careful, she would drive Morgan permanently into Holly's arms.

Dinah was too young and too much in love to be careful. Again and again as spring ebbed into summer Dinah played into the skillful, predatory hands of her older sister. Holly knew how to make herself helplessly appealing in Morgan's eyes, just as she knew how to inflame her younger sister's jealousy. All too often Dinah would feel possessive and jealous, and she would quarrel with Morgan. This was absolutely the wrong tack to take with a man like him, and she knew it. Hadn't he once said he would not allow himself to be bossed by a woman? Every demand Dinah made only drove him further away.

Morgan didn't understand Dinah's jealousy of Holly, and he blamed her entirely. He said that he felt sorry for Holly and that Dinah should try to understand Holly's problems and be kinder. The more he took Holly's side, the more Dinah's jealousy grew. If only Dinah could have felt sure of Morgan's love, perhaps she could have controlled the self-destructive course she sailed. But that was impossible with Holly constantly and so cleverly making her look ridiculous and immature in his eyes. Perhaps Morgan could have seen the truth had he not been under awesome pressure himself because the wine season was in high gear.

It was an uncertain time for all of them, but in between their quarrels Morgan and Dinah made wild and reckless love in the wooded hills above the vineyards, love that was all the sweeter because of the throbbing desperation in Dinah's heart. It was as if she wanted to bind him to her with her body, as if she felt him slipping away, and she had to cling to him all the more fiercely.

Then came the most horrible blow of all.

For months Bruce had been watching his beloved Holly shamelessly chase Morgan. He was delighted that at last Holly was interested in the vineyard and winery, just as

he was equally delighted at the thought of a romance between Holly and Morgan. As always, he wanted Holly to
have what she wanted.

Oblivious to Dinah's changed relationship with Morgan, Bruce confided in Dinah one evening. "Wouldn't it
be perfect, Dinah, if Morgan married Holly?"

"W-what?" Dinah's whole body had begun to tremble.

"It's obvious that Holly loves him, and Morgan wants
to make his future here. No matter how hard Morgan's
worked these past few years, I couldn't disinherit one of
my own granddaughters in favor of him. You and he have
never liked each other."

"Never liked each other..." The memory of callused
hands touching her body intimately brought the most poignant pain.

"It's been tearing at me, this problem of what to do
about Morgan. If he married Holly, I could give her a part
of the estate, and Morgan could stay permanently. I could
retire."

At just that moment Morgan stepped into the library.
His eyes were alight with interest, and Dinah was forcibly
reminded of his ambition where the winery and vineyard
were concerned.

"What was this about my staying permanently,
Bruce?"

Holly was behind him, dazzling in white silk. Dinah
could not stop herself from wondering if they had been
somewhere together. Holly tilted her wineglass in a tri-
umphant salute.

"I—I'm tired," Dinah said weakly. In truth she felt so
nauseated she wanted to flee to her own room.

Morgan did not try to stop her.

The next day a terrible tension ruled the house, and
Dinah knew that Bruce has declared his proposition to

Morgan. Dinah was afraid as she had never been afraid before when Morgan did not confide in her. Instead he left the house earlier than usual that morning for the vineyard, and Dinah knew that he was trying to think out his decision.

By noon Dinah was in an agony of suspense. Holly rushed into the dining room with the mail just as Morgan strode inside with a look of grim purpose on his face.

"Grandfather, there's a letter for you...from the Comte de Landaux," Holly said brightly.

Dinah whitened at her sister's uncanny sense of timing.

Bruce broke the seal and read out loud. "The Comte de Landaux requests the pleasure of Dinah Kirsten's presence at his château in Bordeaux for the entire summer as his son Edouard will not be coming to California and is most anxious for her to come to France." There was more to the letter, and inside the gilt envelope were airline tickets and a second letter from Edouard himself to Dinah, entreating her to come.

"Oh, Dinah, a letter from the Comte himself," Holly exclaimed in excitement. "Who could refuse such an invitation?"

"Yes, who?" Morgan's voice was as cold as ice.

The quarrel between Morgan and Dinah later that night was inevitable. They were alone in the Sauvignanios' ancient, crumbling winery, the darkened interior lit only by the soft glow of moonlight sifting through the open doors and windows. As always, Dinah's emotions were so passionate they overpowered her, and she accused him of wanting the vineyard and Holly.

"Do you really believe I'm that kind of person?" he demanded.

"Well, you haven't asked me to marry you."

"How can you think two people should marry each

other who quarrel the way we do? I keep hoping we'll find a way to resolve our differences. I think you're too young for marriage.''

"And Holly's not, I suppose!"

"At least she's not constantly jealous!"

"Maybe it's Holly and the vineyard you really want."

"Then you believe that I would use a woman as a means to satisfy my ambition?"

"Yes! Yes!" she cried passionately.

"Or are you accusing me so you can go to Edouard?"

"Maybe." Only blind fury had driven her to say that. Too late, she realized her mistake.

He seized her arms, his savage grip crushing muscle against bone so tightly that she gave a little cry of pain.

"Then I'll give you something to remember me by when you're with him, my darling," he said roughly.

Grasping her by her thick black hair, he brought her face against his so that she was forced to look into the blazing fire of his eyes. He was in the grip of the most powerful emotion. As he leaned toward her, his face dark and flushed, his familiar beloved features those of a stranger, she began to tremble.

Never had she seen him so angry, and a new kind of fear crept into her. She didn't know this Morgan. Usually, even in his anger, Morgan was controlled, but now she could feel the violence in him fighting its way to the surface. Vague memories of the terrible things she had read about him in the newspapers so long ago flew in her frightened mind, and she tried to wrench free. He only yanked her more closely against his body, so that she felt the muscular length of his thighs and legs against her own. The zipper of her dress was ripped apart, and his hand slid down the delicate line of sensitive, exposed skin.

"You are mine. You will never belong to him." The

searing heat of his hand exploring her naked flesh rocked her senses.

The warmth of his breath brushed her lips. She inhaled his clean masculine scent.

"Morgan, don't do this." She struggled to stop him from sliding the dress off her shoulders.

"Be still, Dinah!" He growled the command against her soft, protesting lips.

Bending her backward, her dress only half removed, he pinned her even more tightly against his body as he kissed her long and insolently. Dinah writhed in his arms, but her efforts at resistance were useless against his superior strength. Cruelly, Morgan ravaged the lush sweetness of her mouth before his dark head lowered to taste the throbbing pulse beat in the hollow of her throat. His lips followed the slender curve of her neck, his every kiss making a dizzying weakness spread throughout her limbs. Her hands were splayed against his chest, and beneath her fingertips she could feel his corded muscles, latently powerful in their male sexuality.

Morgan's mouth returned to her lips, and he forced her to kiss him, filling her mouth with his tongue, until slowly, the heat of his passion made her own hot anger dissolve into pulsing desire and she was as filled with longing as he.

As her will to fight ebbed, his rough kisses gentled, and his hands on her body sought to caress rather than imprison and conquer. His lightest touch became skillful and tantalizing, until she clung to him, yearning breathlessly for more. Swift, scalding tears coursed down her cheeks, that she should be so in his power. A shudder of emotion swept her body.

"I don't want to love you," she cried. "It hurts too much."

"Only because you can't believe I care," he said, a quiet intensity in his voice. "Don't you see, you're hurting yourself, by not believing in yourself. Why are you so determined to destroy our love? Dinah, you're the only woman I've ever loved. What can I do to make you believe that?" He lowered his head to the voluptuous curves of her breasts and tenderly kissed her pouting nipples. "I love you, Dinah."

Exquisite sensations of pleasure surged through her body, and she moaned, arching her body into his. With an indrawn breath, she felt the world drifting away. There was only Morgan and the ecstasy of his tall dark body, the splendor of his mouth devouring her ever so gently, the pleasure of his voice making vows she couldn't quite believe. A shivering thrill pierced her as his fingers glided lower between her legs.

The time for words had come to an end. She didn't argue when he lowered her onto the blanket on the rough floor in the ancient winery that had so often been their private bower of love.

That night their lovemaking was all the more sweetly desperate because of the quarrel that had preceded it. Her senses passionately responded to his ardent possession. He took her again and again as if the glorious, shattering bursts of frenzied ecstasy he brought her to proved that she belonged only to him.

Afterward, removed from Morgan's passionate embraces, with him asleep at her side, Dinah's doubts returned despite her attempts to subdue them. She thought of how often he defended Holly, of how beautiful Holly was. Most of all Dinah realized that if it were not for her, Morgan would be free to marry Holly and gain the right to make his future permanently at Kirsten Vineyards.

Maybe it would be better for both of them if he married Holly and I went to France, she thought wearily.

It hurt so much to love Morgan because her love for him intensified all of her jealousies and insecurities. Her fear that she was losing him was as great as ever, and she was afraid that when he awoke she would inflame him with more irrational outbursts. She would have to be very careful.

He stirred drowsily and reached for her. At his casual touch, her blood began to pound. If only she loved him less, perhaps she could be more clever at handling him.

"Well, Dinah, do you believe I love you? I damned near killed myself to prove it to you tonight."

"Sex is not the same as love," she said stubbornly.

"Sometimes it is. At least for a man."

"Not always."

"I suppose not, but I wish you weren't such a victim of your personality. Whenever you really want something, you're terrified of losing it. You have to learn to trust, Dinah."

She didn't like the way he always blamed everything on her jealousy and inferiority complex. "What if I won't ever be able to trust you?" Oh, what made her say that? "Maybe it's not just Holly or a flaw in *my* personality. Maybe it's you. How can I trust *you*, Morgan? How can I ever be sure you're not as faithless as your mother was? How can I know you won't hurt me the way you hurt her?"

A muscle spasmed in his cheek; his black glare froze her. "So that's it. You still consider me as some kind of monster." He had not denied her accusation. "I thought perhaps we'd put that behind us. I'll never be good enough for you, will I?"

His hand fell away from her breast. He was angrier than

she'd ever seen him, so angry she was almost afraid he might strike her.

Instead he rose and dressed hurriedly in the darkness. "Go to Edouard. With his impeccable background, he should suit you far better than I."

When Morgan finished dressing, he stalked out of the winery. She lay shivering as she watched him leave, but she was too young and stubbornly proud to go after him and beg his forgiveness. Later when she returned to the house she saw him talking to Holly in the dining room. He did not even glance up at her as she ran up the stairs to her bedroom.

When Morgan continued to avoid her, stubborn pride made Dinah accept the Comte's invitation and fly to France two days later. Stupidly she believed that if Morgan loved her, he would come after her despite his mammoth responsibilities at the vineyard and winery during the busiest season of the year. For four weeks she neither wrote Morgan nor called him. The only letter he wrote her she returned unopened. Her heart was shattered.

Dinah was staring forlornly out of the long windows of the grand salon of the de Landeaux château. She had just returned from a doctor's appointment in the village and was wondering what to do when Edouard rushed into the room. Beneath the window lay the elaborate garden, with its gravel paths, formal gardens, terraces, and sentry-box gazebos. Usually Dinah could find peace in the quiet solitude of the garden, but not today.

"Dinah—"

She turned toward Edouard, the sunlight full on her wan features.

"There's a telegram for you from America," he said.

Her heart stopped, and her fingers trembled so much she could not open the envelope. He whole life hung on the breathless hope that it was from Morgan, that he wanted her, that he loved her, that he was begging her to return, that somehow he magically knew how much she needed him.

She read the terrible words and went as white as death. The telegram was from Bruce, not Morgan. The terse message burned itself like a brand upon her heart.

"Holly and Morgan married today." There was no more. Nothing from Morgan himself.

"What is it, Dinah?"

"Oh, Edouard." She flung herself into his arms. "Morgan's married Holly! And I'm pregnant with his child! What am I going to do?"

Four

An erotic tingle traced up Dinah's spine like a shiver of electricity, and she dropped the fur-trimmed glove she was trying to pull on over her five-carat diamond engagement ring. Only one man had ever made her feel so feverishly afire with sensual excitement, and that had been more than eight years ago.

Until the stranger in black yesterday!

She whirled expectantly. There was no one. Only the snow-capped houses and hotel of St. Moritz beneath a purple, early-morning sky. Though she couldn't see him, Dinah knew he was watching her from some darkened window.

As Edouard lifted her into the Palace Hotel's red sleigh, she felt the thrumming in her blood, was the same odd sensation of thrilling danger that had filled her since the moment she'd become aware of the tall stranger yesterday on the crowded ski slope. She despised herself for feeling giddily young, as if she'd miraculously shed eight years and was a breathless twenty-one again.

A thousand questions formed in her mind. Again she scanned the silent, snow-clad buildings for any sign of the man in the black ski suit and ski mask, the man who had stalked her so relentlessly from the slopes to the streets outside the expensive shops she'd perused, the man who had materialized out of nowhere when her reins had tangled before the start of the *skikjöring* race. His nearness had made her shiver with fiery excitement as she watched him gentle her horse with expert ease while she clumsily fumbled to untangle the reins. Before either she or Edouard could thank him, the stranger had vanished into the crowd of spectators, but the impression of the man's size, of the way he moved, had lingered in her mind. There was something achingly familiar about him.

Who was he, and why could his mere gaze make her tremble? Why didn't he remove his mask? Was it because she would know him instantly? Or was her mind playing a cruel trick on her by making her wonder if it was Morgan? Was her preoccupation with Morgan because of his phone call at her Paris hotel on Tuesday, a call she had not dared return? That extraordinary attempt to contact her after eight years of deliberate silence between them was incomprehensible. She had telephoned her grandfather immediately to make sure everything was all right; and though there had been something off in his frail voice, he had assured her that both he and her son, Stephen, were fine. Nevertheless, ever since Morgan's call, she had not been able to stop thinking of him.

Eight years ago when she'd lost Morgan and remained in Europe during her pregnancy, the sight of any tall dark man had affected her with the same inexplicable course of excitement she was feeling now. For years she had

looked for Morgan everywhere, feeling pathetically
thrilled at any slight resemblance she discovered in some
stranger. Later there had even been a painful period when
she had only dated men who reminded her of him. It was
better that she had settled on Edouard, of course, because
in no way did he remind her of Morgan. Better to banish
ghosts rather than let them haunt her.

Yet the ghost still haunted her, and it was the ghost
who drove her on this mad adventure today. If it had not
been for the stranger yesterday and her dread of seeing
him again, she would have remained cozily ensconced in
her bed instead of rising before dawn.

St. Moritz was still sleeping as the de Landaux helicopter roared aloft early that winter morning and headed
toward the mountains where Dinah could ski unhampered
by crowds. Skis and poles lay in a jumble pile beneath
the seats. Dinah looped her gloved hand over Edouard's
as she stared down at the famed resort that glittered like
a handful of gold and diamonds sprinkled across the darkened valley. Edouard, his expression tense, bent his blond
head over hers. She thought he suspected something was
bothering her.

At twenty-nine, snuggled in cascades of thick lynx, the
cosmopolitan woman scarcely resembled the frightened
young girl she had been at twenty-one when she had lost
everything that mattered to her because of a reckless love
affair. Dinah was strikingly beautiful, and her maturity
had brought an aura of confidence as well. Behind a carefully polished facade, she masked her feelings of insecurity and inadequacy so cleverly that no one suspected they
even existed. The world was in awe of her, and that included the man beside her.

Journalists who wrote infatuated prose about her in
wine magazines said her black eyes and translucent skin

made her face arresting, if not classically beautiful. They said she had the grace and poise of a professional model, and the shrewd talent of a brilliant executive.

How hard she fought to live up to these idealistic beliefs. How important it was to her that people think well of her. It helped make up for her secret feelings of inadequacy.

Except for her full breasts, Dinah's figure was whipcord thin. Too thin, Edouard occasionally admonished her when she stuck with tenacity to her torturous diets.

"You have to be skinny to wear clothes," she would chide him. "And you know how I love beautiful clothes."

"By beautiful clothes, you mean a *haute couture* wardrobe," he would laugh.

"A luxury I can now afford."

"But can I?" Edouard and she were to be married within the week. A crowd of his friends had assembled in St. Moritz for the occasion.

In the past eight years Dinah had become not only a financial success, but a celebrity in the wine world, as well as a darling of the press. These were goals she'd deliberately sought to accomplish. On that long-ago day when she'd lost Morgan and her home forever to Holly, Dinah had vowed that she would never again let her feelings of jealousy and self-doubt bring her to such defeat, that she would rise so high, she would be envied even by Holly. She swore she would be so rich, so glamorous, and so successful that she would no longer care about all that she had lost.

Well, she was rich and famous. If she had not altogether banished the insecurity that always filled her heart, who but she knew? As for Morgan and her son...Dinah tried to work so hard that she never had time to think of them. In rare moments of insight she realized how ironic it was that the same character defects that had driven her to make mistakes in her youth had also driven her to overachieve.

Privately she sometimes laughed about her success to Edouard. "I think the press just likes to glorify my rather modest accomplishments because I am a woman. There are so few women in this business."

"It never hurts to belong to one of the underprivileged minorities, does it, my love? The press so loves the underdog." Edouard's amused gaze had lingered for a moment on her ice-cream pink puckered silk blouse, which Liz Vorzenski had designed especially for her, before dropping to his enormous diamond sparkling on her left hand.

"Not that I've been hurt by being your fiancée," Dinah added fondly. "Where would I be without you?"

"At the top, love. I only helped you because it was mutually advantageous to de Landaux wines and champagnes to tout your brilliance. Having a glamorous woman as a spokeswoman for our company has only enhanced the romance and allure of our product. Besides, I've always known how immensely talented you are. Now with the results of that recent Gault-Millau international tasting, and three of your Texas wines from your new winery walking away with top prizes, the world knows you are a star in your own right. And, of course, you were responsible for two of the de Landaux awards as well. I'm just glad you're on my payroll and not working for the competition."

"You discount Wood Creek Vineyards, then?"

"Why should I worry, when I'm marrying into the business? But even if I weren't, you're only bottling twenty thousand bottles a year, *chérie*. The Texas wine industry is still very much in the pioneer stages."

"That's what makes it so exciting. Experimenting with different soils and grape varieties is challenging."

"And I thought you liked Texas because it was a long way from California and Bordeaux, and the two men you're determined to run away from."

"Don't, Edouard. That's not fair. I am going to marry you."

"I can't forget that we've been engaged over two years and that we quarreled all night before you made that decision. And you don't look particularly happy at the moment."

Any reference to Morgan always brought a dark, haunted look into Dinah's eyes. No matter how hard she tried, she could never quite forget Morgan and the son she had had to leave behind. Instead of fulfillment in her accomplishments there was only an aching emptiness in her heart, a restlessness that drove her to constantly try something new in the hope that this time, she would find what she was looking for. She hoped that if she married Edouard and tried really hard to make her marriage work, she would build a contented life with him. They would have children, and perhaps she would be able to forget the child she had had to give up.

The helicopter hovered noisily as the pilot scanned the mountains for a place to let the skiers disembark.

"I'm so glad we came, Edouard," Dinah cried above the sound of the engine. Beneath, the still, white slopes beckoned. "This is just the thing to make you forget your terrible wine harvest." Just the thing to make her forget a certain disturbing individual in black.

"You mean I won't be alive to remember it," Edouard said, eyeing the razor-sharp cliffs as the helicopter began its descent. His voice softened. "I should be glad of your daredevil passion, my love. It brought you to Europe a week early so we could have this holiday together. And I'm glad you decided to marry me, Dinah. At last you will be here with me where you belong."

"Where I belong…" Her voice had a wistful, faraway sound.

For an instant the vision of vine rows in gilded fields, of hills shrouded in cool Pacific fog, of a small dark boy and his bronzed father tugged at her senses. Unbidden came the memory of the compelling stranger in black from yesterday. The significance of her dreamy expression was not lost on Edouard.

"I think you would have married me months ago, if your sister Holly hadn't died in that accident last year. In the back of your mind, you were still hoping…"

"What are you saying, Edouard?"

"That no matter how many years have passed, you're still not over Morgan, and you're still not sure of your feelings for me."

"That's absurd."

"Then why do you always make certain he's gone when you make your annual visits to see your son and grandfather in California? Why didn't you talk to him in Paris when he called you? Dinah, why are you so afraid of him? And why haven't you married me long before now?"

His questions had brought a sharp, almost paralyzed tension into her beautiful face. "He has no right to call me," she began hesitantly, "and I am…going to marry you."

"Morgan might have something damned important to tell you. He's the father of your only son."

"But Morgan doesn't know that."

"An irrelevant detail, my love."

"Edouard, you know I hate him!"

"No, Dinah, I don't."

"Well, I do! If he hadn't called, you and I wouldn't be quarreling now."

"Perhaps we need to quarrel. Dinah, I'm asking you to make a commitment."

"I said I'd marry you, Edouard. What is it that you want from me?"

How did a chauvinistic French *comte* beg his bride-to-be to love him?

The helicopter hovered four feet above the snow. The pilot looked at them expectantly.

Dinah picked up her skis and tossed them defiantly out onto the snow. Edouard had made her angry with his probing questions. "Edouard, I want to ski by myself."

"So you can sulk."

"For days I've been with your crowd. I want to be alone."

"You're out of your mind. Out here one mistake is death."

"Please, Edouard. You know how it always upsets me to think...of him. You shouldn't have opened up old wounds. Please. I will be very careful." When he hesitated, she knew she had won. She'd always been able to get around him.

The helicopter lowered to within six inches of the snow, and swiftly Dinah kissed him just before she ducked and let him help her jump into the powder where she sank to her thighs.

Edouard shouted to the pilot. "If she's not down in an hour, we're coming back after her."

Powder flew like white skirted wings behind Dinah's graceful form as she swooped down the steep slopes of the mountain. She felt a wild, soaring exhilaration that only a taste of fear can bring. Edouard's troubling ques-

tions were pushed into the back of her mind, and she lost
herself in the challenge of the mountain. Perhaps if he had
not asked them, Dinah would not have skied quite so recklessly. Not that she consciously thought of the dangers of
her speed and the risks of skiing ungroomed slopes where
the possibility of an avalanche always existed.

With her skis slicing snow at a furious pace, she felt
as free and unfettered as an eagle soaring in a vast sky.
Faster and faster she raced down the mountain, skis parallel, her body low and tense when she had to jump.

Edouard had called her a daredevil and the term fit her
too accurately. Since Stephen's birth she'd been careless
of her own safety. She liked fast cars and fast horses. She
skied and she climbed mountains in the winter on
snatched three-day weekends when the wine season was
over. Just as sometimes she combined her love of horses
and skiing by participating in the *skikjöring* races, a spe-
cialty of St. Moritz.

Above she heard the sound of another helicopter, and
she halted her mad flight over snow and ice to catch her
breath and glare at the yellow speck. Someone else had
decided to avoid the crowded runs of the resort, but did
he have to make the same, long, solitary descent among
fairyland Christmas trees she was making? Her heart was
pounding; her toes and fingers felt numb from the cold.
She clenched and unclenched her hands and curled her
toes in her ski boots in an attempt to warm them.

The helicopter hovered several hundred yards on the
slope above her. Dinah's frown deepened, as a lean giant
in a black ski suit jumped from the helicopter. A black
ski mask concealed his features.

It was he! The stranger who had followed her! And she
was alone with him on the mountain. Fear squeezed her

heart, and the icy mountain wind seemed to howl inside her in panic.

She stood rooted in the snow in a state of mindless paralysis as she watched him don his skis. His great body was kneeling. He tore off his gloves to carefully make the correct adjustments. He seemed to move in slow motion. When he finished and was pulling on his gloves, he cast a deliberate predatory look in Dinah's direction that transfixed her. He rose to his feet slowly, and still she didn't move. Only when he began to streak like black lightning down the mountain toward her, did she come to life and point her skis downhill.

She took off like a startled wild thing, racing blindly through the thick drifts of powder. It was like a nightmare, only the nightmare was reality. She skied faster than she'd ever skied before, the chill air whipping her cheeks until they were scarlet.

Filled with a nameless dread, she didn't dare stop. More and more recklessly she pushed herself, and still with the passing of every minute the distance between the two skiers narrowed fractionally in her pursuer's favor. She could hear the whisper of his skis and the crunch of his poles biting into the ice behind her.

Jumps that were difficult for her, he took easily. Slopes that were steep and rugged to her were child's play to him.

Who was this stranger so intent upon catching her? What did he want? Suddenly she was afraid, and as fear and exhaustion possessed her, her reflexes were less sure, her concentration less intense. She was too aware of the danger behind her to avoid the real perils ahead of her.

Across snow and ice he called to her, and a shudder of recognition swept her. The deep, vibrant tone could belong to only one man.

"Dinah, stop for God's sake, before you kill yourself."

Frantically she turned, and her eyes met the brilliant blue fire of his that blazed from beneath his black ski mask. Her senses catapulted in alarm. Too late, as her left ski hit ice, she realized she should never have looked back at him. Desperately she tried to regain her balance, but instead she lost control, falling so hard that both of her skis came off on impact. Her poles went flying. But she kept sliding helplessly, her skis dragging behind her on their straps as she skidded across ice and tumbled through deep powder before she plunged headfirst toward the edge of an awesome cliff.

She screamed, her desperate cry tearing the air like the thinnest blade. "Morgan—"

Despite the risk to himself, Morgan skied after her, leaping between her and the edge of the cliff, attempting to halt her body with the strength of his own. Instead they began to slide down the steep face of the mountain together toward certain death while Morgan struggled, using all his power to stop them. At last he managed to seize a low branch lying in their path.

"Don't let go of me, Dinah!"

For a long moment Dinah clung to him helplessly, gasping hard for breath, her hands tight around his waist, her face pressed embarrassingly against his inner thigh. Finally when she had recovered a bit, he helped her inch her way up the mountain so she could grip the branch as well. They lay there for what seemed an eternity panting.

Miraculously, he was lifting her into his arms. Ten feet beneath them the mountains broke in a jagged wound from a recent avalanche and plunged a thousand feet to the floor of the valley.

Dinah, feeling quite numb, could not utter a word, but

she was aware of the warmth of strong arms wrapping her, pressing her tightly to his long frame.

She felt frozen inside from his touch and from his nearness, sick with the old, feverish longing.

"Are you hurt?" he inquired softly. His warm breath caressed her cheek.

"No." The one word was low and choked. It was a lie, in a way. Just being with him hurt.

He set her down on the other side of a large rock so that she could lean against it for support. Impatiently he ripped his ski mask from his face and stuffed it in his pocket. His compelling gaze held hers as they each wordlessly assessed the changes in the other.

Time had obliterated the softness of youth from his face, making his lean, chiseled features harsher. He looked older, but the lines beneath his eyes and the grooves beside his lips only served to emphasize his rugged brand of virile masculinity.

A shock of black hair peppered with a few strands of premature silver fell across his brow. The California sun had burned his skin a permanent shade of dark umber. His eyes were still the same vivid blue, but there was a new hardness in them as they pierced through the careful veneer of polish and glamor to the soft marrow of her soul. He was as charismatically appealing as ever, and she could not stop herself from drinking in every detail of him like a woman ravaged by thirst.

Her frightened glance met his, and in his eyes she glimpsed some strange emotion before he quickly masked it with anger. His study of her had been equally thorough.

The insolent arrogance she now read in his expression ignited her temper.

"Just what gives you the right to follow me yesterday

and today playacting as Zorro? You scared the wits out of me and nearly caused me to fall off that cliff!''

''The hell I did!'' he whispered savagely, reaching out and grabbing her shoulders, yanking her hard against his body. ''That was your doing entirely. I damn near got myself killed in the bargain, saving you.''

The shock of his touch made her pulse throb unevenly. When she tried to push him away, he held her firmly. Only when she made no further effort to move out of his arms did their pressure ease, but she was keenly aware of his casually possessive embrace, of his hands locked about her waist, of her legs pressing against the length of his thighs, of the way their bodies molded against each other so naturally.

''You shouldn't have followed me up here,'' she said jerkily.

He glanced toward the cliff's edge. ''Believe me. I wouldn't have if I'd remembered your penchant for living dangerously.''

''Why didn't you just tell me who you were yesterday?''

His lips twisted cynically. ''So you could have welcomed me with a kiss?'' he asked, shifting his attention to her lips.

Her cheeks brightened at his words and in shameful awareness of the primitive hunger in his eyes touching her mouth aroused within her. ''You know I would have run,'' she murmured on a breathless note.

''Exactly. Besides, you were with Edouard, and three's never been my favorite number for a rendezvous between old lovers. No, better that I risked life and limb and now have you to myself.''

''A rendezvous between...'' She choked on her unfinished repetition of his sentence as a tide of indignation filled her. "How dare you make such an outrageously crude statement to me!" She tried to struggle out of his arms, but his hard hands burned into her back, their touch intensifying the throbbing ache she felt.

"With Edouard at your side, how could I have found out if the poised woman I've read so much about in wine magazines is the real Dinah Kirsten? Or if any trace of the reckless little hellion I remember so well still exists?" He laughed softly.

"And how do you intend to find that out?" she asked in a strangled voice, wishing frantically she could escape.

"I thought you'd never ask," he murmured. Again his gaze shifted to the tempting softness of her mouth.

He pulled her even more tightly against his body until every muscled inch was pressed into hers, and suddenly she was trembling violently, and not entirely from rage. The ancient excitement that he had always evoked buzzed in her blood.

"Of all the vulgar, disgusting..." Dinah began in an infuriated cry, trying to fling herself away from him. She raised her hand to slap him, but he grabbed it and twisted both arms behind her back.

"It's useless to fight me, Dinah." His voice was soft with an unnatural calm. "Just this once I intend to get what I want from you." His hard, mocking eyes roved over her terrified face, studying her quivering lips for a long moment. "And all I want is a kiss. Consider it payment for your life."

She twisted her face away from his. "Well, you won't have it."

"Won't I?"

Time stood still, in that breathless moment as he towered over her, crushing her to him in a fiercely possessive embrace. There was something primitive and conquering in his stance.

"Dinah, Dinah…I never thought I could still want…" He never finished his sentence, and his unspoken words seemed to anger him. His grip on her arms tightened.

In a blur his black head lowered, and his mouth brutally closed over the lush sweetness of hers. His open mouth was wet and hot, demanding and insulting. She struggled against him, but his arms were crushing steel bands imprisoning her against him. The harder she fought, the more intimately he bound her, until at last she grew passive in his arms. Only after he vanquished all resistance did he let her go.

"I'll hate you forever for that," she hissed.

"You already hate me, love, so what difference could it possibly make if I gave you one more reason?" he replied dryly.

It infuriated her that nothing she said made any difference. "Someone should claw your eyes out, you monster."

"You haven't changed," he jeered, a contemptuous smile curving his lips. "Your sophistication is a pose. You're still the same little wildcat I bedded eight years ago."

"And you're still the same brutish bully I stupidly saved from the gutter!" she cried with loathing.

"Not brutish, surely, love, and Beverly Hills is hardly the gutter."

"Brutish, vile, vulgar…"

"My, my, aren't we a mutual admiration society," he mocked.

In a frenzy of anger, she slapped his brown cheek so hard her palm stung with pain even through the thickness of her glove.

Swiftly he seized her hand, clenching it painfully in his. "Don't ever hit me again."

"I won't," she sobbed, "if you'll just go and leave me alone."

"That's something I haven't the slightest intention of doing, my dear."

"Morgan, I made up my mind a long time ago I never wanted to have anything more to do with you."

"And I'm here to change your mind. I have to talk to you alone. Somewhere more comfortable than where we are now—unless you like making love to me on a mountainside."

"I despise making love to you on a mountainside, you devil."

"Good. Then may I suggest my chalet?"

"No! No!" She kicked the ground in fury. "Why won't you just go? Can't you realize that you and I have nothing to talk about—alone," she finished raggedly.

"Oh, I'd say we do," came the dangerous soft reply. Eyes as hard and brilliant as gemstones met hers.

"What?"

"Our son," he said coldly. "You see, I just found out that you, and not Holly, are Stephen's mother, and that grim surprise is going to change both our lives."

Five

"**G**randfather promised you'd never know!" Dinah cried.

Morgan pitched another log onto the fire. "And that made it all right," he said quietly.

To insure complete privacy the drapes were drawn in the ultra-modern chalet Morgan had rented in Suvretta. Morgan was kneeling before the enormous stone fireplace, while Dinah, still bundled in her snow-dampened fur, watched him warily from across a safe expanse of silver plush carpet, mirrors, crystal chandeliers, and chrome furniture. The chalet was a sybarite's dream, with its breathtaking views and steaming, grottoed indoor swimming pool.

The aroma of fresh coffee filled the air. Morgan's cup was on the mantel; Dinah's balanced precariously in her shaking fingers.

What could she possibly say in her own defense? The

last thing she wanted to do was relive the anguish of the decision to give up her son. She had done it only because she'd believed that it was in Stephen's best interest. He would have borne the stigma of illegitimacy if she'd raised him herself. With Morgan and Holly he had been raised as the legitimate heir to Kirsten Vineyards. She had wanted Steven to grow up feeling that he was part of a real family, that he belonged at Kirsten Vineyards as she never had.

She sighed desperately. "I doubt if I could ever make you understand."

"Try me, Dinah," came his huskily pitched voice.

She fumbled with her gloves, wrenching them from her fingers. There was something so hard about him. It was as if he now leashed his every true emotion. "I...I can't." Her breathing was rapid and uneven, and she avoided his eyes.

"Dinah, this can be easy or difficult. I've come a long way to get some answers." She could feel his fathomless blue eyes boring holes into her. She had the terrible feeling that he wanted more from her than answers.

Reflected firelight danced about the room in a dazzle of flickering phosphorescence. Under different circumstances the setting would have been romantic. As it was, the silent hostility between the man and the woman crackled more ominously than the fire.

Having finished with the logs, Morgan set the poker down with a clatter and turned toward her. He had removed his jacket and now wore only a black turtleneck and black ski pants that fitted his narrow hips and muscled thighs as snugly as a second skin. His bold gaze swept her insolently from head to toe.

She flushed from his rudely evaluating stare. "You shouldn't have come," she said frostily. "And you had no right to drag me up here the way you did. Why, you practically kidnapped me!''

"A rather melodramatic interpretation of the facts, wouldn't you agree?'' was all he said, but his voice was forbidding.

"If you already know the truth about Stephen's birth, that couldn't be the reason you're here. What do you really want from me?''

Again those hard eyes traveled over her body, making her go hot and cold despite her determination to be immune to him.

"Now that depends.''

Something in his look made her shiver. "On what?'' she demanded bravely.

"If we're speaking of what I want tonight or what I want as a permanent arrangement between us,'' he replied with deadly softness.

"I—I don't know what you mean.'' The intimacy in his gaze made her heartbeats skitter rapidly. She remembered his savage kiss. Surely it was impossible that he wanted to resume a physical relationship with her.

"I want you to come back to California and live with me.''

She started violently. Whatever she had expected, it was not this.

"You can't be serious. I'm going to be married this week.''

"All the more reason for you to come back now—before you marry another man,'' he said arrogantly, laughing softly in his throat.

They were little more than strangers now. How could he even suggest such a thing?

"For eight years you have avoided me,'' she said icily.

"You never said anything. Never indicated the slightest interest."

His mouth twisted sardonically. "You forget I was a married man."

"I never forgot that for one minute!"

"Dinah, don't you see? I thought everything between us was finished. I didn't know there was anything to say— then."

"There still isn't."

"Oh, but you're wrong. For seven years I lived in hell because of you, and you say there's nothing we can say to each other? Not a single word of explanation for your callous deceit?" He spoke in a low, biting, cynical tone.

"My callous deceit? I loved you, Morgan. I suppose your marriage to my sister wasn't callous?"

"That was your fault too, in a way," he added caustically.

"I don't see how."

"Then I'll tell you. You left me to go to Edouard. I thought at first it was some bit of foolish childishness on your part and that you'd return quickly enough to me when you came to your senses, but you didn't. Not one postcard from my lost love, either. Even my own letter to you came back unopened. Loving you as I did, I was angry, as well as hurt and disillusioned. That's a very vulnerable position for a man to be in. I thought maybe I'd misjudged you, that you were a woman like my mother who would go from man to man. Holly was there all the time playing up to me. She was lonely, and so was I. Still, I think even then I knew what she was up to, but my pride was injured. I couldn't see past my anger. I found her attention flattering, and in the end, I married her because it was what she and Bruce wanted. I think, in part, I was lashing out against you. A week later when

I realized what a fool I had been, I told Holly I wanted a divorce. She was crushed when I left her and enlisted in the army and left Kirsten Vineyards. I thought everything was finished between us until Holly wrote me a month later with the news she was expecting our baby.''

"Oh, my God..."

"Do you begin to see? I loved you, Dinah, despite what you'd done, and yet I thought I'd made another woman pregnant. There was no way I could leave her and the child even though I realized a marriage such as ours had little chance of success.''

"But I didn't find out I was pregnant until after I learned you were married, Morgan.''

"If you'd only come to me and told me, we could have worked something out. Instead you went to Bruce and Holly, and the three of you worked out this insane fabrication that Bruce finally had the guts to tell me about. I know all about how you entered that San Francisco hospital, registered as my wife, and delivered the baby while I was overseas. Then you gave Stephen to Holly and went on with your own life as if nothing had happened. You made quite a name for yourself in the wine business, didn't you? I came home from the army and tried to make a life with Holly while you became the consort of a French *comte*.''

"I've never been Edouard's consort,'' she cried. "When you married Holly, he was my only friend! I didn't come to you because I didn't want you to think I was using our baby to break up your marriage.''

"Forgive me if I failed to interpret your actions in the same light of noble sacrifice that you did. Your lie trapped me in a hellishly empty marriage to Holly for seven years.''

"I heard rumors that she drank and that she...''

"Saw other men," he finished grimly, his dark look concealing a wealth of remembered pain. He picked up his coffee cup. "She was my mother all over again. In a way I felt sorry for her. There was nothing she could find happiness or satisfaction in. She was consumed with the most terrible restlessness. For a while I did try to make some sort of life with her, but in the end, I'm afraid I gave up and went my own way. I couldn't divorce her because I was afraid she would get custody of Stephen, and she treated Stephen with the same sort of casual, possessive hostility my mother always treated me with. I never could understand her resentment toward Stephen, and that made our relationship even more difficult. You see, she knew she had me because of Stephen. Had I known she wasn't even his mother—" Morgan drank a swallow of coffee and gave Dinah a considering look.

"I'm sorry," Dinah said weakly, unable to meet his gaze. There was a faint tremor in her fingers when she lifted her own cup to her lips. "I really am, Morgan. If I could have known, of course, I would have told you the truth. But now it's all in the past. Holly's dead. You're free to go on with your own life. I'm going to marry Edouard in a few days. I don't see the use in rehashing it all now, and I can't imagine why you came all this way the minute you found out the truth."

His intense gaze made every nerve in her body vibrate.

"Can't you?" he murmured, suppressed violence in his low tone.

"No."

"Stephen is very much alive, Dinah."

"And..."

"He needs a mother."

"But he doesn't know about me, does he? He thinks of me as an aunt."

"An aunt he adores. Even though you only come once a year, he speaks of you constantly. He remembers everything you do together, all the picnics, horseback rides, trips to the libraries and beaches. He treasures his letters from you, the presents you send him. He even framed one of your pictures and keeps it on his desk."

"Did he?" The question was strangled. Frantically Dinah turned from Morgan and went to a nearby window. The hand that lifted the drape aside was shaking. Outside, snow was falling gently, but she could scarcely see the blurred images of chalets and mountains for the hot tears filling her eyes.

"I tried not to take Holly's place," she murmured hoarsely, hoping Morgan wouldn't hear the tears in her voice. "I...I wanted to come see him more often, but it was so painful to have to leave. Fond aunt to one's own son is a difficult role, Morgan." Her voice broke, and her slim shoulders began to heave. Frantically she dabbed at her wet eyes with the back of her fingers. Oh, she didn't want to cry in front of him.

Suddenly she felt the strong grip of Morgan's hands on her arms, pulling her against his body. He turned her around, and through her tears she looked up and saw that his vivid eyes were luminous with compassion.

"Dinah, honey." He wrapped his arms around her, squeezing her even more tightly against him. "I didn't mean to make you cry. I never thought..."

She knew she should twist free of his arms, but their hard comfort was too pleasurably soothing. For eight years, she'd been alone, with no one. For a lifetime she'd wanted to be held as he was holding her. She clung to him as the agony of years gushed from her in a torrential storm. She wept as if her heart were breaking.

He cradled her protectively against his chest, rocking

her, his hands stroking her hair gently as he crooned to her.

At last through broken sobs she managed, "It nearly killed me to give him up, Morgan. You'll never know. I felt like part of me died. And then it was torture to realize every year when I visited all that I missed. His first smile, his first step, his first day at school, all those precious times in his life that would never be mine. I was jealous of you and Holly having him all the time."

"I had to know how you felt about giving him up, Dinah," Morgan whispered into her hair. "It just didn't make any sense when Bruce told me. It seemed so cold, so unlike you to give Stephen up like that. It's unforgivable."

"Well, now that you know how difficult it was, will you just go and leave me alone?" she cried. "It's hard enough without—"

"It doesn't have to be like this," he said softly. "You can come back to California, to Bruce and Stephen — and me."

"I could never do that! You and I—" The flicker of pain in his eyes stopped her. That air was stifling suddenly, and Dinah could hardly breathe. His gaze held hers.

"What was between us has been dead for a long time. I know that, Dinah. Our love died before it had a chance to bloom, and we both played a part in killing it. There was your jealousy and my pride standing in our way, but the fact remains that we have a child together."

"What are you suggesting?" Deliberately she made her tone sound flippant, an attitude that was sharply at variance with the terrible excitement she felt. "Some sort of marriage of convenience?"

"I'm not suggesting marriage at all—yet," he returned grimly. "Come back for six months. We'll see what happens."

See what happens! She lifted her gaze to his, blushing uncomfortably as her gaze went involuntarily to the sensual line of his mouth. His hard features were maddeningly impassive. If only he would give some clue as to his own emotions. Did his own feelings matter so little to him? Desperately she moved out of his arms.

"What you ask is impossible. I have my own life. I'm sure you could find any number of women to marry," she said coolly.

"You're the mother of my child, Dinah."

That disturbing intensity had come again into his voice, and his words ran like liquid fire through her. She cast him another brief, astonished look. Did he still have no idea how unbearably he had once hurt her? How his mere presence hurt her even now?

His beautiful voice continued naturally as if he were not saying these extraordinary things, as if he were not playing havoc with the deepest emotions of her soul.

"There's too much divorce," he drawled almost lazily.

"You and I were never married."

"That was definitely a mistake," he said so gently she began to quiver.

"I don't see how," she cried hotly, determined not to soften toward him.

"Yet Stephen is suffering from the same problems as if we had been," Morgan said. "Children split between parents are robbed of one of their parents. If you think it's a picnic trying to raise Stephen by myself, you're dead wrong. You're not with Stephen fifty weeks out of the year like I am. I don't know what the hell I'm doing half the time. I need you, Dinah. Stephen's not an easy kid to raise. He's too damn much like me. I get impatient when

I see him doing the same crazy things I did. I do things I regret later when I've cooled off, but then it's too late. If you were there—"

She couldn't let him go on! "This conversation is insane," she burst, in a frenzy to have done with it. "Do you think I want to be apart from him?"

"You don't have to be any longer. Stephen has never had a mother, Dinah, and he craves that sort of attention. What he needs, I can't give him. Growing up the way I did, I had to survive without maternal love, but my childhood was hell. Stephen's going through a rough time. If you came home, I think it would help."

"My parents died when I was a baby." Her soft voice drifted off as she remembered the fierce jealousies and insecurity that had always plagued her. Perhaps if her parents had lived, she wouldn't have suffered from those terrible feelings. "I guess I know as well as you what it feels like to be motherless. But don't you see? I can't come back to California. I have my career. There's my own life and Edouard. I owe him so much."

"More than you owe your own son?"

"If it were just Stephen, I wouldn't hesitate. But it's not. It's you. Us. I would have to give up Edouard, and he's been so kind to me. Can't you begin to understand that I can't go back to the suffering I knew with you? It's foolish to think we could ever find any kind of happiness together. There would only be pain."

"Only pain?" An odd light blazed in his sapphire eyes. His handsome face was very still.

"Yes."

"How can you be sure?" His voice was low, and strangely hoarse. His rigid features would have betrayed to her the powerful emotion he restrained had she been less upset herself.

His eyes moved over her body, his look burning her as if he explored her intimately with his hands. Something quivered in her abdomen at his gaze. There was an all-consuming intensity about him.

"You said Edouard can give you kindness," he murmured. "Perhaps it's time for me to show you what I can give you."

Dinah looked away from him, her eyes darting wildly about the room for an avenue of escape, but there was none. His large body loomed between her and the door.

"I still want you, Dinah. The minute I saw you yesterday I knew it."

"But I don't want you!" she cried desperately. She didn't dare look at him. She was too afraid of how his hot blue eyes could melt her.

"Suppose I proved to you that you're wrong," he said in a tantalizing whisper.

"I don't want to feel anything other than dislike for you. Can't you understand that?"

"Do you think I wanted to feel anything for you after what you did?" He ground out the words in fury. "Well, I didn't, but yesterday when I saw you for the first time in that tight blue ski suit with your black hair streaming around your shoulders, with Edouard so obviously in love with you, I remembered how I used to feel when I was in love with you. I can't forget that you once belonged to me. No other woman has ever suited me in that way. You're a wanton, Dinah. A deliciously, sensual woman who can love a man to distraction. I remembered the way you used to kiss me all over with your tongue until I was mad with desire. I still remember everything about that first night on the beach, the way the eucalyptus trees smelled, the sound of the sea, the way you looked in the moonlight, the satin warmth of your body beneath mine, the fragrance of your perfume. But most of all I remember how it was between us, even that first time. You haunt me, Dinah. You've haunted me for eight damn years.''

''Don't!'' The one anguished word was almost inaudible. A single tear trickled down her cheek. He was deliberately stirring her with provocative images she'd fought to forget. Images she had to forget!

He moved toward her.

''Stay away from me. Oh, please—'' Even as she protested, a shiver of heady excitement quickened her blood.

He reached out and took her hand, pulling her to him.

''Morgan. No—''

He stopped her words with a kiss. As his warm mouth fastened on hers, she could hardly breathe, let alone think or struggle. When her lips parted, he groaned softly from the exquisite pleasure of her, and she could not stop herself from returning his kiss, her response only heightening his desire, driving him insane with wanting.

He tore his lips from hers and began to kiss her face, her ears, her smooth neck, even as he huskily muttered love words. ''It's been so long, my darling. I never thought I'd feel like this again.''

Everywhere his eager mouth caressed, tingling waves of fire scorched her sensitive skin. His hands caressed the silken waves of her long black hair. She arched her body into his. Pushing aside her lynx coat, he trailed hot, wet kisses down her neck to the soft swell of her breasts covered by her cashmere sweater.

She gasped as he touched her intimately, but it was a gasp of delight and not the shame she should have felt. Through the sweater he gently squeezed her breasts and teased her nipples to hardness with his fingers. A low guttural sound escaped her lips at his suggestive caresses.

Morgan looked at her. In the gray light her face was

soft in passion, her lips swollen from his lovemaking, her eyes closed in pleasure. Gently he bent his dark head and kissed the throb of her racing pulse in the hollow of her throat.

"Morgan, we mustn't. We can't go back. It's too late," She managed breathlessly, even as thrilling spasms of rapture spiraled through her body. "We could never love each other again."

"Who said anything about love? I thought I made myself clear. I want you back because you're the mother of my child. The desire I feel toward you is the same I would feel toward any beautiful woman, and since we're going to live together, I see no reason why I shouldn't enjoy you."

Six

"Of all the cold-blooded and cruel things to say," Dinah whispered angrily even while she felt taut and yet softly open to him.

Morgan's body was scalding hot against hers, the passion in him barely restrained. "It's only the truth, my love," he drawled, his bitterness seeming to surge through his words despite the great effort he made to suppress it. "Why shouldn't I take the one pleasure you can still give me? I remember how soft you are, Dinah, how your breasts overflow in my palms, how you used to moan and arch your hips into mine right before I took you."

She stiffened against him, but beneath his massaging fingertips her nipples were hard, their condition a betrayal. "I won't let you seduce me with words!" she gasped.

"All right," he whispered. "Then I won't use words."

His breath was hot against her mouth as his tongue glided inside her protesting lips. She shuddered with desire at the rapture of his hard embrace, and he kissed her more deeply. She felt herself yielding to the sweet, all-consuming flame of his passion, and she knew she had to stop him at once before it was too late.

"We're not going to live together," Dinah raged, breaking free of Morgan's fierce embrace. "We're not!"

He let her go, but his hot eyes stalked her. Pride alone held his overmastering passion in check. He would not let her see how much he still wanted her. She had lured him once with her passion and talk of love, and it had nearly destroyed him. He was determined that never again would he give her control. When she clasped the doorknob with shaking fingers and flung the door open wide, he murmured in slow, deliberately measured words. "Oh, but we are going to live together. I intend to have you, Dinah, by fair means or foul."

Only the threat in his low tone stopped her. "Exactly what are you implying?" she hissed, even as a dreadful fear made her heart stutter hopelessly.

"I was merely thinking about this fabulous paragon named Dinah Kirsten I've read so much about in all the wine magazines and gossip columns, this glamorous superwoman who is engaged to a French *comte* whose noble name, I might add, is thus far untarnished by scandal. Edouard has deliberately cultivated the press on your behalf, you know, a foolish and vain mistake on his part. Since you represent the de Landaux name, I think he considers the aura of glamor and perfection that surrounds you as vital. This publicity concept was his brainchild in the beginning, wasn't it?"

"How did you..." She broke off, her face white with horror.

"Suppose I told a certain journalist friend of mine that your past is not as unblemished as the Comte de Landaux has led the world to believe? That his glamorous representative is a fantastic creation of his noble imagination? That she deserted the baby she had out of the sacred bonds of wedlock to pursue her glittering career? Would Edouard continue to employ you in such an important position in his company? Would he back your schemes in Texas? Would he still marry you? Or would you lose everything and damage de Landaux in the process?"

"You wouldn't dare!"

"Oh, but I would."

"That's blackmail."

"I prefer to think of it as the act of a desperate man who wants his son to have a mother."

"It would hurt Stephen unbearably if he found out the truth."

"All the more reason for you to do as I wish and thus prevent his being hurt."

"You would hurt our son to no purpose. Edouard loves me. He would never react as you say he would. He already knows I had your child, and he knows how it hurt me to give him up."

His blue eyes remained fastened upon her person. She looked wildly beautiful with her shimmering black hair tumbling over thick pale fur, with her dark eyes flashing in passionate anger, and had she not been defending Edouard, Morgan might have relented, so great was the power she held over him. As it was, his stance grew rigid and still, his only movement the involuntary clenching of his hand against the chrome rail of the stairway.

"Yes, I was deeply touched when you told me how Edouard stood by you, while I married Holly and lived happily ever after," Morgan said in a hard, sardonic voice. "I can understand his wanting you for himself despite your past. You're undeniably beautiful and smart.

The question is, does he want the world to know the kind
of woman you really are? Can he afford to risk the reputation of his name and company for the sake of love?
You know, Dinah, you could do worse than me. With the
unfortunate beginning I had, I don't give a damn for your
past or anyone else's. There's no one alive who hasn't
made mistakes. It's just that ours have been more con-
spicuous and more interesting than most."

"I won't give in to you. I'll tell him myself."

"Go right ahead. You have twenty-four hours to make
up your mind. I'll be right here—waiting. But remember,
if you come back with me and you stay at Kirsten Vineyards for six months and then you still want to leave and
Edouard will have you, I won't try to stop you. Stephen
needs you, Dinah, more than Edouard does, and I think
you would find being with him far more rewarding then
anything you're doing in Bordeaux or Texas. You can
grow grapes and make wine at Kirsten Vineyards as well
as anywhere else, Dinah. If you come back with me, you
can have both your career and your son, and not even
your understanding French *comte* can give you that last."

Dinah couldn't bear to hear more. Morgan was tearing
her to pieces by offering her Stephen. Yet the price for
Stephen was the beautiful life she had built for herself as
a cushion against thoughts of her painful loss. Without
that cushion, and without Edouard, she would be on her
own and would have to face everything she'd been running away from for eight years. Suppose Morgan wanted
her gone in six months, and she wanted to stay? What
refuge would there be for her then? She knew too well
the feelings of exile and loneliness. It had taken her years
to get past them. Could she survive a second bout of those
dreadful feelings?

Slowly she walked out the door, her ski boots clomping on the carpeted stairs, their sound dying slowly.

Twenty-four hours to decide. How could she make such a choice? Dinah returned immediately to the Palace Hotel. Once back in that clubby, cosseting, fantasy palace of turrets and twisting corridors with its Persian carpets, it was difficult for her to believe that Morgan and his ultimatum were not part of some surrealistic dream. Longing to speak to Edouard privately, she was upset to find his suite filled with members of the fashionable set he so enjoyed on holidays.

Edouard was sipping champagne with a Greek shipping lord and two German steel barons, one of whom had been a college friend. They were trying to decide whether to fling themselves off the mountains on skis or bobsleds, hang gliders or Cresta sleds or whether to go up to the Corviglia slopes and lunch at one of the most important social clubs in Europe, the fifty-year-old Corviglia Ski Club.

Edouard called to her affectionately, and she went to him. His arm slid around her shoulders. "Where have you been so long, darling? Mikki Vorzenski was just telling me he saw you not an hour ago in Suvretta."

"I ran into an old friend," she said, making her voice light and gay. "You know how it is to share reminiscences."

"Who was it? Anyone I know?"

At his question her blood ran like ice in her veins, but when she darted a quick glance at Edouard, she saw no suspicion in his eyes. She forced a gay smile. "Darling, if you don't mind, I'll tell you about it later. Now I'd like to change. My left ski boot is digging into my shin and causing a blister. And after I dress, I think I'll go down to Hanselmann's and buy one of those coiled pastries I

like so much. Then, darling, if you don't mind, there's a
bracelet in Cartier's that took my fancy. So don't expect
me back for a while." If only Edouard wouldn't see
through her excuses to avoid him.

"Careful, Edouard. That sounds serious," said Loel
von Thurn. "Perhaps you should forget hang gliding for
today. Leaving a woman like Dinah Kirsten alone in Cartier's can be the most dangerous sport of all."

Dinah did not stay to hear Edouard's placid reply to his
old friend Loel. She was threading her way with bright
words of greeting through his glittering acquaintances on
her way to her own apartment.

"There's no danger to me, Loel," Edouard murmured
after Dinah had gone. "If she wants the bracelet, Dinah
will buy it for herself, and if she doesn't, she won't. Under
no circumstances would she allow me to buy it for her.
She would consider such a gift compromising."

"I don't understand. I thought you and she…"

"We are engaged, Loel, and she works for me. That's
all," Edouard stated coldly.

"But she's staying in your suite," Loel pressed.

"Her rooms are quite separate from mine. Let me add
that she insists on paying me for them."

"Are you sure she's not after your title or fortune?"

"Very sure."

"This impeccable virtue you allude to her makes her
quite unlike all the other wild women in your past."

"I didn't ask them to marry me."

"No wonder marriages are so impossibly dull."

Edouard laughed.

"Seriously, Edouard, aren't you even a little afraid to
marry a woman who claims to be so virginal at her age?
Women are rarely what they seem."

Edouard chose his words carefully. "I'm not afraid to

marry Dinah. She has never claimed to be anything she's not. You can stop worrying, Loel. I know all her secrets." At this thought, Edouard frowned faintly. "But tell me, if you really want to go hang gliding this afternoon, Loel, why don't we meet at two? Your hotel?"

Loel did not notice that the subject of Dinah had been adroitly changed.

Edouard and Dinah dined that night at the Palace Grill. She was magnificent in a long black gown. A diamond pendant glimmered on her slim white throat.

"There's something I must tell you, Edouard," she said nervously when they were halfway through the second course.

Gray eyes stared into hers quizzically. For a long moment he watched her twist the enormous engagement ring he had given her round and round on her finger.

"Yes," he replied mildly.

"The old friend I met in Suvretta…"

"Was Morgan," he finished. There was a wealth of knowledge in his eyes.

"How did you know?"

"Mikki described him to me. I saw the other helicopter. I saw the man get out. Later I saw the two of you skiing together."

Dinah could not stop herself from wondering if he had seen her in Morgan's arms as well.

"Morgan has found out about Stephen," she whispered. "And…oh, I don't know how to tell you this."

"Just tell me."

"He wants me to come back to California—for six months," she blurted. "He says Stephen needs a mother."

"And how do you feel?"

"I...I want to be with Stephen, but I don't want to be unfair to you. I don't want to be with Morgan. I don't!"

"Ah, so this is a situation where you cannot have everything that you want, little one. Compromises are always difficult."

"What should I do, Edouard?"

"Only you can decide that."

"But we were going to be married."

They both noticed she had used the past tense, and suddenly they could no longer look at each other.

For an instant she felt a poignant rush of sympathy for him. He had loved her so faithfully. She knew she was hurting him more than he would ever let her know. She started to say something and then thought better of it. Any kindness on her part would only deepen his pain.

Though nothing more was said about the subject during dinner, awkward silences often fell between them for the rest of the evening, and Edouard drank far more than he ever had in the past. He was suffering acutely, but he was too proud to inflict his pain on her.

Later, in front of her bedroom door, she slid his engagement ring from her finger and placed it into his hand. "Someday, some other girl..."

"I don't want another girl, but I never really had you, did I?" he said huskily. "You were a dream...that never came true."

Suddenly Edouard's arms closed around her tightly, and he kissed her hungrily, desperately, but the fire in his kiss did not move her as Morgan's would have. Nevertheless, for her there was sweetness in his embrace and sadness as well. He had been her friend. Much much more than her friend. She knew she would never feel his lips on her mouth again. Never would she be able to turn to him for strength in a crisis. Even the comfort of his friendship would now be lost to her.

"I'll miss you," she said softly.

He said nothing, but she felt the powerful tension in his arms that circled her. For a long moment, he held her, his face buried in her hair. Then wordlessly he let her go.

When she closed the door, she was crying.

Seven

Mist and patches of ground fog enveloped San Francisco as Dinah stepped from the private de Landaux jet onto the rain-slick runway. The flight had been rough and because of the fog the pilot had had to circle for thirty minutes before he could land. During this delay, Dinah had grown more and more edgy.

Now, standing all by herself amidst jets and bustling strangers, she felt lost and unsure. In her thin charcoal wool dress, she was suddenly shivering from the combined effects of cold and nervous strain. She paused beneath the plane and slipped into her lynx coat, which she'd been carrying draped over one arm. She hadn't called Kirsten Vineyards, so no one knew she was coming today. She was glad in a way that she hadn't, because she couldn't have faced a crowd at the airport. It would be difficult enough once she was home. How could she step into the role of mother after a seven-year lapse? But now because of her reticence, she had the problem of finding transportation to Napa Valley this afternoon.

Suddenly she grew aware of a tall dark man threading his way through the crowd, and her pulse lurched in shock. Only one man could be so tall, so broad-shouldered. A rush of eager excitement filled her, and before she thought, she smiled and shouted his name, waving frantically. She began to run, and then she forced herself to stop for fear he might think her actually happy to see him.

His black head pivoted, and he caught sight of her. At his wide infectious grin, her heart stood still. Something elemental charged the air that separated them. She brought her hand uncertainly to her lips.

His presence more than anything made her feel that she had come back, and it felt wonderful. As Morgan hurried toward her, this fleeting sensation of indescribable joy faded as she reminded herself that she loathed this man who had forced her to return to her former home. She saw the initial reaction as no more than a bout of foolish sentimentality.

Morgan ignored her tense white face and grim silence and swept her into his arms, crushing her breasts against the wall of his chest and her hips against his steel thighs, his great body curving possessively into hers. To resist him she would have had to make a scene, so she remained stiffly in his arms and endured his powerful embrace.

"Welcome home, Dinah. You're looking beautiful." His voice was as melodically beautiful as she remembered, and she fought to ignore how it stirred her.

She felt the heat of his veiled gaze running over her face and figure in silent admiration. Beneath her straining hands she felt the smooth powerful muscles of his chest. Everywhere his body touched her made her feel warm. It was if a golden heat flowed from his body into her veins.

When his dark head bent solicitously down to hers, she was sure that to everyone who passed them they looked like a couple deeply in love.

"How did you know I was coming today?" she managed weakly.

"Edouard told me."

For the first time she smiled wistfully. "How thoughtful of him."

"It was I who called him, so I deserve credit for being thoughtful."

"You deserve nothing of the sort," she retorted.

"Longing for your noble paragon will do you no good, my love." His blue eyes darkened with purpose. "You're stuck with me." His grip about her shoulders tightened, pulling her toward him.

"I'm well aware of that," she said grimly.

"Good." He lowered his mouth to her trembling lips, the exploring expertise of his kiss coaxing a pliant response from her. At last he released her mouth. He ran his fingers through her long hair, smoothing it down against her neck and throat. "Just so long as you remember who you belong to."

"I don't belong to you!"

"For six months you do."

"I came back because of Stephen."

"Are you sure it was only Stephen?" His blue eyes roamed the exquisite loveliness of her face.

"Of course I'm sure," she began uncertainly. "I hate you, Morgan. I..."

"If only I could hate you," he murmured softly, "everything would be so much simpler. Instead I have other...far more interesting feelings. And you kiss divinely, to be so filled with hatred."

She would have protested, but his insistent mouth claimed hers again, this time more forcefully than before, as though he were crazy with desire for her. Every instinct warned her to fight him and flee, yet she could not. She was as irresistibly drawn to him as he was to her. He held her captive with the hard pressure of his arms circling her. For an instant she almost surrendered to the seductive warmth and sensuality of his passionate lips.

"Can't you be even a little bit glad to be back?" he whispered roughly.

She felt the fierce pounding of his heart. She caught the note of deep, suppressed anguish his low tone attempted to conceal, and she felt startled. Did he care? More than he could admit? Did pride alone force him to pretend otherwise?

Very hesitantly, she murmured, "Maybe I'm glad...just a little bit."

He kissed her in silence then, slowly, deliciously. His hard arms held her body close to his as if she were very precious, and this time she didn't even pretend she wanted to struggle.

After a long while he let her go, and together they collected her luggage from the plane. Then he led her to his truck, and they drove in silence, neither knowing what to say to the other. On the Golden Gate Bridge, with fog rolling in from the Pacific like a great billowing cloud, Morgan spoke for the first time.

"It's about time you came home. I was growing impatient with your excuses, though it was amusing to try to figure out what pretext you'd dream up next. Do you realize it's almost Christmas?"

"They weren't exactly excuses," she argued hotly. "I couldn't just quit working for Edouard without finishing that publicity campaign I'd started. Then I had to go to Texas. There was that problem in the winery. I had to hire a new foreman for the vineyard, and then it turned out he didn't know the first thing about pruning or spraying or anything else.''

"I'll agree your excuses were maddeningly plausible, but last week if I hadn't demanded that you come, you'd still be in Texas.''

Dinah bit her lip. She was too honest to protest further. The real reasons for her delay had been unspoken. She was afraid to come home, afraid to give in to the terrible tug of her heartstrings that had always pulled her to Kirsten Vineyards. She was afraid of failing at real motherhood to a son she scarcely knew. But most of all she was afraid of Morgan, and the dangerous feelings he could still evoke.

When they reached Napa Valley, the late afternoon was dark and cold. Dinah observed her grandfather's vineyards with an uneasy interest. Everywhere there was evidence of Morgan's influence and ambitions. The winery had been expanded and modernized. Kirsten Vineyards now owned three times the acreage it had owned when Morgan had first come. Even on this winter day, the parking lot held several cars filled with tourists. The white house was freshly painted, and a new wing had been added. It seemed that nothing but the valley itself had remained unchanged.

Through misting eyes, Dinah scanned her former home, and was filled with an overwhelming sense of nostalgia. How precious the hills and forests seemed despite Morgan's changes, how beautiful even on this freezing, gray day. No matter where she had gone, the memory of this place, her home that she had never wanted to leave, had haunted her. She had been to places far more glamorous, but no place had ever gripped her as this precious bit of earth did.

Row after row of orderly wines were dormant black statues as they marched away from the towering white house on the hill. A pruning crew in yellow slickers were threading their way slowly through a nearby block of grapes. Dinah's mood changed, and she wondered frantically if she had changed too much from the girl who had loved this place, to ever fit in again. She cast a brief glance at the dark, uncompromising features of the man beside her, and shivered. It would be foolish to expect help from him. Had she been a fool to come home?

Suddenly the dull, frozen day seemed inauspicious for new beginnings, as Morgan drove her through the gates up the long drive to the house. Morgan had barely stopped the truck before Stephen came running out of the house to greet her.

"Aunt Dinah! Aunt Dinah!" he cried as he catapulted across the wide porch and down the stairs.

Her child! Dinah blinked back tears at this thought. At long last he could truly belong to her. She didn't know what to do, what to say. She was aware of Morgan's compassionate gaze, and she whirled toward the door to avoid it.

Morgan jumped out of the truck, ran around the hood, and opened her door, but Dinah avoided the bronzed hand that would have helped her down, just as she avoided the hard blue glitter of his eyes.

Instead she concentrated on the seven-year-old boy who'd gone suddenly shy in her presence. Overwhelmed with emotion, she pulled him into her arms and hugged him fiercely, while Morgan watched them both with an intense but silent interest.

Stephen wriggled free of her embrace.

"Are you staying for Christmas, Aunt Dinah?"

"Yes."

"Great!" he cried. "Did you know this'll be our first Christmas together?"

"Yes, I know," she murmured.

Stephen was bounding up the steps before them like a half-grown puppy. He turned around, his blue eyes brilliant. "How long are you staying?"

"I—I..." Dinah was too startled to answer.

From behind her came Morgan's deep baritone. "Forever."

Stephen clapped in glee and ran ahead of them into the front room. Dinah shot Morgan a look of pure fury. "You're not playing fair," she said tightly.

A wry, crooked smile curved his mouth. "No, Dinah. I'm not. I'm playing to win."

"By fair means or foul." Dully, she repeated the phrase he'd used in Suvretta.

"Exactly," he taunted softly. His hooded gaze swept over her and she felt unclothed by his hot, ravishing eyes. "I'm glad we understand each other."

Flushing warmly, she cried, "Don't look at me like that."

"All right. I'm tired of looking, anyway," he purred in derisive amusement. "You don't have any idea of what sitting next to you in that truck for so long did to me, do you?"

He moved leisurely and put his hand against the door, barring her way. His great body towered over her. He slid his other arm around her narrow waist and then covered her mouth insolently with his. He held her so close she felt his thighs against her slender hips, his chest against her breasts.

The sun came out from behind the clouds and blazed over his body, gilding his black hair, flashing behind him on the windowpanes.

He withdrew his lips, and she gazed up at him, feeling a twinge of doom inside her. He looked like a god in the sunlight. He was her fate. There would be no escape.

He bent his head and took her lips again and again,

releasing her reluctantly at last. "Yes, you were right. It's much more fun touching than looking."

"That wasn't what I meant," she sputtered.

"I didn't suppose it was. But I'm hoping to convince you."

"Well, that's one thing you'll never convince me of."

His hold tightened about her fractionally when she tried to pull away. "Is that because you and Edouard were lovers?" A brittleness edged his lazy drawl.

"No!" she denied explosively, before she thought. Then, when she realized what she'd foolishly admitted, she blushed furiously. "You have no right to ask that!"

"Probably not." A wide grin split his face. "But I'm glad I did."

"I'm back because of Stephen."

"That's what we both keep telling ourselves."

"It's the truth."

"Is it? Dinah, didn't you ever get lonely in the eight years you've been gone? Even once? Didn't you ever want to come back here? You used to love this place. I thought once that you loved me. Was being a celebrity, winning wine contests, and flitting from resort to resort on the arm of your famous *comte* enough to make you forget all this?"

Suddenly his handsome face was blurred because of the tears filling her eyes. "Maybe I wanted to forget! Can't you understand that? You were married to Holly! I'd given up my son! There was nothing here I could come back to."

"That's not true any longer," he said gently.

"What will it take to make you realize it's too late, Morgan?"

Morgan slackened his hold on her and she yanked the door open and fled inside, tears streaming down her cheeks.

His hands reached out after her to pull her back and comfort her, almost touching her before he let them fall back to dangle uselessly at his side. The last thing she wanted was to be comforted by him. At the thought, he slammed down the stairs and went to the winery where he could lose himself in his work.

Two weeks passed, two weeks that did little to ease the tension between Morgan and Dinah. But for Dinah it was an unforgettable time because she was with her beloved grandfather and son, and she could do all the things she'd yearned to do with them for so long. At eighty-four, Bruce was frailer, no longer actively participating in the running of the winery or in the supervision of the vineyards other than the occasional advice he gave Morgan, but he seemed content to spend his days reading quietly, watching television and rehashing the past with several retired old-timers like himself who dropped in to see him.

It seemed odd to Dinah that she'd feared being with Stephen, that she'd feared being unable to reach him, when the reality was so different. Stephen wanted to spend time with her as much as she wanted to spend it with him. He seemed starved for her attention. She helped him with his homework. They went Christmas shopping together. They took long walks and rode horses along the river's edge. Every moment seemed special because he was part of her life.

A week before Christmas, Morgan drove Dinah and Stephen into Calistoga to buy a Christmas tree. That night Dinah helped Morgan move a brown and gold chest from one corner of the front parlor so Morgan could haul in the immense tree Stephen had chosen and set it up there on the Persian carpet. Stephen's eyes were alight with eagerness as he peered first at the tree and then into the boxes of ornaments he held. With Bruce watching from his wing-backed chair, Dinah, Morgan and Stephen began to decorate the tree as excitedly as children.

When they had finished and Stephen had reluctantly gone upstairs with Bruce to bed, Dinah and Morgan, each feeling suddenly awkward to be alone in the other's company, lingered staring at the tree together in silence. The decorations had been placed a little haphazardly; nevertheless, the tree looked wonderful to both of them.

Hesitantly Dinah reached for a Santa Claus in a cluster of ornaments and hung him on a bare spot. She was reaching for another ornament when Morgan's brown hand closed over hers.

It was the first time he'd touched her since he'd brought her home and kissed her on the porch, and the contact of his fingers upon hers was a sensuous caress that sent a shiver tingling through her. She pulled her hand away as if burned.

"Don't," he whispered. "It's beautiful the way it is."

"Did you know this is the first tree we've decorated as a family since you left? Holly always did the tree so it would look perfect. She never let Stephen touch it."

"I just thought I'd balance—"

Dinah failed to see that Morgan was trying to make her feel how special her presence had always been at Kirsten Vineyards. Instead she reacted to the flare of her old jealousy toward Holly his remark sparked. "Holly was always so good at things like that. I couldn't ever compete."

"Damn!" Morgan muttered, flushing darkly with anger. "Will you never grow out of those feelings? I lived with Holly seven years. I was her husband, remember."

Mutely Dinah nodded, seared by his hard look. That one painful fact would always be unforgettable.

"Dinah, what would you say if I told you that Holly was jealous of you?" he asked more calmly.

"What?"

"She was as jealous of you as you were of her."

"I don't believe it."

His grave gaze met her look of astonishment. "Well, believe it," he said grimly. "She said that you always fit in here, and she never could. That you worked in the vineyard and winery, that you were interested in everything Bruce said and did, while she found it all so tedious. She said sometimes she felt that surely it was she who had been adopted and not you. She felt they adopted you because they were dissatisfied with her. She was miserable because she couldn't compete with you."

"She was their real child. Don't you see? I was trying so hard to belong."

"I see, but apparently Holly didn't. I think she made a play for me to put you in your place. She married me and took your son, but she wasn't satisfied. It infuriated her that you constantly made headlines in the wine magazines and that you were written about in gossip columns on the arm of a French *comte*. Believe me, Dinah, Holly could rage for hours after reading one line of newsprint about you. She hated being stuck here with me and Stephen while you were running from one posh European resort to another."

"Its hard to believe that anyone, especially Holly, could be jealous of me," Dinah murmured uncertainly.

"You always thought that Bruce loved Holly more than he loved you, but it was the other way around."

"What?"

"He told me once that he always had to try harder with Holly than he did with you, that he never understood her, that he could never guide her toward any interest. He said that he used to feel guilty for loving you more than he did her, and he made up for it by devoting himself to her in the attempt to change that. But he never could. It was you he loved, Dinah. Not Holly.''

"And all those years, I thought…''

"You're a very special woman when you aren't letting your feelings of inadequacy blind you,'' he said huskily.

Dinah was conscious of an affectionate tone in his voice. "Maybe you're right about Holly and Grandfather. I don't know anymore. I feel so confused. Tonight you've turned everything I've always believed upside down.''

"It's about time. Your beliefs were always topsy-turvy.'' His hands moved onto her shoulders, and Dinah stiffened at the disturbing contact of his fingers touching her skin.

"Thanks,'' she said with a shy smile.

"I've lived through hell because of you, Dinah. When are you going to realize that you weren't the only injured party? I spent seven years with a woman who despised me the minute she thought she'd taken me from you. I'm willing to try to put the past behind me. All I ask is that you meet me halfway.''

The warmth from his nearness and the touch of his hands against her shoulders splashed over her. It was very difficult not to move completely into his arms.

"Morgan, I'm…I'm so afraid.'' There was a betraying quiver in her voice. She lowered her eyes, and her thick lashes lay against her pale cheeks like dark half-crescents.

"Of what?'' he said in a thick, low voice that was as intimate as a caress.

Dinah held herself motionless, her breath running shallow while her pulse hammered wildly. "Of being here with you.''

"Do you want to go back to Edouard? Or are you happy here?''

"I'm happy here. Very happy,'' she admitted almost reluctantly. Still, she could not meet his burning gaze.

Thus she failed to see the look of swift relief that swept his dark features. "But it's hard for me to believe that something won't happen to snatch it all away again. I lost you and Stephen once."

"Nothing's going to happen," he answered softly, "if only you'll stop worrying and start trusting. We're going to find each other again, Dinah. Believe me. It's just going to take time."

"I...I can't believe it." She jerked herself out of his arms and ran across the room to the fireplace. She buried her face in her hands. "Why can't you just leave me alone?" she cried desperately. "Isn't it enough that Stephen and I are together?"

He strode swiftly after her and even before he spoke she knew the treacherous thrill of his hands upon her body again. He seized her shoulders again, and when she didn't resist him his hands began a slow downward descent, exploring the soft flesh of her upper arms. "No, it isn't enough, because I know the reason behind all these barriers you keep erecting between us."

At his merest touch she'd begun to shiver. "What do you mean?"

"We both know you're only trying to avoid this."

He turned her in his arms so that she was facing him. His powerful body was shaking as he pressed her tightly to him, his hot mouth falling first upon her upturned lips before traveling down the graceful curve of her cream-soft throat. He knelt and seared her breast with an intimate kiss.

At the first stirring touch of his mouth on her lips, Dinah had closed her eyes in the futile attempt to block out his existence, but that only made her more conscious of the blistering heat of his kisses, of the raw emotional power that he effortlessly evoked in her. Her stiff mouth began to tremble beneath the onslaught of the soft, wet intrusion of his tongue.

With his body so dangerously close she could smell the clean male scent of him mingling with his spicy aftershave. While her body warmed to his virile brand of pagan magnetism, her mind still attempted to resist.

"Please let me go. I want to go to bed," she managed, pushing him away.

"So do I," he said, a wicked gleam smoldering in his eyes. "For once we're in agreement."

"Oh, but I didn't mean..." she faltered, uncertain.

"Of course you did, darling." He grinned down at her, that insolent, white grin that made her stomach flutter crazily.

He captured her mouth with another long, searching kiss. His arms, which imprisoned her lush body to the hard contours of his, were steel bands.

She braced herself with one hand placed rigidly against his shoulder to hold him away. It angered Morgan that she was capable of such resistance, and Dinah felt the tension in his rippling muscles as she strained against him. He jerked her roughly against him, breaking her hold.

His mouth was both torture and ecstasy combined. Dinah found to her horror that she was responding to him despite her resolve not to. Embers of the old yearning she'd wanted to be long dead were rekindling. Her heart began to pound.

It was mouth against mouth, body against body, and the hate was gone, replaced by the fiery, aching desire that had always lain dormant deep within her. She was on fire to find again the love she had once known with him.

Weakly she tried one last time to wrench free, but he swung her off her feet into his strong arms and carried her toward the back of the house, where his rooms now were. Her head was pressed tightly against his chest, her black hair streaming over his shoulders. She heard the mad thrumming of his heart beneath her ear, felt the raggedness of his breathing. She clung to him, scared, eager.

"Morgan...put me down. Please..."

He seemed not to hear her. He just bore her inexorably through the sweeping darkness of pitch black halls to his bedroom. He opened his door and then kicked it closed behind him once more, carrying her to his bed, where he laid her down.

Perhaps even then she might have made some feeble effort to protest, had he not kissed her with such ferocity that all thoughts of fighting him were wiped from her mind. There was only the white-hot darkness and lips that claimed her with wild, furious kisses, hands that roamed her body freely, intimately, gently.

Covering her with his awesome length he kissed her mouth, her face, her throat, her slender neck, until she was breathless. He murmured her name again and again in broken whispers. She felt his fingers fumbling with the buttons of her blouse, and the flimsy silk garment tearing in his urgency. He removed first her blouse and then her lacy bra, freeing her breasts so that he could lavish them with kisses, his hot tongue hardening her nipples even as he explored their opulent softness with his hands.

Breathing hard, he ripped off his own shirt and unzipped his jeans, stripping completely as she marveled at the bronzed male beauty of him. Next he undressed her as she lay wordlessly beneath him. Then once more her lips and body were claimed by him, and she was clinging to him in the spiraling darkness that enveloped them in a mad, raging sweetness that neither of them could deny.

She was aware of callused hands moving over her skin in small sensual circles that left her aching when he stopped, moaning that he touch her again.

"With pleasure, my love," came his throaty baritone.

Again the skilled hands roved her body while his lips followed and tenderly caressed each erogenous love spot. The liberties he took were wantonly divine and she could do nothing but arch her body to meet his probing, seeking lips. He massaged her full breasts, lowering his mouth to tease and lick her nipples until they were hot wet peaks, pulsating pleasure tips. When she whispered his name with strangled love words, his mouth moved down her satin-smooth belly into the ebony down of her womanhood, where his hands and tongue titillated her with primitive expertise. She lay in a daze of rapture with her eyes shut, feeling the warm pressure of his lips against her pale thigh.

"Love me," she said at last. "Please, love me."

Raising himself over her body, he glided slowly into the velvet heat of her body. He forced himself deeper with each stroke, while her body met each thrust.

The fire of their passion was volcanic and all-consuming, but Morgan deliberately restrained his need. Dinah gripped her arms tightly around Morgan's back just as he withdrew and rolled away from her, breathing hard.

Her dark eyes sprang open in astonishment and hurt. They were luminous black jewels in her pale face. "Why did you stop?"

"I don't want to force you," came his low voice.

"You're not forcing me," she whispered raggedly, her need for him making her feel humiliated. She reached out and touched him.

"How can I be sure?"

"Please," she sobbed quietly.

"Please, what?" he demanded mercilessly, turning toward her. "You always make me force you."

"Please," she faltered. "Make love to me."

Still he did nothing.

"Morgan, I'm begging you."

His fingertips began to expertly tease her moist softness. He chuckled. "I just wanted to hear you admit you want me, darling. Just this once."

"You oaf!"

"Don't insult me, or I'll stop," he said with a chuckle. His hand stopped caressing her.

She heard his hushed, teasing laughter, and a deep shame filled her that she wanted him so much she'd begged him.

"No more insults, little one?" he taunted huskily.

She had to bite her tongue.

Morgan exhaled a deep breath of triumph as he looked into her flashing eyes. He had proved that she wanted him, that she could no more do without him than he could do without her.

Lowering himself over her body, he took her then, his need an immense, throbbing hunger. Deeper and deeper he drove into her until they were both shuddering in ecstasy from the slightest movement of their bodies.

She held him fiercely every time he pulled away. At last he brought her to an earth-shattering crescendo of excitement, and he lay still, deep within her, until the waves of delight washing her slowly faded. Then he clasped her more passionately then before and brought her to a second, even greater peak of fulfillment, before he allowed himself to take his pleasure and pour his warmth into her.

Afterward Morgan fell asleep in her arms while Dinah lay awake, her black hair entwined in his hands, her head against his shoulder while her mind raged in turmoil.

What had she done?

Eight

Dinah awoke, her body tangled in Morgan's arms and legs. She flushed with embarrassment as she recalled the long wanton night. He'd made love to her again and again. The burning, shameful memories made her feel dazed with pleasure as she slid quietly from the bed, careful not to wake Morgan. Her pleasure was quickly being overridden by her doubts about him.

No matter how passionately he'd taken her, Dinah couldn't believe Morgan really cared about her. She realized she'd probably made a terrible mistake to let him make love to her. It would be all the more difficult to fight him in the future.

Later that morning, when Dinah was in the kitchen helping Graciela cook breakfast, Morgan strode inside. Dinah felt mesmerized by his dark, startling good looks, and she almost hated him for his power over her.

A cold chill played around the edges of Dinah's heart.

Was she falling in love with him all over again? She mustn't. She couldn't let that happen. She knew too well the hurt his love had brought her.

"Good morning," he said huskily.

Dinah made no reply to his jaunty greeting. Instead she tried to concentrate on cutting out homemade biscuits with the cookie cutter Graciela had given her.

"*Buenos días* to you, Señor Morgan," Graciela said. "My, but you're not looking too frisky this morning."

"No, I'm not feeling too frisky either. I didn't get much sleep." He groaned dramatically and then chuckled, winking knowingly behind Graciela at a now scowling Dinah. "You might say...I, er...I worked late last night."

"You work too hard, Señor Morgan," Graciela said, taking his remark at face value even as Dinah turned the brightest shade of red.

"Oh, I don't know," he drawled lazily. "Last night I thoroughly enjoyed myself even though it did leave me pretty worn out."

"You're a dedicated man, Señor Morgan."

"Oh, very dedicated. Very dedicated indeed," came that bold, insulting voice.

Rage spiraled through Dinah as she cast a seething glance toward him. In his crisply starched blue gingham shirt, which emphasized the deep blueness of his twinkling eyes and the blackness of his rumpled hair, he looked far from worn out. Indeed, she'd never seen him looking more arrogantly masterful as he grinned insolently at every clandestine opportunity in her direction.

Damn the infernal conceit of that man! Dinah fumed silently. She was the one who had to move gingerly this morning because of an aching soreness in her thighs due to his ardent lovemaking.

"Still, Señor Morgan, you should play more and work less. But I know it's no good telling you what to do."

Graciela swept from the room to set the table in the formal dining room.

"What I need is an enthusiastic playmate, if I'm to work less and play more," Morgan whispered into Dinah's hair.

She stiffened and moved out of his arms. "You'll have to look somewhere else...for your playmate."

"But I thought I'd already found her," he murmured.

"Well, you haven't."

"Last night, you were...er...remarkably playful."

"Can't we change this disgusting subject?" She slashed out another biscuit and flung it onto the cookie sheet with such force it looked like a lump of dough.

"Surely not disgusting, darling?"

"Disgusting," she hissed.

"And I was expecting flattery."

"That's the last thing you'll ever get from me, you conceited oaf."

"Couldn't you at least say good morning to me? And would it be asking too much for a smile?"

"They're in short supply."

"So I see. Last night—"

"Last night was a mistake," she retorted sourly.

"What in the hell did I do wrong this time, love?"

"You seduced me, for one thing. You knew I wasn't ready for that type of relationship with you. But you bullied me..."

"Dammit, Dinah, I waited two whole weeks. Last night you acted pretty ready there for a while," he added grimly. "I seem to remember you begging me—"

"Oh, shut up!" she ground out furiously.

He pulled her away from the counter and her biscuit making. Startled, she looked up and saw that his brows were drawn together in a dark frown, and his mouth was

curled in a sardonic expression of anger. She knew he
was fighting the emotion, not wanting to show his rage.

His tall, muscular frame towered over her. He was so
virile and awesomely all male, he seemed out of his element in such a feminine domain as Graciela's frilly
kitchen.

Dinah felt as if she were facing a stranger instead of a
man she had known most of her life. His deep blue eyes
raked over her with lingering, hostile intensity, challenging her. He had a dangerous way of stripping away her
defenses, until her very soul lay open to his piercing gaze.

She wet her lips to reply, but she couldn't utter a sound.
Instead she turned her head and stared out the window at
the gray hills and rows of vineyards.

"Is what happened last night so frightening you can't
even face me this morning?" he demanded. "Or is it the
truth that you can't face?"

"Oh, why can't you just leave me alone?"

"Because, darling," he exploded. "I love you."

The words burst from his lips before he could stop
them. For a long moment they stood looking at one another, his blue gaze watching her intently for any sign of
reaction, but she gave him none. She went rigid, his three
words producing more pain than anything he could have
said. Then she ran from the room. She heard him curse
softly behind her. The kitchen door slammed.

All through the day, Dinah thought about what he'd
admitted in a moment of anger. She could not stop herself
from wondering if he meant it. Or did he realize it was
the most powerful method of persuasion he could use to
make her yield to him completely? Dinah passed the hours
in a tortured daze of bewilderment. Was she wrong not
to trust him? Hadn't she been wrong in the past? If she'd
trusted him, would their love have ended with his marriage to Holly? Or was that just his rationalization for

what had happened? She remembered the pain of their
separation, her years of disillusionment, and her heart
hardened. She mustn't weaken. She mustn't. But she was
weakening.

Morgan did not appear for dinner, nor for supper, and
Dinah could not bring herself to ask Bruce where he might
be. Once or twice the next day she saw him from a distance going about his duties in the vineyard and winery.
When it was past five o'clock that second evening and he
still hadn't come in, Dinah could endure his absence no
longer. She went down to the winery and asked Richard,
the cellarmaster, if he knew where Morgan was.

"I think he slept in his office last night, Miss Kirsten.
He worked late."

She lifted her skirts and ran up the spiral stairs of the
winery to his office. Hesitantly she knocked on the door.

The deep, achingly familiar baritone welcomed her.
"Come in."

She pushed the door open and stepped partway inside.
Morgan was sitting behind his massive oak desk with a
cup of coffee in one hand and the telephone in the other.
Smoke curled from a cigarette he'd discarded in the ashtray. His eyes darkened as he motioned Dinah to sit down.
He finished the phone conversation and slammed the receiver down on the hook.

Dinah felt his piercing gaze, but she was suddenly too
shy to look at him. He lifted his cigarette to his lips, took
one drag, and then squashed it out.

"To what do I owe this honor, madame?" he asked
with infuriating arrogance.

"I...I..." Suddenly Dinah felt very foolish.

"Don't tell me you were missing me."

She looked up at him quickly and saw a puzzling,
watchful glint in his eyes, a hopeful eagerness. He seemed
to hang upon her next words.

"No. Graciela just wanted to know if you were coming to dinner," she hedged.

Morgan lifted one thick, dark brow in her direction. "The hell it was Graciela who wanted to know!" he said mockingly. "But you're too cowardly to admit it."

Moistening her lips with her tongue, Dinah replied, "I didn't come out here to be insulted, Morgan."

"Then I won't insult you," he said good-naturedly. "I'll surprise you with a compliment. You are very beautiful when you blush like that. It adds a glow to your translucent skin, but I'm sure you know that."

"You said you weren't going to insult me," she stammered, her blush deepening.

"Oh, yes. So I did. With your fair skin and black hair and dark eyes, you'd be stunning if you'd only smile more often, Dinah. Not that I'm complaining, mind you. Nor insulting you." His eyes flashed mischievously. "Who ever said a man could have it all? Least of all me. I think I have enough." He leaned back in his chair in a languid position and let his gaze roam over Dinah's lush figure in frank male appraisal.

She shivered beneath his dark gaze. "You'll never have me," she hissed.

"Really? And I was looking forward to finding you in my arms every morning in the near future the way you were the other day with your warm body wrapped in mine."

Her potent response to the vision his words inspired filled her with fury both at herself and at him. "You don't have to remind me of that."

A warning light flared in his eyes, and suddenly she sensed danger. Dinah made a mad dash toward the door to escape, but Morgan moved more quickly, springing from his chair, grabbing her shoulders, and holding her struggling body close.

"Oh, but maybe I want to remind you, love," he taunted softly.

"Let go of me, you bully!" Her breaths came in quick, uneven spurts. Her heaving breasts pushed provocatively against his massive chest. "You can't treat me like this."

She writhed against him, but it only made his hard body seem that much closer. She was aware of him pressing tightly against her, his hips moving against her thighs, and of her own shameless thrill at his unconcealed desire for her.

Morgan ignored her angry words and buried his hands in her long hair, forcing her face close to his so that her mouth was within inches of his lips. His warm breath fanned her face. "Tonight, you came looking for me, remember? If you didn't want this to happen you should have stayed in the house."

"No...you're wrong. This isn't what I want," Dinah stammered.

"You'd better make up your mind, and quickly, my dear. A man can only be pushed so far, and dammit, Dinah, you've pushed me to my limit. If you don't want me, you need to stay the hell away from me, and if you do, you've got to give yourself to me."

For a timeless moment she hesitated, staring deeply into his eyes. Her pride battled against her love for him. How could she still love a man who'd married another and left her pregnant? *But he didn't know!* a tiny voice cried in his defense. *You left him!* Still, for all his talk of love, she probably meant nothing to him. Hadn't he once taunted her by saying he saw no reason why he shouldn't enjoy her since he still desired her?

But even if that was all he felt, what of her own feelings? Life would hold no meaning for her without him. She knew that now. What was the point of denying herself? Perhaps if she gave herself freely, if she sacrificed her independence, she would someday learn to trust him.

All she knew was that their love had no chance of blossoming if she continued to fight him at every corner. If she didn't take the risk of losing her heart all over again, there could be no chance of winning his love. And if she didn't win it, what would be her future relationship with her son? Would it be an every-other-weekend affair? She loved them both too much not to try for something better.

Arrogant pride crumbled before the mighty conqueror love. He saw it in her eyes, even before she spoke.

"I love you, Morgan," she admitted gently. "I always have, and I always will."

He studied her shining face and then drew her into his arms.

"Oh, I do love you," she whispered, and her arms circled his broad back. "All these years there's never been anyone but you."

His face filled with wonder. "I never knew."

"It seemed so stupid, after what you had done. I wanted to hate you. Oh, how your male ego must be pleased."

"My male ego?" He looked puzzled. "Is that really what you think, darling?" She nodded and he said, "Much more than my male ego is pleased, I assure you." He tenderly brushed his mouth over her throat gently. "The first day I met you, you were scarcely more than a child, yet you saved my life. And when you let me stay here despite your reservations against doing so, you saved much more than my life." He paused. "I couldn't hate you either, no matter how I tried. Through the years I kept remembering your fiery spirit, your beauty, and your strength of character. And I always believed that what went wrong between us was a mistake we would have resolved of it hadn't been for Stephen's birth."

"We've wasted so much time," Dinah said on a breathless note. She locked the door and flicked the light switch that turned off the lamp.

"What are you doing?"

"You'll catch on in a minute, I'm sure," she purred. Seductively she began to strip, lifting her arms high above her head as she removed her sweater, stretching languorously, arching her back so that her breasts thrust forward invitingly. A last scarlet shaft of sunlight filtered through the window and bathed her body in its soft, rosy iridescent glow.

Watching her, Morgan exhaled a deep breath. His pulse began to thud violently. She looked as lovely as a goddess. Lovelier because she was flesh-and-blood and sweet-scented. Lithe, sensual, she moved, letting the light play over her body. The setting sun gilded the voluptuous curves of her breasts and hips and thighs, warmed the sculpted, white flesh, accentuating the bloom of her incomparable beauty.

With a groan, he gathered her into his arms. "You wanton. I do believe you're seducing me."

"Any objections?" She smiled. Trembling fingertips unhooked his collar button.

He pulled his shirt free of his slacks and began unbuttoning it from the bottom up until their fingertips met in the middle of his chest, and a strip of brown torso was revealed.

With her mouth she kissed a line from his throat to his navel. Then she bent her head lower. Gentle lips touched him intimately, and he gasped. She kissed him with slow, languorous motions until he could stand it no longer. He was breathless when he lifted her into his arms.

"I have to have you," he whispered hoarsely before his mouth ravished her lips.

Dinah clasped him in an ardent frenzy of hope and passionate longing. What passed between them were long hours of lovemaking in which they gave themselves to each other with wild, reckless abandon.

For the first time their union was both physical and spiritual, both of the heart and soul and as well as the body. Afterward they lay in each other's arms, happier than they had ever been, a warm glow filling them.

"We're going to have to go inside before long," Dinah teased, smiling through half-lowered lashes.

"Why?" His brown fingers absently caressed her smooth shoulder and breast.

"You have to eat something of Graciela's dinner tonight. You know she'll sulk if you don't."

"Tonight Graciela's sulking is not uppermost on my mind."

"But we shouldn't deliberately hurt her feelings."

"I suppose you're right. But I don't feel like being with anyone except you right now. And what excuse shall we make that we didn't come in earlier?"

Dinah's eyes sparkled with mischief. "Why don't you tell her we were working late? She'll swallow that, since she believes you're such a dedicated man."

"A very dedicated man." Morgan chuckled. "So dedicated in fact I may have to work a little later." His words came out low and husky as his hand slid from her breast down the length of her body. He began to stroke her gently.

"Morgan!"

He silenced her protest with a kiss, and it was a long time before they went to dinner.

Nine

Dinah's acceptance of her love for Morgan brought her a deep, fulfilling happiness such as she had always dreamed and yearned for. The years of stardom in the wine world and the glamour surrounding her engagement to a French count faded into insignificance. She hadn't known what she'd been missing.

Dinah felt that if she could be home and have her son and husband and grandfather, she needed nothing else. The weeks that passed were infinitely special as Morgan, Dinah, and Stephen learned to love each other.

When Dinah thought of the future she was filled with joy. She was home with the people she loved, as well as home in her beautiful Napa Valley. During her years of exile her mind had too often wandered back to the valley, its poetic beauty haunting her, and now it was hers again. She could rediscover the delicate tracery of light and shadow on the craggy face of Mt. St. Helena, roam with her son the same verdant hills she'd roamed as a child, the hills that would be blue with lupine in the spring and tawny with the gold of the summer. Season after season she would watch the vineyards blossom yellow with mustard, grow green in summer, and then wear once again their autumnal robes of purple and gold when the fruit would hang heavy on the vines, swollen with nectar. But most of all, her life would be enriched because of the people she loved. Not in years had she felt so keenly alive, and never had life seemed sweeter.

When the Christmas holidays were over and Stephen went back to school, Dinah regularly began to go into the winery. It had been an unusually good season that year in the vineyard. Every day she worked beside Morgan as he and the cellarmaster conferred on important winemaking decisions, and Morgan listened to her ideas receptively. The first thing she did was to help him taste and blend the famous Kirsten Cabernet that was known around the world for its fullness and softness.

Several journalists interviewed Dinah about her reasons for leaving de Landaux and returning home, and she always spoke with excitement of the opportunities she saw at Kirsten Vineyards. On his way out, one of the reporters, Mr. Davies, a little man with a sharp, brusque manner whom she hadn't much liked, asked her about Morgan.

"Who is this Mr. Smith, Miss Kirsten?"

"I told you, Mr. Davies, he manages Kirsten Vineyards. He's a partner in the business."

"I understand you're going to marry him."

"That's true."

"There's something about him that's familiar to me. I never forget a face, Miss Kirsten. Maybe I did a story on him before?"

"I don't think so."

"Oh, but I do."

An odd, sly look had come into his eyes, and Dinah felt a vague, unreasonable twinge of alarm while the man told her good-bye. She watched him run jauntily down the stairs; the warning feeling remained throughout her long, busy afternoon.

In her spare time she turned a room down the hall from Morgan's office into her own office and furnished it with such decorative flair that he laughingly complained one afternoon as his shoes sank into her thick, plush maroon carpet, "Your office is so lavish everyone around here is going to wonder who the boss is."

From her desk she eyed the stubborn thrust of his hard jawline and smiled. "Somehow I doubt that. You can be awfully bullheaded, my darling. Not that I'm objecting, mind you. A woman can't have everything, you know." She arose from her desk and came around it to stand beside him.

"Look who's talking," he said fondly. A brown hand tipped her chin back and he stared deeply into her eyes. "But you're the prettiest little bullhead on the premises. How about two bullheads exchanging a kiss?"

Their lips clung together a long time, parting reluctantly.

"I never thought I could be so happy," he said at last against her hair in an odd voice. "This was the pattern of life I only dreamed of when I was a child. Two people in love. A real home and a family. Imagine me having all this." His expression hardened from some bitter memory, but she gazed at him silently, not daring to say a word, hoping he would tell her of that time he'd locked deep inside of him. His hands stroked her hair. "You can't know how good it makes me feel to see you and Stephen so happy together. When I was a kid there were people who envied me my beautiful, movie-star mother. They envied us our money and fame, the mansion in Beverly

Hills. They didn't understand. She was a great actress, and she fooled almost everyone. It was a deliberate effort on her part. When my mother was young, stars had to be very careful of their public images. As she grew older, Mother was less cautious. She played the 'bad girl' on screen, and she stopped caring if people found out she was a 'bad girl' off-screen as well. Most of the time Mother ignored me, but I hated that almost as much as I hated the times when she drank and came into my room and abused me both physically and verbally. I was so mixed up about her. She seemed to hate me, and I didn't know why. And then there were the men she constantly saw. In some ways I was jealous of them. I used to wish that she were ugly so the men would stop coming around. The older I got, the angrier and more confused I became, until I lashed out at everyone and everything, including her. What happened in the end was inevitable, I suppose.''

"What about your father?"

"She told me he was dead. She never liked to speak of him.''

"You never explained about that night that made the papers. Your mother said you tried to kill her for her money, and that she was going to change her will and disinherit you. She said you went wild when she told you that. Morgan, she was so badly beaten up.''

His face darkened with fierce emotion. "Do you think I can't remember what she looked like that night?'' His eyes blazed feverishly. "But everything she said about me was a lie,'' he said harshly. "Everybody believed her,'' he murmured in a dull, dead voice. "I don't know why she said those things. I never had a chance with her against me. Like I said, she had been fairly careful of her image. And I had not been careful about mine at all. I had been involved with too many girls and wild parties. My age was against me. No one believed anything I said. That last night was the most galling irony of our entire life together. Someday, maybe I'll tell you about it. It doesn't matter anymore. She died three years ago, and I hadn't even seen her since I ran away from Lawton's except that one time. That's been more than twelve years. I'm just thankful Stephen will never have to go through the hell I went through growing up."

Dinah wished that Morgan would tell her everything, but apparently he still couldn't talk about that time without the horrible memories consuming him. Dinah didn't press him. As time passed they would grow closer, and she was sure that one day he would tell her.

Despite her contentment, and Morgan's constant promises that she had no reason to fear the loss of all that she held most dear, Dinah was still haunted by those vague insecurities that had always plagued her. She just couldn't let herself believe that her happiness with Morgan and her son could last. It was too good to be true. Something was bound to happen that would destroy it.

"Believe in the future, Dinah," he would beg. "Believe in me. Believe in us."

And she tried. Oh, she valiantly tried. But it was impossible to change the psychological habits of a lifetime. She had never believed in herself; she'd only grown more skilled in hiding her lack of self-confidence behind a facade of glamour.

That winter was colder than usual. One Pacific cold front after another blasted Kirsten Vineyards throughout January and into February, and perhaps it was the perpetual chill of the house that made Dinah first become aware that Bruce was unwell. Certainly her grandfather made every effort to conceal his condition from Dinah. He was eighty-four, but his health even in old age had always been remarkably robust.

Suddenly she noticed how pale and thin he was. Recently he'd moved to one of the downstairs bedrooms. He had little strength, scarcely ate, and sometimes remained in bed on especially cold days. Whenever Dinah tried to ask Bruce how he was feeling, he brushed her questions aside, saying he was as well as anyone his age, that he had a cold, that it would pass when the weather warmed up. But he refused to see a doctor. Finally, in desperation, she confronted Morgan.

"I know something's wrong with Grandfather. He's too stubborn to admit it. Tell me the truth, Morgan. He's sick, isn't he?"

"Yes, he's seriously ill," Morgan admitted gravely at last. "Terminally ill, I'm afraid." His blue eyes shone with compassion. "I hate it as much as you do."

"How long have you known?"

"Since right before I came after you."

"And was that one of your unspoken reasons for coming to Switzerland when you did?"

"Yes. I knew you would want to be with him just as much as he wanted you here."

"Why didn't you tell me, Morgan?"

"Because Bruce asked me not to."

"How long does he have?"

"He refused conventional medical treatment, but his doctor says he's strong, and that these things can be slower in someone his age. Maybe two years. Maybe longer."

"Oh, no..." She began to sob quietly.

He drew her into his arms. "There's nothing anyone can do."

"I'm so glad I found out while there's still time."

"Dinah, maybe this isn't the right moment, but maybe it is." He smoothed her hair against her neck the way he always did. His gaze held hers. "I'm sure about my feelings for you. I've always loved you, and that's not going to change. I want you to marry me. I think it would mean a lot to Bruce if we married while he's well enough to enjoy the wedding.''

"Are you sure you won't be marrying me just for Bruce? Sure it's not too soon?''

"I'm very sure.''

"Then so am I.'' She reached up and touched his lips with her own. "Oh, Morgan.'' His name was an aching murmur of tenderness.

Two mornings later a newspaper headline in the second section of the paper made Dinah whiten with shock. She clenched the paper with shaking fingers, fighting to regain control of herself as she read the cruel words.

"Famed winemaker Dinah Kirsten to wed Morgan Hastings' son and accused assailant of his mother, famed film star, Teresa Hastings.''

Dinah cringed at the lurid picture of Teresa's tearful, beaten face and the picture of a young, defiant Morgan, trying to avoid the camera. The article reprinted Teresa's more notorious quotations, told of Morgan's escape fourteen years ago from the school where he'd been sent for rehabilitation, and gave several facts about Teresa's torrid love life, illness, and death. There was information about Dinah's career in France, and a few more facts about Kirsten Vineyards. The byline was Davies.

Oh, that horrid, horrid little man! Dinah tore the paper into shreds and threw it in the wastebasket.

"Do you really think you can get rid of it that easily?'' came Morgan's grim tone from the doorway.

She whirled. His face seemed carved of granite. His blue eyes were cold and metallic, his great body tense. "I—I didn't want Stephen to see it,'' she explained.

"I showed it to him this morning before he went to school.''

"Oh, Morgan,'' she cried. "You didn't...''

"I had no choice. I didn't want him hearing about it from other kids. I told him it wasn't true, and that someday I would try to explain it to him when he was old enough to understand. He said he believed me and that he'd punch any kid that so much as said a word against me. He left looking forward to a fight."

Dinah laughed weakly.

"You know something? I was never prouder of him than then." Morgan paused. "I wonder how our friends in the valley will react."

"It won't make any difference to your real friends."

"And you? Do you still want to marry me now that everyone knows? I'll understand if this makes a difference."

She stared into his dark, unhappy face, not really seeing him through the mist of her own emotions. Gently she put her hand in his, and convulsively his fingers tightened around hers as he pulled her into his arms.

"I love you, Morgan. Nothing will ever change that."

He held her tightly against the hard length of his body, and she hurt for all his terrible, lonely past. She hurt for the embarrassment he would have to face.

"I love you too." His voice was husky with the agony of emotion that tore through him. "No one who knew those lies ever gave me a chance back then. No one...except you." He felt if he said anything more he would fly all to pieces inside. Every muscle tensed to force the bitter memories back down. He couldn't let her see how they ate him raw inside.

"Someday soon, you'll be free of the past, Morgan. I promise."

His lips tasted hers, and she felt a sudden, overwhelming burst of happiness.

Dinah and Morgan were married on the first of March, a cold, clear Saturday afternoon. Outside a blustering breeze whipped the golden acacia blossoms that blazed in full bloom against the house. Inside the rooms were cozily warm. Fires leaped in the fireplaces. Religious music was played upon the piano.

The wedding ceremony was a simple affair held in the front parlor. Bruce had rallied for the occasion and almost seemed his old, hearty self as he led the bride down the stairs on his arm. Beaming with fond pleasure, he gave Dinah away, and Stephen was the importantly proud best man at his father's side, who fumbled self-consciously when it came time to produce the wedding ring.

After the brief solemnity of vows being exchanged, the house came alive with the raucous gaiety of wedding guests, mostly valley people who stayed to attend the reception. If any of them thought any differently of their longtime friend and associate, none of them said anything. Champagne and premium white wines flowed freely.

In her white silk gown and lace veil, Dinah was a radiant bride on the arm of her tall, dark husband as she stood in the receiving line. Frequently the bridegroom cast her a disarming smile that softened his roughly carved features, and she blushed enchantingly, basking in the glow of his love. There were many who remarked on Dinah's singular beauty that day. Delighted whispers floated to her ears. "What a charming couple they make." "It's so fortunate they're marrying. He has a child, you know, and she's very good with the little boy, they say."

A neighboring winemaker pulled Morgan aside to ask him if he could borrow a tractor because one of his had broken down. Morgan and he quickly became absorbed in conversation, and Dinah left them, moving from room to room in a daze of happiness as she chatted and laughed with old friends. After a while she began to miss Morgan and went searching for him. When she returned to the front parlor Morgan was gone. The man he had been talking to told her he thought Morgan had gone with Bruce to the library.

Suddenly worried for fear that perhaps despite Bruce's appearance of heath he was unwell, Dinah made her way quickly down the hall. The library doors were partially open when she reached them, and she could hear their voices clearly. Some instinct of danger stopped her from going in.

"I certainly have to hand it to you, Morgan," Bruce was saying in a warm congratulatory tone. "You were right and I was wrong about how to handle Dinah. I never thought you could talk her into this marriage. This is definitely a better solution than what I had in mind."

"Definitely," came Morgan's grim reply.

Dinah's fingers froze against the cold wood door. What were they talking about? She had to find out. She stood outside, listening warily.

"You needn't look so unhappy, Morgan. Married to Dinah, no one will question your right to run this place when I'm gone."

"You and I both know I wouldn't have pushed Dinah into making a decision so quickly if you hadn't been breathing down my neck."

"I didn't want her pressured either, but I couldn't rest easily with everything up in the air." Bruce sighed heavily. "It's just as well you're married and everything's settled."

"Perhaps."

Dinah pushed open the door. There was an instant, guilty lull in the men's conversation. Bruce went dull red in embarrassment. There was a forbidding hardness to Morgan's dark features, and she realized he was very angry at Bruce. Morgan's vivid blue eyes inspected her in an alertly sweeping glance, and she knew he was wondering how much she had heard, how much she had understood.

Though her dark eyes were shimmering with misery, she forced her most brilliant smile. "There you are, darling. I've been looking everywhere for you," she began teasingly. "What is a wedding reception without the bridegroom?"

"I'm sorry, Dinah," he said gently. His beautiful voice was infinitely tender, and for an instant she almost let herself forget that a moment before she'd believed he might be capable of duplicity. "I didn't mean to stay gone so long." His arm circled her stiff body, and she let him lead her back to the party.

During the rest of the reception Dinah remained agitated about the fragment of conversation she had overheard. Morgan seemed strangely on edge after his discussion with Bruce, and she was practically sure that Bruce and Morgan were deliberately concealing something from her. She was determined to find out what it was.

When the reception was nearly over Dinah went upstairs to dress for their honeymoon. It was to be a brief three-day holiday in a friend's beach house at Stinson Beach. Morgan couldn't be gone long because spring was a time that brought the constant danger of nightly frosts, and he didn't want to leave the vineyards for others to take care of for too many nights. Morgan had selected Stinson Beach because it was close and he had teased, "I definitely don't want to waste what little time we have driving."

Dinah hadn't cared where they went. Anywhere with Morgan had seemed idyllic. Now all that had changed.

She was upstairs in her bedroom and had finished putting on a soft blue wool suit and silk blouse. She leaned closer toward her mirror and with a couple of deft strokes painted her lips.

From the hall Bruce knocked loudly at her door. "May I come in, Dinah?"

"Sure," she called.

Bruce stepped inside and stared at her fondly, his gray eyes as bright as ever. "I wanted to avoid the crowd and tell you good-bye here."

"I'm glad you did." She glanced back at him tenderly. He glowed his happiness. In that moment he didn't look sick at all. "Are you sure you'll be all right while we're gone, Grandfather?" she asked softly. She tossed her tube of lipstick into her blue clutch purse and went to him.

"I've never felt better."

She smiled and hugged him tightly. "We're going to miss you."

"You'll hardly be gone more than three days. Don't waste time missing an old man on your honeymoon. Be happy, Dinah. That's all I've ever wanted for you. Morgan's a good man, no matter what some people might think."

"I know he's a good man." She released Bruce. "And Grandfather, I want to be happy, and I am happy. But—"

"You don't look happy, child. What's bothering you? If it's not those printed lies, then what—"

She stared at him intently and decided to tell him. "I didn't intend to mention this so soon, but a while ago I overheard part of what you and Morgan were saying before I came into the library."

Suddenly Bruce looked very uncomfortable. "You shouldn't have eavesdropped."

"I didn't mean to, Grandfather, but now I want to know what you were going to do or tell me that made Morgan ask me to marry him sooner than he wanted to? How did you pressure him?"

"Child, I don't know what you heard, but the important thing is you and Morgan love each other and belong together," Bruce replied evasively. "You're married now. These things don't matter any longer."

Oh, but they mattered terribly. "Was it Morgan's idea to come after me in Switzerland or yours, Grandfather?" Dinah demanded.

Bruce hung his head. "In the beginning it was mine," he admitted reluctantly.

"How did you make Morgan do it?"

"Nobody makes Morgan do anything."

"How did you persuade him, then?"

"Well, it became obvious to me a long time ago that you two belonged together. There was Holly, of course. I blamed myself, at least in part, for their marriage. But after she died, you two were both too stubborn to ever do anything about it or even admit it. I tried to talk to you about Morgan last summer after the accident, but you refused to listen. When you wrote that you were going to marry Edouard in November, I had to take matters into my own hands."

"What exactly did you do, Grandfather?"

"You know I told Morgan about Stephen."

"Yes."

"I wanted him to understand why you refused to come back. Then I told him I was ill and I wanted you back here with me. When that didn't move him to go after you, I'm afraid I brought up the matter of my will. He can be stubborn, and that infuriated me. You see, I'm leaving my entire estate other than what I settled on Holly, which is now in trust for Stephen, to you. I informed him you would soon own fifty-one percent of Kirsten Vineyards and that he'd better bring you back and make some sort of peace with you before I died, if he wanted to stay here, because you were going to be his boss. Morgan has worked for years on this place, and I knew he didn't want to walk away from all this, just as I knew that once you two were together, you would find each other again. And you have.''

Her throat worked convulsively. It was difficult for her to speak. ''What did Morgan do?''

''Well, at first he refused again, and very angrily, I might add, but shortly after that, Stephen began to have more problems than usual and Morgan didn't seem sure how to cope with them. It wasn't long before he agreed to go after you.''

Dinah's face was as waxen as a death mask. Each heartbeat brought a dull ache inside her chest. Her dark, turbulent eyes flashed with emotion. Had money been the only reason Morgan had come after her, then? He was ambitious. She had always known that. One had only to look at the modernization and expansion of Kirsten Vineyards to realize how he felt about the winery. Could he stand by and let her take over everything he had done? Was Morgan so coldly ruthless that he could marry her for that reason alone? Or was she being unfair? Was it possible that he loved her too? That he had been genuinely concerned about Stephen? She wanted, oh, she wanted so much to believe in him, but she was besieged anew by doubts. As always, her old insecurity wouldn't let her believe that he could love her for herself.

As she descended the stairs to go on her honeymoon trip, her heart was leaden with anguish. Morgan stood at the bottom of the staircase, his broad-shouldered body looking magnificent in a navy blue suit. His eyes, which met hers, were warm and devouring, and she flushed crimson. Never had she been more terribly aware of how hopelessly she loved him. But even as she was torn by wild grief and doubt, she placed her icy hand into his much larger, much warmer one, and let him help her down the last few steps.

His lightest touch rocked every sense in her being. She

met his smile with a trembling one of her own. Time stood still as they stared into each other's eyes. Then they ran outside together beneath a shower of rice. He helped her into his truck, and climbed inside himself. Every nerve she possessed screamed of his presence beside her. She watched his lean, well-manicured hands move to the steering wheel and start the ignition, and she thought of the way those hands had moved over her intimately. The closeness of his body brought to her nostrils the spicy fragrance of his cologne. She ached for him, and it was unbearable to think that he didn't love her.

He looked at her and said huskily, "I've been waiting all day for a real kiss from my bride."

She felt faint beneath his stare. It was torture to wonder if his every kindness was false. She sat very still as he moved closer.

His long, bronzed fingers moved beneath the delicate bones of her chin and tipped it firmly back while his other arm slid behind her back. Her black hair cascaded over her shoulders. He crushed her to him suddenly in a powerful, possessive embrace. She knew their friends were watching them, and she wished frantically that he would start the truck and drive away. But he was oblivious to all save the beautiful woman nestled against his broad chest. His arm was like a band of steel around her, imprisoning her small body tightly against his own. His head lowered and his parted lips moved over hers to claim a passionately searing kiss. His open mouth was wet and hotly demanding as he forced her to part her lips, slowly, languorously teasing her senses with the warm probing of his tongue.

At last the kiss ended, but not before she was trembling violently with both shame and desire. He started the ignition, and when she would have moved a safe distance away from him, he circled her slim shoulders with his arm, holding her close against his body as he drove in silence. Feeling jittery, she watched the road fly past as he headed toward the Marin headlands. She felt surrounded by him, overpowered by him, but he did not seem to know how his nearness disturbed her.

She drew a ragged breath. Oh, how she loved and desired him. But she did not want to trap him into a marriage he did not want except for financial reasons.

What was she going to do? They were husband and wife now. If she said nothing could they go on as they were? Would it be so terribly wrong? She had not forced Morgan to marry her. Couldn't they make some sort of life together? They would raise their child together, and clearly Morgan did not mean to be unkind to her. His desire for her was all too obvious. Why couldn't this be enough for her?

Again she remembered his cruel taunt in Switzerland, when he had said he didn't love her but wanted her back solely because she was the mother of his child. He had not mentioned money, of course, but his words were burned inside her heart. "The desire I feel toward you is the same I would feel toward any beautiful woman, and since we're going to live together, I see no reason why I shouldn't enjoy you."

Were those his true feelings? Now he said he loved her, but did he? Was their marriage no more than a marriage of convenience to him? He had never mentioned her grandfather's will, and the omission pointed to his guilt.

When they reached Stinson Beach, she felt vaguely carsick from the twisting, hilly road. She scarcely noted the quaint, casual charm of the seaside village nestled between its narrow strip of beach and the verdant slopes at its back. Morgan drove straight to the beach house and dropped her off so she could rest while he drove back into town to buy groceries.

"I don't think either of us will feel like going out for dinner tonight," he said before leaving. "You freshen up, and I'll be back soon."

He caught her gaze and would not free it. Even when his eyes lowered to her body, tracing the soft, voluptuous curve of her breasts jutting against blue silk, she could not look away from his dark face. Then once again his eyes met hers, and a small shiver swept her. Her heart began to pound fiercely with emotion.

Tell him. Tell him of your doubts! Maybe he could explain everything. But she was weak and too afraid, and she let him go without saying anything. She was determined to try to go on as if nothing had happened. For eight years she had had nothing; was it so wrong to try to hold on to what she had now?

When he returned he found her outside on the wooden deck sitting on a rough picnic table, staring moodily out at the crashing surf through the glass wind screens. Deliberately he let the back door slam, and when she turned, he smiled that devastating white smile that made her stomach flutter. His face was reddened by the cold wind, and he had changed clothes and was now ruggedly dressed in a bulky turtleneck sweater, jeans, and boots. The rough clothes only accentuated his manliness. With measured tread and long strides he crossed the deck and leaned casually back against the table beside her.

"It's beautiful, isn't it?" he murmured softly, looking down at her.

"Yes." She was watching the water, but he was watching her.

"And you smell so good."

His voice was soft and mesmerizing, and she smiled hesitantly at him.

"Why are you smiling?" Morgan whispered, his warm breath fanning her temple.

"I didn't think you'd notice that I perfumed my hair."

One of his hands circled her shoulders and played with a dark strand of her hair.

"When will you ever learn that I notice everything about you?" he replied in his beautiful, silken voice.

He was dangerously close, and the movement of his fingers upon her neck was beginning to stir her senses. Slowly his mouth lowered to hers for a brief, sweet kiss.

"Dinah, do you want to eat supper or do you want to..." His gaze drifted to the velvet softness of her mouth.

He didn't finish his question, but he didn't have to. She lifted her lids to gaze up at him unhappily, wondering if this was only an act of lust for him. His hand was still on her shoulder, but when their eyes met, his fingers wandered to the silk tie at her throat and loosened it so that the ribbons fluttered in the wind. He unbuttoned the first button of her blouse, and she felt his fingers against the bare flesh of her throat caressing her. His eyes and the velvet touch of his fingertips were seducing her. Her pulse began to race, and she swayed toward him.

His mouth was warm and moist as it seductively claimed hers, nibbling on each full curve of her lips until she sighingly parted them so his tongue could slide inside and taste the honeyed warmth of her. Dinah began to tremble from the intimate exploration of his tongue, and his strong arms wrapped her more closely against his muscled frame.

Morgan continued his slow method of arousal, until Dinah was filled with a searing longing only he could satisfy. It no longer mattered that he didn't love her, that he might have married her only for her money. All that mattered was the burning taste of his mouth on hers, the deep aching hunger he evoked. Oddly, her doubts only made her yearn for him all the more passionately. If only she could claim his soul by pleasuring him with the wanton gift of her body.

He lifted her into his arms and carried her inside the small house into the bedroom and laid her down upon the rustic bed. Her eyes met his, and then his gaze traveled from the tip of her glossy black head, roaming over her dark, sparkling eyes, down to her full lips, and then further to the voluptuous tilt of her breasts beneath blue silk. They seemed to shiver under the compelling force of his hot gaze. It was almost as if he physically touched them.

"You're a beautiful woman, Dinah. I used to wish you were ugly and old...and fat...so I could have forgotten you. Sometimes I think even then that I could not forget you." There was a note of suppressed violence in his low voice.

He was confessing that he had wanted to hate her, and it hurt her unbearably.

But she had wanted to hate him too! Her gaze ran over the powerful lines of his male body. What right did he have being so masculine, so terribly attractive, so devastatingly virile? What right did he have to command her love if he was only using her?

She lay beneath him in a seductively wanton pose. There was stark invitation in her softly brilliant eyes. Her eyes were sending him the most erotic of messages.

"It makes me shiver when you look at me like that," he rasped with a low, sexy chuckle.

"How do you think it makes me feel when you do the same thing?" Gently she reached up to touch the firm line of his jaw. Then the anguished words that she meant never to ask him tumbled from her lips.

"Morgan, why did you marry me?" The question was filled with anguish.

He stared at her for a long time. The intensity of his gaze made her flesh tingle, as if it had been a physical caress. Then he reached down and kissed her tenderly upon the mouth.

"Because I had to," he said at last, little knowing how his answer filled her with pain. "No more questions, love."

She started to protest, but his mouth crushed down upon her lips, this time in a kiss that wiped away the last shreds of her ability to think logically or argue. Liquid fire raced through her veins, making her go limp in his arms, until she was returning his kisses, her passion as ardent as his. Her fingers slid beneath his sweater and caressed the smooth warmth of his naked skin.

No matter what her doubts were, she wanted him too much to resist the powerful magnetism of his male attraction. Desire flamed as he stripped her and plundered the lush curves of her opulent beauty, relearning her most intimate secrets. Her hands tugged at his sweater, and he paused and ripped it off so that her fingers could glide freely over his hard flesh, which was smooth with rippling muscle.

Morgan kissed her more and more demandingly.

Breathlessly Dinah pleaded, "Make love to me, Morgan. Oh, please love me. I can't wait any longer."

"We have the whole night." His mouth moved with deliberate slowness across the curve of her slim shoulders.

Morgan was shaking with desire as he undressed completely and then lay beside her, gently lifting her warm body against his. A tremor ran through Dinah at the contact with his naked skin. Her palms tenderly moved down his shoulders and then closed behind his back, pressing his body deeply into hers. She cried out ever so softly in a little paroxysm of ecstasy as he took her, her own bewildering hunger betraying her. He began to move, his hard thrusting body above hers.

They clung to each other in a whirlwind of passion that

swept them on its turbulent currents until all the pent-up violence in each of them exploded in bittersweet fulfillment, and they held one another even after this shattering release, their bodies entwined, two hearts beating as one in the rich, warm afterglow of mutual bliss.

But the soul of one was left unsatisfied.

Ten

The scent of salt and sea vegetation seeped into the tiny frame house. Outside, the surf thundered incessantly. As Dinah lay in Morgan's arms the smells and sounds of the beach brought back the first night so long ago when he'd made love to her beneath the eucalyptus trees in the moonlight. That time now seemed to belong to another lifetime. It was almost as if the naive innocent she'd been had not even been she, but some strange ebony-haired girl from a romantic dream. That night when she'd given herself to him, she'd known she would love him always. How fervently she'd believed him when he'd said he would love her forever; how completely lost and devastated she'd been when so quickly afterward he'd married Holly.

Her passion receding, Dinah lay in bed feeling cold and empty inside. She pulled the blankets more tightly around her chilled body and moved closer against Morgan for warmth, but it did no good. Not even the blistering heat of his body could warm her frozen soul. She blinked hard, fighting back tears. Her doubts were breaking her heart. She couldn't endure a lifetime of this, of loving him past insanity and yet doubting the sincerity of his response. For his sake, she had to know the truth, even if it cost her her marriage to Morgan.

If Morgan didn't love her, she couldn't stay with him, no matter how she loved him, not even for Stephen. It hurt too much to doubt. She would have to find a way to visit her child regularly, but she could not chain Morgan to her if the only reason he wanted her was because he was afraid he might lose the vineyard and winery. She would give him the control of Kirsten Vineyards he wanted and return to Texas and her work there. Her heart filled with pain at the thought of a future that would be so bleak and barren. Just the thought made her eyes sting with new, hot tears. How would she live without him again? Oh, how.... The mere thought made a sob clog her throat even as she knew she had to set him free if that was what he really wanted.

"What's wrong, Dinah?" came the pleasant rumble of Morgan's deep voice beside her. His long fingers caressingly smoothed her hair.

She jumped in startled fright because she'd thought him asleep. When his arm slid around her, she jerked free of the treacherous warmth of his hand on her body and sat tensely as far from his sprawled, dark form as she could get.

"N-nothing," she replied in a stark, quivering tone. She felt too vulnerable and lost to face him on this issue so soon. How could she even frame the words? "I don't want to talk now."

"There sure as hell is something wrong," he said less gently, "and I do want to talk—now. Something's been eating you ever since we left Kirsten Vineyards. I kept waiting for you to tell me what it is. You're crying in bed, and you won't even let me touch you.''

"We really should wait, until I feel more myself.''

There was a long silence. Then he spoke drawlingly, bitingly in the cold darkness. "I've never liked putting things off. Especially not things like this. We just made love, and you're acting like you despise me.''

"Since you must know, I—I overheard you and Grandfather talking in the library, and when I asked Grandfather about it, he told me everything. No wonder you never told me he was ill, Morgan.'' Her voice was sharp in accusation.

There was an uneasy pause. "Now what is that supposed to mean?''

She glanced toward his carved profile. In the dim light his expression seemed to be harder than she'd ever seen it.

Despite her fear, she said, "You were afraid I might start thinking about why you'd really come after me to Switzerland.''

"Quit talking in circles, and tell me what you're getting at.''

"Grandfather told me that when he dies he's leaving me in control of Kirsten Vineyards.''

"And you think I came after you and married you because I want control of Kirsten Vineyards?''

She felt too wretched to speak. If only he would tell her that was a crazy, far-fetched notion and that he loved her.

"Isn't that what you believed, Dinah?''

She nodded mutely. "I thought maybe...''

"The hell with 'maybe.' Don't soften what you think. I've been handling rejection my whole damn life, Dinah. I can sure as hell handle it now.''

He pitched aside the blanket that had been draped over

his body and swung his feet to the icy floor. She turned and stared at him in the shadowy light.

"What are you doing?" she asked softly.

"What do you think? I'm getting out. If that's what you believe, you can keep control of your precious Kirsten Vineyards for all I care."

"Out." The one word sliced her heart. She watched him achingly. There was a sheen to his bronzed skin. She could see the outline of his broad shoulders and rippling back muscles as he bent over and pulled his underwear on and then his jeans. His steps on the wood plank floor of the little room were soundless, animal strides, like the restless movements of a caged panther. He pulled on his shirt and hastily buttoned it.

"You used to criticize me because you said I was ambitious, Dinah. Would you prefer a man content to let the vineyard ruin and the winery fall down around your ears? I don't know what you want of me, what you expect. Not that it matters, because I can't change, not even for you. Yes, I want Kirsten Vineyards. I've always wanted it, but for what it's worth, in the beginning I stayed at Kirsten Vineyards because I wanted you. You were only sixteen then, but I fell in love with you anyway. I felt a common bond with you. It was as if we were both outsiders and had to fight for our place in the world. But you couldn't see past the lies you'd read about me in the newspapers. Not that I blamed you. When it looked like you were so determined to hate me I couldn't ever have you, I threw myself into my work to forget, and slowly I became involved with winemaking and growing grapes until that sort of work became the only thing I wanted to do. Later, when I thought you loved me but you left me for Edouard, and I was so crazy and sick without you I married Holly, Stephen and Kirsten Vineyards were all I had."

He paused for a long moment before continuing. "In a

way you remind me of my mother, Dinah. You needn't
flinch and look so shocked. In a way she wasn't so terrible. You see, despite her fame and success, she didn't
believe in herself any more than you do. That's why one
man was never enough for her. She needed constant re-
assurance from a lot of men that she was beautiful and
desirable. She surrounded herself with all kinds of syco-
phants who used her. As a result she grew paranoid. She
wasn't even sure of me. I think in her twisted way she
wanted her son to love her, but what I gave her never
satisfied her. I was the one male in her life she could not
drive away. When I was older she thought I struck around
because I wanted her money like everybody else did. She
used to taunt me with that, even on that last night. But I
didn't, Dinah. I wanted her love. It's ironic, but it was my
love for her that got in the way of my common sense that
night. That's what got me in such serious trouble. But for
your information, when she died three years ago, she must
have changed her mind about a few things because she
left me everything. I think it was her way of letting me
know that she did care. It was all she could give me.
Because of her I'm a rich man. I don't need your money,
and I never have. I learned a long time ago that I could
make it in the world without being rich. I didn't marry
you because of Kirsten Vineyards. I married you solely
because I wanted you, but I'm damned if I'll live with a
woman who has so little faith in herself and me. I've been
through that hell once, and I won't put myself through it
again. You left me once before. I imagine it's only a matter of time before you leave me again."

He pulled on his boots.

"Where are you going?"

"What difference does it make?"

"Are you coming back?"

To that he gave no answer. He shot her a fierce look.

Then he stomped down the hall. The door slammed, and she knew he was gone.

Tears coursed in crazily shimmering zigzag paths down her bloodless face. She wadded her pillow and held it close, weeping hysterically, until at last no more tears would fall, and a deathly calm possessed her. His terrible anger had driven all her doubts away, but was it too late to make amends to him? For the first time in her life she even felt different about herself, as if she would never again be blinded by her insecurities. She was as worthy of love as anyone. Why hadn't she ever been able to believe that before?

Feeling numb and empty she arose from the bed and dressed unhurriedly. Morgan loved her. She had been wrong about him. So terribly wrong. She'd meant only to save them from a loveless marriage, and he'd misconstrued everything. She'd wounded him unbearably. He thought she was rejecting him as once his mother had. If he didn't come back, she would have to go to him. Even if he wouldn't have her, she had to try to make some sort of clumsy explanation for her hurt behavior.

Two days passed, and Morgan did not return to the beach house. Dinah was plunged into the depths of despair. Wherever he had gone, he'd either walked or hitchhiked, because he'd left her the truck and its keys. Dinah spent the long, miserable days taking solitary walks on the beach, picking up odd bits of driftwood and tossing them aimlessly into the ocean. She felt she had to stay at Stinson Beach and wait and give Morgan the chance to return. Without a car perhaps he hadn't gone far.

In a moment of supreme anxiety she called home and talked to Bruce and Stephen.

"We didn't expect to hear from you on your honeymoon," Bruce said jovially.

"I was missing you two," she said weakly.

"How's Morgan?"

Her grandfather's question answered hers. Morgan had not gone home alone.

"Fine," she managed.

She talked to Stephen briefly and then hung up, her mind whirling with new questions. Where had Morgan gone? And how could she find him?

Her two days of waiting had filled her with frustration. The walls of the beach house seemed claustrophobic without Morgan. On impulse she decided to take the truck and look for him. Dashing off a note to him and taping it to the refrigerator, she left the door of the house unlocked and got into the truck. She didn't know where to begin searching, so she drove down to Point Reyes, where the waves crashed with violent thunder upon that long, spectacular, eleven-mile strip of dangerous beach. It was a cold, windy day, and the park was empty save for a few hearty tourists bundled in thick coats.

Feeling lost and desolate, she walked the chaparral-covered slopes sandwiched between the silent darkness of the forest and the pounding ocean. The swirling winter mists softened the scrub colors to dull orange, lavender, and beige and grayed the water's surface to a silvery sheen. At last she was so frozen she could endure the harsh climate no longer, and climbed back into the truck and headed once more toward Stinson Beach. Then it occurred to her that the castle that belonged to Morgan's old actress friend, the castle where she and Morgan had first made love, was nearby. She wasn't completely sure how to find it but she decided to try before it got dark, on the thin hope that maybe some shred of nostalgia had driven Morgan to return there. She knew that it was a sort of haven to Morgan, a place he'd gone occasionally when he was younger and felt the need of it.

It took her an hour to find the narrow private road that

led through a thick, pungent eucalyptus grove and curved upward between green hills to the castle. She startled a gray fox, and he leaped from the trees in front of her car and then to safety. The castle stood on the crest of its hill like a powerful, brooding sentinel facing the ocean from its sheer granite cliff. The storm shutters on the windows were closed. The mansion had a look of desolation about it. Dinah jumped out of the truck and ran to the front door and pounded on the door. No one answered her frenzied knocking, and she fought back the childish urge to throw herself down on the front steps and weep. After a long time, she decided there could be no harm in following the bittersweet impulse to wander down to the beach where they had once made love.

The gray day with its opalescent sky lent a strange charm to the familiar landscape. Harbor seals cavorted offshore in the rocks and surf. Thick mists hovered at the fringes of the hills. The terrain seemed rougher, the waves more turbulent than that magic night when she first learned what it was to be a woman in love in Morgan's arms. For a moment she watched the cyclic rhythm of wave and tide gnaw at the slim ribbon of sand. Then she sighed, too distressed to enjoy the view.

As if in a dream, she crossed the beach where they'd once wildly galloped. Sea birds flew low, skimming the wet, freshly washed shore. The damp sand seeped into her shoes as she struggled toward the same eucalyptus grove near the beach where he'd taken her virginity and given her in return a taste of bewildering rapture.

The great whispery eucalyptus trees blocked light, their pungent scent mingling with the smell of the sea, and the poignant memory was so powerful she felt she had to leave quickly before her grief overpowered her.

Stumbling, she turned wildly around. A tall, dark figure was standing in the shadows of the trees directly in the

avenue of her escape. A flowing, scarlet cape swirled in
the wind. The person's face was concealed by a monk's
cowl.

Dinah's heart began to pound. "Morgan," she whispered breathlessly, hopefully.

Long, graceful fingers pushed the cowl aside, and a
woman's voice, one of the most famous in the world, said
throatily, "You are mistaken."

Despite her age, she was beautiful. Without the protection of her cowl, her magnificent flame-red hair stirred in
the brisk gusts that swept through the grove. Hers was an
ageless kind of glamour that transcended mere prettiness.
She had great beauty still, the mystique of Garbo, and yet
her own powerful charisma as well.

"I'm sorry. I didn't mean to trespass," Dinah said hesitantly. "I came only to—"

"I know why you came," came the sensual, raspy
voice Dinah had heard in a hundred movies. The famous
topaz eyes were ancient, wise.

"You do?"

"You have come after him." It was a statement.

"Yes."

"Even after you rejected him."

"I was so wrong," Dinah whispered, wondering how
she knew and yet accepting her knowledge.

"You must love him very much to be so blinded to the
man he is."

"I thought…I believed.…"

"So many people have believed him to be different
than he is. I have known him since he was a little boy. I
never had a child of my own. How I envied his mother.
She was a great friend of mine once. You might have read
that somewhere."

Dinah nodded mutely without interrupting.

"In the beginning Teresa wanted Morgan. He was the

child from the one great love of her life, from the one man she could not bend to her will. Unfortunately, she had a turbulent relationship with this man and he left her and moved abroad. After that Teresa changed. She began to drink more. She went from man to man, seeking something she was never to find. When Morgan was born she blamed him for what was wrong in her life. As he grew older, he looked too much like this father, I think, and because he did, it made it impossible for her to forget the one man who had left her. She didn't want Morgan. She took out her anger toward the father on the son. She abused him, but I think, in his way, Morgan loved her. If he had not, the tragedy that separated them would never have occurred.''

''What really happened that night? Morgan won't tell me.''

''He got tired of telling the truth and being called a liar, but Teresa told me she lied to save her own skin. She had a lover as usual, but he was different than the others. Abusive, inordinately possessive, darkly violent, though in public he could be charming. He was the first man since Morgan's father to have any control over Teresa, but it was a different, terrible kind of control. Teresa began to resent his power over her, and they began to quarrel fiercely at home. Sometimes he hit her, and he threatened to do worse. Morgan was seventeen, and he wasn't home that much. So he didn't realize what was going on. Maybe he didn't want to know. He had his own car, his own friends. He tended to avoid his mother, and he had always resented the men in Teresa's life. When they were around, he tried not to be home. That night Teresa and her lover thought Morgan was out when they began to quarrel. The fight took a vicious turn. Her lover beat Teresa quite badly, and Morgan heard them fighting and tried to stop the man. Morgan was beaten soundly by both of them, and then Teresa told the world that it was Morgan who had beaten her up. Morgan was known for his wildness, and it was easy to make the authorities believe her. She was too afraid of her lover not to lie. This last act of treachery on Teresa's part, when he had fought to save her, completely embittered Morgan toward her until she died. He felt totally rejected. He was trying to save her, and she repaid him by humiliating him publicly and putting him in that awful school that was virtually a jail. It was the worst kind of experience for a boy like Morgan. All his life he has wanted love.''

"Where can I find him?" Dinah begged desperately. "I have to go to him and try to explain...."

"He will be very angry at me if I tell you," the living legend purred gently.

"I can't believe you're frightened of anything."

She laughed her throaty, immortal laugh. "I'm too old to be afraid, my child. He's up at the house, if you must know. Staring at the sea. He's been the most abominable company these past two days and nights. Why do you think I came down for a walk?"

"I knocked on the front door. There was no answer."

"It can't be heard from the upper floors. When the servants are gone, I never answer the door anyway. Go to the back of the house, child. Take the stairs to the second balcony. His room is the last door. I just came down myself. It's not locked."

Dinah began to run. Then she paused, remembering she should thank this world-famous woman with the hair of flame, but the woman was gone, having disappeared into the thick, concealing darkness of the trees. In her overwrought state, it seemed to Dinah that the actress might have been a figment in some fantastic dream.

Again Dinah ran across the thick sand until she was breathless and her pulse throbbed painfully. The howling

wind was against her, tangling her hair with its damp, cold
fingers, biting through her thin garments until she felt icy.
At last she found the stairs and began to climb them.

Before the closed door to Morgan's room, she hesitated,
her heart pounding with the most startling ferocity, her
eyes dark pools haunted with love and pain and fear. At
the slightest touch of her fingertips upon the knob the
wind blew the door open, banging it against the wall.
Dinah stepped inside a small, delightfully furnished room.
Green silk curtains billowed. The fire blazing in the enormous hearth that dominated the room went wild. Sparks
flew.

She fought to close the door.

"A most dramatic entrance, my dear," came Morgan's
deep, sardonic drawl from the shadowy corner near the
fire. "You shouldn't have come."

She ran to him. His tall frame leaned indolently against
the hearth, and he looked down at her so coolly she
wanted to die, his hard blue gaze freezing her.

"I was wrong," she began. "Oh, so wrong. You
mustn't hate me, Morgan. Please." His cold, stark features stopped her pitiful speech. Shaking, she turned from
him, not knowing what to say, nor what to do, feeling
utterly desolate. It was as she feared, much, much too late.
He would never believe he could trust her again, and she
couldn't blame him.

He moved soundlessly. Then she felt his arms slide
around her, and she began to tremble violently as he
pulled her against his body.

"I don't hate you," he said very softly. He crushed her
to him suddenly in a fiercely possessive embrace. "I could
never hate you." He buried his lips in her hair.

"I was so wrong not to believe in you," she whispered.
"I just didn't want to tie you to me with money. I wanted

to give you control of Kirsten Vineyards and set you free."

"I could never be free without you, my love. When will you ever learn that?"

"Oh, Morgan."

They kissed deeply, passionately, clinging. At last he released her. He took her hand in his and brought it to his lips.

"I thought you were never coming back," she managed.

"I couldn't have stayed away. You see, Dinah, much as I might like to pretend otherwise when I'm angry with you, I can't live without you."

"Nor can I without you."

He brushed her hair from her cheek. "Soon we'll have to tell Stephen that you're his mother. *Our* son, Dinah. The thought fills me with indescribable happiness." He clasped her hand more tightly, and she felt the intensity of his eagerness.

"No, Morgan," she whispered. "I don't want to tell him for a long time. He's much too young. He couldn't possibly understand. He seems to be happy now with the way things are. Let's don't shake his world up just yet. Perhaps someday when he's older...."

"It's for you to decide."

Beneath the castle in the fading sunlight, sparkling, dark waves crashed against the pale beach. Morgan drew her toward the window, and, holding each other, they looked down upon the wild, windswept ocean.

"This is where we first found each other," he said gently.

"And it is where we found each other again," she replied, meeting his gaze, feeling tremulously joyful.

"Yes," he murmured. His eyes softened. "We will be happy, you and I. I will work hard at that, I promise you."

"I'm sure you will," she replied. "You have always been such a dedicated man." Her face shone with guileless delight.

He caught her meaning, and his mood lightened. "Perhaps I should begin by dedicating myself to that task now," he murmured, bending his head to her lips. "You are a remarkably beautiful woman," he finished quietly.

Morgan's hands moved behind her head, forcing her lips to slant against his, and his mouth ravished hers, seeking, demanding, plundering as his tongue explored her lips, savoring every intimacy. She moaned softly and began to breathe hard. She felt the heavy thudding of his heart against her breasts, and she was aware of his awesomely hard body pressing tightly into hers, filling her own with a wanton, throbbing ache. Her fingertips moved over his body urgently, and he groaned when her fingers circled him. Her whole body was excited by the taste, the feel, the scent of him, all thrillingly arousing to her.

He was hers. He would belong to her forever.

Realizing there was no time for tenderness, he swept her into his arms and carried her to the bed. Still kissing her, he began to undress her. Then he lowered his body to the searing warmth of hers, and as always the passion that soared between them was something quite beyond love.

* * * * * *

If you enjoyed what you just read,
then we've got an offer you can't resist!

Take 2 bestselling love stories FREE!

Plus get a FREE surprise gift!